The Indigo Girl

The Indigo Girl

A NOVEL

NATASHA BOYD

BLACK STONE PUBLISHING

Copyright © 2017 by Natasha Boyd
Published in 2018 by Blackstone Publishing
Cover and book design by Kathryn Galloway English

Excerpts from letters by Eliza Pinckney used with kind
permission of the South Carolina Historical Society

Printed in the United States of America
Originally published in hardcover by Blackstone Publishing in 2017

First paperback edition: 2018
ISBN 978-1-5385-5292-6
3 5 7 9 10 8 6 4

CIP data for this book is available
from the Library of Congress

Blackstone Publishing
31 Mistletoe Rd.
Ashland, OR 97520

www.BlackstonePublishing.com

For Briony

TRUE INDIGO

indigofera tinctoria

"No time is ours but the present...
and that so fleeting, we can hardly be said to exist."

—*Eliza Lucas,* 1722–1793

Prologue

When I look back upon my struggle with indigo, it appears in my consciousness as a dream.

Impressions are all I am left with—impressions of hands dragging me down, squeezing my heart, keeping me under. Hands that want me to drown in my own creation. In my ambition.

And drown I did.

I sank into the opaque blue abyss.

Yet even though indigo broke my heart, it saved my life.

Indigo ran through my veins.

Blue blood would pulse through my children's veins.

In my later years, when I knew about deep and abiding love and the pride of having sons who would be part of birthing a new nation, I'd look back on that time of my life and thank God for indigo.

How was it that the deepest of blues—the color of the sky in the predawn hours before the warm sticky blanket of the day folded its weight over our shoulders, the hue that made me think of heaven and fine silk, kings and treasures beyond imagining, ancient and unfathomable history—could come from that awkward, dusty weed?

I would thank God also for Essie, and for Quash, for

Togo, and Sawney, and especially for Ben. For the ones who believed in me.

And Charles, of course. Always, I'd thank Charles.

I would also thank my father for his choice to leave a sixteen-year-old girl in charge of his plantations. I never did see him again.

To my dear friend Mrs. Bodicott in England,

I flatter myself it will be a satisfaction to you to hear I like this part of the world, as my lot has fallen here—which I really do. I prefer England to it, 'tis true, but think Carolina greatly preferable to the West Indias.

The people live very genteel and very much in the English taste.

—Eliza Lucas

One

1739

The Negroes were singing.

Light danced over the dark, inky ocean, and I blinked my eyes awake.

No ocean.

Just the faint blue of a breaking day casting over the white walls of my bedchamber.

A dream still clung damp to my bones. Always the same since I was a child. Sometimes threatening, sometimes euphoric.

Breathing in deeply, I fancied the day held the weight of destiny.

I picked out the distinctive low rumble of Togo's voice in the melody, the breadth of his voice in correlation to his size. In our few months in South Carolina, I'd already become familiar with how his deep tenor was the base upon which the other Negro voices blended and danced. I came to know that when they sang, they all worked together on some greater task.

The harvest. The Negroes were singing because they had begun a harvest.

Disliking to rise into the wave of humidity that swelled and crested each day, sapping my energy before I could finish my tasks, I kicked the slubby linens off my legs to get ahead of it.

Esmé had already filled the water bowl and pitcher. After stretching my limbs to wring the last of the dark, sticky dream from my body, there was nothing save the vague sense of triumph that lingered from some unknown accomplishment.

I made quick use of the stone-cooled water to freshen my pale skin. My hands, slightly darker in skin tone from my time spent outside, reached for the small tin bell. A single tinkle, so as not to wake my maudlin mama or little Polly, was enough to summon the dark wraithlike figure of Esmé, whose sight and hearing were as keen as any owl's. She slipped into the room, her cloth-covered feet silent on the wooden boards. Her body in a simple dress of sackcloth, a white muslin wrapped tightly around her head.

"Morning, Essie. I heard singing. Has the harvest begun? Let us make haste."

"Yes. But big Lucas, he be needin' to speak wit ya."

I frowned. Father never asked for me. I already went to his study every morning to assist him with his correspondence after I walked the plantation. I would write his correspondence so he could dictate. His strides across the study seemed to help him find the words he needed to convey things that required a delicate care. Then I would accompany him around our small plantation, pointing out things I might have seen on my dawn inspection. Occasionally I would go with Papa and our driver, Quash, to our other two tracts of land to converse with the managers.

Esmé unbound my coiled dark hair, shaking it out and running the fine bone comb through it before braiding and repinning it up off my neck. She was adept at not taking any longer than I wanted to get myself ready, despite my mother's annoyance that I wouldn't take more care in dressing. Having tended to me since my childhood in Antigua, Essie knew I was not bothered with the primping my mother undertook.

Besides, my still girlish body didn't require much stuffing into any shape-inducing accoutrements.

Essie and Mary Ann and Nanny, the two Negro ladies we'd found in charge of the house when we arrived, kept the home life of the plantation running fairly smoothly. It was just as well, since Mama wasn't in a fit state to do much mistress-of-the-house-ing, and I had been busy insinuating myself into Papa's day-to-day business affairs. I found it a fascinating challenge, and of course my love of plants and horticulture that I'd acquired as a child in Antigua was put to good use whenever the subject of crops was raised.

I hurried to water the small green shoots on my window ledge, the live oaks a gift from a nearby neighbor and fellow botany enthusiast, Mr. Deveaux. Then I made my way downstairs.

"Eliza." My father's voice barked as I approached the open door of the study. He paced in front of the open campaign desk he preferred to use, rather than the polished mahogany one we'd purchased upon landing in Charles Town. Fully dressed for the day, his brown hair, graying at the temples, was waxed yet disheveled. His brow wore a new pleat of consternation.

"Papa. Colonel, sir," I hastily corrected myself.

It had caused my father much amusement when I'd recently informed him I was far too old to be referring to him in the same manner as my baby sister, Polly. Though he seemed to approve. Indeed, his manner of conversing with me had slowly evolved into more partner or friend than that of a father to his offspring. I clung to this new level of respect. He was a fair man, and for the most part stuck to his promises. It taught us children early on not to test his limits.

"Have you had your eggs?" I asked.

He nodded absently. "Yes. I—when I was in town

yesterday, I intercepted a correspondence that was heading this way. For me. A summons."

I swallowed. "A summons?"

"I'm needed back in Antigua."

"Is it time to return already?"

"I'm afraid so. By the end of the month. I was hoping for a little longer to see you all settled, and at least know your mama was improved. I'm afraid this move has set her back."

I pursed my lips. The truth was a sea breeze could set Mama back with her migraines and dull energy. A more different person, I could not be. I often wondered how my vital father had seen the wisdom in a match with my mother. She was handsome, it was fair to say, but Papa favored other qualities. A fact he told me often and with some vigor when he and Mama had sent me off to school in England. I was separated from them with only our friends the Bodicotts to be in loco parentis. My younger brothers, George and Tommy, lived with them still while they schooled.

"So what shall we do with the plantations when we return to Antigua? Do you trust your overseers to manage the business?"

Papa had swung about to face me. One hand grasped his chin, the other absently fiddled with the strings on his shirt. He stared at me deeply as if I held the secret key to a universal problem. With a long sigh, he dropped both hands. "And that you should ask me such a question, Eliza, helps me with this momentous decision." He didn't have to tell me that he hoped to reach whatever decision he was making and have it be irrevocable by the time my mother was up to greet the day.

The idea of returning to Antigua with its emerald green foliage, clear blue sea, and fond memories of my childhood Negro friend, Benoit, was not unwelcome. It was Ben's knowledge of plants that had lit the flame of my own passion for botany. I missed him often as I adjusted to plantation life and grew to know this new and strange land.

Returning to Antigua, or even England for that matter, was of course appealing, but the social expectation of wedding a nice young lieutenant from a strong British family was not. That was surely my lot once I returned to either place.

I searched my father's eyes closely then took note of his clothing and the general state of his desk. "You have not slept at all have you, sir?"

"There hasn't been time." He spurred forward. "Come, Betsey." He cleared his throat. "Eliza," he corrected with a shake of his head, knowing how I tried to grow out of my childhood name. "Let us get you some food, then we must away to meet with the managers at Garden Hill and Waccamaw."

"So, I'm to accompany you?" I was careful to moderate my tone, not wanting to show too much enthusiasm for this "man's work." I followed him to the dining room where I selected a boiled egg and some cold smoked fish from the sideboard.

My father pulled out a chair for me and took his seat at the head of the table. "Tell me, Eliza, have you enjoyed our time here? I know we were hoping the climate of the colonies would be more moderate than that of the islands and be of help to your mama's temperament. Alas." He smiled ruefully. "There's not much to help her feel better."

"I've enjoyed it immensely," I responded dutifully, thinking of what else he would like me to say. "The people in town have been most pleasing," I added.

But mostly I'd enjoyed the time on our lands talking of the potential my papa saw. Slowly, slowly this new world with its dripping, ghostly moss and its marshy brackish water, monsters lurking beneath the surface, seemed to fill my dreams and its very otherworldly essence to find its way under my skin.

In the islands, our holdings—mostly sugar land—had been small and for all practical purposes at full capacity.

Here in the colonies I, like my father, saw potential for so much more. The land was rich. I fancied I could grow anything I put my mind to. Melons, oranges, cassava, benne seeds.

My father's father had left him this fertile tract along the banks of the Wappoo Creek, only six miles by water from Charles Town on the peninsula. With the property came a small bevy of slaves and the not-so-small task of making a family name for ourselves beyond that of my father's armed service to the Crown. An opportunity we couldn't afford to waste, he often said. My father had also immediately purchased two larger parcels farther afield that already had fair production in timber and rice exports.

"Eliza, in order to secure my commission, I had to borrow against the Antigua land and, of course, the parcel here. I'm loath to return there, but the threat of the Spanish has become too strong. And of course, I cannot advance my career from here."

I swallowed a chunk of chalky yolk in a rush as my mind hurried to keep up with his words. We knew the West Indias were an important strategic position against the Spanish, but I couldn't think that he'd accrue more debt to our properties in order to continue his position in the military. While I was sure he knew what he was doing, I couldn't help the panicky feeling that had seized my chest.

"It is now more important than ever before that this land turns a profit." His voice became gruff. Intimate. Imparting some secret I was too young to hear. "Coming here was never solely about your mama's health, though I'm sure we'd both have liked that to be a beneficial by-product."

I dabbed my eyes that pricked from almost choking on my egg and took a sip of tea to clear my throat.

"You asked before if I trust our managers," he went on. "The answer is yes, of course. But if you ask do I trust them to inform me of every decision they make pertaining to our land, our crops, and our yield? The answer is surely not. For we have different end goals. For one man, the goal is to be a good worker. One hopes"—he chuckled—"and receive a wage. For the other, myself, your papa, the end goal is to secure our family for generations and be of economic service to the Crown. We are building a new world here, Eliza. We have a unique opportunity to be among the first to really accomplish something magnificent."

I did so get inspired by his ebullient dedication to serving king, country, and progeny. He'd have to depend on my brothers or Polly for the latter, however.

"But, sir—"

"Let me finish, Eliza. I know this is hard to understand as you are not yet even seventeen years of age, but I've attempted to impart to you the importance of standing for something greater than oneself. To work toward the greater good, be it for God or be it in service to our country or fellow man."

"Yes, Father."

"You have been running the household in your mother's stead already. I have made sure you are educated with certain skills. I have been planning for this eventuality. And now is the time."

My skin prickled.

"In a few years," my father went on, "your brother George will be of age and will come across from England to take over my affairs here. In the meantime, Eliza, I'll need you to act as my surrogate in all matters pertaining to these holdings. You will remain here in South Carolina with your mother and Polly and take charge of my business affairs."

I gasped, this time unable to contain my shock. My back was straight as a punting pole, my hand frozen in midflight toward my cup.

My father continued. "You already do my correspondence. This change of plans will simply mean some decisions and communiqués will be delayed as you relay them to me and await my response. Of course, I understand that some decisions will have to be made quicker than that will allow, but you have managers to consult, and I have asked our friend Charles Pinckney and his wife to look out for you and provide counsel, should the need arise."

I was to run his plantations? "Sir," I finally squeezed a word into his decree, and then failed at adding another.

He raised an eyebrow. "Do you have anything to say that might make the length of a complete sentence?"

For a moment I felt trapped under the weight of the responsibility my father was placing upon my shoulders: to make sure our land would secure our family's wealth, and secure my own dowry for a marriage it was no secret I would never want, or allow my family to descend into poverty. Alone. He was leaving us here alone?

Back home in England, the idea that my father would leave his sixteen-year-old daughter in charge of his estates was absurd. Would anyone even take direction from me? In fact, thinking of trying to explain in a letter to my dear friend and one-time guardian, Mrs. Bodicott, this new turn of events almost made me think this was some ridiculously conjured up fantasy of mine. A wish to be someone of import. To not be owned as chattel by a father or one day by a husband. But this was not England. And something about this place where we'd made our home, where people around us were trying to create a new world from the ground up, made everything seem possible. Perhaps it was my precocity or my simple propensity to dream ambitiously and try to impress my father with the knowledge he'd made sure I learned in school, but I brought my trembling hand down from the table and slipped it under my thigh to press it still.

"Well?" he asked again.

I tilted my chin up. "I shall put the gift of the education you indulged me with to the best use. And ..."

"And?"

"And we shall miss you," was all I managed.

To my dear friend, Mrs. Bodicott,

My papa and mama's great indulgence to me leaves it to me to choose our place of residence either in town or country, but I think it more prudent as well as most agreeable to my mama and self to be in the country during my father's absence. We are seventeen miles by land and six by water from Charles Town—where we have about six agreeable families around us with whom we live in great harmony.

—Eliza Lucas

Two

Had it been just a few days ago Papa told me his news? Everything was happening too fast. We left immediately with Quash, our driver and Father's "man about the land," to visit our plantation Garden Hill, up the Combahee River.

We traveled south along the Santee River and through the treacherous Port Royal and St. Helena Sounds before embarking up the Combahee. We sailed until the oyster banks were no more, and the water inland grew dark, greasy, and still, the trees dense along the banks.

I had only been a handful of times since arriving in South Carolina, but the journey always made me nervous. The rocking of the boat turned my stomach, and between the sharks in the sounds and the great alligators rippling under the surface of the rivers, I was quite spent by the time we arrived. We requested accountings from our overseer, Mr. Murry, regarding the projected rice output and other salables.

Papa didn't say a word to Mr. Murry and his wife about his imminent departure except that "if" he were absent, they could send word to him through me. After all, he hadn't even told Mama yet. Mr. and Mrs. Murry acknowledged the news with but fleeting interest. Absentee owners were common.

Quash stood silently yet intently listening. I could almost feel his questions, yet he voiced none. Quash's once distrustful eyes when we had first set foot on the Wappoo land were now simply watchful.

Papa seemed quite pleased after our visit. "A good sort, that Murry," he'd said as we slid fast and silent downstream on the ferryboat, returning home. "You can count on him."

FATHER TOLD MAMA OVER BREAKFAST the morning after we returned.

Ann Lucas promptly slumped sideways in her chair, upsetting the silver and sending it clattering to the waxed plank floor. Essie lurched forward from her spot against the wall to catch her mistress, Papa leaped to his feet, and I half stood. Polly calmly watched with rapt attention in a rare chatterless moment, popping bite-sized morsels of bread and marmalade into her tiny mouth.

"Oh, George." I heard Mama breathe as my father maneuvered her from the dining table and set course for the stairs.

"Polly," I said, when it was clear Papa was not immediately returning. "If you are done with your bread, please go and wait for me to begin our lessons for the day. We'll try and work on some French before I help Papa."

Polly smacked her napkin down on the table, her curls bobbing, clearly picking up on the mood of the morning. "You are beastly with all your lessons and rules." Her voice rose. "I just want to play!"

My heart thumped under my tight stays as I wrestled with my own temper. "You will have your morning lessons." I modulated my voice. "Then you are free to help Essie out with whatever her afternoon activities are. I believe today we are coring apples for a pie. We received some from the Woodwards," I added.

Rising, I left the room before she could begin to argue. There was no greater skill a young child had than to trap one into pointless argument. Polly was particularly adept.

Meaning to head outside to the veranda, I stopped when impulse led me to the stairs in my parents' wake. I soft-footed it almost to the top before sitting on a stair and hugging my skirts to my legs.

"It is madness what you are asking of us." My mother's shrill voice wafted across the upstairs landing. Perhaps she had meant to start out quietly in her exchange with my father, but she tended to work herself up rather quickly.

"It's necessary," my father corrected, his tone patient.

"Necessary to your ambitions, you mean. And where will that leave us if you are unsuccessful? Where will that leave your daughters? You are gambling with the future of this family. Eliza is almost marriageable."

My breath caught.

"What faith you have in me, madam." My father sounded defeated. "Besides, she has no wish to marry yet."

I let my air go slowly, but my hands had yet to relax from their bunched-up state.

My mother made some sound, and my father continued. "But if it will appease you, I shall endeavor to send some potential suitors this way."

My whole body strained to make sure my ears missed not even one moment of this conversation.

"See that you do," my mother returned emphatically, practically hissing like a bobcat. "We shall be alone out here. What will people say?"

"This is not England, madam. You knew this was our future when we wed. It is a different world here. A new world. If we can make it so."

"A new world doesn't give you the right to gamble our livelihood for your political ambition."

"Ann," my father implored.

"Or indeed to leave your sixteen-year-old daughter in charge of our affairs. And it's not safe! You are a selfish, selfish man."

I heard my father's deep sigh. "Be that as it may, Eliza is more than capable. She will be seventeen by the end of this year. George will be old enough at seventeen to fight for his country. And she has more practical sense in her small toe than most lads I come across in His Majesty's service. And despite your judgment of my selfishness, we moved here for you."

My mother huffed a breath.

My father went on, "None of us wanted to leave the Indias, but it was my mistaken impression it would be good for your health. My intent was pure."

"But I don't understand why we have to stay here while you return there," my mother pleaded. "Surely we are safer with you than in this wild land. Just last week, when I saw Mrs. Cleland at the Pinckneys' Belmont estate, she told us of another attack on a poor soul up near Goose Creek. Bobcat or bear, she didn't say. And never mind the Indians fighting amongst each other, or the rumors of slaves rising up and killing us in our sleep. I'd sooner take my chances against the Spaniards." She'd dropped to a dramatic sotto voce and I could see her in my mind's eye, shivering as she often did when speaking of something unpleasant.

"Ann. I can't advance unless I am there, nor unless *this* land turns a profit. Think of the larger goal. I *must* advance my commission for our success. Eliza *must* stay here and run the business for me to do so. There is no other way."

There was the sound of movement. While I was sure their argument was not done, I suddenly realized how long I had been eavesdropping on things not meant for my ears. No matter it had been about me too. The last thing I needed was Polly leaving the dining room and catching me in the act.

My heart was torn equally between heaviness and joy. Joy because I knew I could perform these duties and also that my father believed in me so readily. Heaviness because I did not have my mother's support, and too I knew my father had no other choice. Would he have picked me if George was of age?

Standing, I smoothed the wrinkles in my linen skirt and quietly descended the steps to await my father.

THE BRIGHT SUNLIGHT DAPPLED THROUGH the large live oaks that writhed and wove together into a sinewy canopy. Such beautiful trees. So stalwart, so strong.

In the distance I could see the work of our field hands as they bent and stood and walked through the rice and alfalfa fields in the beating sun. Beyond that, Wappoo Creek sparkled in a peekaboo with the thick marsh grass. The tide was in.

Another three-quarter turn told me a wagon was approaching in the distance, rattling up the track toward the house. I knew the tall, lithe body upon it. Our driver, Quash. He'd take my father and me about again. This time to our plantation up near Georgetown, along the banks of the Waccamaw River.

A faint breeze cooled the residual warmth in my cheeks left

over from my upset with Polly and overhearing my parents'
conversation. Out of all four of us Lucas children, Polly
needed a mother's firm hand the most. It was unfortunate
she was the only one not to get it. George and Tommy were at
least schooling in England, and Mrs. Bodicott, our guardian,
was fair and kind but stern.

Breathing in one more deep lungful of moist salted air,
I heard the steps of my father joining me outside on the
veranda.

"Ah, Eliza."

"How's Mama?" I inquired without taking my eyes off the
view.

"Fine. She'll be fine. I promised her I'd ask the Pinckneys
to look out for your social life once I'm gone. It seems she
might be more concerned about that than my leaving."

"No doubt." Mama was always on with this angle to
remind me to associate with people my own age. I liked the
quiet life out in the country, even if it was lonely at times.
"Sir—"

"Of course, I assured her I felt the same way. I know you
are young now, Eliza, but in a few years, and certainly when
your brother comes across to take over my affairs here on the
plantations, you will need to be wed. There are only a few
years to find someone suitable."

A lump of dread forced its way up my throat. I hated that
it was a foregone conclusion I would have to marry soon. The
thought of it turned my stomach. Having someone touch
me and expect things of my person. Not forgetting I would
probably have to give up my studies and certainly the business
affairs of my father. "How will anyone be suitable, Papa? I
have no interest spending my days in frivolous pursuits while
a man runs the business of our lives."

"Would that you were my son. But you are not. And you

may feel differently one day, Eliza. Perhaps if you had the right friends you'd enjoy other activities that young girls enjoy. I hear Mr. and Mrs. Pinckney have a niece, Miss Bartlett, who will be joining them soon for a visit. Perhaps you two young ladies might enjoy each other's company and catch the eye of some eligible sons in town in just a few years?"

"I won't," I bit out emphatically. "And what man will indulge my interests when they run so far from the average lady's? Mama often reminds me no man wants to take a lady to wife who will make him feel simple. I have no interest in *japanning* furniture and sipping tea all day long listening to boring gossip."

I finished my outburst and stared at my father's confused face. He had no idea my mood had been worsened by listening to his and my mother's exchange. My emotions were running too close to the surface today. "I'm sorry, Papa, I ..."

How could I explain without him perhaps regretting his decision to have me help with his business affairs? Besides, I had plans for our little acreage here at Wappoo. We already grew rice in the recently purchased Waccamaw property, and we could trade timber for sugarcane with the Indias. I thought of my little horticultural experiments upstairs in my bedroom and also of the dear, elderly gentleman on a neighboring plantation. Mr. Deveaux shared my love of botany, and I couldn't wait to be left to my own devices to see what else we might grow here. I would surprise my father with my industry.

The very last thing I wanted was for my father to second-guess his decision. Or worry about the burden of having a spinster daughter to support once I was no longer needed upon my brother George's arrival a few years hence. Perhaps if I could show my worth, then I might yet have options beyond marriage.

"Pray, what is 'japanning'?" My father finally spoke.

Taken aback, I laughed. "It's a ridiculous pastime performed by some of the other ladies in town. I am sure Mama has already sent for supplies." I rolled my eyes to the heavens. "You paint thick black lacquer on furniture to make it look ..." I paused at the queer expression on my father's face.

"... like it's from Japan?" he asked, a bushy eyebrow cocked.

I giggled. "Yes."

"Well," he mused, "I can see how you think that might be an odd way to spend one's time. Am I to return from the Indias to find all our earthly possessions painted thus?"

"Absolutely. But not the silver." I laughed, and he joined me.

"No, I daresay, not the silver. So, I know you've been out here scheming, Eliza. You can't fool me that you aren't a bit excited at being sole decision-maker around here. What do you have up your sleeve?"

Oh, how well my father knew me. "Just questions, sir. Let us away up to Waccamaw, and I shall interrogate you on our journey."

"Right you will, Eliza." He laughed, his brown eyes creasing with mirth and affection. "Right you will."

THE AFTERNOON WAGON RIDE to the ferry landing up near St. Andrew's church was hot, the scorching sun relentless in its assault.

"Colonel Lucas, sir?"

My father, deep in thought and sitting on a bench with me in the back rather than up front with Quash, looked up. He was troubled by his departure, I knew.

"Will tensions really escalate to war with the Spaniards?" I asked, remembering his conversation with Mama. "Are we safe here? Will you be safe?"

"Well, you are safer here than with me in Antigua. Should they get past us, and past Oglethorpe in Savannah, then you are to ask Charles Pinckney for advice. He'll be amongst the first with information and will be able to advise you whether to stay put."

"And what about other threats, Papa? I have been reticent to mention it, but to leave three females alone ... not that we aren't capable ... but are we to turn to Mr. Pinckney for everything?"

"I know it would be almost unheard of in England. It seems more acceptable here to have womenfolk more involved. And is that so bad, Eliza? Besides, Pinckney and his wife have been wonderful friends to us. To you and your mama. In fact it was he who suggested you would be more than capable of acting as my surrogate in the plantations' affairs rather than hire another overseer."

I whipped my gaze from the road to my father in order to gauge his sincerity.

"'Tis true." He nodded. "Not that I didn't think you were capable myself, of course."

"I know I can do it, Papa."

"You have to. I can't see to my duties, nor advance my commission, unless I am there. And for someone like Charles Pinckney, someone of such ... esteem to agree, and moreover, to approve of you in this role, well, I see you will have an ally in him."

Mr. Pinckney was of an age with Father, though he had wonderfully kind eyes and a merry humor and was considered handsome. More than that, I did so love his intellectual banter regarding issues of the day, much to my mother's irritation.

Which made it twice the fun.

Three

The strong stench of tar required my linen hat tie be brought across my mouth and nose as we walked past the sheds. I listened intently as my father and Starrat, the overseer of the Waccamaw plantation, discussed yield. The heat was damp and relentless, hugging my skin and weighing down my underdress with perspiration.

I didn't like Starrat. Not at all.

Just one look at the whipping post I'd seen when we'd first visited had immediately set me against him. Father had already asked him to remove it once, and had apparently been ignored. A rope was affixed to it now, hanging limply down near the scuffled dirt below. The sight of dried blood and the smell of urine turned my stomach. It wasn't the first such post I'd seen. And certainly, I'd seen them occupied: a poor soul half hanging, half standing as they bore the punishment for some unknown indiscretion or petty crime, blood the same color as my own, running in bright red rivulets against dark skin.

I shuddered. But never on land we owned.

I would speak to my father again about this. Perhaps the previous owner had run his business with a severe hand, but that didn't mean it should stay that way.

Starrat was a portly sort with a brusque manner and the vague odor of something stronger than ale sweating from his pores. His face was a few days past a clean shave, which smacked of laziness rather than the cultivation of a beard. It was still too hot for beards in late summer.

Frankly, there were a few too many small mulatto children running around the slave dwellings for my liking.

I could see Quash watching them too. Their skin color matched his own. Quash's mother, Betty, was of indeterminate age and resided at our Wappoo property. A woman with stronger hands I'd never met. She used those hands for a skill usually undertaken by Negro men: to grapple marsh grasses without cutting herself, twisting and threading them into baskets woven so tight we could carry water if necessary. Those capable hands were black as the pitch in the barrels we were currently inspecting. Sometime in the past, an overseer or some other white man had planted the seed of Quash, who had grown up to become our most trusted driver.

I wondered if Quash knew or cared who had sired him. I was ashamed to admit it had never crossed my mind before now. We'd inherited him along with nineteen other slaves at our Wappoo property. Then Father had bought both this acreage and the one we'd visited a few days ago, deep inland on the banks of the Combahee River, and these properties had far more slaves apiece. *A necessary evil,* my father had counseled me. *Impossible to build a new world without able-bodied help.* Unfortunately, our new world also came with "necessary" hard-handed overseers already in place. Like Starrat.

"You can send word down to Miss Lucas at Wappoo if you have any delays or changes to things we've discussed." My father shook out his kerchief and mopped his brow and the back of his neck again.

The heat was rolling and oppressive. Rather than a cooling breeze off the water, the air off the churning, brackish Waccamaw River seemed to press the heat more firmly upon our shoulders.

Starrat barely glanced in my direction. "Sir, I can just as easily send the note to Beale in Charles Town, it would reach you sooner." That he made mention of our merchant contact, Othniel Beale, with so much familiarity made me wonder how much business he was conducting outside of his official capacity.

"Be that as it may, I'd prefer Mistress Lucas to be aware of all that is relevant here so that she may take it into account. She will be keeping my records."

"And does Miss Lucas have other male assistance at Wappoo? An overseer to help with the business side of things? Or keep her Negroes in line." Starrat glanced at me, his gaze shifty.

Inwardly, I bristled.

"*Mistress* Lucas is more than capable, I assure you," my father returned curtly. Starrat either didn't notice or ignored the warning in my father's tone.

"Well, if you don't discipline these savages, who's to say they won't rise up and overpower their owners. I keep my Negroes well in hand, sir," Starrat boasted with a hard tone that spoke of necessary violence.

It was difficult not to look over at the whipping post while he spoke.

Papa tucked his hand into his pocket and brought out a small case of tobacco and his pipe.

Starrat brought his pipe out also, and my father offered him a pinch of tobacco. They ambled toward a little cooking fire that was left smoldering for much of the day, only stoked up at mealtimes.

"They are *my* Negroes, Starrat," my father said with an edge that brooked no argument. Clearly, his patience with Starrat had been sorely tested.

My father grabbed a piece of straw from the ground and stuck it into the fire. A small flame flared, birthing a smoke tendril that curled and plumed. He lit his pipe, puffing the 'bacca until it lit, then flicked the straw to the fire. "I am the owner of this property and them too. You, however, are employed at my indulgence."

The atmosphere turned frigid, and I tensed at my father's immediate engagement.

"And I would rather receive correspondence from my daughter. She has our Negroes well in hand also," he added.

Starrat sneered, though he attempted to hide it.

Nodding toward the whipping post, my father went on, "Excessive labor or brutal punishment can incite revolt. I'll not have that occurring on my land … or my conscience."

I knew right away I would not be visiting out here much after Father's departure. I only hoped Starrat was trustworthy in business and would be no trouble in that regard. At that moment I had a choice to meet his eyes and show my mettle, but I decided not to throw down the gauntlet and make an enemy. He scared me, and I worried he would see through my bravado. I asked myself if avoiding his look was a cowardly act or a smart one.

I continued to gaze innocently about and my attention was caught by some slave women carrying bundles of sticks back toward the dwellings. "Oh," I exclaimed, genuinely surprised and disentangling myself from Papa. "Look at their skirts. It's just like back home in Antigua."

We all turned to look. The women dropped their gazes to the ground when they noticed us staring at them and hastened their steps, their faded blue sack skirts swishing against dusty dark skin. I was instantly aware I'd made them the focus of Starrat's attention.

Starrat made a wet snorting sound behind me, coughing something up his throat. I turned just in time to see him spit a splat of red-tinged yellow slime to the ground. My stomach roiled, the sight not helping much in the heavy damp heat. "Indigo," he confirmed with a wet growl. "Negro quality. Not quite the stuff you're used to seeing, I'm afraid. I let them grow a bit here and there."

"Interesting. Are you harvesting it?" my father asked.

"One can't grow it in proper quantities if that's where you're headed, sir," he said dismissively. "Many have tried and failed. It's just not the right soil here. And certainly getting it into a tradable form is beyond what these folk are capable of."

"I've heard the French have some indigo growing down in Louisiana," my father mused. "Certainly the terrain in the Indias is different. But I hear Louisiana may be more akin to our terrain and climate."

"Well, they don't get frost down there," Starrat said importantly. "I suppose that's the difference." His stubby fingers, the nails impressed with dirt, scratched at his rough whiskered chin. The color of the stubby growth was mottled like a mangy dog.

I nodded in agreement. "I suppose it is."

AFTER A MEAL OF BREAD, cheese, and peaches that we shared with our overseer, we summoned Quash, who had disappeared to eat his own meal. Bidding farewell to Starrat, we loaded up some supplies of butter and rice and enlisted his promise to send updates to me at Wappoo on a monthly basis at the very least.

After loading the wagon onto the Georgetown ferry, my father and I found a spot on a wooden bench. The water swelled dark in the fading light, the breeze was blessedly cool. Papa turned toward me. "What is being carried on the mill wheel of your thoughts, dear Betsey? I can almost hear the creak and groan as you think." Somehow, with his imminent departure, I clung to the love bound up in that childish nickname.

"We are making much pitch and tar for the shipbuilding industry," I answered. "Should we not also plant many more live oaks for wood? They are the best for shipbuilding, are they not?"

"Yes, the hardest for sure. Though they take fifty years or more to reach a size that can be harvested."

"Well, we should always look to the future. You taught me that. I should like permission to plant more live oaks at Wappoo, Papa."

"Of course." My father chuckled. "Permission granted. Anything else?"

"And I should like to speak to Mr. Deveaux about what other crops we may attempt, perhaps even indigo. I don't believe for an instant that it can't be done."

"Be careful not to make an enemy of Starrat, Eliza."

"I'll be careful, sir." I paused. "Could another be found to oversee the property? He's such a horrid man. I know it wouldn't be easy, but—"

"Horrid though he may be, Starrat knows that land better than anyone. He performs. The land is profitable. For us to remove him now … could set us back irreparably."

"Of course, Papa." I didn't want to appear as though I could not handle the difficulties, so I stopped pressing. "You are right, of course. Thank you for asking him to remove that whipping post. I don't like it. We should have stayed to make sure he obeyed this time."

He dropped his voice. "Not as many people have as free a mind and affection as you do, Eliza. Not many understand that we accord a certain friendship and respect to our Negroes. And 'tis a dangerous pursuit."

My hands gripped the railing of our vessel. "Why, Papa?" I implored quietly. We had had this discussion before on the topic of my dear friend Benoit in the Indias. Ben and I had grown up together as children; of an almost exact age, our friendship was indulged by my parents with amusement. Likened to a fairground curiosity. Indeed, as soon as the novelty wore off for my mother I had been sent to England for schooling, at a younger age than most. But upon my return, years later, our friendship was renewed, stronger than ever, and of sudden great concern to those around us. Especially my mama. I argued that it was simply impossible to put aside fond childhood memories. And Ben was so clever. I learned so much about plants and flowers from him; knowledge passed down by his grandmother. I credited him with my love of botany. It was probably the reason my father allowed it so long. *Why should our friendship with Negroes cause danger?* I'd begged my mother once when I was six years old. *Papa talks business with Cesar. He often tells me how wise he is.* I'd earned a violently smarting backside and no supper for that flippant remark.

After the slave uprising of 1736 in the Indias that had seen the execution, by burning, of our dear Negro Cesar the following year, I was forbidden to continue my friendship with Ben. The failed revolt and its consequences had set our Negroes to wailing and singing in the night for weeks, while I, having just returned from England, shivered in my bed.

Of course that didn't stop a headstrong fifteen-year-old

girl. So I would wander over to the fields under the guise of getting some air as many times as I could get away under my mama's watchful eye. Her increasingly plentiful maladies meant that was more often than not.

My father had been deeply troubled and saddened at the loss of Cesar. And I couldn't help but want to beg why he hadn't intervened to save his life. Even while I knew that politically my father's hands were tied. Even Ben himself had started drawing away from me. It was as if some invisible divide had sprung up overnight, and it took my naïve self a while to realize it had always been present. It didn't hurt my heart any less. For days and weeks I would arrive down the track, past the sugarcane, through the trees, out of breath, to the edge of the field I knew Ben always worked, only to find strangers' distrustful eyes warily watching me. I was welcome no longer.

"The danger is not from the Negroes, dear 'Liza." My father's reply jarred me from this dismal reverie. "But from the folk in town and roundabouts. You must be very cautious; people will be watching."

"That whipping post needs to be removed in any case," I insisted. "You've often said 'one can always judge a man's character by how he treats those beneath him.'" I didn't need to fill in what I thought of Starrat's character.

Father nodded. "It's true. And violence begets violence."

"You don't think there will be a revolt here like there was in Antigua do you, Papa?"

"I fear if there is but even a whiff of some uprising, the suspects will surely be hanged before questioning. You never want to be standing too close to someone accused. Think of poor Cesar. I know you think I could have prevented what happened to him, but it was out of my power." He cleared his throat.

I laid a hand gently on his arm. "I know, Papa."

Glancing at Quash, I imagined I saw his back stiffen. My father wasn't as quiet as he intended. Or perhaps he meant to impart a warning. But Quash would never be involved in such a thing. Surely. Then again, neither would Cesar have done so. Or so we'd thought. And now we would never know if he was innocent or guilty.

"I should hate to lose anyone else," Father added softly. After that he grew very quiet as he often did when we had occasion to talk of Cesar.

Four

The day of my father's departure to Antigua was finally upon us. We'd arrived in town the previous afternoon, in time for supper. It was six miles by boat from our home on the bluff at Wappoo Creek, flowing with the outgoing tide along the creek and out into the wide and more treacherous Ashley River. We rounded the peninsula toward the harbor, our hired pirogue propelled by the rhythmic motion and strength of six Negroes, their dark skin rippling with movement and glistening in the sun. The sound of their labored huffs of breath were lost in the ripple of water and cawing gulls.

A large man-of-war was docked, and people scurried up and down a ramp loading cargo and disembarking for more. This was presumably the ship my father would be sailing upon. Currently, a group of slaves, some Negro, some Indian, and one white man hauled a wheeled pallet weighed down with timber. They moved agonizingly slowly up a long ramp, the rope looking almost as heavy as one of the trunks of wood. Sugar production in the islands was desperate for timber and that had become an export for us from Starrat's operation. I guessed since my father was setting sail on this military vessel there was room to add additional cargo that was also destined for Antigua. I winced at the agony painted on the faces of the straining men.

The loud and foul fish-smelling chaos of the harbor soon had my full attention as we docked and disembarked, seeking out the driver the Pinckneys had kindly sent to collect us.

The dirt-packed roads of Charles Town were ripe with the smell of horse dung, and the heavy, wet heat of the day made sure it clung, wilting us of our last stores of energy by the time we arrived at the Pinckneys' townhouse on Union Street.

All of us, except for Polly, who had stayed behind with Esmé, sat in grim silence throughout the duration of our sweltering trip in the hot sun. My quiet was born of equal parts grief and anticipation at my father's impending departure. I would miss him so, and I hated not knowing when I'd see him again. My mother was practically vibrating with something so heavy you could almost see it shimmering off her. Was she sad? Resentful? She'd held her face averted, her eyes watching the view wherever we passed. I fancied she compared every mile to the rolling green fields of England, and very obviously found them lacking.

Mrs. Pinckney—she'd never offered her Christian name of Elizabeth and so I never used it—fussed over us as soon as we arrived in the cool, calming comfort of her home, clucking and suggesting we stay on in town a few days or weeks after my father left. I readily agreed to a few days as returning to our home at Wappoo knowing my father would not be there for perhaps a year or more was not a happy event to face. However, I was anxious to take over duties, and by my calculation, a boat was expected from our Garden Hill plantation in less than a week. I'd need to inspect and count the goods aboard before it went on to our merchant in town.

"Oh, my dears," Mrs. Pinckney soothed later that

evening from across her waxed dining table, her kind face gently lined. She wore her hair under a white linen cap, her dress the color of primroses. It nicely complemented the pale green brocade curtains and sumptuous furnishings of her home. The table was aglow with the sweet myrtle candles. She was a daisy in a lush evening meadow. I didn't own anything so fine, though Mama, of course, still had some of her gowns from London. My body was slowly filling out, but with my diminutive stature, I wasn't sure I'd even be able to borrow a dress with modifications if the occasion called for it. Perhaps I'd grow taller at some stage too. "How ever will you manage?" Mrs. Pinckney continued.

"You simply must come and visit me in town often. Also, I shall introduce you to Mary Chardon. She's young, though widowed. But she lives with her parents near your stand at Wappoo. I can't bear the thought of you ladies so lonely out there. Charles," she turned to her husband, "you will go and pop in on them often, won't you?"

Mr. Pinckney smiled fondly at his wife. "Of course, dear."

I fidgeted with my napkin. "I can't fathom having even a thought of loneliness with so much business to occupy my time—"

"But of course we shall come and visit you," Mama interjected. "We would be honored. Eliza must—"

I gulped. "And we would welcome getting to know our neighbors roundabouts." I had no idea if Mama was about to hawk me on the marriage mart, but I was compelled to use my age as an excuse for impetuous interruption. "Perhaps I could see what they are growing on their land if their soil is similar."

"I don't suppose there are any eligible young men close to our stand?" my mother tacked on, and I inwardly quailed.

"I have trained Eliza well," my father responded to Mrs.

Pinckney's initial concern, artfully redirecting from my mother's remark. "She has been helping me this last year, and she will be copying all her letters and the transactions of the plantations in her copy book. So should there be any question, there will be a record of events."

"It's not quite the ideal pastime for a girl of sixteen." My mother smiled apologetically at our hosts to show she really was not on board with the preposterous scheme. "But as we are waiting for George to come of age, she'll have to do."

"Nonsense," said Mrs. Pinckney graciously. "We are building a new society, and I daresay, we shall all step outside our normal roles from time to time to get the job done." She glanced at her husband. "Don't you always say that, Charles?"

"Indeed, dear."

I smiled at her gratefully.

"And certainly," Charles added, nodding toward my father, "as far as anyone is concerned, you have all the business set up for production and exports. Eliza will merely be a figurehead. Doing *your* bidding."

I was momentarily incensed. Mr. Pinckney caught my gaze, his twinkling eyes in on some joke. I fancied I imagined him wink. Did he know how little my and my mother's visions for my future coincided? Was he humoring her?

"Quite," my father agreed. My father wisely said nothing of the fact I'd already been running the household in my mother's stead. Not to mention making planting decisions and directing labor when he was too busy.

Mrs. Pinckney smiled indulgently. "No one can fault you for that, Colonel Lucas," she said, making use of his new title.

I squeezed my hands tightly under the table and ordered my features to remain expressionless. But I could see Mrs. Pinckney was directing her observations to appease my mama.

Though I did not know if she believed what she was saying.

Mr. Pinckney withdrew a pouch of 'bacca. His dark hair was pomaded and slightly graying at the temples. A prominent lawyer in town, he was an agreeable and well-read gentleman whose library I always seemed to find myself in whenever we visited. Goodness knew, I'd almost exhausted our small library at Wappoo.

Mr. Pinckney lit his pipe and, squinting through a plume of smoke, rested his keen and deep gray-blue eyes upon me. I was surprised he hadn't left the table with Papa to partake of this after-supper ritual in his study. "I wouldn't underestimate Eliza's industry," he said. "Besides"—he released the smoke in a long fragrant plume—"Eliza is right here to answer for herself. And I have the feeling she doesn't much care for convention. Am I right, Miss Lucas?"

Heat bloomed under the skin of my cheeks and I glanced at Mama, who glared, willing me not to embarrass her. Perhaps she'd hoped the Pinckneys hadn't yet realized my differences from the average girl my age. Or at least what I understood them to be. But it was clear they surely had.

"Well, sir." I rose to the challenge despite, or perhaps in response to, my mother's warning look, and lifted my chin. "If by convention you mean for the eldest child to step into the breach and ensure the legacy of one's family, then I do believe you are quite wrong. I do surely believe in doing that."

My mother's eyes bulged.

Mr. Pinckney sat back, his lithe frame bowing away from the table as his eyes danced with amusement and satisfaction.

"Quite right," my father muttered, earning a scowl from Mama.

Warmth continued to beat in my cheeks. "But if you are referring to the convention that states a *son* should take this on and not a daughter, then you are perhaps correct. I don't believe in conventions. But conventions, by definition, are just that. The conventional way people of like mind do things. Conventions are not rules. And certainly that should allow for some individual freedom with which to conduct one's affairs in the way that best suits. Besides, my brother is not here. And I am."

There was silence around the table.

I blinked and took a breath, then reached for my wine.

"Indeed, you are," came Mr. Pinckney's deep melodious voice. "Indeed, you are."

My mother was mute.

I dropped my eyes and picked at the seam in my brocade dinner gown, noting it needed a needle and thread.

"Eliza has plans for the Wappoo land too." My father jumped in, presumably to rescue the situation. And promptly made it worse. "Don't you, Eliza?"

"Oh dear," my mother muttered, and then to Mrs. Pinckney, "I do apologize. I'm afraid my husband only encourages Eliza's precocious nature."

"And what plans are those?" Mr. Pinckney ignored my mother's conversational exit plan.

"Just a few days ago she asked if she might plant more live oaks for the shipbuilding industry. An eye for the future this one."

"Well, the soil at Wappoo is not the right sort to grow rice on any large scale," I managed softly. "Besides, we already have rice exports from Garden Hill and some from Waccamaw. I should actually like my father to send seeds from the Indias when he arrives there so that I may experiment."

"And indeed I shall," my father said. "If this thing with the Spaniards erupts it may affect our rice exports. We'll need alternatives."

"What crops do you have in mind, Miss Lucas?"

"Well, I know cotton grows fairly well, and alfalfa." I thought of what I'd seen grow in the West Indias. "I should like to try ginger and perhaps indigo. It shall all be a bit chaotic for a while I imagine, while we get to know this new climate. I fear last winter there was a touch of frost, which we never got in Antigua, so I shall have to be very cautious."

"I believe indigo has been attempted here already without much success." Mr. Pinckney indulged my conversation. "I tried some out on our land at Belmont at Mr. Deveaux's urging. It didn't take, I'm afraid. We have orange trees; we could give you some of those seeds."

"Thank you. I should very much like to discuss what you've had success with." I smiled. "Besides, even if we could grow indigo, the actual dye-making is a tricky, and quite frankly, mysterious process," I said.

"Does it have blue petals on the bloom then?" Mrs. Pinckney asked.

I had the feeling that my mother's manners were preventing her from gently reprimanding Mrs. Pinckney for encouraging me. I loved this topic, having learned a small bit about indigo from my friend Ben, so I took the opportunity while I had it.

"That's the absolute marvel of it. Not only does it *not* have blue flowers, but apparently one must harvest it before the flowers even bloom. And the work has to be done fast, very fast. And there is a formula to follow, or all hope is lost."

My father chuckled. "It's true. It's practically a dusty old weed, and the Negroes seem to have brought the knowledge with them from Africa. It is quite extraordinary. Though we never got around to producing much yield or quality on our island plantations before we left."

I thought of Ben and his grandmother. "The secret has

been passed down through generations, perhaps even from ancient times."

Mrs. Pinckney raised her eyebrows. "How mysterious."

"Quite," I agreed.

"How on earth did the first person figure out how to extract the dye?" she asked. "It quite boggles the mind."

"Exactly," I exclaimed, so happy to have another person think as I did.

"Do you think perhaps someone just stumbled upon it one day?"

"I think it's far too complicated a process for that to have happened," I said, thinking back to watching the Negroes beating the dye endlessly, for hours at a time. Not letting it out of their sight. Waiting for the exact moment to … what exactly? I couldn't quite remember. And the smell of fermenting and decaying leaves was enough to turn the belly inside out. Nobody puts up with a smell like that by accident.

"Well," said Mr. Pinckney, looking at me thoughtfully, "it may be a mysterious process, but it is certainly a lucrative one. I do believe I read that London pays the French over two hundred thousand pounds per annum for indigo from their colonies."

My breath froze in my chest at that ungodly amount of money. "For how much indigo? Do you know?"

Mr. Pinckney assessed me.

Mrs. Pinckney raised her eyebrows.

I could feel my mother gritting her teeth next to me at my questions, dying to apologize for my unladylike behavior but not willing to really acknowledge it. My father seemed oblivious to his wife's tension.

"Oh, I do apologize," I backtracked quickly. "My mama always says I am quite headstrong and like to charge ahead. It was idle curiosity, that is all."

"Of course, Miss Lucas. No one thought otherwise," Mr. Pinckney allowed. "However, now that you mention it, I would like the answer to that very question." And then he winked at me.

AS I LAY IN A GLORIOUSLY COMFORTABLE BED that night, in one of the few brick houses in Charles Town, I couldn't keep my mind quiet. It was as if all the events of the last few days had been pointing me to this. The recurring dreams I had, seeing the slave women up at Waccamaw with their blue dyed skirts and finally the direction of the conversation at supper.

A fire had been kindled inside me and no matter which way I looked at it, I knew I wouldn't, couldn't, let it go out.

Back in Antigua, I'd often taken walks over to the indigo fields to watch the Negroes checking the stalks and leaves for the perfect time to harvest. Really, I was usually going to find Ben. But over time, I became enthralled.

It is an ancient secret, Ben would say, his smile broad and blinding against the dark of his skin.

If what Pinckney said about indigo was true, it could save us. It would save *me*. There was no way my father and mother would foist me off on some mean old man needing an heir. There was no way they would give the running of the plantation business to George if *I* was the one who had made it a success and released the property from its debt. At the very least it would allow me my pick of suitors if marry I must.

And how long did I really have? Three crop seasons to get it right. If I didn't succeed by then, marriage was my only option. A marriage not to save the family or our land—a wealthy man could buy himself a more biddable wife than I—but marriage so my family would not have to support me any longer.

I'd need help if I were to try my hand at indigo and succeed. I would need someone who knew what he was doing. The Negroes up at Waccamaw clearly knew a way to do it. But how did it go from small batches of liquid dye to something we could send for trade on a large-scale basis?

I had spent enough time fascinated with the intricate dye-making process that I couldn't help but wonder about whether we could do it here. I wished I'd paid more attention when I'd returned to Antigua from England. Making dye and producing it in a form that was tradable were clearly two very different things. As far as I knew, the dye didn't necessarily keep. We could hardly barrel it as I had no idea what being in wood would do to the dye long-term. I saw large, square, brick vats in my memory but those were for mixing.

An idea had unfurled in my mind along with the fire in my chest. I would speak to my father first thing, and I knew exactly what to ask him. I just hoped I could catch him privately, otherwise Mama would have a fit.

Five

The following morning I arose early as usual, despite my restless night. I could hear movement downstairs and thumping as my father's trunks were loaded. I drew on my petticoats and, without Essie to help me, hurriedly did the best I could with the rest of my dress and hair.

The Pinckneys' home was as nice a home in Charles Town as I'd had the pleasure to visit. Some of the furnishings were of silk from a nearby plantation and damask imported from Europe. I hoped when the Pinckneys called on us at Wappoo they weren't offended by our more simple furnishings. Certainly, they were gracious enough never to mention it. How different from the pecking order of London society my mother lived by.

I slipped from the guest room and padded hastily down the stairs to find my father standing at the open front door supervising the loading of his trunks.

Taking a breath and mustering my best businesslike tone I began, "Father. Colonel, sir."

He turned in the doorway, the blue dawn giving his face a ghostly pall for a moment. For a brief flicker I felt this might be the last time I would ever see him, and the thought sent a sharp pain through me. I gasped and threw my arms about my father.

He caught and held me close against the rough texture of his military jacket. It smelled of pipe tobacco and the linseed oil they used aboard ships to preserve the wood.

"Papa," I managed through my tightly closed throat.

Immediately he withdrew his handkerchief for me.

"I'm sorry, Father," I said, taking it gratefully.

"It's not forever, Eliza. You be strong now. Do you hear? Your mother needs you. Polly needs you. *I* need you."

I nodded.

"As soon as George finishes his schooling and then his commission in the military, he will come and relieve you. A few years at most."

Swallowing, I knew now was not the time to worry him about my thoughts on that score. There were more pressing matters. "Father." Pausing, I tried to form the sequence of words I hoped would have the best outcome. "The conversation last night ... about indigo. I should very much like to try it. But I was thinking we will need a consultant. I remember so much from watching and ..." I went on high alert watching my father's face as I continued. "And from watching Ben and listening to him—"

My father's eyes grew wary as I suspected they would at my mention of Ben. "Where are you going with this, Eliza?"

"There are folks here who know the indigo process. I can learn. I will learn, but we need someone who knows the process well. We can't afford mistakes." I couldn't afford them because I had limited time before I was on the marriage market, and because my father had encumbered our property for his military ambitions.

"I want seeds as soon as possible, Papa. Though I shall start with some seeds from old Mr. Deveaux if he has some. And ..."

"Out with it, Eliza," my father said impatiently.

I took a deep breath and squeezed my sweaty hands into

fists in the folds of my skirts. "I should like you to send Ben."

"Impossible." My father's surprised response was immediate. "And even if it were not, your mother would never stand for it. What is this madness, Eliza?"

For a moment I couldn't gather my words.

"You don't need anyone. I have faith in you, Eliza."

What a heavy mantle about my shoulders, even while I knew his words were simply to deflate my argument. "Please, Papa," I begged, lowering my voice.

"It's impossible." My father's tone was firm.

"It's not," I argued, heedless of the warning in his eyes. "Mama will understand. It will be for the plantations. For us. For our success."

He sighed, his eyes furrowed with concern. "It's impossible because he was sold to an indigo maker in Montserrat around the time we left."

The air left my lungs, my heart falling through my stomach. I struggled not to show anything in my expression. *Oh, Ben*, I thought.

I had a vision of the first time I saw him as a young boy. He'd seemed my age, though I came to know he was a year older. He and his grandmother were walking along the jungle path between the dwellings and the fields. She stopped every few seconds as they walked, pointing out this plant and that, speaking in her soft dialect I had no understanding of. Curious, I'd trailed behind. Once he turned around, catching me in my inspection, and settled his large eyes on me. Eyes so dark that, especially in the shade of the tree canopy, they looked almost black.

Then he turned away.

I picked up a berry and threw it hard at his back.

Why? I have no earthly idea. Perhaps I was cross at being ignored.

He didn't react.

I tried again. My aim was good. I knew he felt it. Why was he ignoring me? When they reached the dwellings, I stopped, deflated and disappointed. I was allowed no farther and suppertime was soon. I hiked up my skirts and began skipping home when a sharp thwack on the back of my dress caught me by surprise. I squeaked and turned around.

The boy was standing on the track behind me, a hand full of berries, and slowly he picked another with his free hand and threw it hard.

Right at me.

The red berry juice exploded on the front of my linen frock. I inhaled in shock, narrowed my eyes, and glared. I knew I would be in trouble for dirtying my clothes. So much trouble, just the thought of it had my backside smarting.

His dark face suddenly split open into a blinding white smile, and he threw another. I dodged with a yelp and he giggled. It was the most mesmerizing sound, a cascading waterfall of glee. I glanced about and spying some berries on an adjacent bush, hastily plucked them up while dodging another volley.

As soon as I was armed, the boy slipped behind a tree. And for the next short while, with squeals and peals of laughter, we played an elaborate game of attack and retreat until I reached for another bush of berries and the boy all but tackled me. Pushing me roughly down to the ground in his haste, he shook his head side to side in a panic.

"What the devil?" I'd yelled at him, and then saw the fear in his eyes. He pointed to the berries I'd been about to pluck. They looked identical to the ones I'd been hurling at him. Then he drew a line slowly across his neck.

I'd gulped, weak with the fear of what I'd almost done. Then I'd heard the bell ringing for supper up at the house and raced away, leaving him alone in the jungle.

The memory, unthought of for years and suddenly so clear in my mind, held my chest in a tight bind I could barely breathe through. All this time, I had assumed he was there. Back where I always thought he would be. Imagining him there gave me comfort. I don't think in the years that had followed, I ever thanked him for saving my life, for surely that was what he had done.

I swallowed. "Was … is the person he was sold to a good man?"

My father's eyebrows snapped together and his head cocked sideways.

I shook my head and thought of a more mundane reason for my concern. "I … I just would hate for his skill with plants to be underappreciated." My voice caught.

"Eliza," my father said gently. With empathy. I could hide it, but he knew what Ben meant to me. My father's friendship with his man Cesar contained a respect that went outside the bounds of slave and owner. But he'd never known that Ben saved my life as a child. He was more than a friend.

"Don't," I said quickly, turning away before he saw the sheen in my eyes. "I'm emotional with your departure, that is all."

"Even if I could have sent him, Eliza, your mother would not stand for it," he said gently. "By selling him to this man, he was being given a chance. A chance to become valuable. Indigo makers are highly prized."

I nodded, buying myself a moment to modulate my tone. "Thank you," I allowed, then gathered my wits. "Father, please just listen. You trust me, I know you do, or you wouldn't be leaving me in charge. And you trust me to find a successful crop. This is it. I know it. I am sure of it. But—"

"Then try it. I have enough faith that you will succeed

without Benoit Fortuné's help." That he used the name I had bestowed upon my childhood friend, Ben the Fortunate, was his way of trying to appease me.

"If you saw it in Ben, then please. Perhaps you can buy him from this man in Montserrat." I grabbed at the opportunity—what I thought was his softening. It was a mistake.

"Enough, Eliza," my father boomed, his eyes flashing with anger and disappointment.

I stepped back at his outburst, my blood pounding with humiliation so loud it rang in my ears along with my father's reprimand. I bit my lip at my stupidity. This was not the adult conversation I had planned to have, laying out my reasoning and sound judgment. I should have simply asked for a consultant. Any consultant. Not thrown my whole argument away on Ben when I knew how long the odds were. My eyes stung and my cheeks burned.

"Eliza." His tone softened in apology. He sounded tired and weary. "I'm not sure you should take on this responsibility."

I snapped my eyes to his, my mouth opening to protest, but he held up his hand. "Let's just take it a moment at a time. I have left instructions with your mama to consult with the Pinckneys at any time to install an overseer at Wappoo if it becomes too much."

"No, Father." I tried and failed to control the tremor in my voice. "I can do this, I swear it. I will make sure you never regret this choice. And furthermore I'll make sure to do a better job than any person you could dream up to usurp me." *Even my brother George*, I didn't say. This was perhaps my only chance to show my father I was destined for more than being some man's wife. Perhaps one day. But not yet. What was wrong with being a spinster anyway?

As if he heard my innermost thoughts of my opposition

to marriage, my father continued. "By the by, you are wrong about one thing. Perhaps back in London men prefer empty-headed wives. But here in the new world, it is all hands on deck. Any man would be lucky to have a practical and educated lady such as you to partner and build his future with."

I swallowed hard at the near impossible dream my father had for me. Oh how I wished it was so, but Mama attempted to disabuse me of the notion as often as she could. I felt my father naïve, though I humored him. "Well, I have you, my esteemed father, to thank for my education. A gift more valuable could never have been bestowed upon me."

"'The very spring and root of honesty and virtue lie in good education,'" My father quoted, his eyes adrift as if he could see the words.

"A Greek?"

"Indeed. Plutarch. I love your headstrong nature, Betsey." My father chuckled, his tension broken. "But I fear I have cultivated far too much ambition in you. And allowed far too much leniency. You may yet get yourself into trouble."

I dropped my gaze, chastened. "I would never dishonor you so, sir."

Six

The scene down at the Charles Town harbor was busier than when we'd arrived the day before. Last minute supplies were being run up the ramp of the large man-of-war that would carry my father away; big bundles and crates hoisted with ropes swung dangerously for outstretched arms. Sailors crawled like ants over the massive vessel, calling out orders and joining with the chorus of early morning fisherman arguing with the fish merchants.

The tide was in and the water lapped at the quays. As soon as it began to ebb, my father's ship would be off. He had left us briefly to go and see about his berth and speak with the captain, and my mother and I waited patiently on the upper harbor wall for him to return and bid us adieu.

"Make sure your purse strings are hidden, Eliza," my mother chided when she could see that I was gazing in awe at the activity in front of me down on the lower level of the quay. She sounded weary as always. Her skin was pale again this morning, and I had the notion she would be abed as soon as the noonday meal was done.

"Yes, Mama."

I watched with rapt interest as a group of Indian tradesmen, their lower garments of animal skins, their upper bodies bare, haggled with a merchant over some fish and deerskin. I had never before seen a man's body. Our Negroes always wore shirts. I knew men's chests were like ours, just without breasts. But though I wasn't close, I could see the lines of body and muscle beneath skin, like you could under the fur of a strong horse.

"Eliza!"

I whipped my face away, cheeks blazing hot. "Sorry, Mama. They look so savage is all. Didn't anyone show them how to make shirts?" I laughed, then cleared my throat at my mother's unimpressed, pursed mouth.

"The tide will soon turn. I must embark," my father boomed as he headed toward us.

My mother was getting paler and paler as the heat of the day rose, her eyes tightening in discomfort. "Is it your head, Mama?" I asked, leading her with my father's help a few steps toward the narrow slip of shade offered by a port wall.

She nodded.

"Let us say our farewells with haste." My father looked toward me, and I answered him with a tight hug.

"Don't worry, Father." My voice caught. I inhaled a dose of heavy pungent harbor air and cleared my throat. Pulling away from his hug while I had the strength not to clutch him and beg him not to leave us, I blinked rapidly. "I will take care of Mama, Polly, and all your concerns," I vowed, swallowing hard.

His eyes too were shimmering, and it almost broke my composure. "I know you will, Eliza. How did I get so lucky to have a capable daughter such as you?"

He drew his finger fondly down my cheek, his head cocked to one side. Then he nodded, satisfied at whatever he saw, and turned to my mother.

I spun away before my eyes spilled over, affording my parents some privacy.

The ship left on the tide with my father aboard.

AFTER LESS THAN A DAY IN TOWN, I was anxious to return to our home on Wappoo Creek. I had neglected my studies and my music, and I missed the deep melodious hum of the slaves working in the fields, and the birds outside my windows at first light. The clatter of hooves and shouts of men in town was not a music I enjoyed.

And more than anything, I was eager to visit Andrew Deveaux that I might inquire after some indigo seeds with which to start experimenting. I would need to ask among our slaves if anyone had indigo knowledge and if not, send for someone from Garden Hill or Waccamaw.

My mission was clear and I was anxious to begin.

It hardly left me with a second to miss my departed father.

WE SET OUT THE FOLLOWING MORNING in the pirogue. White topsails still dotted the harbor and horizon, but the large man-of-war was long gone. The salt wind blustered and bashed at our ears. Mama was as somber on the way home as she had been on our way to see my father off. Only this time she wasn't mute.

"We probably have a year or so, then Papa will be back. Until then, we shall keep your activities in low profile. Perhaps visit Mrs. Pinckney in town more often, especially when her niece arrives."

"I'll accompany you when I can, Mama," I said firmly. "But there is much to be done. Did you see how much timber is needed in the islands? You must have seen them loading the ships. The sugar plantations are in desperate need. I shall visit our other plantations and see about having some sent to Antigua."

"Yes, dear." My mother humored me.

"I think we can do to send double the amount. When I was up at Garden Hill with Papa—"

"Enough, Eliza. I don't feel like discussing business. Just do what has been asked of you, and squash that ugly and unladylike ambitious streak you have immediately. What on earth was your father thinking?"

"Ambition is ugly and unladylike? Who would have thought you would speak so harshly of ambition. You seem to have more ambition for me and my marriage prospects than I for helping Papa." My blood thundered in my ears to speak to my mother so. I swallowed hard but determinedly.

My mother's eyes widened in surprise. "What has gotten into you, Eliza? And that is very different."

"Is it, Mama?" I flicked my gaze away, then further turned my face and body to watch the marshy banks gliding by. Tension throbbed under the surface of my skin, and I marveled that God could have created my character in such opposition to my mother's. It was almost comical. Except it was not.

"Finding a husband and presenting oneself in the best light to a prospective suitor is of the utmost importance. Far from ambition, I'm afraid it is more of a necessity."

Coming around the turn in the wide creek, our home was a welcome sight. *Not for me*, I wanted to reply.

"In case you haven't noticed, there are not a lot of eligible families in this hot, swampy, godforsaken part of the world," she muttered.

I made out Quash in the distance awaiting our return at the small wooden dock. News of an arriving pirogue always traveled fast as the slave children kept a watchful eye on the water at all times. Up at the house, I could see the glimpse of pale fabric upon the veranda and guessed Esmé had deposited Polly outside with her sewing basket. The early afternoon breeze brought the smell of crabs and oysters, and some long-limbed birds gently loped through the marsh grass looking for stranded shrimp.

"Goodness," Mama said suddenly as we got closer.

"What is it?" I asked

"I didn't think. Stupid really. I just, I've never ..."

"Mother," I said, tired, "what is it?"

"Well, it's just I usually have a gentleman's assistance climbing out of the boat. Your papa ..." She trailed off.

I furrowed my brow for a moment knowing full well we had ventured out on small journeys without Papa before. "You'll be fine, Mama. It's a small step up. I'll help you."

"I know." She removed a small linen square from her purse and dabbed under her eyes. "I know. It's a silly thing really. It's always the smallest things that make one realize the magnitude of the loss."

"We haven't lost him, Mother." I forced an encouraging smile.

"Oh it's fine, Eliza. It just had not occurred to me." She gave a dramatic sigh. "I shall simply add it to the long list of adjustments that shall have to be made now that he's no longer here."

It had perhaps never occurred to me how dependent my mother was upon my father. Love? I didn't know. For certain, they were very fond of each other.

Just as Mama would be lonely without my father's presence in the months to come, I would be too. More so, for I would have to work in relative solitude, not sharing my triumphs or frustrations of plantation business with a soul. It would be best if I didn't discuss my plans much with my mama at all. She might have expired if she knew I'd asked Papa to send Ben over to South Carolina and certainly if she knew of the law books I'd pilfered from Mr. Pinckney's library, which currently huddled guiltily in the cloth sack behind the bench where I sat.

"Of course, Mama. And I did so enjoy hearing about Mrs. Chardon and her parents. To think! She lives so close. We shall have to make a plan to visit with her next week. Perhaps Tuesday? I say we should make a standing day of it. It will give us something to look forward to each week."

"How very thoughtful, Eliza." Mama seemed satisfied at the change in direction. "And as she is widowed, she may be pleased for the company. Very well. I shall look forward to that."

As soon as I had settled Mama and bidden a fond greeting to Polly, I went into my father's study to acquaint myself with his papers. He had shown me his ledgers, and now I spent a few hours poring over the accounts, familiarizing myself with our production and outputs.

Then I penned two letters.

One to Mr. Deveaux and another to my father.

Seven

The clatter of our horse and buggy was loud but surely not heard from miles away. Yet, as usual, as we trundled along the straight road that led to Mr. Deveaux's modest home he was already waiting, tall and stalklike. His keen eyes tracked our arrival.

Today I'd brought Polly along in place of her usual studies. If I'd told her she was to have a lesson in botany she would have pitched a fit. Instead, she chattered away above the rhythmic noise of our journey, asking questions for which she never awaited answers before her attention was caught again by some new wisp of thought.

"My, if he stood on one leg he would resemble one of our marsh birds." Polly giggled as she caught sight of our host in the distance.

Mr. Deveaux was a lean, bewhiskered gentleman who walked with a pale yellow ivory cane he once told me was a gift from a tribal chief in Africa, back when he was briefly an agent for the East India Company. He stood with it now, leaning a portion to the right, his clothes hanging from his birdlike body, framed by the lime-washed cottage behind him.

I shook my head with a small smile as we pulled close.

His eyes twinkled in return.

"You make me feel far above my station, sir," I called out. "No matter how often I ask you to await in the shade of the house, you are always out in the noonday sun."

"And let these old geriatric eyes miss a moment of enjoying the light and energy that is Miss Eliza Lucas?" His raspy chuckle warmed my heart.

"You are good for my vanity, Mr. Deveaux." I laughed delightedly and took his bony, outstretched hand as I carefully climbed down, then turned to help Polly. "And you are hardly geriatric. You remember my sister?"

"Ahh, Polly. The youngest Miss Lucas."

She sank into a small curtsy, then tugged on my skirt. "Can I go with Quash and the horses, 'Liza?"

"No, pet. I'd like you to come with me today."

"Please?" she begged.

Mr. Deveaux looked down his nose at her. "Miss Polly, have you ever encountered a macaron?"

Polly glanced up at me. I raised an eyebrow at her and gave a slight shrug, unable to answer myself.

"No, sir." She shook her head, then asked suspiciously, "Is it a bird or a plant?"

Mr. Deveaux guffawed. "None of those, dear one. But let me ask you this: If you were ever to eat a cloud stuffed with a rainbow, what do you think it should taste like?"

Polly's eyes widened, as did mine. "Is it a confection?" She gasped in delight.

"Well, let us go inside and find out."

I instructed Quash to return for me in two hours, and then I followed Mr. Deveaux and the Polly-shaped barnacle newly attached to his arm.

"To what do I owe the honor of a visit from you, Miss Eliza?" our gracious host asked as we found perches in the faded brocade-furnished front room of his home, furniture passed down from his Huguenot ancestors. The room smelled of the eucalyptus and rosemary bundles his house servant hung from the rafters to ward off the insects. Esmé usually confined ours to the kitchen because Mama complained of them so. "Did those seeds not sprout yet?" he asked after we had caught up on pleasantries and the news of the area.

"Oh, they have. I followed your instructions to the letter. They are on my sunny window ledge, lots of water every morning, and they have already unfurled little green shoots. I'm thrilled." I laughed. "I shall transfer them outside at your instruction. Today, I've come to talk to you about growing indigo for dye."

He raised a bushy white eyebrow. "Is that so? Well, I've grown woad, of course, but I'm afraid extracting enough dye to be profitable is not worth the effort."

My heart gave a leap. "So you know how to extract the dye?"

"I confess I find the extraction process something of a mystery, or should I say drudgery."

"When are we going to eat the macky cloudy things?" Polly interrupted. She looked at me accusingly, as if she'd been hoodwinked.

"All in good time, my dear," said Mr. Deveaux. With perfect timing his house servant, a short, plump woman with dark skin and wearing a sackcloth dress and white muslin about her head, came in with a tray and laid it out upon a low table. "Ah, Letty makes these from my grandmother's recipe she brought from Paris. In fact, I believe Letty has even improved upon them."

The woman, whom I presumed was Letty, hid a smile and scurried from the room.

"Let me," I insisted as I saw Mr. Deveaux shifting forward as if to pour. "Polly, why don't you offer the famous macarons?" I suggested and indicated the plate piled with circular items akin to meringues in looks, yet slightly grainier and ranging from pale pink to green to the off-white color of pounded rice flour. Polly clapped delightedly.

"I don't believe the indigo from the Indias is extracted from woad." I returned to our conversation. "The leaves weren't singularly broad. The branches grow as leaves would, and each then have almost a score of leaflets upon them marching up either side."

Mr. Deveaux rubbed his fingers over his chin. "I believe they are using *Indigofera*. The true indigo. I tried some myself several years ago. Bought the seeds from a fellow in town."

I nodded. "Exactly. It grows messily, like a weed or a thicket would. You would never believe anything blue about it. There's lots of it growing in Antigua where we grew up."

"Indeed, I have heard people talk of white indigo. That the substance is colorless before it becomes blue. There's a complicated process to extracting it."

"I've seen it," I said excitedly, a memory from childhood bursting into color. "When they remove cloth from the barrel you can see it turn blue before your very eyes."

"That sounds like magic," said Polly who had just swallowed her third confection and had crumbs about her mouth, but her eyes were wide and listening intently. Ha! Perhaps plants had finally become interesting to the little ragamuffin. I smiled at her.

"Indeed, Polly. It really is some great alchemy. The hand of God or the breath of angels."

"Can we grow magic plants, 'Liza?" Polly asked.

"We're going to try, love."

Polly furrowed her brow. "But how do you get the magic out?"

"I daresay you may need a consultant or some such." Mr.

Deveaux nodded thoughtfully. "*If* it can be grown. It's been tried, you know? Not just by myself. Without much success. And of course it will need to be made into dye cakes to sell."

"I know," I responded and tried not to let my disappointment grow. Again, I wished I'd asked Papa to consider a consultant, any consultant, should it become necessary, and not pushed so hard for Ben. But with the cost of my father's military endeavors it could well be a luxury we wouldn't be able to afford. "That we shall have to figure out. But first things first ..." I looked to Mr. Deveaux.

"I'm afraid I will only be able to give you seeds for woad plants. I don't have any West Indian indigo. The seeds I bought were useless. Only a few came up. Besides, they don't keep beyond a year or so, anyway. They'd be of no use to you."

"But you said woad had some blue in it too," said Polly, and I felt a rush of affection for my little sister who for a moment was clearly as caught up in the idea of magic plants as I was.

"Not as much, I'm afraid. It's probably not even worth the effort to extract. One has to plant and harvest so much of it."

Polly looked disappointed, but I was undaunted. "Perhaps we could use the woad to practice the indigo extraction process while I wait for Papa to send us some seeds from Antigua." In truth, I had already asked him as much in the first letter I penned to him.

"Do you know when one should plant?" I directed the question back to our host, and I began a mental list of which slaves I could ask to impart some of their indigo knowledge. I'd have to visit Waccamaw and speak with Starrat about the Negroes I'd seen there with the blue sackcloth skirts. The thought of having to meet with the nasty, bigoted overseer triggered a small shudder.

"Well, I'm certain that, as with most plants, as long as you avoid the frost times of year, you should be all right. You could plant as soon as possible, I suppose. If there is a particularly special time to plant, it is unknown to me."

"And me," I said, wondering if I could remember the times of year it was planted. Twice a year even, if I remembered correctly. And rain, lots of rain. That would not be easy to predict.

Polly had caught sight of Quash outside, and her attention on our conversation was lost; she sat on her hands, her feet fidgety in their leather travel slippers. "Polly, if you'd like to go and see what Quash is doing, you may. But do not dirty your frock and stay within calling distance. Mr. Deveaux and I will finish tea and then go pick out some seeds from his shed."

"Thank you," she squealed and made to run out of the room then came to a halt. "Sorry. Thank you for the macky things, Mr. Deveaux," she intoned solemnly. "Tea with you was a delightful diversion." She bobbed and then spun out the door.

"You have your hands full with that one." Mr. Deveaux chuckled.

I smiled and took a sip of tea.

LATER, ON THE BUMPY CARRIAGE RIDE HOME, the low sun bathing us through the trees in flickering warm yellow, Polly fell fast asleep, her small body pressed against me. I fondly ran my fingers over her soft hair, brushing it from her temples. I had meant to get to her lessons today; we were to work on her reading, and had brought a few simple books for that purpose, but I was loathe to wake her.

The two of us were jammed up in the front bench with Quash. Now that Papa had left I decided it was less irksome on my stomach for travel. He and Mama would probably think it unseemly.

Quash was quiet as usual. He took direction, reported facts in his unique brand of English, but as per his position as slave, never spoke unless spoken to.

In the year we had been in South Carolina, Quash had become almost indispensable. The thought that he might run away or join some rebellion popped into my head again. Where would I be without his help? I'd have to employ some awful overseer like Starrat to help at Wappoo. There was certainly no other slave who could drive and conduct business and communicate with the other slaves like Quash could.

"Quashy?"

He jerked, surprised.

"Sorry, I didn't mean to startle you," I said with a soft laugh.

"Yes'm," he responded, his eyes never leaving the track in front of our brown horse.

"I was thinking I'd like to improve the dwellings at Wappoo. Are there any that are in need of improvements?"

His face twitched to the side as if he wanted to glance at me. Like it was some trick. Then he nodded.

"Do you think you would be able to take on that extra work? I'd like it done. Just let me know if you need help and how much timber, and I'll get it from Garden Hill or Waccamaw."

"Thank you, Miz Lucas. Mebbe Sawney and Togo. Peter too." I approved of his use of our three largest and most capable field hands. Since there was nothing to harvest at the moment, it would be perfect timing.

"I should like for everyone to be warm and secure for the

winter. Mind they don't neglect the weeding while helping you," I added.

He nodded. Then he seemed to hesitate. "You *send fer* the timber, ya hear? There be no need fer ya to go up on Waccamaw without your father."

I glanced at him. Quash would be with me, of course. Quash always stayed out of trouble. But he might not be able to if I went to Waccamaw. If he had to protect me for some reason.

I swallowed hard.

The reality of taking over my father's business hit home with a thud deep in my stomach. "Of course, Quash. I'll send for it."

And I would have to find a different way to ask the women about their skirts.

We rumbled along and I wished the lowered sun meant the air would get cooler, but it only made it feel denser. Or perhaps that was the weight of the mosquitoes. I had dabbed rosemary and lemon oil about mine and Polly's exposed skin at Essie's insistence before we'd left Wappoo. I hoped it was still working.

"Quash, do you know what time of year is the best to grow indigo?"

"No, Miz Lucas."

"Well, perhaps the women at Waccamaw know. Will you ask if you go?"

He nodded.

"Thank you, Quash. I don't know what we'd do without you."

I said it without thinking and was immediately embarrassed. How could I thank someone for helping me when he had no choice? It was ludicrous. I thanked the servants all the time. I thanked Essie every day. I had never thought twice about it.

But suddenly it was all so odd. Thanking a person who had no other choice than to help you. The comment lay out there like a gasping fish. I opened my mouth to say something, I didn't know what.

"It's good your family done come to the plantation, Miz Lucas." Quash's voice was quiet and rumbly like the wheels of the cart.

I closed my mouth.

Then I nodded and blinked rapidly, but luckily he was looking at the road ahead.

Eight

Over the next few weeks, when he wasn't building, Quash and I picked out and cleared field areas where we might plant the woad given to me by Deveaux and also a new crop of alfalfa and some ginger.

I directed Togo, Indian Peter, and Sawney to till up the soil in the newly cleared areas and fertilize it to make it ready for planting.

We couldn't move the peach trees, of course, so we were confined to a long narrow strip that ran from behind the house back inland away from the water.

I wrote to Starrat and asked for building timber for Quash's work on reinforcing the quarters, and every day I checked the basket we had strapped upon the dock in case a ferry that passed had a letter or package from my father containing seeds he wanted me to try from Antigua. But in the end, we planted the woad.

Quash went up to Waccamaw and returned with the extra timber and materials he needed and the name of a Negro woman, Sarah, who had knowledge of indigo. She would come when it was time to harvest the woad plant and show me how to make the indigo solution. And as we waited for word from my father, Quash, Indian Peter, Sawney, and Togo got to work fixing up the roofs and drafty walls of the houses, rebuilding or sealing any gaps with daub. While we were building I also instructed them to erect another building as a kind of infirmary. I'd seen that the Pinckneys and also the Fenwicks over on John's Island had done this to lower the chance of an outbreak of infection if someone was taken ill. Essie said she thought it would be good to use for expectant mothers too.

The weather had been drier than usual. But as the weeks went on, the alfalfa and the ginger began peeking from the ground.

By the end of August, there was still no woad sprouting and no seeds from my father. The sense of time ticking past fruitlessly became unbearable, and dogged my every waking thought. My mind would slide to Ben repeatedly, wondering what he would say. Did we plant too early? Too late? Was the soil not right? I would imagine walking along the fields behind him as he inspected. I wondered if he had become a man now. He'd always been taller than me, but I imagine now I'd feel dwarfed.

I invited Mr. Deveaux over to inspect my fields where I had planted, and after declaring the land high enough to be sufficiently well drained, he directed that the seeds might benefit from double the amount of watering. The first watering was to be at dawn before the heat of the day baked the moisture away. I put Togo in charge of watering these and the myriad vegetables and herbs we had planted in a newly expanded kitchen garden. The deer were extremely partial to our bounty, and we'd expanded the wood-walled garden so the servants might have their produce protected too.

Mama had been feeling better despite the brutal heat of August that bled over into September. With my busy schedule we had not done much socializing despite a few invitations from the Pinckneys and other families roundabouts. The Woodwards and their widowed daughter, Mary Chardon, whom I'd learned about from Mrs. Pinckney, were one such family I was very partial to.

When Papa had been here we had tried to go to church at least two times a month. I decided that perhaps tomorrow being Sunday, we should go. It was probably five miles inland to the white, plaster-rendered church of St. Andrew's Parish run by Reverend Guy, a congenial shepherd who praised his parishioners for coming to worship rather than "guilting" those of us who hadn't been in some time. At the very least, I might make the acquaintance of more area planters. It was closer to attend there than make the journey into town and attend St. Philip's.

SUNDAY MORNING IN EARLY SEPTEMBER DAWNED cool and clear. I awoke at five as usual and quickly washed.

"Good morning, Essie," I said softly when she appeared at the door.

She bobbed. "Mornin', chil'." Her dark eyes were somber and creased. Everything about Essie was usually light and comforting. She could enter a space and float on the edges of your awareness like she wasn't really there unless you needed her. It was a quality I had come to depend on.

"Is everything all right?" I asked as we got to work lacing me up. "You seem troubled."

"Spirit dreams," she murmured. "There be a warnin' in da air today. You be goin' down to the river, you be careful, you hear?" Essie crushed some rosemary leaves with her nails, then rubbing them between the pale pads of her dark fingers, reached up, running them over my hair and dabbing the sides of my neck.

I frowned but said nothing. I was used to Essie's superstitions. Black crows, comets, dreams … but she prayed to my God too. Glancing out the window, all looked the same as every other morning in the predawn light.

Outside, her warning clung. I walked toward the water to check the mail basket. It was rare that mail was entrusted to someone unknown passing through from Charles Town, but one never knew.

I paused as I got close and looked across the water to the opposite bank. All was dark and still amongst the trees. I stepped onto the creaking dock and made haste to check for mail, coming up empty. The gray water was still, the whine of mosquitoes the only sound. Except … I paused, straining my hearing.

Drums.

A slow, steady, and dark beat.

An iciness prickled my spine.

Nine

I stood still. The distant beat was low and menacing, unlike any rhythm I'd heard. Not a soldier's tattoo. Something almost otherworldly. A tribal beat. The knowledge dropped like an icy shard into my belly. Indians? Or slaves?

A feeling that I was being watched crept over me. A breeze picked up, tickling the surface of the charcoal water, and a sudden loud cry of birds signaled the flight of a skein of geese. The sound gave me a start, and I turned back to the house. The stillness of the plantation around me made me uneasy. Where was Togo, watering the woad fields before dawn as instructed? Where were the sounds of people rising and chattering? Even the birds were silent today.

I veered for the stables. Quash would know what was going on; he would be helping Indian Peter ready the horses for our ride to church this morning. Even if Quash was not there, Indian Peter, who lived above the horses, would be up by now, so I didn't worry about disturbing anyone.

In the dark stable, the horses whinnied softly, their pails of water and seed were full, but the door up to the loft was closed tight. The ladder was removed.

I backed out slowly, my heart beating erratically, then

turned. The figure of Essie hurrying from the house to the dwellings caught my eye.

"Essie!"

She stopped as I ran toward her.

"What's going on?" I panted, my voice breathy with fear and worry.

"You go on inside, and you don't go outside again 'til it's safe, you hear?"

"What? Why? What's going on?"

"You'll be safe here in da house."

"What is going on? Where's Quashy?" My panic grew, and I glanced about wildly, noticing all the closed doors at the dwellings and drawn curtains. "Where is everyone?"

"We'll see where everybody be at the end of the day," she said cryptically. "Go on inside now."

I stood staring at her.

"Go on," she said, her eyes fierce. "You hide. You hear?"

Hide? When my people were at risk? "From who, Essie?"

She shook her head.

Hide.

I'd never had any reason not to trust Essie. "Is everyone safe?"

She glanced toward the creek not answering.

"If I hide," I told her, my heart thumping, "you must all hide. If I see one of you out here, I'll come outside. Do you hear *me*? This is *my* place to protect."

"Everyone will stay hid," she said. "Now go on."

Confused, I turned and then hurried back to the house. The weight of her eyes followed me the whole way until I'd entered the house and closed it up tightly behind me.

Mama was still in bed, but I heard Polly moving about above me. I hurried to the study and pulled open the small armoire in the corner. Father had taught me to use a gun while we were still in Antigua, but I was uncomfortable. The musket stood there, leaning against the back wall of the cabinet. My chest heaved in and out as I stared at the gun. Swallowing, I closed the door again, without touching it. If the need arose, I knew where it was.

THE HOUSE AND SURROUNDS WERE STILL as the morning wore on. I informed Mother and a panicked Polly that we were to stay inside until I understood what was afoot, and after locking all the doors, I rustled them up some cheese, sliced apple, and leftover bread.

The drums, which I could barely hear from the house as it was, faded out for a spell, and I wondered just how long our self-imposed imprisonment would last. I would need answers soon.

Just before noon, the drums grew loud again. I hurried to perch at the window upstairs and squinted as a pirogue laden with dark figures slid slowly up the creek. Negroes, not Indians.

What was going on?

Mama had decided to stay in bed. But Polly sat with me, her needlepoint forgotten as she clutched my hand tightly. Holding my breath, I saw the oarsmen stop and the boat slow. The eyes on board were all trained on our property.

"Don't move," I whispered quietly to Polly. But in truth we were both frozen.

A tall, dark man stood in the boat and brought his hands to his mouth. A sharp caw, like that of a hawk, echoed into the stillness.

Polly and I were still as statues.

The man waited and watched.

There was no movement below me or anywhere I could see. There was no sound.

The drums, which I presumed now came from one or more occupants of the vessel, were silent.

Finally, after interminable minutes, the tall man turned his face away from us and sat. Six pairs of arms began rowing again. The drumbeat started up and faded gradually as the boat disappeared from sight toward the Stono River.

Silence settled over the land and over the house. Nothing stirred. I counted the beats of my heart and knew an intense relief. It was something akin to the tight pressure and irritability one incubates throughout a long day with tight dress stays, the realization they were too tight only coming after they are finally loosened and cool air hits one's skin.

I don't know how long we sat there. My gaze roamed the creek and the trees either side. Every shadow became a question, and the rays of late afternoon sun provided no answers as they revealed nothing but tree limbs and vegetation.

As I looked on though, a dark shape detached itself from a tree close to the river. I gasped then blinked, surprised I had not seen him before now. Quash. His chest was bare and streaked with thick pluff mud dried to gray. All the better to hide, I supposed. A long rice scythe hung at his waist. He looked along the river in the direction the boat had traveled. Then he turned his back and walked onto the dock. I inhaled sharply. I had never had occasion to see Quash half dressed. Thick rigid scars cut across his back haphazardly, making a patchwork of mud and chaos. He knelt at the water's edge and used creek water to wash something from the post. When he seemed satisfied, he stood and slipped toward the trees again and disappeared.

A gasp and a sob jolted me back. Polly was rigid with fear,

tears sliding down her sweet cheeks.

"Oh, Polly. It's going to be all right," I murmured, though with the way my heart was thundering, I felt I could use that comfort myself. I pulled her close, soft curls tickling my nose.

Over her head, Mama, still in her bedrail, her hair braided and hanging like a rope over one shoulder, stood leaning against the doorframe for support. "Was it the Indians?"

"No, Mama," I whispered. My voice had quite disappeared.

"Curse your damned father for leaving us in this wild land unprotected," she muttered. "What the devil is going on?"

Polly's sobs subsided into hiccups, but her little body trembled still. "I think it's an uprising, Mama," I answered finally. "I'm sure we'll know more soon." At the word "uprising," Polly gave another shudder.

"I suppose we've lost all our Negroes." Mama sniffed. "That'll teach your father."

"No, Mama," I said and thought of Quash out on the dock. "I believe … I believe Quash, and Essie too, protected us in some way. And I did not see our people leave."

She made a small disbelieving scoff and shook her head. "You sound more like your father every day."

"A fact for which I am grateful," I responded softly, unwilling to put much heat into my retort.

Had it really been an uprising? In my mind I imagined an uprising to be more frantic. People running, muskets fired, things set alight. But as silent as the approach had been, the atmosphere had wailed and screeched of danger. I knew we had somehow skirted a dire end.

THE SLAVE QUARTERS AT WAPPOO REMAINED CLOSED up and silent all day and into the night. Not even the singsong, chirping voices of Mary Ann's and Nanny's children could be heard.

Mama, Polly, and I scavenged in the kitchen for food. The three of us made a makeshift meal of hominy cakes, apples, and dried venison. I could, of course, be capable in the kitchen, but I kept thinking Essie or Mary Ann would be back at any moment. They didn't return to the house that night. But I knew Essie would be back when she deemed it safe.

Mama decided the occasion was right to open a bottle of Madeira as we would no doubt all have trouble sleeping. For once, I was grateful for Mama's instruction.

By unspoken agreement we used little light before bed, keeping the house invisible against the black of a moonless night. Polly curled up next to me in my room, her small body like a furnace. I rested my cheek on her curls and waited throughout the interminably long night.

I couldn't help but worry for the planters I knew. Had Mr. Deveaux and the Woodwards escaped whatever madness had taken place?

I awoke during the early hours to distant chanting and wailing. The eerie nature of the sounds, and the memory of a similar morning in Antigua years ago, kept me in my bed longer than usual. When I finally met the day, all had returned to normal. And the bustle of plantation life picked up as if it had never paused.

The first thing I did upon entering the study was compose a short note to the Woodwards, inviting them to visit that day. I hoped they were unaffected.

The Woodwards and their daughter, Mary, lived in a modest whitewashed wooden house on a similar sized parcel of land to our plantation a mile or so from us. After the death of Mary's elderly husband, she had returned home to live with her parents.

I knew there was no way I would get Mama to leave the plantation anytime soon. I had moments throughout the day where I thought I must have dreamed the whole thing.

This had been my first true test as plantation manager and I was not sure if I had passed or failed. Could it be considered my success if it was simply luck?

But in my heart there was no doubt that my first instinct was correct—we had been protected yesterday. It didn't stop me from acknowledging how very vulnerable we were, three white females alone out here in the country.

Ten

At noon, Charles Pinckney came charging along the lane on his horse.

I can't say I was not relieved to see that someone had come to check on us. And of course, we were desperate for news as to what, indeed, had transpired.

Mother, Polly, and I came to stand out in the hot yard. In the background Essie, Mary Ann, and Nanny stayed up on the porch, ready to hear the news firsthand so that they could share it amongst the other slaves.

"I must say," Mr. Pinckney called as his horse came to a prancing stop. "I feel weak with relief at seeing you unharmed."

His horse bellowed out hot breath, its coat shining with sweat. Quash came forward to take the reins. Indian Peter was still nowhere to be found.

"I rode hard from Belmont." Mr. Pinckney swung down from the saddle. He wore a more casual riding attire and his dark hair was hurriedly assembled at his nape. "The news is dire. There's been a rebellion."

Mother gasped.

"I thought as much," I said to him. Then I turned to Polly. "Run along inside and help Essie ready some tea for our guest."

Polly pouted a moment but did exactly as I asked.

"Thank you so much for coming to assist us. I'm happy to report we are all well, but it was certainly hair-raising."

Mr. Pinckney dipped his chin. "So they were here then?"

"On the creek. They did not approach."

"Curious. But how very lucky you are," he said. "I'm glad to know my assistance was not needed at all."

We shared a smile.

"Come along," my mother interjected. "Let's get into the house and you can tell us the news."

WITHIN A FEW HOURS, some of our neighbors, including Mr. Deveaux, Mrs. Woodward, and Mary, had assembled in our drawing room. Mr. Woodward was in Charles Town and presumably on his way back if he'd heard the news.

I had Essie and Mary Ann assemble a hearty afternoon tea and shared with everybody what I had seen and heard.

"There will be far-reaching repercussions from this day," Pinckney uttered to the room at large. I hoped none of the so-called repercussions would incite any further rebellion. "A group of twenty slaves took up arms yesterday morning and passed through a score of area plantations, swelling in number as the day wore on. Houses were burned and several plantation owners, though none I knew personally, were killed."

There was an audible gasp around the room. The idea of how close we'd been to certain death sent a chill down my spine.

Charles Pinckney looked grave. "A good many were safely away at church, I presume."

"Was the rebellion subdued?" asked Mrs. Woodward. "Or are they still at large?"

"My sources tell me the rebellion was subdued by late afternoon, but not before a large number lost their lives. Apparently, the slaves had been lured with a promise of sanctuary in St. Augustine by the Spaniards."

"Sanctuary?" I asked.

He inclined his head. "I believe it a trick. I believe the Spanish seek to reenslave any that reach them and turn them into soldiers."

"It makes sense," offered Deveaux. "I've heard the Spanish resolve to use the Indians and the Negroes in their war against us and obliterate South Carolina."

Mary gasped; her eyes were large in her pale face.

And I too felt dread in my blood.

Mama wrung her hands.

"God help us all," whispered Mrs. Woodward.

I glanced at Essie who stood in the corner of the room by the door awaiting instruction, expressionless in present company.

"Mama," I said. "Won't you let Essie accompany you upstairs. Today has been overtaxing."

"Nonsense," said Mama, but she clutched the arm of the settee and attempted to rise. Mr. Pinckney and Mr. Deveaux both surged to their feet. Deveaux, being closer, reached her first.

Turning to Mr. Pinckney, grateful though I was for his presence, I felt a peculiar concoction of comfort and utter loneliness.

As Mama bid adieu to our guests and left the room, he met my gaze. "Have you counted your slaves?" he asked. "I noticed Indian Peter did not see to the horses. You'll have to send word to Waccamaw and Garden Hill also. The militia is calling for a full count."

"Why?" I asked, though my throat felt thick.

Mr. Pinckney winced, almost imperceptibly, his gray-blue eyes troubled. "So they may … *hunt* the deserters."

My hand came to my mouth.

Mr. Deveaux returned to his seat. "What else can we do but to send a message? To make them an example?"

"Kill them, you mean?" Mary asked.

Deveaux nodded.

"It's extreme," I said after I felt composed.

Mary and her mother nodded, as did Mr. Deveaux.

"That aside," I couldn't help adding, "what field hand wouldn't be lured and seduced by the promise of freedom?"

"Yours weren't," said Mary.

"No. No, they weren't. Though the procession came right by here, down Wappoo Creek in the direction of the Stono. I count myself extremely fortunate." I hadn't mentioned Indian Peter or answered Charles Pinckney's question. The truth was I didn't know if he'd been involved. I certainly didn't want him hunted down like an animal. My people had protected me yesterday. And I should protect them.

We'd indeed been lucky yesterday. We might not be so lucky next time.

Not for the first time, I struggled with the burden I'd undertaken in my father's name.

"Well, it's getting late," Mrs. Woodward announced. "There's probably never been a safer time to travel than tonight with all the militia on the roads. But I am tired."

"Yes," Mr. Deveaux added, standing. "I shall accompany you, and then be on my way too."

Charles Pinckney would have a far longer trip than the Woodwards and Deveaux. "You can't possibly attempt the trip back to Belmont this late in the day," I said to him. "You must stay. I'll have Essie prepare the guest room."

"I'd appreciate that greatly." Charles Pinckney bowed his head. "Who knows if the danger is fully passed."

I SAW OUR VISITORS OFF and let Essie and Mary Ann know of our guest. Then I joined Mr. Pinckney in the study. *He's as old as Papa*, I told myself when I noticed how strange it felt to be alone with him in the evening.

"May I offer you some port?" I motioned to the decanter and tumblers. "We opened it last night."

"Thank you, I will." He took three long strides to the sideboard, preparing his own drink with neat efficiency. He tilted his chin at me in question.

"Not for me, thank you."

After pouring his drink, he looked toward the gun cabinet in the corner. "Do you have a gun here with which to defend yourself?"

I glanced over to see the door was cracked open again. I hadn't been able to seal it properly since I'd wrenched it open in my recent panic. I walked over and pressed it closed. "We do. Let's hope I don't ever have to use it. Though Papa did make sure I knew how. Would that I can simply focus on farming, rather than firearms."

"Quite right. I heard Deveaux asking about your crop."

"Yes, he gave us woad seeds to attempt. But no luck, I'm afraid." My shoulders sagged of their own accord. "I don't know what to do."

Mr. Pinckney set his lips to the crystal, taking a sip of amber liquid. "There are other things you can try. There's no need to fret."

"That's just it. I ..."

Lapsing into silence, I wondered at how I felt such ease in talking to Mr. Pinckney.

"Something tells me you have more on your mind than growing indigo, Miss Lucas."

"Well, you know my father has left me almost entirely in charge."

"Yes." He adjusted his cravat, still disheveled from his earlier frantic arrival. "That can hardly be of concern. Hadn't you already made yourself mistress of the house? Your mama, though a lovely genteel lady, would be quite taxed by things you seem to take in stride. I'd say you were the natural choice."

"Mama, would, I'm sure, be first choice were she not suffering so." I felt the need to defend her, though it was a bald-faced lie. "Especially in this heat. It really has been excessively hot these last few weeks."

"Indeed it has. And with all this on your plate, you tell me you can think of nothing but growing indigo?"

"I ... I'm concerned that my father's push to become lieutenant colonel, and now perhaps governor of Antigua, will take all the resources we have. I have looked over all his accounts." I paused to gauge his surprise at my business abilities, or my discussing such a private matter, but to his credit he had no other expression beyond interest, so I continued. "And I don't believe our current output will support his endeavor. Perhaps it may ... but just barely. And that means—"

"You shall have no dowry unless you find a way to make the land more profitable than it is currently," he finished for me.

A dowry was my least concern, but I'd allow him the thought. I let out a nervous laugh. "Precisely. I thought I would try indigo. But my father has yet to send seed."

"So you attempted to grow woad. I have to say it's been tried and it has failed. Not the right soil, I'm told. But I admire your determination. A soul would underestimate you at his own peril," he said. "You are quite determined, and I daresay, resourceful. I have faith that you will succeed eventually."

INDIAN PETER RETURNED A FEW DAYS AFTER THE CRUSHED REBELLION as unremarkably as he'd vanished. I had never reported him missing, nor asked him to account for his whereabouts. Quash trusted him, and therefore I did too.

It was as simple as that.

We accepted an invitation to begin weekly visits with Mrs. Woodward and Mary Chardon. The routine was effective to get Mama out of the house and break up the monotony of winter, and had turned into one I looked forward to immensely. I found I was starved for company outside of Mother and Polly.

On Tuesdays, in the Woodwards' parlor, three pairs of nimble hands worked with furious ease, turning out all manner of exquisitely detailed needlework. The fourth pair of hands produced a rather hopeless assortment of samples. In large part because my eyes would wander to the window, watching the Woodwards' field hands at work and wondering what else I could be doing for our land.

THE DAYS, WEEKS, AND THEN MONTHS that followed grew colder. The marsh grasses faded to brown. The nights grew longer, but the days were more bearable.

The fear of another rebellion faded as each day crept

toward winter. Rebels were hunted and executed. Rumor had it their heads were mounted on pikes lining the major thoroughfares surrounding Charles Town. Charles Pinckney confirmed the macabre and gruesome spectacle, and I grew relieved that I'd never mentioned Indian Peter's absence during the uprising.

From dawn to dusk, I spent as many hours outside as I could spare from my letters and accounts. I studied my surroundings, taking measure of characteristics of autumn that I might remember them for next year. I welcomed rain as it softened and nourished my earth. I watched with fascination as the plants clinging to the gnarled branches of live oaks transformed from baked clay to lush green in the day after heavy rains. "Revival plants" they were nicknamed, according to Mr. Deveaux. Mockingbirds nested outside my window.

I found miracles every day and I clung to them.

A morning in early December found me contemplating the last weeks before my seventeenth birthday. The final stars blinked out in the lightening sky beyond the house before I remembered to go and check the letter basket on the dock. I'd almost forgotten, so caught up was I in my thoughts. Perhaps also because I came up empty most days, and the days I didn't were business correspondence from town or the two plantations.

The leather buckles on the basket were loose. There'd been a delivery. Likely late last night as someone from Charles Town navigated the creek toward the Stono River. I held my breath as I reached inside. One was a letter from the address of dear Mr. and Mrs. Pinckney at their Belmont estate. The other a small package in waxed cloth with a label that read *Miss Eliza Lucas, Wappoo Creek* tied upon it.

My father.

Joy burst through my chest, and I hurried so fast to the house that my braid came loose from its pins.

Skidding on the heart pine floors as I came around the desk in the study, impatience made me want to cut through the twine, but of course I was always in need of it. So I willed my excited nerves to slow and commanded my shaky, determined fingers to work the knot. "By the devil," I cursed softly, my teeth clamped tight. It took endless minutes before it finally came loose, and I was able to unwrap the waxed cloth.

There were two letters, one to me and one to Mama.

And several muslin pochettes containing seeds and cuttings.

Now, which one was indigo?

Please let some of them be indigo.

I dipped my fingers in to sample the contents, drawing out a brittle pinch of black, sticklike objects, shaped like garden pea pods, but on a minuscule scale. Seed pods themselves. Some were split open, and small black seeds tumbled out. Indigo seeds!

Eleven

The wait for the season to become warm enough to plant the indigo seeds my father sent was interminable.

Unable to be patient, I had Togo till the land on a mild day in early March. Mr. Deveaux came by unannounced to "check on us women" and I was relieved to be able to let someone know of my plans.

After tea and a walk round the fields, Deveaux held a small black seed up to the sky at arm's length as if he could focus better. "It seems so hard-cased. I wonder …"

"You wonder?" I prompted.

"I wonder if you might soak or score them as we did the woad seeds."

"I certainly don't want to chance them not coming up," I agreed. "I'll do it. Come, let me show you your live oaks before you go."

Over the next few days, Togo, Quash, Sawney, and I sowed rows upon rows of the soaked indigo seeds.

For the rest of the month, the weather dipped back to winter, and I prayed it would be over soon.

I RECEIVED WORD FROM OUR MERCHANT BEALE that the rice I had sent into town had settled some of the outstanding accounts for tools, materials, and a portion of the essentials we'd had to purchase upon arriving in Carolina.

It was a relief to be out from under some of the debt. And it marked my first bold fraud, whereupon I had insisted that my father had requested a full three quarters of all rice production be barreled up and sent to town for export and sale at the markets. Of course, he had suggested nothing of the sort. Though I assured myself he would agree if the suggestion were put to him. I would still need to visit Starrat, as the Waccamaw plantation had not heeded my requests as well as Garden Hill had done.

We kept up with our visits to the Woodward home. Certainly after the rebellion it seemed imperative to maintain a connection with others in our area. And we traveled to town to visit with Mrs. Pinckney as much as Mama's nerves would allow.

"Oh!" my mother suddenly exclaimed one day as we spent a quiet afternoon with Mrs. Pinckney and her close friend Mrs. Cleland in Mrs. Pinckney's private parlor. "I quite forgot! Colonel Lucas, far from neglecting his fatherly duties, has informed me of a suitor for Eliza's hand."

My attention flew up to my mother's face. "Ow," I yelped as I jabbed the needle into the pad of my finger. "Dash it all," I snapped, sucking my finger into my mouth. The vaguely salty sweet taste of blood coated my tongue. I grimaced.

"Well, no need to be quite so dramatic, Eliza. It's not like this plantation business could go on forever. George is only a few years away from coming over to rescue us."

I kept my lips pressed together, trying not to react to my mother's needling.

"Though, I daresay, your brother will be quite pleased

with the state of his inheritance upon his arrival," Mrs. Cleland murmured and I smiled gratefully at her, even while my heart turned inside out.

Mrs. Cleland resided north toward Georgetown and had vowed to keep an ear to the ground regarding our rice interest on our Waccamaw plantation up there. Or at least to ask her husband to do so. She was older than Mrs. Pinckney in looks and manner but they had been friends for years, and in mannerism could almost be taken for sisters. They were two of the kindest ladies I had ever met. "Do tell us about the suitor," Mrs. Cleland directed at Mama.

"Oh. Well. I don't know much about him. Mr. Walsh, I believe." She looked up as if to peer into her memory banks. "Yes. Mr. Walsh, that's it."

If it was the same Mr. Walsh I'd had occasion to meet when we had visited the Pinckneys' Belmont estate during the Yuletide festivities, then I had about as much knowledge of him as Mama. I hadn't given him a moment's thought. Nice enough man, I supposed. But entirely forgettable. What on earth was Papa about? He knew how I felt about this. I could only imagine it was Mama's doing.

Mrs. Pinckney smiled blandly, not endorsing nor vetoing this vague Mr. Walsh fellow. That, to me, spoke volumes.

"May I see Papa's letter when we return home?" I asked my mother.

She gave a small smile. "Of course, dear. I would have thought he'd have mentioned Mr. Walsh to you also." Of course, she didn't. And she'd waited until we were in polite company to reveal her announcement.

"I'm surprised you haven't thrown your hat in for William Middleton," Mrs. Cleland directed at me. "He was extremely dashing at the Yuletide ball, didn't you think?"

I thought back to the splendid affair. The candles all

alight, gleaming silver, the polished brass buttons of the gentlemen and sparkling jewels on some of the dames. William Middleton had indeed cut a fine figure. We had been able to procure new dresses for the event too, from a seamstress recommended by Mrs. Pinckney.

"And I've heard the Middletons' Crowfield plantation is absolutely magnificent," Mrs. Pinckney added. "As an amateur botanist, Eliza, surely you must be eager to see the gardens we've heard so much about. One would almost think he was the perfect match for you. Imagine, you could garden all day long and wander about the grounds and never see the same flower twice."

I chuckled at the image my friend had conjured. "I think I rather bored him with my take on plantation affairs. It's one thing being interested in flowers, quite another to be interested in crops, or what makes money."

"Oh, Eliza," Mama said with despair.

"In fact"—I paused in my stitching as I remembered—"I do believe he said, 'Why would you worry your pretty little head with a gentleman's affairs?' Then he told me to hire an overseer so I may rather enjoy the many parties and diversions town has to offer."

I must admit, I'd been quite stung to be so summarily dismissed. Anyway, he seemed to have an eye for Miss Williams, an heiress in town.

"Quite right. You see it's not just me who notices, Eliza. I fear you are getting a bit of a reputation. What gentleman is going to want you if you carry on like this?"

Why would I want a gentleman who doesn't respect my interests? I wanted to ask but gritted my teeth instead. But of course, tears pricked my eyes. As only my mother's words could so effectively cause. I was ashamed to be spoken to like this in front of our dear friends.

Mrs. Pinckney was too polite to acknowledge my mother's comment. "Shall I ring for more tea?" she asked instead.

I cleared my throat. "That would be lovely, thank you, Mrs. Pinckney."

To my dearest Father,

As to Mr. Walsh, you know, sir, I have so slight a knowledge of him I can form no judgment. A case of such consequence (marriage!) requires the nicest distinction of humors and sentiments.

But give me leave to assure you, sir, that a single life is my only choice. And I hope you will put aside thoughts of my marrying yet these two or three years at least.

Your most dutiful and affectionate daughter,

—Eliza Lucas

Twelve

"Come look, Miz Lucas," Togo shouted excitedly as soon as I set foot outside our Wappoo home in the cool March morning. He was walking stooped with the watering buckets hanging from the yoke across his shoulders, heading for the kitchen gardens when he saw me. He laid his burden down and gestured over to the fields.

The indigo!

I picked up my skirts and hopped down the steps from the veranda. In a few moments, I stood on the edge of the long tract and squinted. Togo headed along one of the rows of what looked to me still bare turned earth in the low early morning light. A few feet along he stopped and lowered to his haunches. I followed and then, picking up my skirts, did the same, following his dark finger as he pointed.

"Ha!" I exclaimed as my eyes adjusted, and I made out the tiny green speck. Cautious hope bubbled in my chest. My eyes went along the row and sure enough there were more. I cast about and saw others, some a little more than a speck. And all of a sudden I could see them everywhere.

Yes! A burst of joy squeezed my chest, and I laid a hand upon it as if I could temper my excitement.

I looked up and saw that Togo was smiling ear to ear,

mirroring my own expression. At the end of the field Sawney and Quash stood smiling too.

We'd done it!

I couldn't wait to let Mr. Deveaux know. And Charles Pinckney would be so impressed. And my father too. Surely now he'd consider it a worthwhile investment to send a consultant. It needn't be Ben, but someone, anyone, who had experience with the crop and who might protect us against the pitfalls would be prudent.

I sighed with happiness and stood. "Thank you, Togo."

He rose also, unfolding to his towering six-foot frame. "Yes, Miz Lucas." He smiled, showing his two front teeth missing.

I wanted to sing and dance and yell with happiness. I thought about whom I could share my news with and came up empty. Neither Mama nor Polly, despite her earlier fleeting interest, had any inclination toward my planting efforts.

I made myself a promise. When the shoots made it through the end of March and were clear of frost, I would beg my father to send a consultant.

I feared if he didn't send someone, we wouldn't even know when the perfect time to harvest would be. I knew it was before the flowers bloomed, but when exactly? What a waste of all this energy to grow it perfectly if we ruined it by not harvesting correctly. And what about time to build all the infrastructure a dye-making operation might need?

In the days that followed, the promise of success with indigo went to my head. I was ashamed to admit to sins such as vanity, pridefulness, and no small amount of greed when I let the idea of its worth cross my mind. But yet, I was too excited. I prayed for humility in my evening prayers, still I was proud of our efforts.

I made plans to head into town and visit our banker, Mr.

Gabriel Manigault. He held the deeds to the mortgage on the Wappoo plantation. I would get an understanding of where we stood with respect to paying some outstanding amounts back. I had been diligent with the accounts and ambitious in the sales of our rice with more still to come.

My father, even though he'd been made colonel, had made mention of perhaps being able to switch commissions with Major Heron, who was in Oglethorpe's regiment near Savannah. It would be a demotion, and no doubt Major Heron would extract a steep price, but after it was paid, it would allow my father to remain close to us and more importantly, no longer require as much capital from our estates on an ongoing basis. Or so I hoped.

It all felt as if things were coming together just so. In a right kind of order. And so I finally gave in to my instinct concerning the indigo and wrote to Father about finding a consultant, anyone who had the skill and knowledge to produce the dye. *It is time*, I wrote, and laid out our success and my worries about squandering such a fortunate chance. Without asking directly I described all the attributes I knew Ben had.

As I lifted my quill, I let my mind linger on my childhood friend. I thought of him as I'd last seen him, silent and brooding, on the cusp of manhood with no more time for the silly shenanigans of a plantation owner's young daughter. My skin flashed hot. Silliness. That was all. Two children separated by culture and circumstance. Of course we would grow apart. But I could barely ignore the way my belly turned and twisted at the thought I might have a chance to see him again. To have someone about the plantation with whom I could share these triumphs. Someone who understood my love of the land. Someone I was so fond of. I said a silent prayer as I sealed the letter.

IN THE MEANTIME, I ALSO WROTE TO STARRAT and requested he send Sarah down from Waccamaw, if he could spare her, as I had need of another female. A sloppily written response came back announcing that he could not spare her. And I grudgingly made plans to perhaps visit there again if I could find someone to accompany me.

But one morning in April, I opened my eyes and as I felt the frigid air my heart sank. By the time I made it outside, Togo was already in the field inspecting the rows. He looked up when he heard me and slowly shook his large head side to side.

I gasped in despair when I saw the blackened and brittle little shoots.

"I'm sorry, Miz Lucas."

Bitter tears of disappointment sprung to my eyes against my will. I blinked rapidly, taking deep breaths through the surge of disappointment threatening to choke me.

"It's all right, Togo." I fought to control my voice. "It's not your fault. I forced a smile for his sake. "We shall make another go of it. We simply don't know the right time to plant. And certainly we had no idea there would be a frost this late in the year." I lifted my hands then dropped them in despair. "We shall keep trying. Please go ahead and till up the soil again. I still have some seed. We'll plant next week, when I am sure the frost won't return." I injected as much confidence as I could into my request.

We were to leave that very day to Charles Town for my meeting with Mr. Manigault. I resolved to keep the appointment nonetheless, even though I now had no news of a new income-producing crop. I would make the best of it.

"Oh, it is so lovely to see you again." Mrs. Pinckney beamed as she drew me into an embrace in her front parlor.

Today she wore a dress in a natural hue woven of the finest Dutch flax I had seen, a pale green that matched her eyes and edged with a pale pink lutestring the color of an ornamental rose I had encountered once on an outing to the botanical gardens in London with Mrs. Bodicott.

I smiled. "Thanks to you and Mr. Pinckney for having us to stay with you yet again."

"Absolutely," Mama agreed as I joined her on the settee. "I was just telling Eliza the other day what a wonderful prescription your company is."

"And it is most fortuitous," Mrs. Pinckney directed at me as she poured some tea. "Mr. Pinckney and I want to introduce you to our niece, Miss Bartlett. She is staying with us for a few months. We visited the markets this morning, and I fear I quite tired her out. She has gone to lie down. She's just a few years younger than your age, Eliza. I do hope you'll be friends."

"Will you be having a soiree to introduce her, then?" Mama asked, accepting a cup and saucer.

"Oh, I hadn't thought of it, but what a splendid idea. We shall have it while you are here." Mrs. Pinckney sat down on a beautiful brocade chair across from us, her skirt draping elegantly to the floor. I did so admire her. She was always warm and elegant, with a clever wit and intelligence dancing in her eyes. I fancied she and Mr. Pinckney were a love match. They showed such respect and affection for each other at all times, I wondered for a moment how much more so it must be behind closed doors.

My stomach gave a little lurch, an odd sensation slipping through me. Was that what I wanted? A love match? I almost laughed out loud at the absurdity of the stray thought. Perhaps it was simply my age. I'd noticed a sort of fever that overcame friends as they attended balls and soirees and swooned over potential suitors. I'd thought myself immune to such flights of fancy. I was certainly far too busy.

Both Mama and Mrs. Pinckney looked at me expectantly.

My cheeks bloomed with heat as though they'd heard my train of thought. "Did you ask me something?" I said quickly. "I do apologize, my mind quite disappeared."

Mama pursed her lips. "Mrs. Pinckney was just asking if there was anyone we would like to invite to meet Miss Bartlett. I suggested Mary Chardon and her parents, Mr. and Mrs. Woodward."

"Oh, quite yes," I agreed with enthusiasm. "That would be a lovely addition. Mary is so very agreeable; she would be a good friend for Miss Bartlett."

"Just what I was thinking," said my mother, satisfied. "And I know she is too young yet, but what eligible young men might we invite?" she asked Mrs. Pinckney.

As they named some of the prospects, most of whom I'd never heard of, I wondered what kind of gentleman might make me seriously consider marriage. If I loved someone would that be enough when I no longer had the satisfying business of a plantation to run? My drive to succeed and improve our lot, as unattractive a quality as Mama said it was, couldn't be helped. Would this ambition, for I'd come to accept that was truly what it was, be replaced by something sweeter and more tempered? A simple need to love and be loved?

I snorted. And quickly covered it with a cough as I realized I'd expressed myself aloud.

"Is everything all right, Eliza?"

"Oh, I caught a funny breath is all. I'm fine, Mama. I think I just need to stretch my legs then maybe lie down.

You know how I get rather bilious in the boat, and then the carriage here, I—"

"Yes, yes. Fine. Go and rest before dinner." She shooed me off, no doubt eager to discuss my marriage prospects in more detail.

I gathered my skirts and excused myself.

Perhaps one day I could ask Mrs. Pinckney the secret to her happiness with her husband. Just in case I should ever have need.

I stepped out into the hall and moved toward the stairs. The Pinckney home gleamed with deep-hued wood and beautiful furnishings. It was a happy home. Warm. I'd never asked, of course, but I felt sure they longed for children. What an added dimension to their joy that would bring. I said a silent prayer that such wonderful people would be kindly blessed.

The sound of a throat clearing caught my attention just as I'd rested my hand upon the newel post and gathered my skirts in the other hand preparing to ascend to my room. I paused and looked along the entryway hall. The door to the library was ajar.

To my dear friend, Mrs. Bodicott,

I have the business of three plantations to transact, which requires much writing and more business and fatigue of other sorts than you can imagine. But lest you should imagine it too burdensome to a girl in my early time of life, give me leave to answer you: I assure you I think myself happy that I can be so useful to so good a father. And by rising very early I find I can go through much business.

Lest you think I shall be quite moped with this way of life, I am to inform you there are two worthy ladies in Charles Town, Mrs. Pinckney and Mrs. Cleland, who are partial enough to me to be always pleased to have me with them and insist upon my making their houses my home when in town and press me to relax a little more often than 'tis my honor to accept of their obliging treaties.

—Eliza Lucas

Thirteen

"Eliza!" Mr. Pinckney greeted me with a surprised grin after I knocked gently on the doorframe. "Come in, come in."

I returned his smile, my heart warming, and slipped inside the open door of the library.

Charles Pinckney stood against the backdrop of the floor-to-ceiling bookshelves. His dark hair was pulled back and powder free. He really was a handsome man. Mrs. Pinckney was a lucky lady.

A text was open in his hand as he angled it toward the window, his formal overcoat removed, revealing his shirtsleeves and dark waistcoat. He leaned casually but straightened as I entered, making to close the book.

"Don't stop reading on my account," I said. "I simply wanted to say hello."

After my unexpected thoughts of his and Mrs. Pinckney's love marriage, I was surprised to find myself more observant of his person. Such kind eyes. Those I'd always recognized, of course. The color of a stormy sea. But strong shoulders too. He was tall, but not overly, and had the most irreverent dimple in his chin. As though his person sought to remind the world of his humor, even while his hair was wigged or powdered for his very important job of lawyering for the province.

He'd always treated me with respect, rather than as a mere girl standing in for her father, so I felt almost as comfortable around Charles Pinckney as I would a family member.

"How are you, Eliza? How are your experiments going?"

"Rather disappointing, I'm afraid." I scrunched up my nose. "The plan for our trip to town was made in a rash state of mind. I was excited we had growth in the indigo fields. Alas, the frost of last week put paid to my excitement. Next year we shall plant later."

"So, you're not fine. Bitterly disappointed, I imagine," he said kindly. "Come. Come and have a seat and tell me about it. I'm glad you decided to call upon us even though your purpose changed."

I perched on a club chair next to the open door. "I'm all right. I didn't sow it all; we shall merely try again."

"We?"

"Ah well, I have rather ignited a cause amongst the Negroes. I'm not sure how it came about, but I believe they are as excited to see this project to fruition as am I!" I laughed.

"So industrious and clever," he said approvingly. "And what is the plan once you succeed? As I'm sure you will."

"Well, I have written to my father to send a consultant from the West Indias. *If* I finally succeed, it will be more important than ever to make sure we don't squander the chance to produce good quality dye."

He strolled back to the window. "Have you heard from your father?"

"I have. It seems tensions are rather high. Do you think it will escalate?"

"I don't know for sure. But I imagine so, if it hasn't already."

My heart lurched with fear for my father's safety.

"We have been on and off at war with the Spanish for

decades," Charles Pinckney went on. "If there are further embargoes, trade will become difficult. I would advise anyone who asked to diversify their crops. You are attempting that already." He smiled. "I think I shall nickname you 'the little visionary.'"

I raised my eyebrows, both amused and warmed by his praise.

Mr. Pinckney waved his hand dismissively. I decided since I had his ear to talk of something that had been very much on my mind since the rebellion. I'd come across a copy of the hurriedly enacted Negro Act and sought to understand it.

"I was gratified to see that part of the Negro Act strongly advises against the use of brutality or physical punishment for slaves," I commented. "I've been after my overseer Starrat to remove the whipping post up at Waccamaw for some time, though according to Quash, Starrat blatantly ignores my requests."

"I'm of like mind. There's not much to be gained from a servant by treating him thus and expecting loyalty in return, it is true. I'm afraid most don't agree and will continue to run their plantations as they see fit. We can only choose to do the best thing for ours."

"I wonder if I might beg a boon. I find myself in the curious predicament of disliking someone. I speak of Starrat, of course. And I can assume he doesn't think much of me running Father's affairs either. I need to visit, and I find the thought of it rather ..." I hated to admit I was afraid of Starrat. I stopped and thought how else I might phrase my request.

As if he could sense my predicament, Mr. Pinckney came to my rescue. "I happen to need to visit Georgetown in the coming months. I do believe if you are in need of some company, and your mother approves of it, we may well travel that way together?" He raised an eyebrow at my presumably surprised expression. "Unless of course, you were not just about to ask me to accompany you on your mission to dole out instructions to your overseer?"

I snapped my mouth shut, my cheeks warming.

He grinned. "I'm sorry. I should have waited for you to ask. Has anyone ever told you that you wear your thoughts as clear as day? Please don't ever take up gaming. You would lose a fortune."

I swallowed hard. Knowing he was merely teasing me, I could hardly be mad. Though I did feel quite foolish. I let out a small laugh, then a larger one. "Goodness, you are direct."

"As you normally are too. Promise me that if you ever require my help, you will simply ask."

"Then I shall. Here is my formal request: Would it be too much of an imposition for me to accompany you and Mrs. Pinckney the next time you have need to visit Georgetown? I should like to visit Starrat and our land on Waccamaw personally, and I'm afraid I do not wish to see that man on my own."

Mr. Pinckney frowned. "He has not behaved in any untoward manner, has he?"

I shook my head. "I simply do not like the man. And I have to trust my intuition where he is concerned."

"Well, certainly." He nodded. "As I said, I have to visit there soon. I shall send word or come to collect you from Wappoo."

"Thank you, Colonel Pinckney. Only if it's not too much trouble."

"I do wish you'd call me Charles."

"Charles," I murmured, and it felt oddly intimate. I knew at once I would not stick to it.

Giving a half laugh, I rose. "I'd best get rested. I'm

looking forward to meeting your niece. And I'm afraid my mother and your wife are at this very minute planning some evening frivolity to introduce her about. And of course, to identify potential marriage material for us."

"Indeed?" he asked, his head turning sharply toward me. "And who do they have in mind for you?"

I lifted my shoulders. "No one, if I can help it."

He laughed, his eyes creasing at the corners. "What a waste."

And I left with an odd feeling in my belly.

MISS BARTLETT, THE PINCKNEYS' NIECE, was a small, buxom girl with a dear and pretty face. She had a dimple in her chin that reminded me of her uncle. I was allowed to think of her as buxom because next to me she looked womanly despite being almost two years my junior. She had dark hair like her uncle too and the same stormy blue eyes that seemed to hide the gray of a winter ocean in their depths.

We took tea with Mrs. Pinckney and Mrs. Cleland in the Pinckneys' parlor the next afternoon as we got to know each other and discussed further plans for the soiree.

We spoke of recipes, music, and the latest town news; which ladies were coming up for marriageable age and which planter families might align. Of course, I did not have much to add on that particular subject. William Middleton was in the marriage mind and the guessing game was on as to who would bear his name. While I'd made the acquaintance of the young man, and clearly put him off with my talk of crops and outputs, I had no knowledge of the many other people of whom Mrs. Pinckney spoke. I had spent, and would continue to spend, most of my time in the countryside seeing to our business.

Our friends, Mrs. Woodward and Mary Chardon, arrived the next day, and soon it felt wonderfully festive. I did not realize until I was surrounded by these charming ladies how very lonely the countryside was at times. But regardless of the momentary joy, I knew my heart would always yearn for the solitude of our Wappoo Creek plantation and the beauty of the land.

"It is so lovely to see you, Mary." I hugged Mrs. Chardon's slender frame, and then we made our way to the drawing room where I introduced her to the Pinckneys' niece, Miss Bartlett.

"I'm so glad you finally agreed to start calling me Mary," she said, settling herself on one of the comfortable chairs. "All due respect to my late husband, but carrying around Isaac's name has been a wretched weight. Aged me before my time, I daresay. Half the day I feel forty-six, not twenty-six."

"Ha," I said. "If only we could return to our maiden names upon the death of a spouse. But then, I suppose no one would know who we belonged to!" I laughed and drew out the small ring of embroidery I was attempting to keep my hands busy with while I had no business to attend to and no figures to add.

"You don't make marriage sound very appealing," Miss Bartlett tittered. "So will you be acquiring a spouse of your own soon, Eliza?"

"Oh goodness, no. Who has time for that? I have been too busy with our plantation affairs to consider the concept." Not true, of course. There was not enough work in the world that could dislodge the dread of marrying from the back of my mind. And certainly my mother was reminding everyone she could that we all had a mission to find me a suitable match.

"Did I tell you we have planted indigo?" I went on to avoid further discussion of husbands.

Mary chuckled, drawing out her own embroidery. "Only a dozen or so times. I am glad that you are not too busy to keep up with our weekly Tuesday visits. Mama is worried about your many responsibilities. She says you asked if you could watch our rice harvest. Is that true?"

"It is indeed." I rummaged around in the small basket I'd brought. "I can hardly do an effective job at supervising the harvest if I do not understand the process or where it might be improved. I do need to be more involved."

"Oh, you are so clever, Eliza." Mary shook her head as if she could not quite understand my predilection for business. "Pray, tell me what other little experiments are you conducting over there?"

I sighed and shrugged. "You do flatter me so. Although, I know you think me quite peculiar. And really, I'm simply following my papa's instructions to grow his enterprise. He sent some lucerne grass, which is said to be good for cattle. I'll let your parents know if it proves to be so."

"Do. Oh, did you hear about poor Mrs. Daniels?" Mary asked, referring to a woman who lived in our part of the parish. "Her husband got the fever and died suddenly. Left her with two young'uns and no will." Mary's deft fingers nimbly worked her embroidering needle. She had churned out several beautiful cushion covers in the months we'd been visiting. I didn't know Mrs. Daniels, but her tale made me sad. How irresponsible of her husband.

Upstairs, I imagined our mothers with Mrs. Pinckney in her salon, discussing their daughters' marriage prospects out of earshot before joining us downstairs.

"Most of these poor country folk don't have the means to call for a lawyer to draft estates and such." Mary frowned.

"She'll be quite turned out on her ear, I imagine, unless she can find another husband. But I fear she's beyond childbearing age. So who would want her?"

The simple tragedy sent a cold chill over my skin, and I let out an involuntary tremor.

"Are you cold, Eliza?" asked Miss Bartlett, taking on the role of hostess in her aunt's absence. "Should I call for the fire to be laid?"

"Oh no. Thank you. Not at all." I jabbed my needle into the small embroidery sample. I thought of the law books down the hall in Charles Pinckney's library and resolved to learn how to at least draft a simple last will and testament should anyone in our local area have need. It couldn't be that hard. I might need some more specific texts though and perhaps some guidance from Charles himself.

Mary sighed with amusement. "Pray tell, what are you thinking about as you murder that poor piece of cloth?"

"Dead husbands," I said with a theatrically dark look, and my two friends laughed.

I FEARED NEXT TO MISS BARTLETT, Mary Chardon and I looked rather plain. I took this as rather a boon when we sat down to dinner with the Pinckneys' dinner guests, Mr. Laurens and his son. They had called that afternoon and, after much prodding from my mother, apparently been asked to stay for dinner.

Mama, borrowing a silk scarf from Mrs. Pinckney to lend her attire a heightened level of elegance, was ecstatic to make the acquaintance of men so clearly in need of wives now or in the future. I steeled myself for a long evening.

Henry, the younger Laurens, was a skinny fellow of perhaps a year or two my junior. His hair slicked back and a slight curl to his lip lent him the air of an imp who would think it hilarious to set a cat's tail on fire. He was like a boy playing a man. And while he was courteous as he made my acquaintance, I couldn't help feeling a level of superiority emanate from behind his careful gaze.

I traded glances with Miss Bartlett, and she surreptitiously stuck out her tongue in the universal gesture of distaste. It was a struggle to keep my expression neutral.

Henry and his father were dressed impeccably with cloth of the finest I had seen, even in London.

"So, Mr. Laurens—" my mother started as we were presented with delicate quail at the supper table.

"John, madam, please." The older Mr. Laurens was quite rotund with a shiny nose and watery blue eyes. I fancied he was put together of features of differing age. His hair was perhaps older than my father, as were his eyes and teeth, but his complexion seemed young. Perhaps the wrinkles were stretched smooth over the fatty deposits beneath. And he did not seem to sport as much bristle as perhaps a man should. I looked for the smile lines at his eyes that might show his humorous temperament and saw none obvious—I'd recently noticed them on Mr. Pinckney who exercised them often and decided it was quite a lovely way to assess the nature of the person to whom one was being introduced.

My mother tittered. "John, it is."

I glanced away and accidentally caught the gleaming amusement in Mr. Pinckney's eyes as he noticed my discomfiture at my mother's antics.

"John," my mother reiterated, "how do you find yourself at the home of my dearest hosts? Do you live roundabouts?"

I thought it would have been more efficient to ask him

his trade and his assets in a more direct manner. Not that it would be acceptable etiquette to do so, but it was simply so obvious.

"Oh, Mr. Laurens here is the best saddler in the Carolinas, perhaps the whole land," Mr. Pinckney interjected. "He has become quite an important merchant among the businessmen of Charles Town."

"You do flatter, Pinckney," Mr. Laurens chided but puffed up nonetheless.

I could feel my mother calculating how much money a saddler made and whether she might support John's son, Henry Laurens, as a candidate for my hand in marriage should the moment arise. I barely contained a shudder.

That my mother was busily attempting to forge an inroad and assess the potential wealth and worth of someone who in years past she would have considered beneath our status regardless of his apparent wealth, was an indicator of her absolute and vehement opposition to our current state of affairs orchestrated by my father.

"And, Mrs. Lucas," Mr. Laurens returned, "your husband, I hear, has returned to Antigua. Rumor has it he'll be making a bid for governor. Is that true?"

Mama smiled, her shoulders straightening a fraction. "Well." She dipped her head. "I suppose that would make my Eliza the daughter of the governor of Antigua. How ... politically interesting ..." she mused. And so, supper that evening reminded me clearly of the campaign she'd undertaken to see me safely married regardless of my father's wishes.

As well as seeing to the business of three plantations, I would also be fending off my mother's various machinations. I smiled faintly as I ground my teeth hard enough to brew a headache.

"I feel very fortunate to have been seated next to you, Miss

Lucas." The voice came from my right. I turned to look into the boyish face of John Laurens' son. His auburn hair was pomaded back, leaving a rather shiny expanse of forehead.

"Master Laurens," I acknowledged him.

"Henry, please."

"Are you old enough to attend, Henry?" I teased and winked. Instead of the amused response, I felt sure I had immediately stood upon a sore issue. His lips tightened, but in a moment the look was gone, replaced by a rueful grin. "I know you mean no harm," he said thinly. "But it is upsetting to be reminded of my youth repeatedly. My father does it often enough for everyone."

I bit my lip, instantly embarrassed at my faux pas. "You are correct, I *was* jesting. But I apologize nonetheless."

"I'm sure you have no such concerns since you have been left in charge of your father's business affairs. He must think you quite mature enough." I detected no malice in Henry's tone, but his words didn't sit well.

"Oh. Well, to be honest, there was not much other option. My brothers, George and Tommy, are being schooled in England, and my mother not being too well, it had to fall to me," I said self-effacingly. And then in an attempt to find common ground, I added, "But I too struggle with the notion of being taken seriously due to my age and, I'm afraid, my gender. At least you are your father's oldest and only son."

"That's true enough." Henry Laurens smirked, a glint in his eye. Then he cleared his throat, a flush crawling up it. "I, I do so admire you. As I am sure is obvious. I was wondering if, uh, if my father and I may come and call upon you at Wappoo in the near future?"

"Oh." I was rather taken aback. Have Henry and his father visit us at Wappoo? I could hardly say no. "Certainly," I offered. But I didn't want to have to offer them lodging. Not that I'd thought twice about it when Charles Pinckney had arrived to check on us after the slave uprising. Somehow the thought of Henry and his father staying with us at Wappoo set me at odds.

Henry grinned.

"The quickest way is by boat," I went on quickly. "It's easily there and back in a day. It will be a straightforward evening return. Actually quite beautiful as the sun sets. So long as it is pleasant weather."

"Indeed?" Henry asked. "I shall let my father know."

Mr. Pinckney called for the men to repair to his study and Henry pushed back from the table.

He glanced from me to Mary Chardon, who was seated on my other side.

"Ladies." He bid us adieu and drifted off.

"What an odd creature, that boy is," whispered Mary. "He acts like he is of age, and his father brings him about these soirees, though we all know he is but sixteen years old. In fact, fifteen, if rumors are true. It's rather creepy, the child playing a man like that."

"It's worse," I muttered under my breath to her, to avoid wagging ears. "I believe he just informed me of his intent for my hand."

Mary gasped, her eyes round. "No," she said disbelievingly.

"Yes." I nodded. My nose wrinkled. "He asked if he and his father could call upon me at Wappoo."

"What are you going to do?"

"First, I suppose I'll hope I'm mistaken. Although, I'm afraid my mother did rather lay the groundwork didn't she? It is most peculiar. I thought Henry's father planned to apprentice him in London. What on earth would he need with a wife then?"

"Unless ..." Mary stopped and shook her head.

"Unless, what?" I asked and glanced around the remaining womenfolk at the table, all ensconced in lively conversation secure with their own stations in life.

"Unless it isn't for the boy," Mary whispered, "but for his father?"

Fourteen

"Mr. Pinckney! To what do we owe the honor of your visit?" I was delighted to see he had just pulled up on his horse as we returned one Tuesday afternoon from the Woodwards' house. It was again late spring, and while warm, there was a refreshing breeze off the waters of Wappoo Creek. Polly, Mama, and I had walked the short distance of a mile and seen no traffic until thundering hooves came upon us as we turned into our drive.

"Greetings, ladies." Charles Pinckney's dismount was lithe as he dropped to the ground from the handsome animal. His hair was windswept, his cheeks pink from the sun.

"Oh my, what a horse," exclaimed Polly. "He looks very fierce and very handsome all at once."

"Why, thank you, Miss Polly." Charles chuckled. "I'm sure if Chickasaw could blush, he would. Before I left town, a letter came for Eliza from London via our shared merchant, Beale."

He presented it with a flourish.

"I do hope you didn't ride full tilt the seventeen miles from town just for a letter to me." I laughed, taking the thick letter from his hand.

"How lovely to see you," my mother joined. "Will you stay

for the night and dine with us? I see Mrs. Pinckney is not accompanying you."

"I was leaving for our estate at Belmont when I came upon the letter. I had hoped you wouldn't mind the letter a few days late if I could deliver it in person after I saw to Mrs. Pinckney. She is there enjoying some country air."

"That is twice the fortune for us then." I smiled and looked at the handwriting on the envelope. "Oh how wonderful! I daresay, the letter is from my former guardian, Mrs. Bodicott. She and her husband were very kind to me during my schooling in England."

"Does she still look after your brothers?" he asked.

"George and Thomas." I nodded. "We've been desperate for news of them. Especially Tommy. He has been very poorly."

"We certainly have," agreed my mother. "Let's hope she has enclosed a letter for me also."

I handed the letter bundle to her and she headed to the house, no doubt to let Essie and Nanny know of our guest. Charles Pinckney's horse was gleaming with exertion, his dark flanks heaving like bellows in the heat.

"Come," I offered. "Let us take Chickasaw to the stable so Peter can rub him down and give him some oats and water."

My heart gave a thump of happiness at the arrival of our guest. "I am so glad you are here, sir," I started as we led Chickasaw to the stable. "Pray, look to your right," I couldn't help adding with pride.

Mr. Pinckney turned.

I waited, my smile impossible to hold back as I watched the sight of the fields register on his face.

He turned to me, eyes wide. "Your indigo?" he guessed.

I sighed happily and nodded. "My indigo."

He looked at me a beat longer, then returned his gaze

to the field. The afternoon sun turned his gray-blue eyes translucent. "Well done. I wondered what was keeping you so busy that you hadn't returned to town in recent weeks. Now I know."

"Togo, Sawney, and I, and even Quash, patrol these fields endlessly." I chuckled. "There have never been more cosseted plants in all of Christendom."

"I imagine there haven't."

Peter took Chickasaw from Charles, and we turned back to the house.

"Last year, after the initial crop was lost to frost, we were somewhat successful in growing it. Not all the plants reached maturity, but some did and we collected seed. However, with no one to whom we could ask for knowledge of indigo-making, we did not even attempt it. But Quash tells me there is a woman on our plantation at Waccamaw who might know, although the overseer has repeatedly declined to send her when I make my request by letter."

"I have to go to Georgetown," said Charles. "Mrs. Pinckney cannot accompany me as she is not feeling herself. It sounds like you have reason to visit your overseer?"

WE GLIDED UP THE WACCAMAW RIVER. The marsh grasses were vibrant and acidic in their new growth. There was the sound of a puff of air, and Charles Pinckney and I both turned to see a mother porpoise and her baby undulating through the grasses at the water's edge.

Nearing the banks where the Lucas land began, Quash called out to a small boy who was scaring off birds along the fields that bordered the river. He was dispatched to tell Starrat of our arrival. "Do you know his name?" I asked Quash as we watched the boy look at us wide-eyed and then run away like there was a bobcat on his tail.

"Lil' Gulla."

I exchanged a glance with my traveling companion. *Charles.* Even though he'd asked me to call him Charles many times, I knew I still could not say it aloud.

"That's certainly an easy one to remember." Mr. Pinckney chuckled.

The fields were all plowed and presumably sowed with rice, the last few being worked upon heavily. Glistening dark heads and strong bodies dipped and stood repeatedly, moving in lines down the rice stands.

We had spent an enjoyable evening the night before as guests of Mr. and Mrs. McClelland, whom Charles knew through his law practice. Although I had not met them previously, they'd fussed over me, and we'd lamented together on Mrs. Pinckney not being able to accompany us. After a hearty breakfast, the McClellands had sent us on our way, begging me to stop in on my next visit.

The ferry glided up to the weathered dock, and two large ferry hands hopped out to rope up and assist.

The boy was still visible in the distance as he ran up to the door of the overseer's cottage, banging on it.

"Starrat, suh," he yelled at the top of his lungs. "The white lady, suh." His voice carried on the breeze down to the water.

Charles requested the ferry master wait for us.

I was surprised Starrat was inside and not out doing rounds, but the rice harvest was heavy work for all involved, so perhaps he had been about earlier and was taking a short rest. They must have already started threshing the rice heads off the stalks. It seemed like such a bounty of rice, I could hardly imagine how much work it was. After seeing the Woodwards' small rice plot, and how overwhelming the work seemed to be to get the rice table ready, it was hard to imagine the effort involved in an operation this size.

Beale had informed me how much rice he was expecting from Starrat based on his calculations, and from the looks of it, we were producing much more.

Up at the cottage, the door finally opened. The little boy scampered backward but not fast enough to avoid the hard clip over the head he received for his efforts. I winced, watching as the boy, holding his head, hustled back down to his post at the river's edge. I'd have to find him before we left and make sure he was okay. Beside me, Quash made a small clicking sound in his throat but said nothing. He didn't have to.

"Whose boy is he, Quash?"

"Sarah's boy," he said stiffly.

I glanced at him. "Sarah who knows about the indigo?"

Quash nodded.

Just then a dark-skinned woman came out of the door behind Starrat and hurried off toward the dwellings.

Starrat's frown turned toward us and then dropped, to be replaced by something more neutral.

"Charming fellow," Pinckney murmured as we approached.

"Good afternoon, Starrat. May I present Mr. Charles Pinckney, a friend of my father's."

Starrat wiped his hands down the front of his coarse waistcoat and then held one out to Mr. Pinckney. "Delighted to meet you, sir."

I requested updates on the harvest, and Starrat answered me curtly and directed most of his conversation to Charles. Charles neatly volleyed back to me, and I thanked heaven he was so well versed in diplomacy.

Talk turned to the pitch production and the cattle. I told Starrat of the high hopes we had for the lucerne grass my father had sent, which I had planted at Wappoo. If it did well, I would be sending some, at my father's request, up here and to Garden Hill for the cattle. We walked as we talked, and I was careful to begin every sentence with "Colonel Lucas asked, said, requested, wondered."

Eventually we came to my first order of business, and I informed Starrat how many barrels of rice would be expected in Charles Town.

He blustered for a moment. His eyes grew narrow, and he drew a stained rag hanging from his pocket and mopped his forehead shiny with sweat. "That's not possible. We never send that much. Besides, some of it is scheduled to leave from the new Georgetown port."

"Well, I'd prefer it all go through our man in Charles Town. And it *is* possible because you just informed me how much rice was harvested. By my calculation—"

He gave a short bark of laughter. "Your calculation?"

"Yes, my calculation. Or are you not the same Starrat who was present during that last visit with my father?"

"Yes, with your father. He's the one what pays my wages. Not some girl child." He glanced at Mr. Pinckney as if to say, *What is the world coming to that a girl could be so brazen?*

My skin blazed with heat from a temper that was starting beneath my skin. "Be that as it may," I managed, my lips tight, "You'll quickly find out I hold the purse strings."

My tone was calm by sheer force of will.

Charles held up a hand.

But Starrat ignored it. "Is that so?" he growled and took a sudden small but menacing step toward me.

I gasped and reared back from him. I immediately realized my mistake at the flash of satisfaction in Starrat's eyes.

He was a bully, plain and simple.

Charles Pinckney was between us in an instant.

I found myself staring at a broad back, close enough to see the individual stitches of a finely woven linen shirt. Charles' dark hair was tied in a small queue at his nape.

My heart still pounded with the sudden fright, but I swallowed and, unthinking, reached up to lay a hand on Charles' shoulder to let him know it was okay. He jerked under my touch and I withdrew my hand. I stepped up beside him.

Starrat held up both hands, but with a smirk that smacked of a secret he was hiding. "I meant nothing by that. Not used to taking orders from a girl is all."

"Well, take orders from me then," said Charles.

"It's all right, gentlemen," I appeased. "The good news is these are not my orders. They are my father's orders. So please, just do as he requires, and I'll let him know of your success in this year's harvest. I'm sure he'll be very pleased with you. And rest assured, I will ask nothing of you that has not my father's approbation." I smiled as meekly as I could possibly manage.

I motioned to Quash, who walked ten steps behind us. He called to one of the children and spoke in low, rapid tones. The child scampered off toward the fields.

"I'm sure you received my notes about the whipping post?" I asked casually as we headed toward the dwellings.

"I did," Starrat answered but offered no more and as the offending equipment came within sight, I stopped.

"And yet, it still remains standing."

"It does."

I glanced toward Starrat then exchanged a quick look with Charles. Did I want to fight this battle now? I needed to. Or perhaps there was another way to deal with the problem. I'd have to think on it.

Starrat turned to me. "I find it is better to leave it. Even if I do not use it."

I didn't believe him for one moment, but I remained silent as I assessed him. "If I hear of it being used again, I will chop it down myself," I said and was saved having to see his reaction when my attention was diverted by the arrival of the person I'd sent Quash to fetch.

A woman carrying a small girl with light skin approached warily. It looked to be the same woman who I'd seen slipping out of Starrat's cottage earlier. Sarah.

I frowned.

"What do you want with that one?" Starrat's voice was brusque.

"I have a few questions for her."

Fifteen

"She's not reliable." Starrat stood, legs akimbo. Attitude all sorts of defiant. "Having trouble keeping her in line. Thinks she's some kind of priestess or something from her tribe." He slipped his thumbs into the waistband of his breeches and rocked back on his heels.

"Well, my questions don't concern her conduct or her alleged station," I murmured, but wondered what exactly he meant by keeping her in line. I hoped it had nothing to do with the cursed whipping post.

The answer came as Sarah got close. Her head was bowed but it wasn't hard to see she had a fresh purple lump under her left eye that was partially split and a swollen lip.

I gritted my teeth. It wasn't *her* conduct but Starrat's that was under question by me.

The babe was quiet, her large eyes taking in the scene.

"I'll be wanting Sarah at Wappoo right away," I said immediately, surprising everyone, including myself. I had only planned to speak with her, not relocate her to Wappoo. But the words, born on instinct, were out of me before I could think. "And any children she has." I looked at her. "How many children do you have?"

She raised her eyes.

Her gaze was filled with defiance and bitterness. Toward *me*. Straining to keep my gaze steady, we continued looking at each other.

I swallowed down a gasp of surprise.

Starrat spat, a rough wet sound. "Answer the lady, bitch."

The harsh word slammed through our group, and I struggled to show no reaction.

Her gaze wavered on the impact, and her spirit seemed to sink imperceptibly.

"That boy," Starrat answered when she didn't, indicating Lil' Gulla. "And the brat she's holding."

The light coffee-skinned little girl.

Sarah's eyes had dropped from mine again. She shifted the small girl on her hip. I had no doubt who had sired her.

Charles was still and quiet beside me. I was filled with gratitude at my friend's support. And his silence.

I dared not look at him, but his strength was a solid wall as I dealt with the horror curdling my blood as I understood the relationship between Sarah and Starrat. Or rather, Starrat's relationship with *her*. I had no doubt it was not reciprocal. Nor consensual.

A chill was moving through my body and shuddering along my bones. I knew nothing of the relations between a man and a woman firsthand, but my mother was never bruised in my recollection. Mrs. Pinckney was never bruised. I understood it wasn't exactly enjoyable to submit to a man's baser needs, but I knew it was not supposed to be … violent.

I willed my mind blank.

"I require her and her children at Wappoo. We have need for help at the house." I turned to her. "Gather your things and your children. You are coming with me."

She locked eyes with me, her glare mutinous.

I was aghast. I was saving her; how could she not see that?

"We need her here. You can't come and just move our Negroes around. We depend on each one of them," Starrat said angrily.

I turned to him. You *depend on her*, I wanted to say.

"I can and I shall." I crossed my arms, hating how childish and petulant I sounded. "You will just have to … to make do with one less … pair of hands," I finished. My voice was raspy, my cheeks hot with embarrassment.

Sarah turned to Quash and spoke in a staccato dialect, so I only understood a handful of words. Her body language was all wrong. She was agitated and angry. Quash answered her calmly, and the two of them seemed to battle it out before she turned and stalked away, her back stiff and head high.

"See what I mean? She's trouble." Starrat snorted and spat onto the dirt. "Take her then, but don't complain to me."

The easy way he accepted his defeat rattled me further. And a curious sense of foreboding rippled over me as he opened his mouth to speak again.

"Course, it won't be long now before you don't make the decisions about this land."

I swallowed. "What is that supposed to mean?"

"It means, I was in town just a few days ago." A slick, satisfied smile slid across Starrat's face. "In Mr. Manigault's office."

Surprise, confusion, and dread dropped heavy in my bones.

"For what purpose?" I demanded.

Starrat chuckled eerily. "Why, bearing witness to a mortgage being placed upon this plantation, of course. Since I oversee it, I was the natural choice."

"What?" I gasped.

Starrat raised his eyebrows innocently. "Oh, you didn't know your father encumbered yet another property? I thought you were in charge of all his plantation affairs?"

Shock had rendered me mute. My heart thumped heavily in my throat, which had somehow forgotten how to work in any capacity. No words were there to be formed, no saliva to be swallowed, and no breath moved through me.

Starrat rocked back casually, then stuck his thumbs in his breeches before turning and walking away.

I let out a long shuddering exhale, my stomach in rebellion, and turned to my silent companion. Swaying slightly, Charles crooked an elbow for me to hold on to, and I accepted it gratefully.

"Did you know?" I croaked. "No, of course you didn't. I—"

"Come, let's get you into the shade. Perhaps sit down." Charles' brow was furrowed, his kind blue eyes seemed gray with trouble. He looked around, then obviously spied a place to do that, for he turned and led me to the long branch of a live oak whose weight had caused it to grow snaking along the ground. For the first time realizing my legs had lost their strength, I sat where indicated. In fact, perhaps my whole body had been robbed of its essence. I felt hollow and bloodless.

"How could my father do this? I was making it work," I exclaimed. "With rice we would have … I … I just saw Manigault a few weeks ago when I was in town. Why did he not mention this?" My breath came in gasps. My tight stays and the growing heat of the morning threatened to stop my breathing altogether.

"Take a slow breath," Charles ordered calmly. "Perhaps he didn't know at that time?"

"Oh, he knew. I'm certain. And why would Manigault ask Starrat to be the witness and not inform me?" I choked out the last word on a squeak as the burn of tears seared my nose and eyes.

"It's fairly common practice, I'm afraid, to have the overseer bear witness to any encumbrances upon a property. But as to the reason he didn't inform you, I can't say."

"It was the most frustrating meeting. To be treated like a daft child with a harebrained scheme. Now I know what was behind that indulgent smile. He may as well have patted me on the head." My temper flared to a new heat in my chest, and I battled not to give in to the tears of frustration that were beating at the doors to get out. "And it's not that he sees me as a child. It's that I'm ..."

"A woman," Charles finished for me softly. The strength of Charles' hand closed around mine and the gesture sent a shock through me. I didn't remove my hand. He squeezed gently, and it almost undid me. The comfort and kindness as he seemed to lend his strength made me instead want to crack apart. My stomach swirled. I closed my eyes tight as I fought to control my emotions, grateful we could have this moment that could never have happened without the privacy of where we were. The words I didn't voice were the ones about my father and his military ambition that was bleeding us dry. An ambition born of a sense of duty and love of country that I understood as equally as I now began to resent it.

"Thank you for not coming to my aid with Starrat," I said softly, opening my eyes. "I needed to mark my ground with that man on my own. Even though he bested me."

He started to speak, then stopped and cocked his head. "Well, I was about to apologize for not coming to your aid sooner. Are you sure about this? About taking Sarah to Wappoo?"

"I—" My shoulders sagged. I felt hollow and confused. "No, I'm not sure. But how can I leave her here? He's ... he's ..." A shudder rolled over me again. "I need her anyway. Quash tells me she has knowledge of indigo. So, it just has to be." And I felt sure if we didn't leave with her, he would exact revenge just to mark my notice.

Charles nodded and stood, drawing me to my feet. "We need to go if we're to make it back to Belmont by nightfall. Mrs. Pinckney and Miss Bartlett will be happy to see you." Then he let go of my hand.

I made a fist as if to keep some of his comfort imprinted upon me and pressed it to my belly. "I shall be glad of their company after a day like today. You mentioned Mrs. Pinckney was unwell?"

We turned to walk back to the ferry landing.

Nearing the river, Charles paused, looking out over the wide channel to the marshy island that made up the other bank. Then he looked at me. "We wish for children, as I'm sure you know. Every time God decides we are not to be blessed, it breaks Mrs. Pinckney's heart further." He looked away, pain clear in his eyes.

I thought of the easy way Starrat had deposited his filthy and prolific seed in Sarah's womb to create life.

"I've come to believe that a completion of happiness is not attainable in this life. And that is all I will say on the subject." Charles smiled valiantly. "Your company will be just what she needs."

We stood upon the dock and waited. Sarah, Quash, and Lil' Gulla holding the hand of a chubby small girl no more than two or three years old, walked from the dwellings. Sarah held a bundle upon her head. All her earthly possessions. My heart squeezed.

"Why do you think she was so angry about the chance to leave here?" I murmured.

"Who takes care of her children while she works?" Charles responded to my question with his own.

Immediately, I understood the ramifications of my

decision that had seemed so simple. There was a structure and a hierarchy among the slaves, and I was removing a piece that would have to be reinforced or worked around.

"And—" Charles broke off.

"And?"

"It shouldn't be mentioned."

"In such genteel or innocent company as myself?" I asked and turned to face Charles. "You wonder who will fulfill his ... needs ... now that Sarah is not available?"

Charles' cheeks flushed, and then mine did too.

"I'm sorry," I muttered and turned away, mortified for having addressed the issue aloud.

"So did your father really give orders to barrel up so much rice?" Charles cleared his throat.

"Not at all. You caught me in a bald-faced lie." I grinned ruefully, gratefully accepting the neat change of topic.

"I knew that." He smirked. "I told you I can read your expressions. You are a terrible liar."

"Well, *needs-must*. It worked for now."

Charles nodded. "For now."

I WOKE BEFORE DAWN AS USUAL. But this morning, rather than the normal routine of running through my list of things to be done that day, I lay in cold, dark, paralyzing fear. Sweat was icy against my skin. The weight of the fear upon my chest was so heavy, it was almost impossible to breathe.

What was I doing? I needed to simply do as my father instructed. Just that and no more. And wait. It was only a few years. And really how bad would it be being married to some curmudgeon, being allowed to exert my influence only over the household and its affairs? To improve my musical ability. To spend time reading. Ahh reading! And doing needlework. It was a relaxing way to spend time. *Waste time!* I could call upon people and spend more time visiting and making friends and talking about … what exactly?

The panic hit me anew. If that future was suffocating, then the reality was I had to change it. But even if I made Lucas land the most profitable in all of Christendom, it might not make a difference.

I threw back the covers, forcing the panicky feeling off my chest. I imagined it dropping to the ground in a greasy thud, writhing around and disintegrating without a host from which to suck sustenance.

Almost unconsciously, I slid my hands down my chest. Then I held open the neck of my gown and made out the mounds of my small girlish breasts in the dim light. Curse these things that dictated how my mind could be utilized. I let out a long sigh. Though if I was a boy, I'd be off like my brother George would be soon. To train to be a soldier just like my father. If I was a boy I wouldn't be here. I wouldn't have been charged with this duty.

Being a woman was my lot. But it was also my difference.

I reached for the bell, giving it a brief tinkle, and washed my body with a muslin at the cold basin of water as I waited for Essie.

When I was washed, I sat naked on the edge of my bed awaiting Essie's arrival. It was relatively bright outside, and I'd thought dawn so very close, but it was the moon, full and bright white, low in the sky that had put me ahead of myself.

Understanding now that Essie wouldn't be up for an hour or so at least, I pulled a fresh chemise from the armoire. I took hold of my braid and wrapped it around itself in a tight bun at the back of my head. My dress had been laid to air on the rack against the wall. I did the best I could with my stays, pulled the dove-gray linen dress on, and secured the skirt strings.

It was time to write to my father.

Dear Sir,

... I know how ready you are to fight in a just cause as well as the love you bear your country ... in preference to every other regard ...

I put down my pen, worrying my lip between my teeth. I was frustrated, but there was no point taking it out on my father. He was doing what he saw fit. And I was aware that every word I wrote to him could be the last words he would ever read. We were at war. I'd have to temper my emotion.

I have high hopes for this crop of indigo. It will save us, Papa. And if what I hear is true, it could very well be a boon for the Crown, your beloved country. Please find an indigo maker with utmost haste as I should hate to miss the chance to perfect the dye. I have been frugal. We have a little extra set aside to help with the cost of such a consultant. And perhaps, if needed, a little of the proceeds from mortgaging Waccamaw might be diverted to this cause.

My Dearest Eliza,

... I had hoped to spare you the concern about my decision to mortgage the Waccamaw plantation. I wrote to Manigault to take care of it privately as I had no wish to add undue concern or pressure on your already burdened shoulders. Please forgive me.

I have contracted a man from Montserrat to aid us in our indigo endeavor. He has been running a successful indigo concern for the French a good many years. He is obligated to see our crop through to the successful production of dye. I hope this will go some way toward assuring your forgiveness of my folly in attempting to conceal my financial concerns from you, my most trusted daughter.

Also, I must let you know that Mr. Laurens has written to ask permission for your hand ...

Your affectionate father

Sixteen

Polly was practicing her scales inside and Mama was resting. The bees buzzed lazily around the jasmine and lavender.

I was too excited by half.

Seeing the tall, wide frame of Togo in the distance, I took off down the track at a fast clip.

No running.

Ladies didn't run.

Papa was sending a consultant! Though, goodness knew when he would arrive.

This third crop of indigo had reached two feet and looked hardier than anything we had produced before. Still everyone was on alert for any weed or pest that might possibly interrupt our endeavor.

After sharing the news about the consultant with Togo, I sought out Quash to let him know also.

At my request, Quash had asked Sawney to help construct a room for Sarah and her children. We would build an additional two dwelling cabins with a shared chimney. Sarah and the children would have one side. The extra space would be needed if we grew our indigo operation. Sawney had been reinforcing the chicken coop to keep out the foxes, so work on Sarah's cabin had been delayed. In the meantime, she was staying with Mary Ann and her children, as well as helping out in the house and kitchen. Which, according to Essie, had set Mary Ann to muttering in the kitchen all day long. "Too many what ain't got no sense 'roun' here," Mary Ann would say at least four times a day.

"It's just until the indigo harvest," I told Mary Ann. "Then Sarah will be helping outside."

Mary Ann grunted.

Essie, for her part, had gifted me a small talisman one morning before sunup. A desiccated chicken foot. I squealed in disgust when I saw the thing sitting on my palm, yellowed and scaly, and promptly dropped it.

"Hush up," Essie had admonished. "It's for luck and protection."

"I have a small crucifix and a prayer book for that."

"A body can' have too much."

"What am I supposed do with it? Wear it?" I shuddered.

Essie had shaken her head. "I'll be leavin' it under your bed."

"Is this to do with Sarah thinking she's a witch?"

"A priestess? None that we ever heard of. But I'm not likin' her thinkin' she is."

Settling Sarah and her children into Wappoo proved difficult. She was surly and caused confused and restless murmuring amongst her peers. Perhaps that was the problem; she didn't see them as peers. More as underlings.

When I asked her simple questions, her topaz-colored eyes met mine with silent hostility and challenge. Do you recognize the indigo plant? Do you know how long it takes to flower? Do you know the signs that the leaf is ready to harvest for dye? All of it met with mutinous silence.

She expected to be punished, I imagined, for defying me and was daring me to do it. And while my level of frustration grew with every encounter, I simply prayed harder for humility, kindness, and patience. I would wait her out and earn her allegiance.

Now that we had a consultant coming, Sarah's indigo knowledge might not even be needed, but I was sure more knowledge was better than none.

The honest truth was I admired her grit. And worse, I admired her stubbornness. She held herself in a certain manner I envied. No matter that she was in bondage, it was as if her spirit would not submit to the reality of her position. And she held her power the only way she knew how. In a way, I came to understand how that must have incensed Starrat, causing him to try and break her.

While Sarah found it hard to accept her change in geography, Lil' Gulla had gravitated immediately to the stables and now shadowed Indian Peter all day long taking care of the horses. After a few weeks he stopped going to sleep next to his mother altogether, preferring to wake up early in the stable.

Sarah's little girl, Ebba, had joined Mary Ann's two daughters in the kitchen, but being too young to do anything worthwhile, she was more of a distraction than anything else.

Her chubby tanned hands grappled at Mary Ann's skirts, causing irritation and muttering, until Sarah would fashion a sling from a piece of sackcloth and tie Ebba into a little cocoon on her back. There, the baby girl would press her cheek against her mother's shoulders and for a while fall into a wakeful stupor, watching the goings-on around her while Sarah continued sweeping or doing whatever chore Mary Ann had assigned her. Eventually the constant movement would set the baby's eyes to slow, long blinks until they closed altogether.

Every day, the indigo plants grew taller, the leaves more

perfect, the color changing so incrementally to a deeper green that some days I think I imagined a blue tinge. I couldn't believe this field of chaotic thickets that had no structure, no order, could be capable of so much promise. Indigo was a weed, pure and simple. It was the kind of plant one threw up on makeshift borders or found on the side of well-worn roads to town where the comings and goings of man kept the wildness of nature only temporarily at bay.

The heat of summer pressed into autumn. Overdue for rain, the afternoons had started swelling and emulsifying with humid weight even beyond a normal Carolina summer. Each day I'd look west and see the dark iron of swollen clouds, but they never came close enough to break our heat.

Thinking of the late frost that had killed our first crop, and news from my brother George about how it had been so bitterly cold in London as to draw a snow in May, I realized the scales of justice would mean this summer would drag by and extend well into fall, roasting us slowly at the spit. I told myself it did not matter as long as the indigo continued to flourish.

Then one day, the reality that we were missing our chance hit me. This crop might go to seed without our ever getting a chance to try.

I sent for Sarah, asking Essie to please dispatch her to my father's study.

Wiping damp palms upon my skirt, I waited at the window until I felt her sullen presence enter the room.

I turned and was struck once again by Sarah's presence.

Proud bearing, I'd already noticed, eyes lighter than usual and gleaming with a thousand emotions, but also smooth brown skin over perfectly symmetrical features. It was funny. I had never looked at a Negro in terms of attractiveness. But part of me recognized this woman's beauty, and it was intimidating.

She stared at me, wordless.

I stared back at her.

"Sarah," I finally said. "I know you have no reason to trust me. I moved you away from Waccamaw because—"

Sarah spat on the floor.

I jerked. Shocked.

I told myself to think and to school my expression. Charles' noting that I wore my emotions clear on my face rang in my ears.

Tilting up my chin, I refused to look down at the product of her disdain pooling up in a globulous mess on the floorboards. Instead, I picked up my skirts and walked forward, careful to avoid her spittle. I kept coming until I was a foot away. And a foot smaller than she. Then I stepped up even closer.

The smell of her skin was meaty and tinged with musk and salt. Heat wafted up from her person.

"I can see you are not afraid of me. I'm not afraid of you either."

Her gaze was dead and unwavering.

"Now, I'm sure it wasn't quite the same between you and Starrat."

As I said his name, I saw the most fleeting movement in her eyes.

I stepped to the side and walked around her. "No, in fact, I believe that—"

"I'm no' fear of him," Sarah snarled, her words clipped and underlaid with a French patois. Essie still had a tinge of the same. She was here via the islands and had obviously been resold into the Carolinas.

I finished my circuit and again stood in front of her. Our eyes locked. "I was going to say that I believed he was afraid of *you*."

Surprise registered for a moment before it was replaced again with her impenetrable glare.

"You don't agree?" I asked and was met with continued silence. "Men do not like strong women." I let that sink in for a moment, then put my face close to hers. "Starrat does not like *me* either."

She remained quiet.

"I would like your help harvesting the indigo. I know Lil' Gulla is happy here. He is learning a skill with horses that will make him very valuable. But if you would prefer to be at the mercy of Starrat, I can send you back to Waccamaw."

"Do you sell my chil'en? Do you give my son skill and sell him?"

Her question surprised me.

"Was that the nature of the deal you made with Starrat? That he would not sell your children? *His* children?"

She was quiet. Some of the fire had dimmed from her eyes, but her body emanated a rigid defensiveness, as if she had constructed weaponry around herself that would be set off at the slightest threat.

Perhaps that was the deal she'd made, but the truth was he would have taken what he wanted anyway.

"Did you know that he has no right to sell slaves that do not belong to him?" I asked. But my mind whirled. How many children had been born on that plantation who had never been reported to an absentee landlord? An easy matter to sell them then and make an extra penny. That man's audacity knew no bounds. I felt sick.

Sarah made a snorting sound of disbelief.

I went through the reasoning in my mind. Slaves were a commodity. I knew my father, no matter his sympathies, believed so. There was nothing to be gained by us selling any slaves at present. Certainly not while I was trying to up production from all of our land.

I made a decision then and there. If I had need of extra hands and moved Negroes from one plantation to another, it would be on a temporary basis only. "While I am in charge here, no children will be sold from any Lucas plantation, nor separated from their mothers."

She stayed silent. Perhaps she didn't believe me.

"You have my word."

I would have to earn her trust. Somehow. But I sensed her spirit was broken and defiant in a way that might never be fixed.

She said nothing.

"You may go," I finished eventually, knowing that day wouldn't be the one I'd win. She was insulting and insolent, but I chose to overlook it. I'd be the same in her position.

I prayed again for patience with her.

———

I am resolved to make a good mistress to
    my servants,
To treat them with humanity and good
    nature;
To give them sufficient and comfortable
    clothing and provisions,
And all things necessary for them.
To be careful and tender of them in their
    sickness.
To encourage them when they do well and
    pass over small faults.
Not to be tyrannical, peevish, or impatient
    towards them
But to make their lives as comfortable as
    I can.
So help me, oh, My God! Amen.

—Excerpt from prayer written by Eliza Lucas

———

Seventeen

After yet more frustrating days with no help from Sarah, and my refusal to force her assistance, I called upon Mr. Deveaux. But he was unable to give us helpful advice.

"You soak the leaves. And there's lime involved. Though how much I don't know," he said.

I'd sighed. I knew those steps too. But how long. How much?

But then it didn't matter because a virulent little worm made a feast of our beautiful, tired indigo plants.

For several days, Togo and I furrowed our brows and plucked a few little yellow creatures from the leaves. A week later we were fighting a losing battle, and we had to admit defeat.

We were left with a third of our crop.

I asked Togo to leave me a moment.

The urge to collapse to the ground in my hoop skirts and cry with frustration was so strong I could feel it like hands pulling me down.

I stood still in the middle of the field. The ground beneath my feet was mortgaged. Waccamaw was mortgaged. In time Garden Hill would be too, if it wasn't already. I had yet to get a straight answer from Mr. Manigault or my father.

I looked to the east across the fields and the corner of our home and out to the sparkling waters of Wappoo Creek. The cool air off the water caved to the heat that flooded upward from the ground to stifle my body. Sweat slid in a tickling rush down my cheek and between my breasts. To the right, Quash was showing Sarah, Ebba strapped to her back, her finished room.

A wave of bitter frustration and anger washed over me as I watched her. It was so strong it took my breath.

As if she felt it, Sarah suddenly looked up.

I swallowed.

We stared across the fields at each other.

Then I saw her say something to Quash, and he too looked at me and said something back to her.

Later that afternoon as I made copies of my latest letters into the copy book, Essie appeared at the study door.

"Sarah here to see ya," she said with a cryptic look on her face. A smile, but not quite.

"Did she say what she wants?"

"Better she tell ya."

Again Sarah walked into the room. Like last time, her personality emanated a range far outside her stature.

"Hello, Sarah."

She dipped her chin.

I sighed. "I'm sure you are happy to be moving out from Mary Ann's room?"

She stood a few moments and I waited. Was I expecting a thank you?

"I gon' show you how I make my dye."

A tingle of euphoria trailed up my spine.

I tamped it down. I hadn't been through the last few disappointments without learning not to put too much stock in any one avenue.

She looked at me expectantly.

"Can you make dye cakes?" I asked instead.

Her mouth tightened and she shook her head.

"But you can extract the dye from the leaves?"

She nodded.

Who knew when the consultant would arrive in Charles Town? Tensions with the Spanish were rising. Already Oglethorpe in Savannah had put a call out for able-bodied young men in Charles Town to take on the Spanish in Florida.

A ship headed this way might never get through, and we had indigo ready now.

At least I'd know part of the process. I wasn't sure I trusted Sarah; she might yet exact a price. But what choice did I have? It could be my only chance to learn anything related to making indigo. She couldn't teach me exactly what I wanted to know, but it would be something.

I nodded at her. "Okay. Show me."

EARLY THE NEXT MORNING, Togo and I trailed along behind Sarah as she inspected all the damaged leaves, clucking and shaking her head. "Did we leave the leaves on too long?" I asked.

Sarah shrugged.

I looked at Togo, and he shrugged too.

She was enjoying her moment of power, I knew. And I thought how few she'd probably had. I allowed it.

Sarah indicated we needed a very large shallow container and after coming up empty, I finally sent Quash to ask Essie and Mary Ann to bring out Mary Ann's round wooden washing tub. I'd be fielding questions about it later, I knew, but needs must. It was to be filled with fresh water and left out in the sun to warm.

Sarah picked leaves here and there, and as we made our way to a less blighted area, she motioned for Togo's reaping hook and began hacking off whole branches. I pulled out my small dirk that was only useful for smaller stalks and I began to copy her, despite incredulous looks from both of them.

Many of the little worms had started spinning cocoons indicating their feeding frenzy was over. But where they still roamed free, we picked them off into a cup that Togo was to go and burn.

Before long, we had filled the sack slung across Togo's chest with stalks of leaves and he went to empty it and return. Some plants were deemed in good enough shape to be allowed to go to seed. While I wanted to harvest as much as we could, I could see the value in having our own seed. Who knew how much longer the small remaining quantity I had from my father would stay viable?

All the branches with cocoons were burned as well, and the remaining bushes inspected carefully and cleaned of the blight.

The sun was high in the sky when we were finally done and dripping with sweat.

I'd ruined a dress, having torn the hem and slashed open a sleeve. Mother would be spitting mad if she caught me. "Do you want to wait until tomorrow for the next stage?" I asked Sarah when I felt the weariness in my body and saw the tired faces of those around me. I wiped the dust-caked back of my hand across my sweating brow, no doubt painting myself with a mud mixture. For my part, I did not want to stop now that we'd started, so anxious was I.

Sarah clicked her tongue at my question of waiting, shaking her head.

We had collected Sawney and a couple of other field hands

in our quest over the past few hours, and now they watched our exchange carefully.

I was saved having to respond by a commotion out on the road. The clatter of hooves and a carriage I didn't recognize. We weren't expecting anyone that I knew of.

Quash glanced at me, then down at my dress, and a barely discernible wince flickered across his face. I grimaced too, just imagining what I looked like.

"Do not begin without me," I aimed at Sarah. "I will see who this is and then return. Quash, stay and watch her." Not waiting for her response to my mistrust, I turned and picked up my skirts and hurried toward the house. Any thought I had of taking a turn for the back door was interrupted when two gentlemen immediately alighted from the carriage.

Master Henry and Mr. John Laurens nodded at Indian Peter, who had taken the reins from their driver and now stood staring at me aghast. A third gentleman, his entire bearing showing his exhaustion, was being assisted down by another Negro I couldn't see on the other side of the carriage.

I came to a halt. Oh dear. Bitterly disappointed that it was not the man from Montserrat, but the Laurens and an acquaintance of theirs, I quite ignored the expressions on the men's faces.

Then John Laurens was striding toward me. "I say. Is everything all right? Do you need some assistance?" He scowled over my shoulder at my ragtag group of helpers, then back at me, his face grim as he took in the dirty and torn state of my dress. "Did they attack you? Henry," he tossed over his shoulder as he strode past me, "get my gun."

"Oh goodness, no," I called out in a panic and tugged on John Laurens' sleeve.

He shrugged me off and walked forward brandishing a wicked-looking cane that he didn't seem to need.

"Mr. Laurens! I demand that you stop this instant."

The group of slaves stood rooted to the spot, terror and confusion on their faces.

He turned back to me, an eyebrow raised, skin mottled in agitation. My outburst rang across the yard.

"I'd heard rumors that you were out here without an overseer," he huffed, incensed and wide-eyed. "And I thought '*that can't be true,*' and yet … here you are being overrun by these Negro heathens and not coping at all. Defending them, even. Have you quite taken leave of your senses? What were your parents thinking leaving a helpless girl in charge? Have you been … compromised?"

"I beg your pardon," I mustered, my chest ballooning with indignation. "I have not seen you in over a year, sir. What right on earth do you have to come to my father's plantation and tell me how to run it and make such wild accusations?" I spat the question.

The words were out of my mouth before I could process the impudence and caution myself. I slammed my lips together, breathing heavily through my nose.

A glance at young Henry saw him wince and avoid my gaze.

John Laurens was dumbstruck.

"Forgive me," I said quickly. "I'm afraid the heat has quite gone to my head."

The familiar whine of the porch door on its closing swing signaled my mother had now borne witness to the exchange also, and I could feel the blaze of angered humiliation scorch my back.

News of my radicalism would be around the countryside and into town before noon tomorrow, and my mother would blister my ears … and presumably write a scathing letter to my father.

The third gentleman stood impassively, arms folded

across his broad chest, graying hair greasily slicked back from a ruddy and tanned complexion. He eyed me with a look of awkward pity and assessment.

John Laurens took a deep, steadying breath and with a pained expression opened his mouth. "We were headed this way and received word that this gentleman"—he motioned to the third, as yet unknown man—"had recently arrived by packet from the islands, sent by your father. Miss Lucas, may I present Mr. Nicholas Cromwell of Montserrat ..."

My stomach lurched in surprise. Emotions laced with dismay, elation, and relief struggled over each other. The indigo consultant!

"And his ..." Mr. Laurens' lip curled up with distaste, like he had a sour apple seed trapped between his yellow teeth. "His apprentice, Mr. Ben Cromwell."

A man stepped from behind Nicholas Cromwell, almost of his height, his skin burnished walnut, and dark, dark eyes I'd seen in my dreams since I was a girl.

My mouth dropped open in shock.

His jacket of dark and beautifully dyed indigo was incongruous and shocking against the skin of a Negro, the white of a linen shirt stark against his corded neck. He was dressed formally. Like a free man. Not a slave.

Only a fraction of time passed as the surprise shot through me, and I took in his person and felt a tightness in my chest. A sting burned behind my nose and eyes. I blinked and tried to close my mouth, but only my teeth met.

He made a small shake of his head that was barely perceptible.

Then Mr. Nicholas Cromwell was stepping forward, his hand held out to receive mine, any evidence of his earlier pity eradicated. Perhaps I'd imagined it after my heated words with Mr. Laurens. "Miss Lucas, I presume. The indigo girl."

He smiled. "I apologize for our unannounced arrival."

I swallowed, my eyes peeling away from Ben with difficulty, and shook my head to clear the shock. But my mind was a turmoil of questions and excitement and an emotion so foreign, sharp, and overwhelming, I had to close my mind off to avoid giving myself away. Every inch of my person itched and prickled with the urge to throw myself into my friend's arms to test the reality of him. I hadn't missed the small shake of his head. I was to pretend I didn't know him? But surely my surprise and recognition must have been clear on my face.

I placed my scratched and soil-caked hand into Mr. Cromwell's, and to give him credit, he didn't flinch, but instead bent over it. "A pleasure to make your acquaintance. Your father says you have a knack for botany, and I am to help you produce indigo dye."

"A pleasure to meet you," I said to Cromwell, my voice shaky. "You came in the nick of time. We were just, I was just ... we were harvesting the last of our crop. There's not much, I'm afraid. It was afflicted with a little pest."

My mother came up at my side and then Polly flew out of the house. In the shade of the distraction brought by my sister, I saw Ben step back slightly behind Nicholas Cromwell's frame. To avoid my mother? I wasn't sure she would recognize him. Certainly not out of context. However, he was still using his given name, Ben, although he had adopted the last name of his owner as all our slaves did. I had so many questions.

Mr. Laurens greeted my mother, introducing his son and Mr. Cromwell.

Before he could introduce Ben, I stepped forward. "Come, let us get out of the sweltering heat to the shade of the house. We have fresh-squeezed lemon water made just yesterday to cool your travel-parched throats. Though I'm afraid we are low on sugar so this will be the last of it."

"Your father had us pick up two barrels for you," Mr. Cromwell informed, thankfully not noticing I had all but cut off the introduction of his apprentice. "Though they are still at the Charles Town wharf, I'm afraid. We did not want to hold up these gracious gentlemen who offered a ride to Wappoo."

Ben had sidled to the back of the carriage and was busying himself with unloading two cedar trunks. Quash joined him to assist.

If my mother wondered who the "we" of which Mr. Cromwell spoke was, she said nothing.

"Well." I spoke on a rush of air, eager to move us on from this awkward encounter. And then broke off as I realized with dismay the Laurenses had come by carriage the seventeen miles from Charles Town, not by boat as I'd suggested, and so would be overnight guests themselves. My stomach fell. "I'm afraid we don't have a lot of space, Mr. Laurens. Would you be able to share with your son? There is a sleeping porch attached to the upstairs bedroom, so perhaps one of you might enjoy our Wappoo night air this evening?"

"That should be fine. Right, Henry?"

"Yes, Father," Henry responded dutifully.

Mr. Laurens glanced about his surroundings, then back at the state of my dirty and sweat-caked dress. "Just a brief visit. We shall be on our way first thing in the morning."

I struggled not to show my relief.

But what was I to do about Ben? Where would he sleep? With the other slaves? Why not with the other slaves? I'd need to take direction from Cromwell.

"Mr. Cromwell."

"Nicholas, please."

I smiled politely. "Nicholas, I'm sure you are weary from

your travels, but if you wouldn't mind starting your job right away and taking a quick look at today's harvest before we go inside?"

Cromwell raised his brows. "Well, uh, of course. As you say, it is my job. And I suppose you *are* dressed for it."

It was said with a twinkle of amusement, but my mother made a small sound I recognized as horrified resignation. "Come along, gentlemen," she offered politely to John and Henry Laurens.

Cromwell and I turned toward the fields. Polly was pestering Henry, and the last thing I heard as distance separated us was, "I heard you were coming here to court my sister? Is that true? Is that why you're here?"

Why ask one question when you can ask it three different ways? That was my chatterbox sister. I was saved having to hear the response, which of course I would tickle out of Polly later.

I felt the burn of eyes in my back.

Ben.

Eighteen

My mind careened like an out-of-control carriage pulled by a spooked horse.

Where did I even begin my questioning?

"I do have to apologize," Mr. Cromwell began almost immediately. "It is always a shock for people to be introduced to my Negro, Ben."

I cleared my throat, grateful he had taken over the opening. *Ben was here.* "Not at all, I—"

"You are too gracious. Really. I saw the surprise on your face. People do not expect a Negro accompanying a white man to be anything but a slave. Not a well-dressed one, and certainly not to be introduced to one as if they were meeting a gentleman in a drawing room."

"Oh well, yes, I suppose it was a surprise. Unexpected."

"It's my brother's fault, I'm afraid. He bought Ben for our plantation in Montserrat due to Ben's proficiency with indigo, and gave him airs and graces above his station." He sighed. "Including making him an apprentice with an agreement to buy his freedom."

I stayed quiet, listening intently. A rush of pride for Ben swarmed through me. "So, he is not a harsh slave owner then, your brother?"

"Not at all. Quite the contrary. Thank goodness Patrick is away on trading business most of the time these days so I could get some order back into the place."

I breathed a sigh of relief that Ben had been with a fair and just owner, at least before Nicholas Cromwell had taken over. "So, if you were running the indigo business there, how could you afford to take my father's offer to spend time here?" I asked, genuinely confused.

He chuckled ruefully. "I'm afraid I have rather a weakness for cards, and I may have gotten us into a bit of a pickle. Your father's offer came at an opportune time. My brother all but forced me to answer the request." He paused. "So now you know my sins ... Will you share yours?"

"My ...? Whatever do you mean?"

We'd reached the site where I'd left my gaggle of helpers. All that remained were Sarah and Togo, who were still sorting the indigo leaves.

"Well, you clearly have a fondness for fieldwork. A hardy nature. One I find quite comely in a member of the fairer sex." I sucked in a breath at his brashness, but he seemed oblivious. "I hope you won't find this too outspoken, but it is clear you are not a lady suited for the likes of John Laurens with his societal airs and graces."

While marginally impressed with Cromwell's astute observation, I was offended on so many levels. Then Mary's observation came back to me.

"Well, I see you have me at a disadvantage," I said, swallowing my indignation. "I had been led to believe that Mr. John Laurens sought to approve of me for his son." Even though the thought of that too was enough to turn my stomach. Henry was nice enough, and while only a little younger than me, seemed but a child.

Mr. Cromwell nodded. "Yes, well. I believe it is their

intention to have you believe such. But I happen to know the reverse is true. I know his kind. He's bought his position as far as he can in the drawing rooms of Charles Town but cannot get much farther without becoming a planter and owning land. That's where it seems you come in."

Marry John Laurens? I shuddered. Would my father sell me and our land to the highest bidder? And the subversive nature of their courting had me extremely ill at ease. Why not just press his own suit? Did he think I was so dim-witted he'd be able to switch one groom with another? Surely he wouldn't go to such ridiculous extremes. It must simply be a misunderstanding. But more importantly at the moment was the irreverent and disrespectful wretch in front of me. "Why are you telling me this?"

"Did you not wish to know? I assumed you would want a level of trust between us if we are to work so closely together." His tone and expression rang with truth and innocence, yet I felt as if something shadowy lurked beneath his earnest demeanor. Perhaps it was his admission of a passion for gambling that had me distrustful of the intent behind his words, whether they were true or not. I'd never trusted games of chance, nor those who could so easily put their faith in them.

But without wanting to, I felt indebted to Cromwell for this confirmation of Mary's suspicions. It was perplexing to wonder why John Laurens had gone to the trouble to use his son as proxy. And frankly with the arrival of Ben beating everything else out of my head, I couldn't spend much time thinking on it at present.

"Thank you for advising me," I offered, deciding to let him believe I was simply grateful for his counsel. "Now, about your apprentice."

Cromwell smiled with satisfaction at my easy acceptance

and change of subject. "Well, you needn't worry. He's a good sort. He'll do as he's told. I have a firmer hand than my brother."

"You mentioned him buying his freedom? Is he free now? Are you paying him?"

"Patrick used to pay him a meager amount, but now with this current appointment, he is working off his remaining indenture. When he is finished here with us, however long that takes"—Cromwell winked to let me know he dictated the terms of Ben's tenure to suit himself—"I have agreed to *consider* his manumission. Much as it pains me, I'm afraid I've given my word. He really is a remarkable Negro. A fast learner, though arrogant. Even has some skill with lettering and figures. Where he learned that, I have no idea."

I swallowed my surprise, and happiness for Ben, and scowled instead. "I see."

"Of course, I shall refrain from mentioning that in polite company."

Memories flittered into my mind of me as a girl scratching my newly learned letters into the dirt, with Ben standing next to me rubbing his head while my baby brother George tugged on my skirts to get my attention. "Buh-eh-nnn," I'd sounded out, pointing at my scrawl. "Ben. That's you." My name was harder. But over a few weeks he learned it, and other words too. Simple words first. *Tree, bee, happy, sad.* Then harder ones. *House, field, flower, indigo, friend.*

I pointed toward Sarah and Togo. "Let's have a look."

Cromwell noticed Sarah as she stood up, and I watched an appreciation for her form cross his face. Men were such simple creatures, it was rather frightening to know they held the complicated nature of civilization in their hands.

"This is Togo, one of my chief gardeners and field hands," I said. "And this is Sarah. Sarah was brought down from our Waccamaw plantation due to her knowledge of growing indigo in South Carolina. They'll be working closely with you. As will I."

To Sarah and Togo, I indicated the white man at my side. "And this is Mr. Nicholas Cromwell."

Cromwell nodded at them, and unused to being introduced or perhaps worried at having a new white master, both sets of eyes acknowledged Cromwell then immediately angled down to the ground.

"He is an indigo consultant from Montserrat," I informed them, making clear we were not installing an overseer. "He is here with his apprentice, Ben, whom I'm sure you will meet shortly, after he has assisted Quash with unloading their belongings. You are to treat both men with respect as I know you will," I added for Togo's benefit, seeing his large head cock ever so slightly. "And adhere to their instructions regarding indigo production."

And so I neatly inserted Ben in superiority over Togo. And winced internally, saying a quick prayer. I wished I could assure them that they would still be treated well. But I didn't know how to say that in front of Cromwell. And the truth was I didn't know. It would be something I'd need to pay close attention to.

I just hoped Ben was welcomed and easy to like. I couldn't remember if he was well liked among our Negroes in Antigua. I just knew that at one time he was my best friend. And if the truth mattered, I'd never had another friend, male or female, I considered such. I couldn't believe Ben was here, my insides felt as if they would spin out of my body.

Cromwell crouched next to the bushels of cut stems. Fingering the leaves and casting through the piles, he made clicking noises of disappointment in the back of his throat.

"What is it?" I asked.

"Well, apart from the poor condition of the leaves left over from your pest and the small quantity, it was also left too long upon the bush I'm afraid." He tutted again. "Very poor quality, indeed. This will only make a few pounds of very bad quality dye. There's almost no point in wasting the effort."

I bristled. "Well, we harvested what we could. We can still attempt the process, can't we?"

"Who was in charge of deciding when it was ready to harvest? This one here?" He indicated to Sarah.

Her gaze was defiant.

"Actually, no one was put in charge until yesterday. So it's quite my fault, you see," I said quickly, pulling his attention away from her. And it was. Though I felt smarting irritation that she ignored my plea for help so long, it was my fault that I had decided not to coerce her. Could a woman like Sarah even be coerced?

Cromwell looked over his shoulder at me. "I see." He stood, clapping the dust off his hands. For a moment he glanced around us as if looking for something. Presumably not finding it, he then reached into the tub of water, dipping a hand to the wrist. He withdrew and flicked off the water, before dunking his hand again, and frowning thoughtfully.

"Not the right temperature either." He shook his head. "You cannot wait on these things. There's barely a point to these proceedings. I can see why you needed me. One must know the exact hour the leaves are at the height of potency. Then they must be stripped and submerged within the day, in perfectly temperate water. It takes years of practice to foresee the peak of the leaf coming so that the water may be ready. Then, well ... then the real test of a dye maker begins."

He removed a yellowed handkerchief from his pocket and dried his hand before using it to dab sweat from his neck. His head continued to shake from side to side. "And that's not even the half of it." His tone continued to increase in exasperation as my spirit continued to sink. "Where are the production facilities?"

"We—we have none yet. That's why—"

"Your father had me believe you were running an operation here that needed my expertise, not that you were starting from nothing. Simply a hopeful young girl without the slightest idea of what you are doing? And you say you are in charge of three plantations? I hope to dear God, and for the sake of your father, you have overseers installed on the other two. I see the scope of my work shall have to extend to far more than just overseeing the indigo production."

My throat was tight with offense, and I was reeling with his abrupt change in demeanor. How he'd transformed from someone trying to get into my good graces to this horrible, superior prig in mere moments put me at a loss for words. To avoid a tremor in my voice that would reveal my dismay should I find any words, I turned away for a moment to regain my composure.

Ben was at the stables with Quashy and Peter. They were within earshot, and while Ben was not looking at me, I felt his attention.

There was a small overseer's cottage that sat away from the dwellings in the trees on the other side of the well. It had stood unused for goodness knew how long. I'd often thought about letting Quash stay there, but I was nervous about creating envy amongst the slaves, and he had such a calming presence, I felt he was almost the glue that kept us all in harmony. Cromwell could stay there, though. And Quash, in building the new dwelling for Sarah, had built in the style of our others. Two cabins with a shared chimney. So there was an empty cabin for Ben. It would be private too, being at the far end of the dwellings by the woods. I could probably visit with him a little without worrying my mother.

The thought of covertly visiting Ben slipped into me with sharp, uncomfortable edges. It created an unbalanced feeling within my person, and I knew it was something I should avoid. But I also knew immediately I would do it anyway, and it would be beyond my control.

I took a deep breath, tamping down my dangerous thoughts and dealing with the things within my control. "I'm sorry you are so disappointed in any perceived misrepresentation of your job here," I said firmly to Mr. Cromwell and was gratified when his expression morphed to surprise at my subtle rebuke that placed the blame squarely upon his shoulders. "But it remains true that you are here to help us produce good quality dye. So we'll just have to begin where it's necessary to begin. And if that is at the very, very beginning, then so be it. I'm sure a man with such considerable intelligence and experience as you can handle it." I smiled sweetly. "I have extremely talented helpers and a carpenter of superior skill." I nodded toward Quash. "You'll just have to let us know what to build, and we'll do it. Now, if you'll excuse me, I have to see your apprentice settled in one of our newly built cabins and you in the overseer's cottage. And prepare for supper, of course. I'm sure you are hungry after your long journey."

I looked toward Sarah and Togo, not waiting for an answer from Cromwell. "Sarah, you can continue to work on this batch of indigo with Togo and teach him what you know."

I wanted to know too, but today had dealt me an emotional as well as physical blow, and no doubt I'd learn much from Ben and Cromwell in the coming months that would eclipse Sarah's knowledge anyway.

And I wondered how long I had before Mother put two and two together and got Ben.

Nineteen

Knowing Ben, *my Ben*, was here fairly caused my spirit to vibrate. It was impossible to keep myself together, and so I channeled it into the most efficient organizing and doling out of instructions I had ever undertaken as our newly arrived guests took tea with Mama in the drawing room.

Chickens were slaughtered and defeathered for dinner, courtesy of Sawney. Mary Ann made quick work of readying our two guest rooms, and I joined her to help tighten the ropes on the bed frames. Then she returned to the kitchens to work on supper.

Essie was the only one I could ask to help me take special care of getting the extra dwelling ready without causing fuss and whispers.

When we stood in the doorway, I turned to her and said, "It's Ben, Essie. My Ben."

She set her deep brown eyes upon mine, the corners crinkled with years of smiles and wisdom. Then she pressed her thumb to a spot between my eyebrows and muttered something before shaking her head.

I didn't ask her what she was thinking. I never did. And she'd never tell me. But she insisted on putting some kind of mark on Ben's door to ward off haints and spirits. She and Quash were so funny about their chicken blood, bones, and feathers.

The overseer's cottage was swept of mice droppings and spiders and polished with lemon oil. Rosemary was to be hung from the rafters, and I dispatched Mary Ann's two daughters to fetch some. I had them get extra for Ben's dwelling too.

I had a field hand come and make sure the chimney was clear by climbing up on the roof and sticking a large straight branch inside and swirling it around. By some miracle only one old nest that had been abandoned a long time ago fell down to the cooking hearth.

New wood was laid, and I fetched one of our medium-sized cast-iron pots from the kitchen, smiling apologetically at Mary Ann, as well as a pitcher of rainwater and a basin. I made a mental note we needed more pots, pitchers, and basins the next time I was in town. Perhaps I'd send Quash to the market next week. Ben would need provisions too.

I returned to the house, passing my mother on the stairs as I finally went to my room to get cleaned up. If Mama knew something was afoot, she made no mention.

I'd not seen Ben again and guessed he'd been helping where needed with horses and trunks and being shown about by Quash. Quash would also show him to his cabin. I didn't know what he'd been used to in Montserrat, but I hoped he was comfortable here. Certainly it was roomier than the cabins I knew of in Antigua.

All through what felt like the most boring long-winded dinner I'd ever endured, as John Laurens and Nicholas Cromwell tried to outdo each other with overblown trading stories from various parts of the world, all I could think about was whether Ben was comfortable in his room. Did he need anything? Did he wonder why I hadn't sought him out to greet him despite his initial warning? Was he as surprised to see me as I was to see him?

Even more, I couldn't help thinking how different Ben looked. He was always self-assured, and that had emanated strongly as long as I'd known him. But he'd gone from boy to man in the few years since I'd seen him. I'd no doubt gone from girl to woman, but to be fair, I saw no change in my appearance. Womanhood had bloomed and peaked early on me. I certainly wasn't growing out or up anymore.

Ben, on the other hand, had.

Mama was clearly having one of her "good days" and hung on every word of our guests as they put on their show.

"You seem distracted this evening," Henry murmured at my right-hand side. "I know my father's bluster is boring, despite half of it being made up, but is something troubling you?"

"The things on my mind are also rather boring, I'm afraid." I smiled politely at him. "I do apologize for my lack of manners. Did you have a good journey here today? I trust it was incident-free?"

"Valiant effort, Eliza." He grinned and took another small bite of sage-roasted chicken. I did the same, smirking. It was quite nice to have someone my own age with whom I could commiserate about the tedious generation above us.

"So half of it is made up, is it?" I asked, teasing.

"Probably three quarters."

"Truly?" I asked, surprised.

"No, not really. I think the majority of the basic facts are true, but handsomely embellished. For example, I do know he was once held captive by an Indian chief while trading for deerskin."

I couldn't help my small gasp of surprise.

"But the man did not threaten to scalp him," Henry

continued. "Nor hang him over a cauldron with the threat of being boiled alive. He simply made my father stay for dinner and partake in a smoking ceremony before he let him be on his way in the morning with his procured skins."

We laughed softly at his father's attempt at aggrandizing the ordeal.

Henry continued. "The Indians are quite resourceful with nature. Corn comes from them, you know? One day, when I have land, I shall have Indians work upon it."

I took a small sip of wine. "Indeed? You think you will be so successful you'll be able to have paid workers? I admire your ambition. And I'm sure we have much to learn from the people who've worked this land centuries before us."

What a thing to aspire to. I should also like it if Lucas land were profitable without the need for enslaved labor. Imagine being able to reward Quash or Togo or Essie … My mind drifted toward the radical thoughts in the way one might indulge an unrealistic dream of basking in the success of indigo. A dream that seemed so very far off after seeing another failed crop today.

"Thank you. I admire yours also."

"My what?"

"Your ambitions."

Heat burst into my cheeks, and I glanced at Mama to see if she'd overheard.

"It is a compliment, Eliza."

"It is not seen that way by most."

"Are not the mothers of the young girls paraded about at tedious balls ambitious in their own way? Anyway, I plan to have enslaved Indians. Though I'm rather waiting for them to continue warring amongst themselves and make their numbers more manageable."

I swallowed a hard nut of disgust at his words and quite

forgot my previous train of thought. To wish hardship and war upon a people to be able to enslave them? Oh, how very different we were. Being of a similar age and sharing a laugh or two at the expense of our parents did not a lifetime companion make.

"Are you all right?" Henry asked, concerned.

"Yes." I gave him an insipid smile, thinking of an excuse. "Yes. Only I fear the turmoil of this day has rather gotten to me."

"And so," John Laurens announced from his position to my mother's left. "It is my recommendation that Cromwell act as overseer while he is here to relieve the burden on Eliza and then Colonel Lucas will appoint another."

Cromwell sat up straighter upon Mr. Laurens' pronouncement.

"Excuse me?" I piped up. "I missed part of that. Are—"

"It was merely a suggestion, Eliza," my mother interrupted, putting me in my place as her daughter. "One I happen to agree with. Certainly by the looks of you today, you could use the help."

I stood. My emotions were too frayed and thin to face the world about me a minute longer. "Actually, regarding today. I fear I am quite fatigued. I hope you will all forgive me as I bid you good night. Breakfast is usually served between six and ten. Simply ring the bell on the sideboard. I shall see you all tomorrow."

My mother dabbed her mouth. "Very well. I have told Mr. Laurens you will give him a tour of our holding here in the morning. You may be excused."

In my bedroom, I stripped down to my chemise. For a moment I stood at the window staring out to Wappoo Creek reflecting silver from the darkening sky. I wished I could see the dwellings from here. Was Ben settled? Perhaps he was already asleep, exhausted from his long journey. I hoped the slaves had been accommodating and shared their supper. Things such as this had never occurred to me before.

I said a quick prayer, thanking God for the miracle of this day, and for Ben's presence, although he was part of the aforementioned miracle, and asking for patience in the face of condescension. Oh, and patience with my mother. Oh, and wits to handle both Henry and his father and avoid a marriage to either of them. Oh, and one more thing, apologies if I was asking too much.

I couldn't get Ben out of my head. He'd grown taller. Stronger. His head was shaved close. His dark skin was burnished and smooth, though I imagined he shaved whiskers upon his jaw now that he was a man and not a boy. Not that I'd ever touched his face. The thought of it now sent ribbons of curiosity looping through my insides. My fingers tingled as if I could feel the rough texture of skin.

Sucking in a breath, I was shocked at myself.

I was marveling, that was all. Marveling at the miracle of seeing a person I'd thought never to see again. It almost felt as if he was a mirage.

I would have to set or find new boundaries for us. Or perhaps he'd set them for us already by the subtle shake of his head. It was as if he'd known what I'd been feeling in that moment. That I wanted to throw myself upon his person. To prove his reality.

Impossible.

I could never let anyone know how I felt, but I would remain his true friend even if no one ever knew. Even if *he* never knew.

I reached for my prayer book and grabbed the quill I set by my bed for working on my task list. By the last light of my lamp, I added to a prayer I had written while asking God for patience with Sarah, this time promising to try and love all of mankind.

Having washed earlier, before dinner, all that was left was for me to lift my knees from the hard wooden floor, crawl blissfully onto my stuffed bedding, and pull the rough cotton sheet over me. It was hard to calm my racing heart so that sleep would overtake me. My life felt on the very cusp of some great change. Some movement toward destiny.

THE MOCKINGBIRDS THAT HAD SEEN fit to build a nest near my bedroom window stirred early the next morning. I struggled to hang on to my dream as I peeled my eyes awake into the soft blue darkness. I had dreamed of the blue water again. Indigo. This time Ben was in my dream. I couldn't see him, but I knew he was there, and it left a swirling hive of warmth in my belly.

I sat straight up, my heart pounding with newly rediscovered joy.

Ben was here at Wappoo.

The memories of yesterday fell over themselves. Did my father know that the man he sent from Montserrat was the brother of the man to whom he'd sold Ben? It was either mercy on the part of my father, or divine mercy on the part of God.

Of course, this morning I would have to give Mr. Laurens a tour of the property he thought might end up being his dowry. Also it was Tuesday, the day we visited Mary and her mother. I'd have no time to see Ben.

Remembering the indigo that Sarah and Togo worked on

yesterday, I hurriedly got up and dressed, not bothering to ring for Essie. I could do my rounds of the fields and check on the indigo before breakfast was served and still manage to avoid having to share another meal with our guests. They were bound to be abed until it was true daylight.

Of course, no sooner was I around the fields that I found myself gravitating toward the far end of the slave dwellings.

I paused and turned away, forcing myself toward the sheds where the vat of soaking indigo had been left.

It was covered with a piece of sackcloth held down by broken bricks and large stones. I removed a few and looked inside. The water was dark and full of stems being held submerged by yet more heavy stones. The sour stench of the fermenting process I could remember so well from my childhood had yet to happen.

Carefully replacing the cover as I'd found it, I stood.

There was not yet a soul about. The dwellings were still, though they wouldn't be for much longer. Stars were blinking out one by one as the sky on the horizon turned silver to match the water.

I couldn't visit Ben, but I could walk the long way back to check the fields one last time. I found myself stopping yet again near the woods and looking at the newly built cabin.

Straining for the sound of movement inside, or the flicker of movement in the dark window, I stood in the still silence. It was then I noticed how very quiet it was. Not a bird, nor rustle of a small animal, nor even a breeze could be heard through the leaves.

"Whach you waitin' fo?"

I leapt, a stifled scream strangling in my tight throat, and whipped around. Luckily the fright had quite robbed my breath, and the scream had died on its way out or the whole plantation would now be awake. My pulse beat hard in my neck.

Ben was sitting on a tree stump to my right on the edge of the woods. His bare dark chest had blended in with the surrounding shadows. He held a small knife in one hand and a piece of wood in the other. He'd obviously been whittling, though must have stopped as I approached or I would have heard him.

My hand was at my throat, and I slowly removed it, my heart still furious. I let out a nervous laugh, light-headed with relief. "Well ... you."

"And here I be."

Finally, I could say hello.

I smiled, starting toward him.

He raised the hand holding the knife, four fingers opening to put his palm out and halt me. When I complied, he let out a long breath and looked away.

I began to fiddle nervously with my dress strings, but when his eyes returned to me and followed the movement, I let them fall and wiped my palms on my dress.

My mind was ridiculously blank. I could muster nothing to say, so I let my gaze feast on the happy miracle of my friend sitting in front of me.

"I missed you," I said finally, whispering the words so they would never be overheard. "Are you comfortable in your cabin? Is there anything you need? I'm so happy to—"

Ben's eyes narrowed on me. Then he stood, his lithe and hard-worked body unfolding.

Curving his hands around the hilt of his knife, he turned abruptly and punched the blade down into the stump. It slammed home with such vehemence, it was a wonder the small blade didn't snap.

I gasped in surprise and stepped back.

Then he stalked to the cabin and entered without a backward glance, leaving me staring after him in stunned silence, my heart ballooning painfully against my ribs.

I am resolved to be a sincere and faithful
  friend
Wherever I professed it,
And as much as in me lies
An agreeable and innocent companion,
A universal lover of all mankind.
All these resolutions by God's assistance
I will keep to my life's end.
So help me, oh, My God! Amen.

—Excerpt from prayer written by Eliza Lucas

Twenty

John Laurens, his son Henry, myself, and Polly made a slow procession around the property. Polly was sitting sidesaddle on her small, fat mount being led by Pompey, one of our younger slaves, who had recently started shadowing Quash whenever he could.

Pompey had shown an aptitude for carpentry and it seemed Quash was quite enjoying having someone to teach. Quash drove our wagon while Mr. Laurens, Henry, and I sat enjoying the breeze of the sunny morning.

"It's remarkable how much cooler it is out here than in town," Henry commented.

I adjusted my bonnet to keep the low-riding sun from my face. "I imagine all the buildings in town buffet the breeze from the Cooper River."

"With more going up all the time," Henry agreed. "It shall be nice to have space in the countryside to get away to in the height of the summer." He cleared his throat. "One day."

Not Lucas land, I chided in my head, though my mind still couldn't leave Ben alone. Had I upset him? Surely he knew I'd had no idea he was coming.

"It is rather more stifling at some of the up-country

plantations, however," Henry bungled on. "You have a fortuitous spot here on the bluff."

"I was interested to discover last evening at dinner that you had planter ambitions." I glanced at John Laurens who studied the surrounding landscape, but whose ear I knew missed nothing, certainly not my seizing upon his son's misstep. His son had played their hand.

"I seem to remember you like your books, Miss Lucas," John Laurens interrupted us. "Ever read any Aristotle?"

On alert for a trap, I hesitated in my answer. It was unseemly for a lady to read like I did, as much as I did, as well as the texts I chose to read. Yet, he knew my propensity, having met me while staying at the Pinckneys' in town and he'd witnessed me fairly raiding Charles' library.

"I confess I have borrowed a volume from Mr. Pinckney."

"So you'll have pieced together how Carolina sits on a veritable climatic Golden Mean. In the most temperate part of the globe. It would be a sin not to partake of God's bounty, would it not? God helps those who help themselves."

I nodded. "I had the same thoughts about Carolina myself after reading Aristotle's cosmography. It is little wonder Charles Town was settled."

"Indeed." John Laurens' shrewd eyes assessed me, then roamed briefly upon my person, making my skin burn. It was over before it began, and I barely controlled a small shudder.

I glanced to see if Henry had noticed.

He was frowning up ahead to see Pompey turning Polly's horse. "Are we at the boundary already?"

"I'm afraid so." I quite enjoyed his disappointment. "The Wappoo land is only six hundred acres." *Therefore not worth your time*, I wanted to add. And hoped it also meant *I* was not worth their time.

My eyes stayed firmly ahead as we passed the woods and

Ben's cabin. His strange behavior this morning had been relegated behind an iron dungeon door in my mind, lest I drove myself mad.

By the time we got back to the house, after enduring many more comments from John Laurens on how we could best use this plantation and questions about the other Lucas holdings, I was barely keeping my composure together. I felt like I'd spent a morning at the market, only this time the prime auction items were me and the land upon which I was paraded about.

"Thank you for the delightful turn about the property, gentlemen," I managed stiffly. "I fear I must ready Polly and Mama for our weekly outing to the Woodwards. I shall ask Mary Ann to prepare you a meal to take on the drive back to Charles Town."

"Oh, your dear mama kindly invited us to stay a few days." John Laurens smiled. Henry looked uncomfortable. My legs wanted to give out. I didn't know how much longer I could continue the farce of politeness. "But, please," he continued, "we shall not impede your plans. You go on ahead. Henry and I will enjoy your mild country air and catch up on correspondence. Your mother said I could use the study, would that be all right?"

"Of course," I responded enthusiastically, giving him a smile. I bet Charles Pinckney would be impressed at how much I'd learned to school my expressions in the last day. "Well, I must hurry. Come along, Polly. Oh, gentlemen, do look at our wonderful walled kitchen garden. I quite forgot to add that to our tour." I pointed in the general direction, hoping they would go now and give me the time I needed to hide Father's ledgers from prying eyes. Correspondence, indeed. I was almost offended that he'd underestimated me so.

🌾

"JOHN LAURENS IS ABSOLUTELY DESPICABLE, MARY," I confided in my friend the moment Mama went upstairs to tête-à-tête with Mrs. Woodward in her private sitting area.

I want a private sitting area, I mused, as Mary and I made ourselves comfortable. I debated pulling out my volume of Plutarch but instead fished out another needlework sampler. If my indigo plan ever did grow to success, I vowed I'd have my own sitting area filled with books ladies weren't supposed to read. Oh, and I'd build a greenhouse like Mr. Deveaux's. And a wonderful planned garden like the Middletons'. *Now I am getting greedy*, I admonished myself. I'd settle for a sitting area.

"He can't be that bad, surely."

"Oh, he is. He and Henry quite think they have me outwitted."

I filled Mary in on the arrival of Cromwell, the discovery that she'd been right in her harebrained thought after all. Of course, I left out any mention of Ben beyond the fact Cromwell had brought a Negro with him.

At that, Mary frowned. "You'd best consult with Charles Pinckney, but I do believe part of the Negro Act prohibits importing slaves for one's personal use."

I glanced up, surprised. "Truly? Goodness, I clear forgot that Negro Act. Perhaps because it didn't apply to me at the time. Anyway, this Negro is Cromwell's apprentice, not owned by me, so perhaps that's a special case. It's a curious law though." I jabbed my needle through the fabric. "I suppose newer slaves are more apt to rise to rebellion than those born here into the system. Can't say I blame them. Poor things."

Mary gasped. "Eliza."

"Sorry, but it's true. You can't say you think it's right that we enslave human beings."

Mary sucked the end of a red thread and held a needle up

to see the eye. "Yet, you own slaves and so do I."

"Actually, you don't and I don't. Our fathers do. What I can do is be fair and just while they are in my care."

"Well, Father says some folk in town have counseled that it's not the same as enslaving normal human beings. They are of inferior intellect and without our structure pressed upon them, they would still be savages in Africa, no better than animals killing each other. So in my view we are doing them a favor."

I felt as if my eyes bulged, they opened so wide. "Truly, Mary, how dense do you think we'd seem if no one had ever taught us lettering, or basic numbers, or French, for that matter? That doesn't make us less than human."

I thought of Essie with her keen intelligent eyes that saw so much. A mother to me more than my own. Quash and his skills with carpentry that could grow into who knew what if he was educated. Ben. Ben who was smart and knowledgeable and would one day be free. The thought was still exhilarating to me. If it were ever in my own power to free him, I wouldn't hesitate.

"Oh, I suppose you are correct in your way." Mary sighed, busy with her embroidering and oblivious to how feverish my thoughts were. "But it is a moot point, for we are not to teach them to write either, else they may be able to send messages and organize another rebellion."

I sat nonplussed at our exchange, feeling at once confused, small, and powerless. And I was equally surprised yet unsurprised by my friend's words.

She was only a planter's daughter, what other opinions could she have?

Then again, so was I. And I had so many.

I had, obviously, read the Negro Act. Had even had Charles explain the finer points of law. But it never fully hit home to me in a personal way until just that moment.

On the way to Wappoo, we prolonged our day and stopped in at Mrs. Hill's. An aging widow, she had married off two daughters and the last was almost out the door. She had a small home, without much land, and was our closest neighbor. We dropped off apples and salted pork from the Woodwards, and I politely stood by while she expounded on the dangers that my reading too much would make me old before my time. To which my mother nodded all too enthusiastically. I was becoming infamous in the area, it seemed.

Then we were on our way back home. "Mother, I do wish you hadn't offered Mr. Laurens and his son to stay on. It is such a burden on Essie and Mary Ann. Especially now that we have the permanence of Mr. Cromwell to deal with."

"Mr. Laurens quite put me in a difficult spot where I couldn't say no, I'm afraid. It was hardly my idea. I find the man quite tedious. Polly, do not repeat that," she added to my sister.

My sister grinned.

"I am relieved you think so," I replied. "I find him insufferable."

BEFORE MAMA, POLLY, AND I COULD ENTER THE HOUSE, a commotion at the sheds drew my attention.

I hurried over to where Sarah, Cromwell, and Togo stood over the indigo vat, leaving Mama and Polly to go inside the house alone.

"What happened?" I asked as I approached.

Cromwell shrugged. "This batch is useless, I told her to throw it away."

Sarah stood, her eyes blazing, then picked up a tranche of wet, bundled indigo that had obviously been fished out of the vat and threw it angrily so it scattered all over the ground.

"Well, she's a feisty one," said Cromwell grimly. "You'd better keep her in line. Or I will." Then he shook his head, striding off in the direction of Ben's cabin without a backward glance.

Ignoring him, and not wanting to dismiss Sarah's offer of teaching me the process, an offer that had been so hard won, I refused to react to her ire. "Keep it if you want to, Sarah," I offered.

I needed to get supper ready and see off an unwanted suitor as soon as possible. I didn't have time for an argument. If she wanted to continue with the batch so be it. But I too was concerned with the quality, sure in my gut it had been left too long before harvest.

She marched past me, brushing aggressively against my shoulder as she did so.

"What is the meaning of this insolence?" boomed John Laurens who was nearly upon us as Sarah stalked past him.

Before I could comprehend what he was doing, he'd pulled his cane out to the side of his body and brought it hissing through the air to crack hard upon the backs of Sarah's knees.

The sound of wood hitting flesh and Sarah's sharp cry as she pitched forward, sprawling onto her front, pierced the late afternoon and hung in a stunned silence.

Twenty-One

Everything slowed as the cane sliced through the air. Too fast and unexpected for me to stop it, I'd simply stood there watching in shocked disbelief.

Then the horror ricocheted through me, galvanizing me to action. In my periphery I saw Quash start forward, then Peter, then Togo.

Strength in numbers.

Almost as instantly as they'd started forward, they stopped. Years of ingrained deference to a white man.

John Laurens stood over Sarah.

Her face had mashed into the ground, and she peeled it up, attempting to get to her hands and knees.

His cane came up again.

Finally released from the clutch of paralysis, I rushed toward John Laurens, screaming. The backward swing of his cane proceeded in slow motion, and I knew the cane would hit her before I could make it. Somehow, I held my dress and lifted my booted foot planting it squarely against Mr. Laurens' frame and pushed, kicking him back as the cane came down, barely missing Sarah.

John Laurens stumbled backward but never lost his footing. I cursed my lack of strength against his bulky frame.

He dropped the cane in his surprise and stood gawking at me.

If there'd been stunned silence before, now you could have heard the cries of the fish hawkers six miles away at the Charles Town market.

The rashness of my actions immediately overcame me, roaring into my ears, and my heart leapt into a pumping cannon ball in my throat.

I didn't know myself.

I was aware of eyes from everywhere watching this exchange and understood I had stepped over some imagined line and things would never be the same. *I* would never be the same.

"Well." I laughed, shock making me light-headed and hysterical. "About your strange little plan to press your suit, how would you like to marry me now?"

A lock of hair had escaped and fell across my eye. I angrily swiped it out of the way. I took another step closer to Laurens, and he actually took a step backward. I must have looked like a witch in my state of attire and my madness.

"This is, this is … monstrous," he bellowed. "I—"

"Let me save you the trouble. I absolutely reject your suit. Yours and your son's." I sent a mental apology to Henry for dismissing him too, without explanation. But the chances were he'd grow up just like his sire. At the very least I'd have John Laurens as a father-in-law. Unacceptable. "You'll be hearing officially on the matter from my father. Thank you for your interest, but … no."

John Laurens' face grew purple as he sputtered and tried to form words. "If you think—" He looked around as if to find a witness to back him up or perhaps to see how many had witnessed his humiliation. "Consider my suit rescinded," he announced.

I ignored his vain attempt to save face, there were bigger

points to make. "*I* am in charge of what happens on Lucas land. No one else. Togo?"

I kicked Mr. Laurens' offending cane the short distance across the ground toward him. "Break it."

I was out of control.

It was so unlike me, but yet, it *was* me. Something was unfurling within me from behind the fear of societal expectation. Something true and deep. A part of my soul I'd always known was there but never acknowledged. I knew I'd never completely stop playing the role assigned to me in this life, but I would never, ever, let it compromise me. I knew also that Mr. John Laurens was currently paying the price for all of my frustrations and the cruelties of others, including Starrat, and even Cromwell, but yet, I felt justified.

In my periphery, I saw Ben coming over and helping Sarah to her feet and moving her away from us.

"Don't you dare," Mr. Laurens yelled at Togo. I thought for a moment he might be in danger of an apoplexy.

It was too late. Togo, obeying my command without question, had already brought the cane across a raised knee, and the strength in his bulky arms was no match for the item.

The crack of splintering hardwood was as satisfying as the crack of it against Sarah's skin had been horrifying.

"I'll see to it you pay for this." John Laurens' eyes swung between me and Togo. "This is, this is … unnatural. You wait until people hear of this."

"I'm sure they will all believe you were bested by a mere helpless girl. You are trespassing on Lucas land," I hissed, ignoring his threat. "I suggest you get off it."

"We did no such thing." Spittle flew from his mouth. "We were invited."

"Consider the invitation"—I stepped forward—"rescinded."

Father,

As you proposed Mr. L to me I am sorry I can't have sentiments favorable enough of him to take time to think on the subject ...

Pay my thanks to the old gentleman for his generosity and sentiments of me and let him know my thoughts on the affair in such civil terms as you know much better than any I can dictate.

The riches of Peru and Chile if he had put them together could not purchase sufficient esteem for him *to make him my husband.*

Your most dutiful and affectionate daughter,
Eliza Lucas

Twenty-Two

After the hasty and incensed departure of Mr. John Laurens and his son, I sat alone in my father's study. The leather of his chair had grown warm under my person, but my bones felt chilled.

I'd written to Papa immediately of course, and then busied myself with the accounts and painstaking recording of all our correspondence into the copy book that was a few days overdue.

Sitting in here, with the smell of cypress wood and waxed pages, I could almost imagine Father's fragrant pipe 'bacca drifting gently through the room. Oh, how I missed him. He would have taken one meeting with Laurens and the whole debacle would have been avoided.

I'd neglected Polly's studies the last few days too but didn't feel like seeing anyone just yet, not even my vivacious chatterbox sister.

The muted rustle of skirts at the doorway drew my attention.

My mother stood on the threshold.

Bracing myself to hear her wrath about my outlandish treatment of our guests, I laid down my quill. I squeezed my hands into tight balls and pressed them in my skirts.

"I'm not sure why your father acted against his sound judgment by sending that cursed Negro," she said, surprising me with her tack. "But you are no longer a child, Eliza, and ..." She paused as if changing her mind from her original intent. "We live in turbulent times." She closed her mouth and lifted her chin.

I snapped my brows together and swallowed heavily. *Ben?* Ben was her issue? Well, I no longer had to worry about whether she'd realized he was here. I waited for her to say something else as we stared at each other. Perhaps she waited for me to speak.

I had nothing inside me.

Was there no admonishment for my actions today?

My fingers, still curled into their tight balls, began to throb.

As abruptly as she'd appeared at my doorway, she turned and left. And I was left staring after her. Some days I knew my mother, and some days she fair surprised me.

Ben.

I'd managed to keep my mind busy since the altercation this afternoon. But now I ruminated on his presence here. Though my heart was glad, the joy was weighted heavily with a jangling mess of barbed hooks. His actions early this morning had confused and hurt me. And perhaps they had set the tone for my day, which had resulted in me acting as I had.

I didn't know how to move forward. And I wanted more than anything to run back to the past. All the way back. To being a carefree child who had a best friend.

Instead I sat stuck on my father's chair, in my father's study, coming to terms with the person I'd birthed within myself today.

I was different.

Different from other women. The crushing paralysis that came from being stuck between a past I couldn't return to and a future I couldn't have was heightened by the realization there was nothing to be done about it. I couldn't change the fact I was a woman. Or that I had to be civil to men like John Laurens. I couldn't change the fact that I was merely caretaking my father's enterprises until he could give them away to my brother. His eldest *son*. I couldn't change the fact my father owned other humans as chattel, chattel that indirectly included Ben now and also—a sob of breath escaped my chest—included *me*.

I'd crossed a threshold today. A line I'd never be able to step back over. There wouldn't be any more suitors coming my way. That was certain. The Laurens men would, of course, see to that.

One day I might marry. Maybe if someday I had a dowry that made me an attractive prospect. But no one would come calling. Not anymore.

The confirmation of all my realizations was in my mother's lack of admonishment.

It was done.

It was too late. All she could do was offer me a warning not to make more enemies. I sensed her feeling of failure, as if her motherly efforts had fallen short, and my conscience twisted with a pang of guilt.

I thought of my sister, Polly, who would one day be looking for a husband if I didn't ruin it utterly for her. I thought of my father at war with the Spanish and what might become of us if something happened to him. My heart constricted in imagined grief. My brother George was still too young to take over the family. Besides, he was in England. My brother Tommy, younger still, was in poor health. And I thought of the slave revolt. And the Negro Act, hastily thrown together by fearful people, prohibiting teaching the poor wretches to read or write or even gather to pray. What kind of a world were we living in? *We live in turbulent times,* Mother had said.

We did.

And it had never been clearer to me how utterly rash and selfish I had been by refusing to ever consider a husband. How would I protect my family on my own? It seemed I'd gotten my wish, and only now did the consequences truly weigh in.

On a whim, I pulled out a fresh sheaf of paper and addressed my brother George.

> Congratulations. Papa's last letter informs me you are to take up your commission in the army. I hope you will forgive a girl at my early time of life presuming to advise you but beware false notions of honor. One must make the proper distinctions between courage and rashness ...

I looked about the room, not really seeing anything, but trying to recall my brother's nature. My heart squeezed as I remembered the dimple upon his cheek, his boyish enthusiasm, and his indignation on small conflicts. How trying must it be on Mama to be so separated from her children, wondering if their characters would be intact upon seeing them again. I sighed and put ink upon parchment again. I would write to George and Tommy more often, I decided, and perhaps be of some guidance in that regard. And attempt to subscribe to my own advice.

> ... And the proper distinctions between justice and revenge. As you enter into life one must be particularly careful of one's duty to our Creator, for nothing but an early piety and steady virtue can make one happy.

Yes, I'd do well to follow my own advice. I needed to learn piety myself.

George would be here to take over our affairs. And I would have nothing. Without a husband, I would be nothing but a burden.

Indigo.

Indigo was what *I* would have. I didn't know what it would bring me, bring *us*, but it was the only thing I could think of that I could contribute.

It was surely a gift. I couldn't be mistaken.

My studies in botany, a father who supported my pursuit, my childhood and friendship with Ben, my dreams, meeting Mr. Deveaux who'd encouraged my amateur experiments. Even my father's circumstance, leaving me in charge.

God was giving me a gift. A chance. A destiny. And I recognized it as such.

While I didn't know what that chance could do for me, I knew I couldn't squander it.

And I needed Ben's help.

My chest tightened at the thought of him.

Ben, who for some reason didn't want anything to do with me.

MANY RESTLESS NIGHTS AND EARLY MORNINGS FOLLOWED that I spent ruminating on whether it was better to let Ben be. But every day as the sun rose, so did my selfish need for his friendship. And I knew it was selfish. What good would it ever do him? Or me? What was it exactly I wanted beyond his expertise with indigo? We would never again have the easy laughter and companionship of childhood.

Yet, after that first morning where he'd surprised me in the woods, I'd never attempted to see Ben alone again. Even during the day, and my work with Cromwell, I studiously avoided him as best I could. But I was aware of exactly where he was at any given moment, even if my body would have to turn around for my eyes to find him.

Initially, Cromwell inspected the remaining indigo plants daily with Ben. I often followed behind. Occasionally, they would disagree on something. I'd hear the deep soft rumble of Ben's voice and Cromwell's terse response. I'd watch Ben carefully finger the seed pods. I came to understand that Ben was the one to whom Cromwell deferred on all indigo knowledge. In fact, Cromwell was nothing without Ben. However, knowing that made it even more imperative that I only addressed my questions to Cromwell.

"When does one harvest seed?" I'd asked Cromwell.

"We don't. We wait for the seeds to drop. Then we must leave them on the ground to dry before picking them up."

I couldn't help glancing at Ben because that seemed a little ridiculous.

"Why not just gather the seed after it falls and dry it on trays in the open shed? Surely it would dry faster."

Ben made a dismissive snorting sound and glared at me. The longest he'd actually looked at me in days.

I narrowed my eyes back at him.

"And why don't we plant again right now?"

Ben opened his mouth, then snapped it closed and looked at Cromwell.

"We'll plant when I say so," Cromwell said importantly.

Ben snorted again before turning away and walking off, his shoulders proud.

Cromwell raised his eyebrows and shook his head. "Please forgive him. He's been acting out of sorts and surly. If I didn't depend so much on his innate knowledge of these things, I'd teach him a lesson in respect. Unfortunately, as history has shown me, that gets me even less from him."

I cringed inwardly, turning away as if to survey the field and biting down so hard I thought I might crack a tooth.

How could that question have possibly irritated Ben so much? Was it that he thought I'd addressed him and he didn't want me talking to him? He'd made that clear the first morning, and I'd adhered to it.

"He has these superstitions," Cromwell went on, oblivious to my discomfiture. "As all these Negroes seem to, about the seeds needing to come to know their soil, so that they will grow to their fullest selves when they are themselves planted."

That sounded like the Ben I knew. And I'd bet that little piece of mystical wisdom had been passed down from his grandmother. I couldn't help a small smile.

Cromwell shook his head. "It's ridiculous, I know, but I humor him."

I thought it actually quite insightful, but kept quiet. And now I knew why Ben had just been annoyed with me. He probably thought I should know this.

In fact, I was suddenly convinced that if I asked him he would tell me the reason our crop had failed was we were using orphaned seeds, separated from their comfort zone, and planting them in foreign soil and expecting them to thrive. They needed to be gently coaxed. They would adapt. Eventually.

I would succeed with indigo, little by little. Every attempt would teach me something new. I only hoped it was enough and in time. It would be a long few months waiting until we could plant again.

"I'll ask my father to send more seed as soon as possible for next year. And we'll have the seeds that will drop from our plants here so we'll be prepared. Perhaps sowing them together next year they will draw strength from each other."

Mr. Deveaux had often mentioned to me how similar plant specimens could adapt together, cross-pollinating for strength.

Cromwell puffed up. "Miss Lucas, you have no idea what you are talking about. It's endearing for a woman to have such an interest in horticulture. Charming even. At times."

The insult rolled off me. "You are being paid to be here for a specific purpose, and I do not want another year to close out without you having a chance to show me your expertise in indigo-making. But alas, pestilence has forced me to be patient. Next season can't come soon enough. And I'm sure a man with your considerable talent won't let it fail again." I was certainly counting on his pride.

The next question was, how would I keep Cromwell busy until we could sow again? "Let us go and speak to Quash about the plans to build all the production facilities so we can be prepared for our next harvest."

"Lead on," said Cromwell stiffly.

OVER THE NEXT FEW MONTHS, Cromwell began to take the boat into Charles Town. As winter came, he stayed away more and more frequently. Sometimes he took Ben, and on those days sleep eluded me almost entirely. And I'd be up hours before dawn, checking our oaks and walking the property.

I knew Cromwell was probably losing his shirt in gambling dens or frequenting unmentionable houses. But what was Ben doing when he went with Cromwell? The same? My stomach clenched tightly at the slightest thought.

I had taken to joining Ben and Quash every moment I could when he was at Wappoo and finding excuses to ask as many questions of Ben as I could creatively summon. I probably drove him crazier than I had as a girl. Luckily, he and Quash worked closely together, Ben making himself useful before the next indigo season, and they seemed to have become good friends. And so, it was easier to hide my inclination to spend time near him since there were always plantation matters to discuss with Quash.

Of course, nothing fooled Mama.

Somehow, even though Ben rarely spoke to me, it was obviously clear to my mother that when I was out in the fields, I revolved around Ben like the Earth around the sun. And worse, it obviously didn't much concern me who cared to notice.

Weeks where we went to town for business and social functions were distractedly endured by me as I counted the moments until we could return to Wappoo. Only staying at the Pinckneys', where I experienced Mr. Pinckney's enthusiasm for my ventures, could come close to the pure happiness I felt when I was about the land.

Mother had obviously inked an extremely concerned letter to Papa, for I received a cautionary letter from him a month later. He reminded me of my duty "*as his surrogate,*" and how my brother George's legacy "*rested in my hands,*" and lastly, but by no means least, that any impropriety would demolish any hopes we had of a social standing in Charles Town or of finding me a husband "*when the time came.*"

Incensed upon receiving it, I hastily worded a strong letter back to him.

To the Honorable Colonel Lucas,

Father,

You are so good to say you have too great an opinion of my prudence to think I would entertain an indiscreet passion for anyone, and I hope heaven will always direct me that I may never disappoint you.

What indeed could induce me to make a secret of my inclination to my best friend? As I am well aware you would not disapprove it to make me a sacrifice to wealth, and I am as certain I would indulge no passion that had not your approbation.

Your most dutiful and affectionate daughter,
E. Lucas

Twenty-Three

"Quashy?" I asked one morning the following spring as he and I headed to check on several projects I'd asked him to set into motion. Togo had just given us the bad news that our lucerne grass was not thriving. And my mood was melancholic which somehow managed to weaken my resolve not to think about Ben. "How is ..." My voice cracked and I cleared it. "How is Ben settling in?"

"Fine, Miz Lucas. Jus' fine."

"Only ..." We'd made our way past the dwellings and headed down the dirt path to the cattle fields. "Do you think ... well, does Mr. Cromwell treat him well? And the others?" I added hastily. "I want to know what kind of master he is."

I mashed my lips together.

"He's fine, Miz Lucas. Jus' fine."

Losing my nerve to ask more, I changed tack. "And how is Sarah doing? I haven't seen her much at the house." In fact, I'd thought about her a lot over the winter. Her being right next door to Ben.

"Fine, Miz Lucas."

Sighing in exasperation, I put my hands on my hips and came to a stop. "Are you going to say that about everything?"

Quash's mouth twitched. "Yes, Miz Lucas."

"Well, Quash. That's of no use to me, now is it?" I turned back to the path and strode on, deciding to leave the subject of Ben alone again. "Tell me," I tossed over my shoulder, "did Cromwell show you the plans for finishing the production facilities?"

Quash didn't answer, and I paused to look back at him. He'd stopped and folded his arms over his chest. His light brown skin furrowed upon his brow. Scratching his chin, he looked around.

"Well? Did he?"

Quash nodded.

"And?"

Quash stayed silent.

I walked back to him. "What is it, Quash? If you don't understand the instructions, perhaps you can ask Ben. You two seem to get along. And of course he should know all about the facilities required." In fact, as I spoke, it seemed odd that Quash had not sought Ben to fix whatever roadblock he'd run into. I frowned and waited for Quash to answer me.

He bowed his head as if he struggled mightily with what he was about to say, then he looked up, his face a myriad of confusion, hurt, and also hopefulness. "How come Ben done able to read?" he asked.

My sleep had become increasingly fitful since the day Quash had asked me why Ben knew how to read. My dreams were even more vivid than they had been in the past.

One night, memories from childhood seemed to flitter in

and amongst my imagination so that every time I awoke as the night wore on, I wondered what was true and what was not.

We stand in the shadow of a lean-to, the fronds of jungle palms slapping against the wood, the sound of birds cawing.

"*Un mystère por un mystère*," Ben says, his wide mouth quirking with mischief. I've never heard Ben speak true French.

Ben at eleven years of age is very tall. His features are angular, almost European except that his skin is dark as charred coffee.

"It's no mystery," I say importantly. "They're just letters."

Then Ben is older. More serious. We are outside though it is nighttime now. I feel nervous, my palms sweaty, and I glance back toward the still house almost invisible against the sky. I'm not supposed to be out here.

"You are daylight, I am night," Ben whispers.

We are sitting side by side.

"Your eyes are rivers," I respond, joining him in our game. We have read poetry with a small flame as our light, and now we play with words to find different ways to say normal things.

"Like mud?"

I laugh nervously.

"Yours are green stones," he says.

"Emeralds? My eyes can hardly be compared to fancy emeralds."

"It is true, I have no use for fancy stones," Ben says, his voice low, confusing me with what he means by that. As if he had need for my eyes otherwise.

"I am uncomfortable with your words," I whisper.

"We sit en secret." He slips into the French nuance his grandmother uses when she speaks. "And the color of your eyes makes you uncomfortable?"

I swallow. My heart flutters against my ribs. "Not the

color of my eyes ... The way you see my eyes."

Ben studies me intently. I can see the reflection of our small flame dancing in the dark of his irises. "I see the eyes of a woman no one will ever forget."

I suck in a breath. "I'm hardly a woman. I'm but a girl."

"It's no matter. I see what I see."

"The future, you mean? Is that part of the gift of your eyes? That you can 'see' like your grandmother?"

He shakes his head and after a long pause where conflicting thoughts seem to pass over his face like clouds, he finally opens his mouth. "Today is my day to say goodbye."

"Why?" I frown at his words.

"You are going away. Far away. To the place they will never forget you."

"I am most certainly not." I'd only come back from England recently. There were no plans to leave Antigua.

He shakes his head patiently. "I will see you again."

"What are you talking about?"

"One day you will need my help. And I will come." He shrugs. Then he lifts two fingers and lays them against the small leather pouch at his chest.

"Benoit Fortuné, you are the most peculiar boy. Of course, you'll see me again. You'll see me tomorrow."

I WOKE WITH A START, my heart pounding, my throat parched. Replaying my strange dream, I knew that beyond he and I reading a few poems together he'd found difficult to understand, the entire conversation in my dream was definitely not from a memory. Yet, I still held the nervousness within my belly and remembered the intense look in Ben's eyes.

Sitting up, I swung my legs over the bed. A glance to the window told me it was time to get up anyway. I was relieved.

As soon as I was dressed, I went over my list of chores, writing in new ones and prioritizing others. Then I crept downstairs and out of the front door, into the dim breaking daylight. I breathed in the fresh salted air of Wappoo Creek that was mingled with sweet yellow jasmine and made my way toward the indigo fields. I checked the small green shoots incessantly to make sure they were pestilence-free.

Movement at the dwellings caught my eye. Someone had already been up and stoked the large cooking fire. The smoke curled up, becoming invisible against the gray sky. I stopped and discerned the tall, proud form of Sarah quietly making her way into her cabin. She slipped inside without a sound.

For a moment, I thought perhaps I'd imagined it. I mashed my lips together as I contemplated where she had been. And, I knew without a doubt where she had been. Next door.

I hadn't had breakfast, but my belly didn't feel empty. It felt as though I'd partaken of a hearty helping of coarsely ground oyster shells.

I headed toward Ben's cabin before I could change my mind.

The door opened, and the fleeting expression that crossed Ben's face was one of minor surprise. As if he was expecting someone else and got me. Not as if he didn't expect me at all. I took it as an encouraging sign, but I was so nervous my pulse pounded in my throat, making it hard to swallow. Or talk.

Ben, bare-chested, held a wet rag in one hand. The bitter smell of lye soap perfumed with myrtle mixed with the salty smell of fresh sweat and musk.

I'd interrupted his morning ablutions.

Moments passed in silence. His face was so familiar, yet so much a stranger's.

A small pouch on a thread of leather rested against his breastbone, and I felt a jolt of recognition upon seeing it.

He stepped back to allow me room to enter.

The gesture, shocking, turned my feet to stone, heavy upon the earth.

"I'll be out," he said when I didn't move.

The door closed in my face.

I let out a breath and crunched over dead leaves and pine needles, settling on a fallen log.

He came outside a few minutes later and took a seat at the other end of the branch. He rested his elbows on his knees, hands hanging between his legs.

My cheeks felt warm, despite the cold morning air. The image of Sarah hurrying into her cabin assailed me again.

I should leave well alone. Sarah deserved happiness. Ben deserved more even than that. "I saw her." I wanted to bite my tongue off for bringing it up.

He looked at me. I could tell he wanted to ask what I meant. The terrible part about his habit of not talking to me, combined with his propensity to only speak when answering a question, was it resulted in this silent torture. He was slave and I was master.

"I saw her leaving here." I swallowed. "Sarah."

Mortified that I'd brought attention to my confused reaction upon seeing her, I snapped my mouth closed before I said anything else inappropriate.

It was none of my business. He ignored my statement, pulling his small knife and a piece of wood from his pocket.

God above, there was so much I wanted to ask. *Why are you angry with me? Do you miss our friendship, or am I the only one? How's your grandmother?* Except, I didn't want to ask that. He didn't know how his grandmother was. How could he know when he'd been sold to another island? Separated from her. Families were routinely separated and sold and they never saw each other again. It was something I wanted to avoid here at Wappoo. I'd made Sarah that promise.

Sarah.

Sarah who'd watched my movements around Ben with an eye that crawled over my skin.

"Is that the same pouch your grandmother made for you?" I asked, indicating the talisman that hung from his neck. A brief flash of the day I began to teach him letters crossed my mind. Ben sprinkling a pinch of dirt from the ground upon which we'd stood into the little leather pouch at his neck.

Ben nodded.

"Did—did you know where Cromwell was bringing you?" I'd been unaware this question was something I needed answered until the moment it left my mouth.

Ben glanced to the side. "Yes." He nodded once and sighed.

"I mean to me. Not just South Carolina."

"Yes," he repeated. "He is here because of me."

"How?" I stuttered in surprise. "How did you know?"

"You need my help," he said and slid his blade against the wood in his left hand.

The eerie similarity to what he'd told me in my dream sent a chill through me. I held my hand up in front of my face to make sure this too was not a dream.

It looked and felt real.

"I do need your help, but you won't talk to me. And Cromwell is a pompous bully. And ... and I want my friend back. I miss you."

Ben snorted with derision and the heat in my cheeks flared, my stomach feeling nauseous.

"Why you not teach Quash to read?" he answered me

with a question of his own, his chin tilting up in challenge. "Or the chil'ren?"

His question took me by surprise. "I—"

Quash's question had been on my mind constantly though, which had probably been the instigation behind my strange dreams.

I'd waited impatiently for Ben to come back from wherever it was he'd disappeared to with Cromwell the last few days. To ask his advice? To ask him to help Quash finish the indigo-processing facilities? To ask him why he'd told Quash he could read?

I got to my feet, pacing back and forth. "I—it was different when it was you and I. It was different there. I was young. There are rules. And laws. I—"

Ben stood and took a step toward me, bestowing more eye contact upon me in moments than he had collectively since he'd arrived. "*Lâche.*" He hissed. "You a coward."

Blood seemed to drain from my head, and I sucked in a sharp breath. "How dare you."

He raised an eyebrow. "Why you teach me? To anger your mother? Maybe it was a game? You change my life. You no do the same for Quash?"

I couldn't believe I was being spoken to this way.

And yet I could.

This was Ben.

The lines of white and Negro, servant and master didn't seem to exist here between us.

"Do you want indigo?" he asked.

"Yes," I whispered.

"Why?"

"I—" I put my hand upon my throat as if I could control what came out of it. My pulse fluttered wildly beneath my fingertips. How could I explain my selfish need to succeed and yet ask him to help me in the same moment?

This wouldn't make *him* rich. Or Quashy. I wondered if Cromwell would *ever* free him. What incentive did Ben have to succeed here with me?

"Why—" He grabbed the pouch against his chest as if seeking strength from it. His eyes closed briefly, his nostrils flaring. "It is a gift. Why do you deserve it?"

"Does Cromwell deserve it?" I shot back.

"No," he said firmly, a snarl to his full lips. "But Crom'all, he holds my future. My freedom."

I took a step closer. Closer than propriety should allow. And I had the bizarre urge to press my lips to his, to soothe the twisted anger I saw there.

Ben's eyes flared. Perhaps with alarm.

The instinct to look around for observers was strong, yet I held his eyes and reached out a hand to rest on his forearm. My fingers landed on his warm skin and I inhaled involuntarily, shocked at myself. Yet determined. "Benoit Fortuné," I said softly and watched his eyes flicker at my use of his childhood nickname. "Someone else may control your future." My hand squeezed his sinewy forearm. "But you control *mine*. You just said you are here to help me. So help me. Please. I'll do what I can for Quash and the children here. But please."

We stood that way for long moments. Then he shook my hand off his arm and stepped back. Chilled air moved between us and he swung around and went back into his cabin, closing the door on me for the second time. I would have been incensed or disappointed, but I'd seen the acceptance on his face. His barely perceptible nod.

He'd agreed.

Now how was I to keep my end of the bargain?

Twenty-Four

"I need your counsel, Mr. Pinckney," I said quietly, sitting on the very edge of a pink damask-covered club chair in the Pinckneys' library at Belmont.

Mama, Polly, and I had been graciously invited to their country estate for a summer house party that included several families from the surrounding area. I still got along famously with Miss Bartlett, the Pinckneys' niece, on the occasions we saw each other. She'd turned out to be intrigued rather than horrified by my role on my father's estates. It made a refreshing change from most of genteel society. My reputation had apparently preceded me, certainly made more newsworthy since the Laurens incident. It was valiant on the part of Mr. and Mrs. Pinckney to continue to include me among their social set.

It was just as well I'd never gotten my hopes up for William Middleton either, as we were also celebrating his engagement to Miss Williams, an heiress. Something I was most definitely not. No, after the Laurens incident, I'd come to peace with the idea of spinsterhood.

My friend Mary Chardon had recently caught the eye of Reverend Hutson, and I knew our days of Tuesday embroidering and companionship would perhaps become few and far between if they were to marry. In fact, we had not seen as much of each other since the day we'd returned from her home and I'd had my altercation with John Laurens.

Mrs. Pinckney; her friend Mrs. Cleland, who seemed completely unflappable; and Mrs. Pinckney's niece were among my only female friends. Indeed, the friendship of Miss Bartlett, though she was younger than I, had come at an opportune time.

I'd come to the realization that no matter I lived with my mother and sister and Essie and all our helpers, I was lonely. My heart yearned for friendship. For solidarity. For the rare beating wings of belonging. Part of me felt that it was Ben's presence, along with his unbearable distance, that had made the feeling all the more acute.

"I must insist you call me Charles. Please. My counsel?" he confirmed. "I'll help any way I can. I'm glad to know you don't just seek me out for access to books." He chuckled.

"Oh well, that too," I teased and felt a rush of fondness for him. Charles. Charles was my friend too, though I'd still refer to him aloud as Mr. Pinckney. A very, very dear friend.

We had spent two Christmases now without my father, and I was so very grateful he'd seen fit to make a friend of Charles Pinckney before he left. In fact, the only joy I felt when we left our home in Wappoo was for the time spent with the Pinckneys. "I did so love the Plutarch," I answered. "Though I'm not quite done. I learn something important each time I pick it up—"

"That you feel you must reread it several times," Charles agreed, stealing my thoughts.

"Quite." I laughed. "No, it is your legal counsel I seek."

He walked to the chair beside mine and lowered his lithe body, dressed in an exquisitely tailored suit. His dark hair had grown slightly longer and was pulled neatly away from his strong features. Not for the first time I wondered his exact age. Older or younger than Papa? Probably twice my age. But so very pleasing on the eye and the sentiment.

I hesitated a moment and chewed my lower lip. "Well the thing is, we have had a development in our indigo endeavor. The man from Montserrat arrived late last year, as you know. Nicholas Cromwell. And he brought a Negro man with him. I ... I know this man."

"The Negro man, you mean?" Charles looked at me so intently, I dropped my gaze.

"We, ah, I'd like to think we were friends growing up." I swallowed and looked back at him to gauge his reaction.

A faint vertical line appeared between his eyebrows.

"As children on the plantations in Antigua," I clarified. "His name is Benoit. Ben. He has a very special knowledge of indigo. Unfortunately, my father had sold him to an indigo maker in Montserrat, but by some divine twist the gentleman Colonel Lucas hired, Nicholas Cromwell, brought him to South Carolina."

"That is a coincidence." Charles assessed me with a narrow-eyed gaze. "When last we spoke you made mention of the Negro Act and the provision regarding importing Negroes for one's personal use. Is this why you asked me to look into the matter?"

"Well, yes. The thing is, I know I've probably made an enemy of Mr. Laurens, and I want to make sure I'm able to do what I must to make my endeavor succeed, but within the confines of the law. My father expressed concern when last he wrote, and I assured him I would seek your legal judgment."

Charles continued his scrutiny, and I wished I knew all the conjectures he was sorting out in his head. "I did look at the provisions, and I believe it was proposed in the assembly and rejected. For now. And hearing your explanation of how he came to be here, without your intent, I believe you are perfectly within your right even if it had been accepted."

My chest relaxed and I let a relieved breath escape.

"There's one more thing. There's a provision in the act I read that prohibits educating a Negro so that he may not convey messages. Presumably to avoid another orchestrated rebellion like the incident at Stono."

Charles nodded. Though I sensed a wariness in his person.

My eyes flicked down to my clasped hands. He always made me feel as though I could confide in him, but I feared this time I needn't tell him all my plans or motives.

He let out a breath and stood.

The disturbance of air sent the faint smell of his pipe smoke and sandalwood over me. A smell I had come to find comforting.

He walked over to a campaign desk and pulled a sheaf of papers, going through them slowly as he held them to the window light. The afternoon had turned gloomy and didn't offer much additional illumination. But clearly it was enough.

"These were in my study, but I found myself going through them again last evening in anticipation of your arrival. Somehow I knew you would have more questions. It says here that you may not teach slaves to write."

I played his words over again in my head. "And it says nothing about reading? Just writing?"

He looked down again. "Yes, it would seem so."

"Well, that certainly seems odd. I'm not sure one can learn one without accidentally learning the other."

"I'd have to agree."

An idea came to mind that would perhaps get around anyone who became concerned with my project. "But I suppose one would need to be able to read in order to learn the moral principles of the Bible."

"And pray what scheme have you concocted?"

"Just a little project. Teach some of the Negro children to read so they may seek counsel from the Bible." I knew the lie was written all over my face.

"All right." Charles' eyebrows were sky high, causing a ladder of lines upon his brow, his mouth twisted to a smirk. "Well, you'll let me know how you get on?"

"Of course."

"In fact, I should very much like to hear about all your endeavors. I have a feeling I'll be much entertained." He frowned. "But I fear if we correspond too frequently, it might seem ... odd."

"Me being an unmarried woman?"

"Well, yes. Mrs. Pinckney is so fond of you." He cleared his throat. "As am I. But others may not approve."

Such as my mother. "I must thank you and Mrs. Pinckney for being so accepting in light of my hoydenish reputation. And I have gotten along famously with Miss Bartlett," I said, immediately realizing a solution. "We have talked about keeping in touch. As a dutiful uncle, I'm sure you must read her correspondence?"

He looked up sharply. "Indeed, I do."

"Well, then. I shall write her detailed missives on my exploits. That way you can be sure to hear about my endeavors."

"I'm not saying you can't correspond directly with me."

"I know. And I'm just saying there are many ways to let you know of all my business endeavors without needlessly raising the eyebrows of people with too much time on their hands. Especially since I gave my last suitor the boot, quite literally, and I shall remain an amateur spinster botanist for as long as I have land upon which to practice."

Charles' eyes flicked away. "About Mr. Laurens ..." A smile played around his lips. "I must say, he told quite a grand tale. But then he's always been known to embellish."

A fact for which I supposed I must be grateful. I raised an

eyebrow. "So you didn't believe him?"

"Oh, I believed him." Charles let out a chuckle and shook his head side to side. "But then, I think I see a part of your personality no one else does."

"I—what would that be?"

"Well, I don't believe you have ever met an obstacle you felt you couldn't overcome." His eyes were fond but still thoughtful.

I tried to smile, though my lips were tight. I had. I had met an obstacle I couldn't overcome. "I can't be a son. And there isn't much I can do about that. I'd say that was a rather large obstacle."

Charles let out a puff of laughter, and then his warm eyes grew somber, though no less fond. "I know," he said quietly. "I often wonder what a visionary such as you could achieve if God had seen fit to make you a man." His eyes flicked away again, his strong shoulders tense. "But I ... I ..." His voice was low. "I ..." he tried again.

"What is it, Mr. Pinckney?" I asked softly, confused at his strange expression. His usual self-assurance seemed rattled.

He looked up, his expression pained, then let out a long sigh. "I, for one, am glad you are a woman, Eliza." He shook his head. "For you are a remarkable one," he said simply.

Warmth spread through me. I wasn't quite sure how to respond.

Voices sounded in the hall. Charles cleared his throat. "I came across a book you may like. *An Essay Concerning Human Understanding* by John Locke. Unfortunately, it is in town."

"Thank you. I believe I'm sending Togo into town in the next few weeks for some supplies, can I ask him to stop by your home? I believe I may have some correspondence prepared for Miss Bartlett by then too."

Charles smiled. "I'll look forward to seeing him."

Dear Miss Bartlett,

　　'Tis with pleasure I commence a correspondence with you …

　　　　Best respects wait on Mr. Pinckney and lady,
　　　　Your most obedient servant,
　　　　E. Lucas

Twenty-Five

Upon my return from Belmont after my informative chat with Charles Pinckney, my days about the plantation were imbued with renewed energy and purpose.

I arose at my usual predawn hour, but now, on days I felt too much temptation to veer near the woods, rather than take a turn about the property, I would wake Lil' Gulla and have him saddle a mare. He was always so happy to see me and do the job of Indian Peter that I didn't feel bad rousting him. I had no desire for a repeat of my horrible encounter with Ben. And no desire to put proof in my suspicions that Sarah and Ben were growing closer. I rode up and down the lanes and enjoyed the coming fall coolness that was clothed in the wind that whipped my face.

At my direction, Quash, Sawney, and Pompey were building a covered but open-sided gathering place on the other side of the dwellings, out of direct view from the house and visitors approaching. It would become a schoolroom of sorts. I'd thought briefly of asking Mary Ann's girls and Lil' Gulla to join me in the study each morning, but they were so unused to being in the house, I thought they'd be too distracted. Certainly, Polly was hard enough to direct; she would lead them into a fit of distraction all by herself.

Transacting the business affairs of the plantations and recording everything into the account books took a fair chunk of each day. The boat from our plantation up at Garden Hill was now expected daily on its way to Charles Town. Murry, our overseer at the plantation on the Combahee River, had risen to my challenge and production was as good as could be expected. In fact we were sending a substantial amount of bacon and salted beef over to the West Indias with the next timber shipment. And we continued to run a full schedule of imports and exports. But whichever way I looked at our accounts, I couldn't escape how flimsily our life was built. One failed shipment or a drop in production or demand and a mortgage payment might not be met. Curse Father. But, oh how I missed him so.

The investment in indigo was no mere trifle. Between the cost of employing Cromwell and building the infrastructure we would need, we were in a critical balancing act.

Extra luxury expenses such as attending the King's Birthday Ball, to which all of Charles Town was invited at the end of October, and the dresses we would have need of ordering since Mama insisted we attend, added to my already burdened mind.

I felt more dread than joy in the imagining of attending such a grand affair.

A note from Mr. and Mrs. Pinckney arrived insisting we stay with them while in town for the ball. And Mrs. Pinckney, like an angel from heaven who could hear my panicked thoughts from so far away, had suggested that if we had the fabric, she would ask her seamstress Bettina to make our dresses. I had responded gratefully that, of course, we would be very much obliged.

The rest of my day that was not involved in business was employed in educating the little parcel of Negroes and then rewarding myself with two indulgences: music and following Ben along the rows of indigo.

Dear Mrs. Bartlett,

Why, my dear Miss B, will you so often repeat your desire to know how I trifle away my time?

In general then, I rise at five o'clock in the morning, read a little, then take a walk in the garden or fields and see that the servants are at their respective business, then to breakfast.

After that, I spend time at my music, French, and shorthand. I devote time to our little Polly and two little black girls who I teach to read, and if I have my father's approbation (my mama's I have got) I intend them to become school mistresses for the rest of the Negro children.

The remainder of my time until the evening meal is employed on the business of the plantation.

I practice my needlework until candlelight and from that time to bedtime, read or write.

I hate to undertake a thing and not go through with it; but by way of relaxation from the other, I have begun a piece of work of a quicker sort which requires neither eyes nor genius, at least not very good ones. Would you ever guess it to be a shrimp net?

Oh, I had like to forgot one last thing: I have planted a fig orchard with design to dry and export them. I have reckoned my expense and profits to arise from these figs, but if I was to tell you how great an estate I am to make this way, you'd think me too far gone! Your good uncle, I know, has long thought I have a fertile brain at scheming.

Pray, tell him if he laughs at my project, I never intend to have my hand in a silver mine and he will understand as well as you what I mean.

If my eyes don't deceive me; you, in your last letter, talk of coming very soon by water to see how my oaks grow. Is it really so? While 'tis in your head, put it speedily into execution. It will give me great pleasure!

Your most obedient servant,
Eliza Lucas

Twenty-Six

Ben tolerated my presence in the indigo fields, and often it was just the two of us walking through the rows, inspecting each plant. As weeks went on, he began to speak more and more. I learned the quieter I stayed, the more he spoke.

"Here," he said, touching a particular branch that caught his eye, the leaflets marching proudly up each side. "See how the branches go every direction? They chase the sun. Not one of them is hiding in the shade of another."

"That explains why they always look so wild and undisciplined," I answered.

"Not everything got to seem perfect. But you look closer, see how perfect they are." He lowered himself down to his haunches and pointed out three branches, which due to the way they hung, could easily be compared. "The same count of leaves on each side. All the same shade. But see how … different is each leaf?"

I held my skirts and crouched beside him as he pointed to one of the leaves, gesturing as he spoke.

"Look how full the leaf is becoming. How the edges start to curl down, its body pressing up to the sun. The time is coming soon. Maybe just weeks."

I looked, and frankly, didn't see what he meant. His eyes

were dark and expressive, his face sharp and proud. But I nodded anyway, perhaps more at the melodious rumble of Ben's voice than what he was saying.

He impressed me.

At times like this, when Ben spoke and it was just he and I, I wished Andrew Deveaux or Charles Pinckney could know what a remarkable intelligence Ben had. Mr. Deveaux, in particular, would very much enjoy chatting with Ben. It had been too long since I'd paid Deveaux a visit. Perhaps next time I went, Ben could accompany Quashy. Oh, the discussions they could have about plants!

"You do not see it." Ben sighed.

"I do," I protested. "I'm sorry, my mind was elsewhere."

A fleeting look of disappointment flittered across his face, and his hand let go of the small branch as he made to stand.

"Wait," I said. "My mind was on you, just—" I reached out to stop him, coming forward onto my knees, my hand grabbing his.

And then I couldn't let go.

I watched in fascination as my fingers slipped between Ben's like the keys of a pianoforte.

My palms burned.

The heat of his hand, the rough texture of his skin, the shocking and contrasting visual. My head grew light as I realized I hadn't drawn breath. The air was so still, I thought perhaps Ben hadn't either. I tore my eyes away from our linked hands and looked up. Ben was equally mesmerized. For a moment his grip grew tighter on mine, then as I watched, he blinked and reached out with his free hand, taking my wrist and pulling my fingers free as if only part of himself had the volition to do so.

He stood.

Avoiding looking at him, I scrambled up too, awkwardly when no assistance was forthcoming. That would necessitate touching again.

My face throbbed with mortified heat. With a gasp of delayed reaction, I turned and ran back toward the house.

Twenty-Seven

"It is intolerable." Mama's voice reverberated around the small study. We'd enjoyed a lovely autumn meal of venison and pumpkin and now retired to the study to enjoy the fire after Polly went to bed. "You spend far too much time with that … that …"

"Ben, Mama," I said patiently and walked to the fire roaring in the grate, giving the embers a poke. It was remarkably cold for October, and I worried constantly about an early frost. The sooner we harvested the better, but Ben and Cromwell kept saying it needed a few more days. How they could tell, or rather how *Ben* could tell, was still magical to me, an alchemy beyond my understanding even as I learned all the facts. I'd filled Mama in on the progress of the indigo, but it had been days since I'd been in the fields following Ben. "His name is Ben. And you've known him since he was a child. You know he is a good, kind person. You know he is my friend. My *best* friend."

At that my mother gave a shrill squeak and leaned back against the settee cushions.

I looked to the dark heavens outside the window.

When I didn't indulge Mother's theatrics, she sat back up. "*And* you've been teaching the Negro children to read." She shook her head. "To read," she echoed in disbelief as if she wasn't quite sure she'd uttered it the first time.

"Yes, Mother. That's been going on for quite some time now. They're just children, it's basic lettering. They're hardly about to organize a slave revolt."

"It's against the law."

"Are you going to tell someone about it?" I asked. I drew the green brocade curtains closed against the windows to keep the chill out of the room.

"Of course I'm not going to tell anyone about it. They'll fine us, and then what will we do?"

"Quite," I said blandly. "Money is stretched tight as it is."

"You mustn't mention a word of it, Eliza. Do you hear?"

"Yes, Mama."

"It's bad enough I had to tell your father about you spending time with that … that …"

"Ben, Mama."

"Well, you'll be hearing from your father."

"Spending time with my best friend is no secret, and there is nothing untoward." But her admission that she'd complained to Papa yet again set me on edge.

She huffed. "So says you. I know you, Eliza. I'm your mother. Your passions for life and people and all God's creation run deep. I fear you wouldn't recognize a line when you saw one. How many have you already crossed? And I've seen the way he looks at you."

My insides flipped upon themselves, and I turned abruptly to my mother under the guise of her having come to the end of my patience. In truth it was shock at her observation.

"Oh, please." I modulated my voice through an unexpectedly strangled throat. "If he is my best friend, then I am his. It is nothing more. Besides," I added, though my throat closed up farther at what I was about to give voice to. "I believe he's been spending more time with Sarah. Perhaps …"

I cleared my throat and walked to the fire. As much as I wished to ignore it, Sarah's belly was growing round. "Perhaps that is where the so-called passions you speak of lie."

Mama pursed her lips. "It's not right. Not to mention I can't help but feel he causes unease amongst the rest of the Negroes. What must they think, for goodness' sake? To see their mistress about with one of their own as if he were her equal."

I didn't answer.

"The sooner your father fetches us back to Antigua the better."

"You know as well as I, there are no plans to do that. He needs these plantations to turn a profit. His career depends on it."

"So says you. And if they fail, and they don't seem to exactly be succeeding right now, we shall have to return regardless. What's the point in dragging it out?"

"We're not dragging it out, we're turning it around. Albeit very slowly."

We're gambling on an idea, I mentally corrected myself. An idea that was all mine, where the success of it sat very firmly upon my lone shoulders.

Walking to my desk, I shuffled amongst my papers. Pulling out what I was looking for, I went to take a seat next to my mother. "To put your mind at ease, I'll go ahead and read you the exact letter of the law."

I settled myself upon the settee and cleared my throat, reading from the paper I'd painstakingly transcribed from Charles Pinckney's copy. "Be it therefore enacted by the authority aforesaid, that all and every person, and persons whatsoever—"

"It should be *whosoever,*" Mama interrupted. "If they are talking of people."

"They are." I smiled and continued. "*Whatsoever, who shall* hereafter teach or cause any slave to be taught to *write*, or shall use to employ any slave as a scribe in any manner of *writing* whatsoever, hereafter taught to *write*, every offense forfeit the sum of one hundred pounds current money."

I finished and laid the paper on my lap.

Mother was silent for a few moments.

"You see, Mama? I'm not breaking this law. I am only teaching how to read, not write. Besides, how will they learn about God if they cannot read the Bible?" I took her hand as I delivered the final move.

"You are a smart, smart girl, Eliza. You really should have been a boy." Mother shook her head as if she'd failed some utterly simple task. Some of the time I knew how she felt. Other times I almost *blamed* her. It seemed a ridiculously careless accident that made me female rather than male. The rest of the time I wondered why it should make a difference at all. But it did.

"Just for the record, Mama, while I'm not breaking *this* particular law there are several others we are breaking that you might want to keep quiet about, lest we become destitute from paying fines. Slaves are not allowed to grow their own food—"

"That's ridiculous."

I smirked, amused, and continued. "Gather together for any reason—"

"Not even church?"

"No."

"Well, I never ..."

"Play musical instruments, wear nice clothes." I thought of Ben when he'd first arrived. Nowadays, of course, he wore clothing more suited to fieldwork.

"Do you mean to tell me this has all been unlawful?"

I nodded. "Unlawful."

"But no one reported us?"

I blew out a breath and shrugged. "I can only assume those like us in the country find the laws as tedious as we do. I can't speak for town in general, but I know Charles agrees with me."

"And he is a very accomplished lawyer. He would never steer us wrong. He has such a soft spot for you, Eliza."

"And I for him."

"I can't imagine who came up with these ridiculous things," Mama said. "The scaremongers, I'm sure. Well, the rules will be overturned when people see how silly they are."

A knock sounded on the study door followed by the tenor of Nicholas Cromwell. "Ladies? May I enter?"

I raised my eyes. "Come in," I called. The man was still as supercilious and tedious as ever. But we had all grown used to his presence on our plantation and at our dinner table over the past year. It was a distraction, a buffer really, from the monotony and itchy discord of three females living in the house.

"How cozy it is in here. I'm quite chilled to the bone this evening." Cromwell came immediately to the hearth, holding out his hands for warmth.

"Would you like some rum? We received it from Antigua. Eliza, pour the man a drink, would you, dear?"

"Of course." I headed to the sideboard and unstopped the decanter. "So ... how are we doing?" I asked.

Cromwell turned from the fire. "I've just inspected today's progress. I believe the indigo vats may be ready in a few short days. As soon as they are done, we will need to fill the main vat with water so we can begin to monitor the temperature. The time to harvest could come any day, and we'll need to be ready."

Knowing Ben, I understood there was some art form

to the harvesting of indigo and the production of dye, but Cromwell made it sound so difficult and said it with such a superior air, it was hard not to roll my eyes.

"Wonderful," I stated. "We are so grateful and of course anxious for our first batch so we can prove we can produce it."

Cromwell shifted and took my proffered tumbler.

My mother cleared her throat and got to her feet.

"What is it, Mother?" I asked.

"Oh, I'll leave you two to talk business. I am very weary."

Frowning, I went to her side. "Come along," I said, not wanting to remain alone with our consultant. "I'll accompany you. Mr. Cromwell and I can discuss business in the morning."

THE MOMENT QUASH HAD FINISHED CONSTRUCTION on the school shelter for the children, I'd asked him to meet me in my study an hour before dawn every other morning. He'd nodded without asking why.

The first morning he arrived, his field cap in his hand, his brows had furrowed as he glanced this way and that before following me down the hall and into the study where I'd lit a small lamp. I'd set up two chairs side by side next to a demilune table by one unshelved wall.

Quash stood awkwardly, looking at the two chairs and then around at the books on the shelves that lined the other walls. "Knowledge, Quash," I whispered. His eyes found mine, and I smiled encouragingly. "We'll take it slow. We'll see where you are, then go from there, all right?" I indicated one of the chairs. "Have a seat."

Quash continued to hesitate, a myriad of emotions

crossing his face. I hoped none of them were distrust of me. Eventually, he seemed to reach some internal conclusion and moved forward quietly, lowering himself into a chair.

I had one of the simple letter books that had been Polly's and had somehow made the trip from Antigua. I hadn't shared it with the children in our schoolyard, lest it be pulled to pieces.

Taking a deep breath, I sat down and opened the book to the first page, which listed the twenty-six letters of the alphabet. I pointed to the letter B. "Do you know the sound this makes?"

Quash looked at it, then at me. "Ben?" he asked.

"Yes." I nodded encouragingly. "Ben's name starts with B. Ben has three letters in his name." I pointed them out, sounding out each one. "So you see the sound this B makes is 'buh' and words are really just sounds strung together. Once you know all the sounds, you'll be able to read."

Mostly.

I'd save the tricky exceptions for later, if we got that far.

Time flew by those first few mornings. And I didn't miss my quiet time about the land at all.

Quash, his keen intelligence not missing a thing, astounded me time and time again with his quick grasp and also his aptitude for arithmetic, which I'd incorporated toward the end of the first week.

However, even with his progress, there were still some frustrations. The thing that annoyed Quash the most, in the first few days, was learning his own name. Q had to be used with another letter, and the SH sound had to be yet another two-letter combination. His irritation made me giggle.

"I don't think I've ever asked, but how did you come by your name?"

We were sitting in our side-by-side chairs.

Quash seemed more at ease now. Less furtive.

"I know there is a Quash family farther south of here," I went on. We still spoke in very low tones to avoid discovery. "Planters ..." I left the thought hanging, not wanting to assume.

Quash nodded, rubbing the back of his neck with a toffee-skinned hand. "My mother. She were a slave on the Quash plantation afore she was sold here to Wappoo."

I cocked my head to the side. "Then I'm imagining she was with child, you, when she came here?"

Quash nodded.

Sarah's situation so closely resembled that of Quash's mother, I couldn't help but draw a parallel. But for her to name him Quash was almost diabolical. That was like if Sarah had named her daughter Ebba after Starrat. I tamped down the urge to shudder.

My brows must have still betrayed my confusion.

"My mother, she did not want to leave," Quash answered my unspoken question.

Of course. She was settled there. Had family, presumably. Again this awful practice of selling humans and wrenching them away from their families made my heart hurt. "She didn't want to leave family?"

"She did not want to leave my *father*." Quash's voice was stiff.

I swallowed. "She—she *liked* the man who did that to her?" Visions flashed through my head. A large white body like Starrat's, with his grim eyes, covering Quash's mother's dark-skinned, small-boned body. This time I couldn't hold in the shudder.

"It was not the master. It was the master's son." Quash's eyes gleamed in the low light of our reading lamp. "She *loved* him."

I sucked in a breath.

The implications of his disclosure seemed to shimmer in the air before me. As if I could see each intricate part of a picture, yet couldn't quite see the image as a whole.

"Is our lesson finish?" Quash broke the protracted silence.

I started. "Yes. Yes, that's fine." I stood, absently brushing nonexistent dust off my dress. "I—how is the building of the indigo vat coming along?"

"Fine, Miz Lucas. Jus' fine."

"You have enough bricks then?" We'd had to have three boats deliver the bricks from Charles Town at huge expense. An investment we could ill afford yet equally couldn't afford not to undertake.

"Yes, Miz Lucas. But ..." Quash hesitated.

"What is it?"

He scratched at his head. "Sarah say brick will give too much red in the dye."

I felt my eyebrows elevate. "And what does Ben say?"

"Ben say do what Cromwell say." He shrugged.

"Indeed?" I turned to the window. I wasn't sure, but I felt indigo was graded on the variations of color. An indigo that was not *true* and held a purple cast was perhaps not as valuable. Or perhaps it was more so? I let out a frustrated breath at coming up against yet another gap in my knowledge and no source from where to glean it. Except from the man who had experience trading it, and who could lead us any way he chose. Cromwell.

Dear Miss Bartlett,

Won't you laugh at me if I tell you I am so busy in providing for posterity I hardly allow myself to eat or sleep and can snatch just a minute to write to you.

As well as the indigo, I am making a large plantation of oaks which I look upon as my own, whether my father gives me the land or not; and therefore I design many years hence when oaks are more valuable than they are now, which you know they will be when we come to build fleets.

I suppose according to custom you will show this to your uncle and aunt. "She is a good girl," says Mrs. Pinckney. "She is never idle and always means well." "Tell the little visionary," says your uncle, "come to town and partake of some amusements suitable to her time of life."

Pray tell him I think these so, and what he may now think whims and projects may turn out well by and by. Out of many, surely one will hit.

Your most obedient servant,
E. Lucas

Twenty-Eight

Cromwell sought me out one morning in Papa's study a week or so before we left for the King's Birthday Ball in Charles Town. "May I have a word?"

I was penning a short missive to my father, updating him on plantation affairs and letting him know we soon planned to harvest our next crop of indigo.

The seed pods from the plants that had survived the pest last year had been gathered and dried. We had planted them with new seed sent from my father. So we had high hopes for this crop.

I laid down my instrument and gave Cromwell my full attention. "Of course. How can I help you?"

He shifted uncomfortably. His skin was sallow and brushed with powder that did nothing to hide the old pox scars on his cheek. His mustache was worked into two sharp points on each side. "We don't have enough hands to harvest when the time comes," he said. "We'll do our best but unless all the leaves are harvested and put into the vats within a day, the dye will be inferior."

Irritation surged.

"I'm sure you understand," he went on, "how woefully underprepared you are here to succeed in this indigo scheme."

"I'm sure *you* understand that we have already covered this issue, and I will give it no more credence. You have a job to do."

"Which is impossible in these conditions," Cromwell blustered.

I frowned, confused by this resistance again from him and not understanding his lack of will to succeed. "Everything is prepared as you asked. In time. For you to suddenly tell me now that you believe we haven't enough help borders on irresponsible neglect for the job you are being paid to do."

"I do apologize. Ben and I had spoken about it, and I was led to believe he, and perhaps Quash, had spoken with you. You are with him alone in the fields fairly regularly. It was only made clear to me today that the subject of additional help had not been broached." He took a seat in a club chair without being invited. "We'll do the best we can, of course, but I fear that's all I can promise."

My head throbbed, and I realized I had been gritting my back teeth together as he spoke.

"Certainly. It must have slipped Ben's and Quash's minds." My voice was stiff. "But I can't get cross, can I? As it is *your* job, not theirs, to tell me what is required for this to be a success. I'm sure it was a simple misunderstanding."

"So you are prepared for the expected outcome to be somewhat disappointing? Next year, I'll—"

"Of course I'm not all right with it. I will have to move some help here from one of the other plantations." I sighed heavily. "Please excuse me while I compose my request."

I pulled out a fresh sheet of paper and dipped my quill. I couldn't write to Murry. His operation was performing so perfectly, I didn't want to upset his balance. My hand trembled with barely controlled emotion. A year of waiting and then this. Starrat, then. "You may be excused," I said, not looking up.

I heard a sound of what could have been indignation gurgle from Cromwell's throat. Then he rose and left the room.

So this had been his final attempt to prove to me I couldn't do this. It was beyond comprehension that he would so perjure his own integrity to make a point. What purpose could it serve to cause me to fail? I imagined he'd thought he'd timed it perfectly. That I'd be unable to procure more help.

Cromwell proved himself quite correct. Despite my plea to Starrat to send Negroes down from Waccamaw, Starrat's response was that he was unable to help due to the fall rice harvest. A valid excuse. But somehow I knew he could have managed.

Quash informed me he had never heard from either Ben or Cromwell of the need for more help.

Each day that passed brought us closer to the day it would suddenly be deemed harvest day, and I didn't want to miss that moment when it came. But with the end of October and the King's Birthday Ball bearing down upon us, it seemed I might.

There was no way I could be absent from the largest social event Charles Town had ever seen. It would put the final nail in my coffin of spinsterhood and probably seal Polly's fate as well. Besides, Mama wouldn't allow me to back out, I was sure of it. I wanted to see Mr. and Mrs. Pinckney. She had, after all, been so generous in having her seamstress, Bettina, make our dresses, we could hardly not attend. We needed to be there for fittings a few days prior to the event.

I hadn't been alone in the fields with Ben since the day I'd grabbed his hand, but I couldn't avoid being near him forever. Now I found myself seeking him out.

Ben was facing away from me, inspecting the rows with

Togo, talking softly, pointing out certain plants. From the looks of the buds, the indigo would soon burst into bloom. I had a feeling this was what we were waiting for. For the indigo to be at its most potent and its most creatively fertile; moments before it burst forth into flower.

I waited on the edge of the field. Togo saw me and nodded his head. When I didn't summon him, he kept moving. Ben did not look up. On a whim, I looked around at my feet and spied a small pinecone. I picked it up and taking careful aim, I let loose and hurled it at Ben's back.

He stopped.

My heart pounded with nerves.

Ben resumed his walking without turning around.

If Togo noticed what I'd done, he didn't give it away.

I felt stupid for replaying our silly childhood game. I didn't know what had come over me. It was a childish gesture and now I simply felt ridiculous.

After a few more minutes, Togo left and Ben turned to me.

"I don't like being kept waiting," I said when he finally approached, his gaze guarded.

"I not like things thrown at me," he responded.

"You didn't used to mind so much," I half spoke, half whispered, my voice feeling oddly choked up.

He breathed in through his nose. "I was a child then."

I looked away. The energy between us, unable to become anything resembling what we'd once had, was almost physically painful in its impotence.

Swallowing, I cleared my throat. "Did you tell Cromwell we needed more hands for the harvest, or did Cromwell tell you?" I already knew the answer. It was Cromwell I didn't trust.

Ben cocked his head to the side. "You do not have more workers coming?"

"You didn't answer me. But no. No, we don't. Because no one told me."

Ben shrugged. "We will manage."

I narrowed my eyes at him, not giving him the satisfaction of a nod. "When will it begin?"

He turned to the stalks nearest us, fingering the small buds. "Sunrise in three days. Maybe before."

Exactly what I was afraid of. I'd have left for the ball. I swallowed in disappointment. At a loss as to what else to say, I began walking away, blinking rapidly.

I felt like I was holding on too tight to everything. My ambitions, my emotions … I feared they would soon slip through my fingers and unravel at lightning speed.

A thump hit my lower back. I gasped and turned around. Ben stood, a small smirk playing around his mouth. Two more pinecones in his hands.

I swiped at my eyes, betraying myself.

He stilled when he saw my tears and was quiet a few moments. "It be alrigh'," he said finally. "I'll make it alrigh'."

I let out a long breath that wobbled and hitched as it left me. "Thank you."

He nodded and brought two fingers up, laying them gently to the pouch at his breast.

I didn't know what it meant. It was familiar, though. I felt a chill move through me that I would have dreamt something so foretelling. It must be a memory.

A gasp from my right drew my attention, and I saw Sarah, hand on her swollen belly, swinging her gaze between us.

And somehow, with dread, I knew Ben had made a terrible mistake.

Twenty-Nine

Again, I was awake before dawn.

Impatience for the indigo harvest was driving me to madness. I felt as if any one of a hundred things could go wrong at any moment. Sarah and the way she had looked when Ben made that promise haunted me.

The new batch of live oak shoots I was growing in a box on my window ledge would soon become trees if I didn't take them outside and plant them.

I gave them a bit of water in the half light, then holding my shoes in one hand and the small container in the other, I padded down the stairs and out into the cool early morning. I was surprised Essie hadn't seen to me yet.

Not only my mind, but my body was restless too. I waited anxiously for the harvest of course, and I was keyed up about having to leave for Charles Town soon, but there was something else. Something I couldn't pin down. A sort of *aliveness* that ran under the surface of my skin and just out of reach from my thoughts. It was hard to concentrate on anything, let alone relax enough to sleep. And it was hard to keep still.

A late rising moon shot a twinkling path toward me across the water of Wappoo Creek. I donned my shoes, lacing them tightly, and grabbed a small trowel from the basket at the end of the veranda.

Seeking out a spot near the water on the southernmost part of our land, in a spot rarely trampled upon, I methodically planted a spaced-out stand of what I hoped would become beautiful, tall, and strong live oaks. The earth was damp and gritty, dark and fertile. I was careful not to plant in the line of sight between the house and the creek, lest they should one day block the view.

There was a live oak near Lord Fenwick's land across the creek that, rumor had it, was a thousand years old. The trunk would take the arms of six men to encircle it, its gnarled and curving branches almost too heavy to hold themselves up. What majesty and mystery must a specimen hold to affix itself upon the earth in such a hardy manner, come thunderstorms and hurricanes. I hoped at least a few of these oaks I was planting would see out whatever became of this land a thousand years hence, sentinels upon the banks of Wappoo Creek. Others, I knew, would doubtless be harvested for ships. That was my intention, anyway.

I'd ask Quash later today to create a barrier of sorts with sticks and twine so that nobody damaged the small saplings.

Quash's lessons were going well. I thought I might try to procure some books on architecture for him if Charles had some. It seemed his knack for arithmetic, along with his carpentry and building skills, had coalesced into a burning fire. His thirst for knowledge had been well and truly ignited.

I blew out a breath and tramped back to the house just in time to hear an almost inhuman scream that froze the blood in my veins.

THE HUT WHERE SARAH AND HER DAUGHTER, EBBA, LIVED was dark as I entered, lit only with a small oil lamp I recognized from the house. Essie was within, hovering over Sarah, whose normally dark skin seemed leached of color and polished with sweat. Her eyes were squeezed tight, her teeth bared.

The smell of camphor and Essie's herbs did little to diminish the sickly sweet and metallic smell of bodily emissions. I hurriedly pulled out my small hanky to cover my nose and mouth.

Essie's face was grave.

"What happened? Is she all right?"

Sarah moaned, the hoarse, guttural moan of a wounded animal bleeding out. It was then I saw the dark blood staining the sheets around her lower body.

My chest seized, my stomach flipping over in protest. Her baby! I lurched forward. "Oh, my sweet Lord." I made the sign of the cross upon my body. "What can we do?"

Essie shook her head. "It is too late."

Sarah seemed to hear Essie and cried out again, her back arching in agony.

"No. It can't be. I shall run to the house for wet cloths. We'll bathe her and give her willow bark for the pain. She will be all right!" The baby wouldn't. My breath hitched. But she would be.

I turned and fled, hurrying toward the kitchen block. Mary Ann was there already. Ebba, unaware of the situation with her mother, sat with Mary Ann's daughters at the scarred wooden table eating corn cakes and drinking cow's milk. Hopefully Lil' Gulla would stay oblivious in the stable block.

The pot of water was already heated, and I went to the shelves that held the lye soap and cloths, grabbing a handful and dumping them in the pot. "We need some willow bark tea too please, Mary Ann."

Sarah had lost her baby. Ben's baby perhaps. I could not identify my feelings on that score. How painful must it be to have a life wrenched from your body? Surely there was no sin that would warrant that act from God.

I thought of Mrs. Pinckney and what Charles had told me. Was it better to have the babe taken from your body before you knew him or her or for the babe to die as an infant? What was God's plan to invoke the miracle of life under even the most difficult of circumstances, and then cruelly rip it away? Why? I blinked rapidly against the horror and bloodiness of the scene I had witnessed, even though I was headed back to it. *God grant that I may never have to endure such a thing.*

I drew the cloths out with a wooden ladle and set them into a pail, and then also spooned some water into the tin cup Mary Ann had set on the table.

Approaching Sarah's hut, I saw Ben crouched outside. He sat upon his haunches, his indigo-dyed trousers stretched across his thighs and a tanned leather work vest upon his upper body. The charm that normally rested against his breastbone was clutched tight in his fist. He watched me approach, his eyes dark.

I swallowed, at once sympathetic but with a pain in my heart I couldn't fathom. Shaking my head, I stepped past him. "Excuse me," I muttered and holding my breath, entered the hut. I thought I felt him reach out to me as I passed, but I did not slow.

There was quiet from the bed. Sarah was perhaps unconscious at last. "Come, leave the pail. I must wash her," Essie instructed, indicating the bucket I had brought.

"I'll help."

"She would not want that." Essie shook her head and took the tea from me, setting it upon a low table. There was a small collection of artifacts upon its surface. Bones, some rocks, twigs, and dried berry husks. It looked like the bits and pieces Ebba liked to collect. Essie's movements knocked a horse chestnut hung with twine, and it rolled from the table to the floor and under the low platform that served as Sarah's bed.

I bent to retrieve it. Movement and light caught my eye. A blown glass jar was pushed under the bed. Curiously, I brought it out, seeing it was covered in cloth and tied with twine.

Then I almost dropped it in fright at the contents, mottled and distorted through the thick glass. Caterpillars.

No. Not caterpillars. I shook my head, not believing. Stuffed into the jar were indigo leaves and dozens of the awful pests I had seen only once before in my indigo fields.

I looked up and saw Essie staring at the jar in my hand, looking as aghast as I. Then my gaze slid to the bed and Sarah, who should have still been asleep but now lay staring at me. Her eyes were narrowed to slits and filled with such hatred, I could feel it slicing across my skin.

"How could you?" I asked, too shocked to feel anything but confusion. "I ... I saved you. Didn't I? Why would you do this?"

She didn't answer.

The hatefulness of her actions, her intent, was almost too much to bear. It was hard to breathe under the assault of such malice. I blinked at her and thought she smiled, though her lips were pale and cracked, white against her dark skin. I wanted to be angry, but as I looked at her I couldn't summon it.

"I'm sorry for your loss," I whispered with as much meaning as I could muster.

"She make it on her own self," Essie muttered as she rang out the washcloth and peeled the sticky darkened sheets from Sarah's legs.

I looked away, my stomach rolling at the sight. I had to swallow down a retch.

"This here dark magic. She done practiced a charm upon a body who is protected. Mighty protected." Essie glanced at me meaningfully as if I was to know of what she spoke. "It come back upon *her*."

My gaze darted back to Sarah's face at Essie's words, my gut still churning. But Sarah was passed out again. Taking the jar, I stepped outside into the now bright dawn, my eyes creasing against the assault of light.

Ben stood and looked down at what I held in my hands. I watched the realization take hold. His jaw hardened, and he made a short clicking sound. Reaching out, he closed his hands around mine, so together we held the jar. The warmth and roughness of his skin soothed me, and I felt the delayed emotions inside me lurch for the surface. I let out a hiccuped breath, looking up at Ben's kind and beautiful dark face. With all my might, I wished for Ben to draw me close and hold me against his strong body. I wished for two friends to be able to take comfort from each other. I yearned for it with such a fierce desire, I trembled, my heart hurling itself against my rib cage.

"Why does she hate me so much?" I whispered instead.

Thirty

The low rhythmic melodies of field songs drifted with me as I emerged from dreaming to wakefulness.

I opened my eyes and sat up in bed, straining to hear in the darkness. Sure enough, the low sound of African voices and one melodious voice belonging to Togo dancing over the top of it floated in from outside.

We were harvesting.

Oh, thank the Lord.

I turned my face to the door. Essie materialized as if summoned. "Hurry, Essie. I want to go down and see." I kicked off my covers, tangling my feet.

"Slow down, chil'." She chuckled her warm treacle laugh.

"I'm too excited, Essie. I've waited for this day for far too long. Make haste." Harvest had come early. I'd get to see it after all.

I WAS OUTSIDE IN THE DARK MORNING, racing toward the harmonious voices. We were succeeding at last! Nothing could stand in our way now. We had avoided another pest attack, though Ben had assured me there wouldn't have been time to do any real damage. When I let myself think of it, I felt enraged. Fortunately, Sarah had survived the loss of her baby. I knew Essie tended to her each day, but I had not seen her since. And it was almost a relief to know she was not present at this momentous moment.

Dark figures moved through the rows of indigo, dipping and rising like waves as they tended to their work. The whisking sound of the blades lent a percussive undertone to the harmonies.

I searched for a familiar outline, even as I picked out voices. A beautiful vibrato stood out, and I pinpointed it coming from Togo. His voice was deep in parts and beautifully falsetto in others.

My eyes found Ben. My heart thumped erratically in excitement. As I started toward him, I noticed Cromwell too. Pacing nearby, a dim orange glow from his pipe was occasionally visible. He raised his hand in greeting, and even though Ben was the person I wanted to check in with, I changed course toward Cromwell.

"It will be a long day," he said.

I nodded. "But an exciting one."

He made a sound of dismissal. "It will get tedious for a lady soon enough, I am sure."

I ambled away from him to see where I might be needed.

LIGHT SEEPED OVER THE LANDSCAPE. Work paused as the first ray pierced the trees at the creek's edge and shot over the field. The cooking fire was going, Quash's mother standing over a large, suspended pot, stirring constantly. Stone-ground cornmeal with hog's lard and salted pork and greens from the walled garden. All our workers, young and old, played a part.

Hours passed. The atmosphere was one of camaraderie and excitement. We were united in a common cause. I'd shared with Togo one day, when he returned from the market in town, how I was depending upon the indigo crop to save the plantation. Perhaps it was pointless to explain something of such a personal nature to one's slave. Anyone, even Charles, might have questioned my judgment in doing so. But in the end, I was glad. For whether Togo had chosen to share the information among his peers, or Ben had shared how Sarah plotted to destroy the crop, the feeling that morning of a team united and excited in the pursuit of a common goal, *my* goal, was beautiful satisfaction.

Every available pair of hands, including my own cased in cowhide gloves, worked until the field was green no more. We worked until every last leaf and all my hopes were bundled and laid out on sackcloth.

There were two large, square, three-foot-deep brick vats built adjacent and attached to each other. One was built up higher than the other, so liquid might be drained into the lower vessel. Ben climbed up the ladder to the higher of the two vats and returned shaking his head. Cromwell went up and returned too, though he looked less perturbed.

"What is it?" I asked, approaching.

"The water is perfect and ready for the plants." Cromwell nodded as he spoke.

Ben's stare scorched the side of my face. I swallowed and turned to him. "Ben, do you agree?"

Cromwell's head bobbed backward in surprise that I would rather defer to Ben's expertise.

"Well?" I persisted, ignoring the undercurrent.

"Master Cromwell says it is ready."

I narrowed my eyes at him.

Cromwell grunted in satisfaction.

"The water, it is not warm enough," Ben murmured, glancing sideways at Cromwell.

"Well, the sun is not strong enough, it will be. Come along. We haven't got all day."

"Wait," I said. I struggled with whether to call Cromwell out by giving credence to Ben's belief. But it was obvious Ben was the master indigo maker here. "Can I feel the water? I'd like to get a better understanding of the process."

"Suit yourself. But if the indigo gets too dry, it will not be for my lack of advisement. I'm going in the house for some refreshment. I'll be out momentarily."

Ben gave me a reassuring look with a subtle shake of his head.

There were two ladders, made by Quash and Pompey, one each on opposing sides. I approached one and climbing gingerly up to the rim, I peered into the clear water. Dipping my fingers in, I was surprised when it felt neither cool nor warm. "It feels perfectly temperate to me."

"Lower your hand." Ben's voice next to me at thigh level surprised me. "You must feel the water here."

I looked to where he lay two fingers across his wrist. "Here to your arm, where you feel the ..."

His brow furrowed.

"My pulse?" I offered.

Ben nodded and touched his chest. "Where you can feel your heart pulse. That's where you must feel the water."

I lowered my hand, and sure enough, the water that had felt neither one thing nor another, at once had a small bite of coolness as it slipped over the joint from my hand to my arm.

"You should not feel it here, if it is ready." I startled as I felt Ben's fingers against my wrist that hung at my side.

Hidden from anyone watching, his fingers moved lightly across my skin, indicating where he meant. "This water need more heat."

I snatched my wrist away from him. "You're right," I said, attempting to react normally. My voice was tight.

"It feels cool," I said and descended backward down a rung, my legs feeling weak. "So what do we do? We can't wait, can we? What are we to do?" My toe slipped and I gasped.

Ben's strong arm was about my waist to steady me. I was enveloped in an aroma of salt, clove, and warm safety. The heat of a body at my back. In an instant his arm was gone and my feet were firmly on the ground.

My heart pounded with adrenaline, and I sucked in air, reaching a steadying hand out to the brick side of the vat.

I quickly glanced around to see if Cromwell had seen Ben catch me. But he was almost at the house ... where my mother stood upon the wraparound veranda, turned in our direction.

My heart, already racing, seemed now to drip acid. I felt ill. I was, at once, a child caught in an act of stupidity by an unforgiving parent.

"I have bricks in the fire to warm the water." Ben's voice snapped my attention back to him.

"Pardon, what?"

"The water. It must be warmer." His face was impassive and stony. Was this the same Ben whose fingers had just gentled across my skin and steadied me as I fell?

I swallowed, embarrassed.

He went to the fire, calling out something to Togo and Sawney who joined him. Poking through the logs with a large set of iron tongs, he withdrew a brick-shaped object covered in ash and glowing embers. Walking quickly to the vat, he climbed up and dropped the stone with a hiss and a plume of steam. Sawney and Togo worked more bricks hidden in the fire free with sticks, and Ben hurried them to the pool.

Ben had carved what he called a "beating paddle." He grabbed it and agitated the water in the vat, pausing occasionally to check the temperature again.

"It's ready," he said at last.

Sawney called out, and bodies emerged from huts and shady corners heading back to the bundles of indigo leaves. As people materialized, Togo began a low singing. Moving to the bundles, they formed a line.

Ben positioned himself at the top of the ladder and Togo mirrored him on the other side.

As bundles came up, one hand to the next to Ben, he'd throw them in and direct Togo to move them here or there with the paddle. Togo nodded as he sang, and before long all of the plant cuttings had disappeared over the edge of the large container.

I took Togo's place, so I could see inside the vat again.

Ben stayed at the top of his ladder facing me. He pushed, prodded, and heaved the paddle to and fro as he made sure all the indigo was lined up, the stalks like sacrifices lying side by side on the battlefield. Long, heavy, bark-stripped branches were passed along the line and fed up to Ben.

He laid their pale lengths crosswise to keep the stalks submerged under the weight.

"Amazing to watch, isn't it?" Cromwell's voice came from beside me.

I glanced down at him, and he indicated the chain of humans. I climbed down, more carefully this time, and slapped my palms together, dusting them off. "It is."

"Ben could command an army of slaves. Neither you nor I have to tell anyone what to do. Ben just gets it done." He shook his head. "Remarkable."

The chances of Ben being manumitted by Cromwell and

becoming a free man were slim, and I was sure every time Ben showed his worth, the chances grew slimmer. I bit down a kernel of despair at the idea and focused on the wonder of my scheme being so close to fruition.

"When do you leave for the ball?" Cromwell asked.

"Tomorrow. I'm grateful the harvest came upon us so suddenly. I would have hated to miss this part." I pursed my lips. "I hate to miss any of it. And despite the lack of extra hands, it seems they managed quite well," I couldn't help adding. "Tell me what is the procedure next?"

Cromwell cleared his throat importantly. "Now it soaks. Anywhere from fourteen hours or more. Depending on the sun tomorrow it could take days. It will be watched and checked constantly for the leaves to give up their 'offering' as Ben calls it."

"Their *gift*," I agreed and gave a small smile. "He called it a gift once."

Cromwell snorted irreverently. "Exactly. We'll then remove the stalks and beat the water to get the air moving through it. Once it turns dark then we add the lime. I'll watch it closely to make sure it's done right."

Togo and Ben worked together to secure a cover across the top of the vat that had been made from stitched-together sackcloth. To keep the heat in, I surmised. I'd seen Sarah do the same.

Finally, it seemed Ben was satisfied. He straightened and climbed down to us.

"They must eat well and rest tonight," Ben said approaching, wiping his hands and his brow on a piece of muslin. "When it begins, the beating is hard work."

Once again I was desperately sad I would be missing it. "I'll have Quash speak with Mary Ann about what we can spare to add to their dinner."

Ben nodded and made his way to the dwellings.

My eyes followed him as he walked over to the rainwater barrel. He stripped off his white shirt, revealing his black skin burnished from sweat.

"His form is certainly formidable," Cromwell commented.

My cheeks burned with fire. And I swallowed, my mouth suddenly dry, and looked away. A glance to Cromwell showed his eyes narrowed on me.

"Certainly," I managed. "You must be pleased to own him."

"Indeed," Cromwell mused, his hand rubbing his chin. "Indeed, I am."

"Well," I smiled, "I must go and see about dinner and begin packing for tomorrow. It was quite an exciting day." With that I realized I was starving, having not eaten since breakfast.

"If it goes well, you should have some drying indigo pigment cakes awaiting your return. We shall leave a sentry posted all night. I believe Ben will want that honor."

"It *will* go well," I said stiffly. "I have no doubt that you'll live up to your reputation. It would be unfortunate not to be able to recommend your expertise."

KING GEORGE II'S BIRTHDAY BALL was a magnificent occasion. Despite my reticence to leave the plantation, I was filled with such wonder at the sparkling elegance of Charles Town society, their wealth on full display, that I couldn't help being glad I'd attended.

Burnished buckles, jewels, and formal military regalia

glittered wherever one looked in celebration of a regent thousands of miles across the sea.

Bettina had turned our lackluster fabric choices, all we'd been able to afford, into exquisite apparitions. Mama was regal in dark green, alternating bolts of silk and velvet that must have been a donation from Mrs. Pinckney, catching the light. And I felt like a confection in dusky rose shot through with gold thread.

Essie had traveled with us and spent the better part of the day curling both my and Mama's hair with hot irons. That was after she'd made sure I kept my farming hands wrapped in oiled muslins for most of the boat journey to soften them back to girl's hands. We'd bathed in orange blossom–scented water and become as primped and primed as any of the Charles Town ladies.

As we left our room, Mama stopped me. "I'm counting on people's short memories of your incident with Mr. Laurens … If ever you are to catch the eye of a future husband, tonight will be the time. You are a vision."

Surprised, I felt overcome with emotion at her kind words, even couched in a reminder of my folly. "Thank you, Mama. You look beautiful also. I wish Papa could see us."

She nodded as if it were her due. "Don't mess up your chances by talking about your indigo," she added then tapped my arm with her fan and proceeded ahead of me to the stairs.

I couldn't think of anything *but* the indigo. If it would succeed. If Ben could succeed. What that might mean for our family. To my father. My thoughts were all braided together and as tightly wound as a grass basket.

Sighing, I followed.

Thirty-One

Mama needn't have worried that my mouth would ward off potential suitors. I never even had the chance to hold back. While I had noticed a few second glances, I feared most of them were out of curiosity. John Laurens, while not always part of the Charles Town society elite, obviously served enough of the families in his merchant capacity for his spurned outrage to have had far-reaching consequences. In fact, I saw him chatting with Mr. Manigault and wondered if John Laurens was, perhaps, borrowing to buy some land of his own, having lost his chance with me. Or at least looking for a deal from someone who couldn't redeem his mortgage. Perhaps he'd get his hands on our property after all. I forced back a shudder of worry.

Andrew Deveaux was a welcome sight, and I approached as soon as Mama had taken her umpteenth trip to the punch table to soothe her headache.

"Miss Lucas." He beamed. "What a delight. Tell me your news."

"It's most gratifying," I told him. "And I must thank you for all your counsel regarding seeds and such in the past."

"Nonsense. I'd hardly say I gave you much direction behind cheering you along."

"Even the little pointers helped. And don't underestimate what your support of my endeavors has done for me."

"In that case, you are welcome."

I quickly and eagerly filled him in on the progress of my indigo and promised him some seeds for next season.

Mother returned and after chatting with Mary Chardon and her mother, we sought out the gracious hostess of our stay in town, Mrs. Pinckney.

Mrs. Pinckney, Mrs. Cleland, Miss Bartlett, and I had occasion to find ourselves alone when Mama finally repaired to the ladies' rest area for respite.

I took the opportunity to thank them.

"Nonsense," said Mrs. Pinckney.

"Thank us for what?" asked Miss Bartlett. At barely seventeen years of age, I still enjoyed her youthful enthusiasm and also her obliviousness to underlying current. Though I rather thought that was less to do with her age and more her design. It was part of what I found so wonderful about her. She was a true friend. There were no hidden meanings behind her words or her actions.

I smiled, not really sure how to explain.

"You'll find," said Mrs. Cleland, addressing me, "that we have nothing to prove. We are both well, and grandly, married. Mr. Pinckney is so very well respected in town, in spite of his shenanigans in court this week, but frankly none could be his equal in understanding of the law. That gives he and Mrs. Pinckney a certain inoculation against petty social grievances. For my part, I simply don't care." She fluttered her hand-painted chinoiserie fan. "I think you are wonderfully smart, Eliza. And a dear, dear girl. Would that we all had been given your opportunity. I am your largest, most vocal supporter," she finished and took a small sip of her punch.

My chest expanded to bursting, and I was quite unable to respond.

"Well said." Mrs. Pinckney smiled. "I'd say *I* am too. But I do believe we both lose that title to *Mr.* Pinckney." She laughed.

At that moment, the man in question was upon us. "My ears are burning and I do believe I heard my name. What is afoot?" He laid a hand fondly upon his wife's shoulder, and I felt a shot of melancholic yearning to know what it felt like to have such a relationship. So trusting. So mutually uplifting. So tender. Or to at least know what it would be like to be the offspring of such a tender union. Even though I knew Papa was tender with my mother, it was clear to me in that moment that my parents did not even come close to the magic that flowed between this man and his wife. The simple physical affection alone was enviable. A brief vision of Ben gently touching my wrist startled me, and I shook it away.

"Oh, do dance with me, Uncle," Miss Bartlett pleaded. "I can't keep up with the cryptic conversation of these ladies."

Charles chuckled. "Come along then. And, Miss Lucas, do you wish for a turn about the floor when I am done?"

My face flared with searing heat.

"Oh, do go on," said Mrs. Pinckney. "Charles does so love to hear about your latest exploits. Take pity on the man."

"All right." I nodded, even though the thought of making a spectacle of myself by dancing with Charles Pinckney caused my stomach to knot upon itself. "I'll wait here."

Miss Bartlett giggled as Mr. Pinckney bowed formally over her hand, and then they were off.

"You are sweet to correspond with my niece." Mrs. Pinckney sighed after them.

"It is a pleasure, I assure you. And I'm sure you know it is as much a way to keep your husband up to date on my endeavors as Miss Bartlett." My eyes flicked to Mrs. Cleland at my admission, but she looked unsurprised.

"We surmised as much," said Mrs. Pinckney, also glancing at Mrs. Cleland, and then smiling gently at me. She squeezed my hand. "Tell me, Eliza, do you keep up much with politics?"

"As much as I hear or that affects my plantation business," I answered with a shrug.

"Then you must have heard of Oglethorpe's tyrannical government at Georgia. And also the late act of Parliament that extends to all America to dissolve our private banks or be liable to lose our estates and put ourselves out of the King's protection."

My blood chilled in my veins. "What d—does that mean?"

"Oh, you won't be losing land, I doubt. You'll have to ask Charles. He was quite forthright before the judges this week. He was held in contempt, and the six of them unanimously fined him twenty shillings!"

"And poor man," said Mrs. Cleland. "To fall off his horse *and* get in trouble with the judges in the same week. Luckily his pride is robust. He's quite right though," she added. "It's ridiculous for some act of Parliament in London to apply to us. We are already underfunded in the war against the Spanish, and now they seek to tell us how we best conduct our affairs?"

My head swung between the two of them. We, the Lucas family, had our money in the private bank. I'd needed the ease of paper money to transact. We had personally become dependent on the paper money system, and our accounts were in good standing, thanks to my pained efforts to keep them so.

"Of course, regardless of his thoughts on the matter, Charles' associates did stop issuing notes upon learning unofficially of the law."

"Are you all right? You look quite pale." Mrs. Pinckney dipped her head toward me.

"She does," added Mrs. Cleland, reaching to squeeze my hand. "Shall we repair to the ladies' resting area?"

"I'm fine. I, uh, I have so much plantation business on my mind. And I do wonder how this will affect us."

At that moment Charles Pinckney returned with Miss Bartlett.

"Thank you, Uncle," Miss Bartlett gushed. "Oh, Auntie, I do believe there are several handsome men here tonight. Who is that, for example?" She pointed across the room. Mrs. Pinckney immediately took her niece's hand and lowered it, causing her to giggle. "Sorry."

We all looked across the room, and I saw Middleton and Drayton talking, their heads bent together. "Well, only John Drayton is still unattached." Mrs. Cleland had raised her monocle on a stem and was peering across the room. "And barely so. A fortnight or so and he will be married to Lieutenant Governor Bull's daughter, Charlotte, of Ashley Hall."

"Oh, drat," breathed Miss Bartlett. "They shall all be married off by the time I'm of age next year."

"I daresay there'll be another crop of young bucks gallivanting about by then," offered Mrs. Pinckney.

Mrs. Cleland clucked. "As long as they are not all sent to their deaths fighting the Spanish under Oglethorpe."

I shuddered and squeezed Miss Bartlett's hand. "I wish all men were as great cowards as myself, it would make them more peaceably inclined." I thought of my papa, and then of dear George already following in his footsteps. "I could moralize for half an hour on the wickedness and folly of war and bloodshed, but I do believe Mr. Pinckney offered me a turn about the room." My mind was still racing at the news about the private banks, my skin feeling at once sweaty with panic.

Charles Pinckney was grinning with amusement at me, and no doubt at my outspoken opinions. He leaned down to give his wife a brief touch to her cheek with his and then stood and held out a hand for me, his head bowed. Again I was struck by how much their public affection for each other affected me.

I dropped into a curtsy before allowing my friend's husband to lead me to the dancing area. My eyes must have looked like the rabbits I surprised sometimes in the early morning, catching them in Togo's vegetable garden.

We paused as the small accompaniment struck up a minuet.

"I see you are fully recovered from your fall off Chickasaw?" I posed the statement as a question.

Mr. Pinckney nodded gravely but with a twinkle in his eye. "Indeed, it was my pride that was most bruised. Blasted horse." He stepped forward and the dance began.

"Please tell me about the private banks," I asked, unable to wait a moment longer. "And how this will affect us."

Charles Pinckney raised his eyebrows.

"Mrs. Pinckney and Mrs. Cleland," I explained.

He chuckled. "I should have known. I did mean to discuss it with you before you heard the news and panicked. Are you all right?"

I bit my lip as I realized it would tremble in my attempt to speak. Swallowing, I shook my head slightly, blinking and pasting a smile on my face as we turned by the edge of the floor and near to watchful eyes.

"I—" I swallowed my words.

"How is your indigo scheme coming along?" Mr. Pinckney asked as he stepped forward again, purposely diverting my mind.

"We just completed the harvest." I tried to keep up with

the intricate steps as I spoke, grateful to speak of indigo while I composed myself. "We transferred the plants to the vats before I left with Mama."

"Will they wait to continue until you return?"

"Unfortunately not. I'm afraid the process apparently requires expediency and vigilance." I grimaced at my disappointment.

"Oh," he sympathized. "After waiting so long to learn the process, I'm sure you were loath to miss out by attending the ball."

"Well." I smiled at him as we crossed paths. "Yours and Mrs. Pinckney's company more than made up for it."

"Somehow, I think that is not entirely true. But I shall wallow in your flattery."

My worries of our earlier conversation must have still been painted on my face, for his smile turned thoughtful as he appraised me. "I'm afraid there will be a devaluation in our currency," he confirmed. "Though I hope it's temporary."

"The rice values have gone down somewhat too," I said. "I'm sorry to unburden myself so. But I … we," I corrected, "are quite precariously balanced at the moment, and I'm not sure we can sustain a devaluation in currency as well as our exports." I blinked again rapidly as my chest tightened and my eyes stung.

Glancing up at Mr. Pinckney, I saw his eyes fixed heavily on mine.

"I would that I could comfort you," he said quietly as we passed each other again.

My heart squeezed painfully. Me too.

"We all need someone to share our burdens," he said. "To verbalize them, at the very least. I'm painfully aware that you have no one at home to whom you can turn."

I nodded. At any moment I could be in over my head and drowning. I needed Father to tell me everything would be all right. I needed someone's embrace. I'd never felt the need so strongly. It quite took my breath away.

"Or tell you all will be well."

My eyes pricked under the weight of worry. For the millionth time, I thanked God our indigo harvest was underway. "Me too."

"How precarious is it? Your situation? If you don't mind my asking."

I shook my head. "Both Wappoo and Waccamaw are heavily mortgaged. And Starrat refuses to send more tradable goods regularly. I believe the Garden Hill estate up on the Combahee is the only one unencumbered at present. And Murry has been most excellent. Thank heavens for him. His boat came daily in the summer months. And we expect the last rice harvest of the year from him in the coming weeks, and I do hope the income from that, despite the lowered price, will see us through until one of these other ventures bears fruit."

"I hope so too," Charles Pinckney said gently.

The dance came to its conclusion, and a quick look saw that my companions must have retired to the ladies' resting area to join up with my mother.

"I'll walk you to them," Mr. Pinckney answered my unspoken question. He offered his elbow and I slipped my gloved hand into the crook of his arm.

His warmth seeped through to my chilled fingers. Fear had taken hold of me again in the wake of admitting the state of our affairs.

"I do have people who comfort me," I said softly. "Though it may not seem proper. And perhaps they are unaware they do it."

"Your slaves," he guessed, his kind eyes burning down to mine.

I breathed out. "Yes. Is it strange I consider them friends

of a sort? I trust them more than I trust almost anyone else. You excepted, of course."

"I hope you know you can always trust me, Eliza."

"I do."

"Let me know how the indigo endeavor goes. I have a man in town who may be able to test the quality. Or I could send some to England to my contact on the stock exchange."

Some of the tension eased from around my chest. "You would do that? I would be most grateful."

"I imagine we could get you an evaluation and perhaps a promise of an order quite quickly. Do you think that might help with the instability you are currently experiencing?"

Relief danced a pirouette through my head, making me dizzy. "Yes," I exclaimed, glancing up at his handsome side profile. "Yes, it would. Thank you so much." The promise of an order would allow Papa to invest in more seed, and after we learned from this harvest, we would be well prepared for next year.

My fingers reflexively squeezed Mr. Pinckney's arm as I said another thank you to God.

He patted my hand. "I said I would help you, Eliza."

Warmth spread through me at his affection. "And you have helped. So much. I'm forever grateful."

I had a plan now. Despite my father's expensive ambition, Starrat's stubbornness, Cromwell's resistance, and a volatile financial world around me, I had a plan.

Ben was on my side, making indigo in spite of Cromwell's stalling.

Charles Pinckney was on my side, giving me an avenue of opportunity upon the success of this indigo venture.

I would put my family back on stable and hopefully lucrative footing. I would see to the success of this indigo crop, wait for our final rice export of the year to pay off and simply hang on. Perhaps, after next year's crop, we could even release the mortgages. George would come to South Carolina still, of course, but it would be *I* who ran the day-to-day business. He was young, after all. Even if he married and another woman became mistress of Wappoo, he would still leave me in charge of business. I was sure of it.

"You know," Mr. Pinckney said. "There are quite a few of us who are rooting for your success with indigo. Not just for you, but for what it might do for our colony."

I swung my face up to look at him.

"Several of you?"

"Some planter families." He pursed his lips. "Some you know, some you don't. The thing is, Eliza, this currency issue, among other things, serves to remind us that our King does not always have South Carolina's best interests at heart. At some point or another, as our fledgling colony flourishes, we may find their governance a hindrance to our progress."

I sucked in a breath. What sedition at the King's own Birthday Ball! The feeling of being out of my depth took over me again. And this time, the water seemed so much deeper. "What are you saying?" I whispered, again pasting a smile upon my face as we moved toward the stairs up to the resting areas. Never in my plans for trying to save our family fortunes and stabilize my own future had I need to worry over affairs of state.

"Just that we will all have to diversify in order to survive as a colony ... as you know rice will continue to devalue ... and to build wealth, we will have need of other crops. Silk perhaps ..." He raised an eyebrow.

"Or indigo," I murmured.

"Or indigo," Charles agreed.

I couldn't wait to return and see the fruits of our labor. So very much depended on it.

Thirty-Two

We didn't have to wait long to return to Wappoo from Charles Town. Upon waking the next morning, Mama believed she was feeling one of her episodes coming on. The sky looked ominous too, so we decided to get ahead of the weather and take the boat home.

The talk on the docks was of a wild storm out at sea that could be heading this way. The water was choppy and gray to match the slate sky. We were bundled tightly in wool and fur against the wind.

Mama gripped my hand the six miles by boat, and I fought to keep the contents of my stomach settled by staring out as far as my eyes could see. But nothing could dim my excitement. I'd even worn a small piece of yellow ribbon Father had sent me in my hair as an outward expression of my joy. It was incongruous against the wild gray day, I was sure.

This morning I had awoken with a sense of purpose unlike anything I'd ever experienced. My success would be for far more than just the Lucas family.

What had Plutarch said? Empire may be gained by gold, not gold by empire.

Indigo was my gold and my silver. The empire was more than the Lucas family. It could be South Carolina.

If Cromwell was correct in his estimation, I could have indigo dye cakes awaiting me upon my return. Though we were coming home earlier than expected, I still hoped that was the case. Although if the sun didn't shine for many days, I supposed the dye cakes wouldn't fully dry for a while.

As soon as they were ready, and as soon as the storm had passed through, I would immediately send Togo with some of them back to Charles Town. I'd also send some to Father! The excitement brewed to a bubbling mess in my belly.

I had managed it in the nick of time too. The heavens must have been smiling upon me to bring me Ben and this harvest at a time when things had gotten so precarious in the economy around us. I sent a grateful prayer up while I thought of it.

"What has gotten into you?" Mama snapped, and I realized I was smiling into the wind. Thoughts of family fortunes restored and my father's proud approval couldn't be contained, they had manifested into a physical giddiness. Not to mention how my success would help the colony. And Mr. Pinckney would be so impressed when he saw I had succeeded.

"Well?" Mama continued. "I'd think after your utter lack of effort in attracting a suitor last night, you'd be a little more shamefaced today."

"No one is interested in me, Mama," I offered, exhausted by this recurring topic.

"If that insipid Mary Chardon could find herself a husband, even if he did up and die, surely you could have at least tried."

"Mama," I exclaimed, shocked. "How can you visit with her and her mama every Tuesday, taking of their hospitality, and speak of her so poorly? And she's my friend!"

"I'm not saying anything untrue. And to look at her or

converse ... well, she's as dull as dishwater. Honestly, Eliza. It's like a slap in the face to me and your father for you to behave thus."

"Behave like what?"

"The way you carry on consorting with the slaves. Treating them as equals. There are rumors, you know. I heard them more than once last night. People whispering and whatnot. What should have been a glorious affair was utterly ruined by your past conduct."

My eyes and nose burned in muted frustration.

"Why can't you be proud of me and what I am trying to accomplish? I don't know how to be any other way. I wouldn't be doing a true service to myself to pretend to be some stultified society miss. I'd never pull it off, anyway." My voice wobbled. "Can't you just love me for the girl I am, Mother?"

No matter how much I disagreed with what she thought best for me, I couldn't help but feel the rejection of a child by her own mother. "Father manages just fine," I added.

Mama sighed heavily. "It's got nothing to do with love, Eliza."

"I'm sorry you feel that my gift for botany and my determination to help this family succeed is a curse. Or that being a decent human being is bad conduct. I'll not change for you or anyone. Besides, once we get home and see the first indigo crop, you'll understand. Papa will be so proud of me. I'll have no immediate need of a husband."

"Eliza, darling. You are a smart girl. Too intelligent for your own good, I'd say. You are living in a dream world. Do your best for your father, of course. Do your best for our family. But if you do not have a husband"—she paused and leveled me with her gaze—"you will have nothing."

"That's not true, I—"

"It *is* true. What did you honestly think? That you would run your father's holdings so well that he would simply turn them over to you?" She barked out a shrill laugh. "Besides, they are mortgaged to the hilt."

My head felt light. I hated quarreling with Mother. And the longer it went on the smaller and more insignificant I felt. "It won't matter," I got out breathily. "Next year, with the indigo we'll be able to unencumber the properties—"

"That damned indigo will not save us!" Mama shrieked, spittle flying from her mouth.

I started, my heart lurching.

"And you are not allowed to own land, Eliza. You are a woman."

Overcome by her outburst, I couldn't respond.

She fixed her eyes upon me. The color so like my own, the whites, though, slightly yellowing. "You will *never* be allowed to own land. *Ever*."

I swallowed. "I know, Mama. But I—"

"Do you? Do you really know, Eliza? If you want land you will need to *marry* someone who has some. This ridiculousness will stop. Immediately."

Why was she being so obtuse? "Papa believes in me, he even sent a consultant! Why would he do that if he didn't believe in what we are doing?"

"He's humoring you. And he feels guilty for leading you to believe you can be more than you are."

I shook my head. There was no way Papa would do something so underhanded. He was honest to a fault. He would tell me if he wanted me to stop.

She smiled sadly. "It's true, I'm afraid."

"You are lying. Father will always let me work upon his land. He needs me. George will need my expertise. Especially after this crop. And if I am successful perhaps I will be able to choose my own husband," I added to appease her tired quest to marry me off.

Mama cackled and shook her head. "There will be no land for you to work upon long before you finally realize you need a husband. Regardless, it doesn't matter. We're heading back to the islands."

"We're not. Where did you get such a notion? Besides, it's dangerous to return there now with the Spanish aggression."

"More dangerous than here with the threat of slave uprisings hanging over us? And the Spanish are just as much of a threat here as they are there. At least in Antigua we'll be with your father."

"He'll never agree." I swallowed heavily and took a fortifying breath of cold, wet wind.

"He will when you don't succeed and the property at Garden Hill has to be mortgaged too. Then what?" She smiled in satisfaction as if she had won the argument.

I said nothing. I *would* succeed. Had already succeeded. And Garden Hill wasn't in danger yet. The last rice export was still expected and that would see the plantation through until next year.

WHEN WE APPROACHED THE LANDING AT WAPPOO, however, I saw Quash waiting and Togo pacing agitatedly back and forth. Lil' Gulla must have been posted as sentry to look out for us. My bilious stomach fraught with seasickness, emotional upset, and nerves seemed to crunch in upon itself like a tight ball of twine at seeing the men agitated and not joyful.

The boat bumped our small plantation dock and dark hands deftly moved to moor it. The wind had strengthened, and the normally calm creek was whipped into a frothy soup. If we'd waited even mere moments longer to leave Charles Town after the ball, we never would have made it.

I took Quash's outstretched hand, bracing against the deck from the lurching craft, and then turned to help Mama. We were damp and bedraggled from the mist-soaked wind, our cheeks ruddy with cold. My ears stung.

"Essie, please go on with Mama," I said hurriedly before turning to the grim-faced men who'd been awaiting my return. "Well, what is it?" I gritted my teeth. "The indigo? Quick, let's go up to the warmth of the house," I added before I could read confirmation on Quash's face.

Our world got darker as the storm rolled closer.

Quash's brow was furrowed then he shook his head against going up to the house. "Go on, Togo. You tell the mistress."

Togo looked to me and then at Mama.

Mama, after a brief hesitation and a nervous glance at the weather, turned and hurried away, dragging her soaked voluminous skirts through the wet grass.

"Cromwell and Ben, they was fighting," Togo said, raising his voice, clutching the "nail bone" he wore from the leather at his neck he used to weave tight threads of sweetgrass.

Quash nodded. "He think it be about the indigo."

"Where's Cromwell?" I frowned.

"In da house." Quash pointed.

I nodded at both Togo and Quash, thanking them for letting me know. "Now go on and get warm and dry. Take shelter. I don't want anyone outside working in this weather, you hear."

"Yes'm."

I pulled my shawl tighter around me, squinting as the first thick drops of rain began to fall and then ran up to the house to avoid getting soaked. Essie clucked at me as I came inside, the door banging shut behind me.

Voices came from my right. A fire roared in the study grate. Mama was already standing at the hearth warming her hands. Cromwell sat in a wing chair. They fell silent as I entered.

Cromwell didn't meet my eye nor greet me, and my stomach tumbled with dread.

"We have to get out of these damp dresses," Mama said, grabbing my attention. "Mary Ann is laying things out for us upstairs. Though I believe I'll repair to bed. My head is entirely too troublesome. Will you send up a plate for supper, dear?"

"Of course," I responded. The air was oppressive, and it wasn't from my heavy, damp, wool traveling dress. It was from words unsaid. I'd interrupted their exchange.

She turned and nodded at Cromwell who returned the gesture.

I took her place at the fire. "Well?" I said impatiently. "What happened?"

"Everything went according to plan."

"What did you do?" I turned and faced him. My body shuddered with a chill, and I told myself it was my iced skin raising gooseflesh as it met the heat from the fireplace. I fixed my gaze upon him.

He frowned. "What do you mean?"

I waited.

His face betrayed nothing, but he laid his hand on the chair arm and took a step toward me.

I moved away as he approached.

He smirked. "How did you know?"

The confirmation that something was amiss was a blow to my stomach.

"Sweet, little Eliza." He reached out and took a strand of hair that had been plastered to my cheek. His forwardness was so unexpected I was unable to react, frozen with disbelief.

"So trusting. So ... naïve. So innocent." His eyes dropped to my mouth, and his fingers drew around my jaw.

The shock of his touch finally registered and broke through my haze. I swung my hand up, smacking his away from my face. "What is the meaning of this?"

I swiveled my head to the door. It was closed. Mama had closed it behind her. My mouth dropped open in surprise. It occurred to me it was her second attempt to leave me alone with Cromwell. As horrible a thought as that was, the most pressing one was the state of the indigo.

"What did you do to the indigo?" Whatever it was he would tell me, and we would fix it. If he'd taken it or sold it, I'd make him get it back. I set my jaw. "Tell me. This instant. Where is it?"

Thirty-Three

Cromwell's eyes widened, and he shrugged. "The indigo is here of course. Where else?"

I breathed out, confused, ignoring his proximity. "It's here? So you didn't take it and sell it?"

Now Cromwell looked confused. "Where on earth would you get such an idea? There's nothing to sell. The solution was too diluted, the indigo never separated from the water." He shook his head.

"What do you mean 'diluted'?"

He cocked his head. "Apologies, the way you asked, I assumed you knew. Such a shame. After we worked so hard. It was quite ruined, I'm afraid."

I gasped.

Cromwell went on, but I could barely hear him as my ears seemed to have a roaring ocean pressing in from all sides. My vision was dark and inky. Needing support, I reached out to hold the mantel.

"I've been trying to get to the bottom of what happened," he finished.

"Ruined?" Forming words was a struggle. "How?"

"Well, it's a mystery, isn't it? It's such a delicate process. If one's not paying attention it could be turned too soon, too late, so many things can go wrong. Perhaps Ben got distracted with that striking Negress, Sarah."

He shrugged again while my heart squeezed painfully. I ignored the bolt of alarm at the thought of Ben being anywhere near that conniving viper Sarah. Even though she was recovering, and seemed more docile, I had yet to figure out what to do with her.

I kept looking for a sign that Cromwell was lying to me. The dishonesty purled off him in waves. My chest tightened and breathing became difficult. If what he said was true, the financial ramifications were too much to think about. This venture had to work. It had to. I had to prove I could do this. And if he was lying …

I closed my eyes, praying for strength.

Why would he lie? How could it be ruined? I wobbled where I stood.

"Here," Cromwell said silkily, and his hand was around my waist leading me to the couch.

I jerked away. "Unhand me. How could this have happened?"

"There is nothing to say." He lifted his hands, palms up. "The plants were inferior. The batch was poor quality."

"You said that last time. This time I know the plants were good. They were harvested correctly. Ben said they were perfect."

Cromwell snorted. *"Ben said they were perfect,"* he mimicked with a snarl. "You do spend an inordinate amount of time with him, don't you?" His face grew flushed. "I am the indigo maker, not that black-skinned son of a bitch. *Me.* Do you hear?"

"Perfectly." I walked to the door and wrenched it open. "Essie," I called and startled as she materialized, obviously hovering close by. "Essie, please send someone to get Ben. I need to see him immediately."

She nodded and scurried back into the shadows. I needed answers, and I wanted both my indigo makers present. I was astonished to find myself on the verge of tears, frustrated anger and worry clearly having no other outlet. I turned back to the room.

"What are you doing sending for him? Are you saying you don't believe me?" Cromwell snapped, his tone indignant. "How dare you insult me so."

The lamps did not give much light against the darkness outside. Despite it being afternoon, it felt like dusk, so heavy were the clouds. The quiet roar of gusting wind rumbled the windows. *We should have put up the hurricane planks*, I thought absently as my mind spun as fast as a water spout.

I sank into a corner of the love seat and tried to modulate my voice. "Pray tell me. We have followed all the directions to the letter." My voice was pleading. "We've done everything you said." My voice hardened. "Despite your deliberate attempts to thwart my progress."

"I don't have to listen to this. Your mother was right. The sooner you are done with this ridiculous essay, the better. You have become far too ambitious. It's a rather unflattering quality, I'm afraid. Though, with effort, I may be able to overlook it."

"My mother?" I was outraged. "You will keep her and her opinions out of this." The rest of his words registered. "Overlook it. What are you talking about?"

"She's of the opinion you should all return to the islands." He sat and settled his frame against me, his hand closing over my wrist.

I balked at the close contact. Wedged in and unable to move, alarm raced through me. I arched away as best I could, pulling my wrist back without success.

"I've been wanting to talk to you about something. A proposition, if you will."

A knock sounded on the doorframe. Cromwell slid away, breaking his constraint of me.

I took the opportunity to leap to my feet and swing around to the open door.

Essie, soaked through, bobbed a quick curtsy. Her gaze was fixed to mine. Any guilt I'd normally feel about sending anyone out into a torrential downpour was absent. Thank God they were here.

Ben stepped into the room, rivulets of rain running down his face and off his chin, his clothes dripping upon the floor. I searched his expression, hoping for something to comfort me, but it was blank, his gaze averted to the fireplace.

I was living a nightmare. No one was acting as they should. "Ben?" I whispered, and my voice shook.

Essie hovered by the door, and I was grateful to have her near me.

"Tell me about the indigo," I begged him. "Is it ruined?"

Ben glanced at Cromwell, then his eyes finally met mine. "Yes."

A small cry escaped my throat, and when I felt the slide of moisture on my cheeks I knew my body had given up trying to contain my anguish. "How?"

"Too much lime was added to the solution." His voice was quiet and sad.

Cromwell tutted. "Now then—"

"Too much lime? I don't understand." I glanced between them. Cromwell glared at Ben. "But Cromwell said it was because the crop was inferior quality," I told him.

"Well," interjected Cromwell. "What I meant to say was if the crop was good, the lime wouldn't have been too much. But as it was, it can have a rather diluting effect. No way to know until it's too late."

Ben dropped his gaze, and I knew Cromwell was lying.

"But it seems to me, an expert would know that," I said. "So which of you deliberately ruined my indigo?"

I DREW THE CURTAINS together to somewhat drown out the dismal scene outside the window of the study and allow myself a moment to regroup. Then looking back and forth between Ben and Cromwell, my two supposed expert indigo dye makers, I tried to make sense of what could possibly have caused either of them to deliberately sabotage my efforts.

Who had done it? And what motive could either of them have had?

Togo said he saw them arguing. The only way I could reconcile that information was to assume that Ben must have been trying to stop Cromwell.

Ben shifted uncomfortably, no doubt waiting for Cromwell to say something. Why hadn't Ben tried harder to save my indigo? I knew why. Just arguing with Cromwell could have been cause for whipping, or worse. I didn't blame him. But I did blame him. *I did.* He had said he would make it all right. He'd promised me.

So, in the end I focused my attention on Cromwell. "Well?" I asked him.

"As I said, I've been trying to get to the bottom of what happened." Cromwell cleared his throat.

I took a deep breath and pressed a fingertip to each of my temples in an attempt to bring myself down to a more peaceable temperament. Because now that the shock was wearing off, I had outrage pulsing through my veins. "Of which would you rather be accused? Deliberately misleading me and sabotaging my attempt? Or that you are not the expert you purport yourself to be? It is rather an explicit mistake for one who claims such expertise."

Cromwell's face blotched red. "How dare you speak to me in such a manner? You deserve a thrashing. If you were my wife—"

A sharp bark of laughter erupted from my throat. "Your wife?"

Cromwell's mouth snapped closed. Then he seemed to change tack. "But no matter, I wonder whose hand was the one to perform the ruinous deed?" He raised his eyebrows.

Energy was radiating off Ben, and I turned to him. He flinched as our eyes made contact.

"Why don't you ask Ben what happened? It was his mistake," Cromwell purred.

My heart thundered in my ears. My wet dress had kept my body from fully absorbing the heat of the room, and I was chilled through to my bones. But this coldness had nothing to do with temperature.

Not Ben. Surely not. Ben and I, we were beyond such petty connivances. Ben had said he would help me. That he would make it succeed. What mistake could he have made?

I realized Ben and I were staring at each other. His eyes were connected to mine in a way I couldn't break away from, and I didn't care that we had an audience. My success would have been Ben's success. My failure was his failure. Of that I was sure. He might say whatever he needed to in front of Cromwell, but I'd know the truth from his eyes.

Our friendship was the friendship of two connected souls who'd met in the shade of trees on a sugar plantation when our hearts were pure.

"Ben," I pleaded, stepping even closer to him, desperate to discern any hint of dishonesty that would tell me he was lying to protect his master.

Ben's eyes flickered.

I pressed on. "Was it your doing?"

"Yes," he answered without hesitation.

Of course it was what he'd say.

Essie had a hand over her mouth as if she believed him.

"Try again."

"Yes. It was me," he said. His voice was hard.

"I need to speak with Ben alone," I said to the room.

Cromwell tutted. "Come now, I don't see what difference that will make. The surly bastard just admitted it."

I lurched forward and grabbed Ben's arm, marching him toward the door of the study. I burst through into the hall slamming the door closed behind me. Ben was maddeningly silent, allowing me to manhandle him. There was no way my diminutive frame would have been any match for him if he had resisted.

There was even less privacy out here if my mother was listening, so I yanked open the front door. It flew back on its hinges, and I dragged Ben with me out into the wild blustering wind. Wind that instantly grabbed the breath from my lungs and pulled my hair loose from its bindings.

"Please," I managed. "I just need to know if you had anything to do with it. I know you will say anything in front of him." My words shuddered out as my body was wracked with spasms from the cold. "Just tell me you tried to help me. Please. My heart is aching with the thought you did this to me. I know it can't be true. Just tell me the truth, just for me to know, and I'll deal with Cromwell."

Trying to keep myself together, I breathed heavy and fast. The rain drove sideways under the veranda roof, slapping against us.

"On the soul of your grandmother," I pressed. "I need you to answer me honestly."

Ben's dark chocolate eyes were fastened on mine, and I saw anguish there.

I shook my head. "Oh God, please. Tell me you didn't betray me also."

"I—" He swallowed. "I want to be free."

A sob escaped my throat from the depths of my chest. "So you sabotaged me for a promise of freedom?"

Ben didn't answer. His arms hung limply at his sides.

"How many times has he made that promise? Answer me? How many times?"

His stony silence enraged me.

"He will never free you!" I screamed in his face. "He needs you. He is nothing without you. You called me a coward once, but the only coward I know is the one I'm looking at right now."

"I ..." Ben spoke through gritted teeth as if he was in pain. As if he was physically swallowing words he should say. His gaze dropped from my eyes to my mouth. His face inches from mine. "I *need* to be free," he said.

"Me too," I choked out and saw my anguish reflected back to me in his eyes. "You were closer to freedom than I ever was. I want to be free too. And you ..." My tears were hot knives against my icy wet cheeks. "You, Benoit Fortuné, just took *my* chance of freedom away from me."

Thirty-Four

I couldn't face Cromwell when I went back inside. I called for Mary Ann to place warming bricks in my bed and sent Essie to change into dry clothes. I changed out of my heavy soaked dress myself, and when Essie returned I had her help me dry my hair. It took hours for the shaking in my body to subside, and I didn't know whether it was from cold or emotional shock. Essie gave me a draught of herbs to ward off the chill she expected me to catch and brought me a small sprinkling of sugar and told me to let it melt on my tongue.

I wrote in my copy book as soon as my hands were steady and composed a letter to Father to update him. I spoke of the magnificent ball, and I decided at the last minute not to let him know about the indigo. I would, in time, but for now, until I was sure he wouldn't reflexively mortgage Garden Hill, I told him the indigo wasn't quite dry. A half truth at least.

My sleep was dead and dark. There were no dreams to lose myself in. And when I awoke to the bleak landscape, the failed indigo endeavor was a weight upon my chest.

"Miss 'Liza?" Essie's soft voice came from the door.

I turned my head in the bed.

"Come, chil'. Essie hep you rise."

"Thank you, Essie." My heart squeezed. I wanted to ask her to hug me. I wanted to crawl onto her lap, like I had when I was a child.

"That storm be ragin'. An' there be more comin'."

She shook her head and clucked, breath huffing in and out. "You got challenges comin'. It's gone take a fireball from the sky afore things to be gettin' better."

"That's ominous, Essie." I scowled. "I feel hopeless enough without relying on heavenly portents." Hopeless was an understatement. I was devastated by the loss of the indigo. It was almost too big a loss with so many repercussions that I thought I might prefer to stay in bed than have to face a day where my dream was over. An urge that was entirely unfamiliar to me and so frightening that I made myself get up immediately.

I dressed, still feeling the chill in my bones. "Let's get all the fires going today. This house is freezing." A thought occurred to me. "How are the dwellings? Are they holding up in this weather?"

"Yes'm. Quash done make good fixin' 'em up when you tol' him. They's be warm and dry."

"Oh, good."

SOMETHING ABOUT CROMWELL'S WORDING the day before was bothering me too. I'd have to speak to him again today and get to the bottom of his motive. There was no doubt in my mind that he'd been the instigator behind the sabotage. And that I'd been unfair to Ben expecting him to choose my indigo over his freedom. But I'd been right in pointing out to Ben that his freedom from Cromwell was a mirage. My heart ached when I thought about how my harsh truth must have cut him.

I found Cromwell in the breakfast room. His pompous air made me want to hurl the silver candlestick at his forehead.

He stood as I entered. "Good morning."

"Is it?" I asked.

"Perhaps it will be better after we talk. We never did get to discuss my proposition."

I selected some warm chamomile tea and honey and a piece of corn bread. "Why would I entertain any ideas you had? I think you've done enough, don't you?"

He sat as I did. "Well, yes, I can see how you'd think that. Perhaps I should first apologize for the manner in which I went about it. It's only ... I thought that if you had no success here you'd be more amenable to my suit."

I gaped at him, my breakfast forgotten. Then I laughed. Because, what else was I to do? Here a man sat before me, telling me he'd deliberately ruined my dream in order to sway me for my hand. It was nonsensical! What was it with men and their ridiculous notions that I would be only too ecstatic to have someone relieve me of the burden of being alone? Besides, he couldn't be serious. He didn't even like me. Wasn't I too ambitious for starters?

Cromwell appeared nonplussed at my amused outburst, his face flushing.

"Oh," I sobered. Then my hysterical panic at the reality of what he'd admitted became too much, and I laughed again, but with tears in my eyes. I was mad with it. I laughed until the tears came hot and fast down my face. "You thought—" I choked. "You thought if I didn't succeed I would marry you?"

Cromwell's face was enraged. I'd seen a humiliated man's face before.

"Why, for God's sake?" Why would that make me marry

him? What on earth did he have that I would want? What did *I* have that *he* would want? How could he ever think I'd marry a man who'd forced my best friend to drown the one thing most important to me? I swallowed, my laughter dying on a hiccup as I remembered my mother's comment about going back to the islands.

My conversation with her on the way back from the ball suddenly took on a new and hideous gravity. I grew light-headed and held the table for support. "Did my mother promise you a wife in exchange for a failure so we could return to the islands?"

"You were just a bonus," Cromwell said.

So it was true? My mother had sold us out for the chance to wed me to this … this …

Iciness swept across my neck as I prickled with sweat. I added my mother's betrayal to the bag of stones that was tied around my neck and pulling me under.

I struggled to breathe in and out.

He shrugged. "Something to show for my time here. The daughter of the soon-to-be governor of Antigua. A bonus that, on second thought, seeing your disdain for me, I'd rather not have to endure."

A relief for both of us.

The thought of this supercilious and cruel man sharing the rest of my life, touching my person and forcing me to bear his progeny and bend to his will, made the one bite of corn bread I'd eaten feel like a handful of crushed oyster shells. "So if I was the bonus, what was the real prize?"

"For a girl doing her best to play the part of a plantation owner, you are rather naïve, aren't you? I'd thought you smarter." His insult and condescending manner, which I was so used to, rolled right off me. He was attempting to recover his pride. As men often did.

"Where am I from?" he asked patiently, and I wanted to smack the smug smile from his face.

"Montserrat," I answered woodenly, though I knew of course what he was about to say.

"Which, as you know, is a French colony. Why on earth would you think I'd deliberately set you up as competition against French indigo? Do you know how much my brother is paid for our indigo? Of course you do, that's why I'm here."

"You are right." I made a show of resuming my breakfast, spreading a dollop of honey on my bread, though I had no stomach for it. "I *was* naïve. But only because I'd considered you more mercenary than patriotic. Of course I knew you and your brother sold to the French. *You* are naïve if you thought otherwise. It's a shame though. Now you have ruined relationships with the governor of Antigua *and* your indigo-making reputation. I'll make sure of it."

"Who would take the word of a petulant little girl playing above her station over the brother of one of the most preeminent indigo makers in Montserrat? There are plenty of men in town I've sat across from in cards who would gladly take me and my expertise in indigo rather than listen to a girl who has already made herself unwelcome. I may have a damaged reputation from gambling, but so do you. And *your* misdemeanors are far more egregious. I'm still a gentleman who'll be given an ear. You will be nothing but a footnote."

My ears and cheeks burned. "Well, I'm glad we cleared up the fact you were mistaken in wanting to marry me."

I realized the other reason I hadn't told Papa of the indigo affair was that I was sure he would demand we send Cromwell back. By sending Cromwell back, his reputation in tatters, I was sentencing Ben as well. And sending Ben away. Away from me. If only I could afford to buy him out of bondage. But we had nothing until we sold the last rice from Garden

Hill. And truly what price would a man with Ben's knowledge fetch? He was priceless. And sending him away now, when I'd never see him again, would hurt worse than the knowledge he'd been an accomplice in ruining my indigo.

My threats to Cromwell were empty.

Ben was Cromwell's only asset. Even if I wanted to, I doubted I would be able to persuade Cromwell to let Ben go. So Cromwell would have to stay here. I wished I could have him take over Waccamaw from Starrat. But what would replacing one devil with another accomplish?

Cromwell laid down his fork and narrowed his eyes. "Are you ... in a relationship with Ben? My Negro?"

I stood abruptly. "Don't you dare—"

"Or Quash, perhaps? After all, you have had several opportunities ... *alone* with them." He tutted, shaking his head side to side. "Oh, you think I don't notice? It's been quite fascinating to hear about your reputation in town, and then be able to see it for myself. What is it you *discuss* with Quash in the study every other morning?"

I laid down my napkin. "You have been paid for your expertise and been a guest in our home, and you have just outstayed your welcome."

Essie came back into the dining room, Togo trailing behind her. "Miz Lucas. Togo say he need to speak wit ya."

Togo's face was grave. "Ben. He done gone."

Thirty-Five

Ben was gone. His cabin was empty. I stood in the doorway to see for myself. There was nothing to suggest he'd even been here except for the smell of clove I often associated with him.

Wet wool clung to my body, having run across the property in the rain again. My feet scuffed the dusty plank floors. For a moment, I wondered if it had all been a dream—Ben being here, getting to know him again. This time as an adult. Ben with his pride, his broad shoulders, his stoic expression no longer full of the mischief of youth.

A twig snapped behind me, and I turned my head. Quash. Whatever he saw in my face had him pursing his lips. He looked past me.

"He's gone," I whispered. "It's my fault. I blamed him for everything. When it was Cromwell who manipulated the whole thing." *And my mother*, I didn't add. I backed out of the doorway, leaving Quash to go inside. The rain stopped.

I walked to the indigo sheds Quash had constructed with open walls to allow air and stacked shelving. Stepping inside the dim interior, I saw the empty trays that were supposed to be filled with drying indigo paste. My heart squeezed anew to have been so close to success.

I could blame whomever I wanted, but I should never

have left for the ball. I'd gone for Mother's sake and look at how she repaid me.

My own mother had set me up to fail. Not just me, but *all* her children. She'd destroyed George's legacy too. I thought maybe she was going mad. Maybe her symptoms all these years were the beginning of an irrational madness.

There was no one whom I could trust anymore, and no one to blame but myself.

I DIDN'T KNOW IF IT HAD REALLY SUNK IN that Ben ran away. But it was clear by the next day he wasn't coming back.

I hadn't spoken one word to Mother since finding out what she'd done. She had walked into my study after the disastrous breakfast with Cromwell where he'd admitted his intent, and I had promptly walked out, leaving her openmouthed. I took breakfast in my room and lunch and dinner in the study. I had also taken to locking the door, turning the large iron key in the lock, relieved when it actually worked and wasn't just for looks.

Mother had tried to talk to me through the door, telling me I was being stubborn, or childish, or shortsighted. But not once had she apologized. I decided I'd need to tell Father the truth of what happened after all, before Mama made up a story to suit herself. Besides, now that Ben was gone, I needed to send Cromwell far away from here. I couldn't tell Father about Mama's involvement though. No good would come of causing such strife between a man and his wife, no matter how much I yearned to unburden myself fully.

I drew out a fresh piece of parchment and filled the small inkwell from a stoppered bottle. Charles would be waiting for the good news regarding the indigo. I had to disappoint him too.

Polly ran past the open study door. I'd been neglecting her studies altogether recently, and even today I had no heart for them.

"Polly," I called. "Where are you off to?"

She came to a stop, out of breath. "Lil' Gulla's teaching me about horses."

She and Gulla were the same age, and I immediately thought of Ben and I. My eyes stung. I blinked. What was the point of her building a friendship only to have it bastardized by societal mores as she grew up?

"I don't think that's a good idea." I frowned and rubbed my temples.

"But you've been wanting me to be better at riding. I don't understand." Her sweet face took on a frown of its own. "Anyway, now that the big scary horse is gone, it's not so bad. Gulla says the other horses are calmer."

"What do you mean the big horse is gone?" A thought occurred to me. "A horse is missing and Indian Peter hasn't come to tell me?"

Polly's cheeks bloomed crimson, and I knew right away she'd been supposed to keep a secret.

"Sister, I—"

My heart hammered and my stomach fell. As much at the idea that Ben might have stolen a horse and my own slaves had hidden it from me, as at yet another financial blow. "It's all right, Polly. You did the right thing now." I motioned her inside the room. "You should have told me right away. I'll send for Quash."

"Please don't let them know I told you," she pleaded. "Please?"

"Polly, I—"

Her lip trembled. Her blue eyes were wide.

"I'm sorry. But you understand that you can't keep secrets about stolen horses or anything that could affect the plantation. Or keep secrets at all. Secrets can get you into trouble." I came around the desk and walked to her, my arms out. "Come here."

Enveloping her in my arms, I soothed the crown of her soft hair, and she shuddered into tears.

"I got everyone in trouble." Polly was taller than I ever was at her age. Her voice was muffled into my shoulder.

"Polly, love. Ben is a runaway slave on a stolen horse. It's better that I know, so that if he gets caught, I can rescue him from being whipped."

"Or murdered and beheaded," Polly wailed. "Just like those runaways from the Stono Rebellion."

My blood turned to ice. What had I been thinking? I needed to send someone after him before he got caught.

"Are you going to whip Lil' Gulla?" Polly sniffed, turning her tear-streaked face up to mine. "You can't. Please say you won't. Gulla said if I told you, you would whip him 'til he bled."

I swallowed and held her out at arm's length. "Polly, you know that's not how we do things here. He came from another plantation."

"But it was our plantation. He said so."

"Well, it won't happen to Gulla, all right? How about you go find Quash for me, and I'll have him inquire about the horse to Indian Peter. That way you won't be in trouble with your friend."

Polly wiped her nose and eyes with the back of her hand. "You'd do that? You are the best sister. The very, very best."

"Good and trustworthy friends are worth keeping, I say." I pulled out my muslin cloth to wipe her tears. "Maybe one day, he'll do you a good turn. But, Polly, I want you to go and find Quash right away, you hear?"

"Yes, Sister." She pulled away and headed outside to find Quash.

I returned to my desk and finished off the letters to both my father and to Charles. I'd send Togo to town with them as soon as possible.

A knock sounded on the doorframe, and Quash entered as I looked up, pulling his field cap from his head.

Quash's eyes were troubled. He'd lost a friend too.

"There be a horse gone too," Quash said before I could open my mouth.

"Did Peter know?"

"Indian Peter, he knows. He told Ben about St. Augustine."

"About the rumor the Spanish will give freedom to those who can get there?"

"Yes'm."

"Do you think it's true? They are allowing slaves to live free?"

"No, Miz Lucas. Not to them with no skill. The others, they be good soldiers. Men who know the land."

"Ben has a skill."

"Yes," Quash agreed. "If he's taken a horse, then he will go by land. He know about Garden Hill. I think he go there for shelter and food before going on."

"Why are you telling me this?"

Quash was quiet.

I knew what he was telling me, he could go after him. Was willing to.

I was torn. If Ben wanted to be free, who was I to stop him? I was also worried. Worried for his safety. Who would listen to him if he were to be stopped on the way to St. Augustine?

He would simply be reenslaved and sold or arrested for being a runaway. There just weren't any Negro men riding around on horses on their own without a letter or something proving they were on an errand for their owner.

Oh, Ben! What are you doing?

"Thank you, Quash. Come and see me before first light tomorrow. I need to think."

He backed out the door. Quash was willing to go after Ben, and I was the one stalling. What would Cromwell do to Ben if we fetched him back? And would Ben ever forgive me for thwarting his attempt at freedom?

I thought about nothing else all afternoon and evening. Every minute I agonized over the decision Ben was getting closer to freedom or danger.

My dreams that night were vivid and frightening.

Dreams of marrying John Laurens and his sweaty, large body upon mine on our wedding night. Dreams of his son, Henry, laughing somewhere nearby. I glanced around for Mr. Pinckney. Charles. He would understand. Surely he would stop the farce. Then I was dancing at a ball, the ceiling miles above me. Candlelight and glittering crystals. *It's all thanks to you,* whispered Charles in my ear. *Everyone wears blue silk. All the indigo is thanks to you.*

But look, I said, they are wearing nothing but rags. I failed!

I turned back and saw only Ben standing before me in the middle of a road. The glittering ballroom was no more. The earth was dusty and red. Ben wore sackcloth pants and no shirt. Gone were his fancy breeches and buckled shoes. There was no charm around his neck.

His body streamed with water. Rivulets and droplets glistened on his dark skin and sparkled upon his coarse, nubby, close-cropped hair. His eyes stared, but there was no life in them. They were dark, pitch lagoons with monsters lurking beneath. The earth around him turned to mud as the water flowed down his body.

I had to get to him. I stepped forward but my feet were unable to move. My heart kept going and lurched toward him, wrenching against whatever part of my body held it tied in my chest.

I woke on a gasp, my chest tight and painful.

I held a man's life in my hands. I couldn't waste another moment.

I STOOD AT THE STUDY WINDOW, the night still dark outside, the land washed clean from the nonstop rain. The cold draft slipping in through the seams of the house made me pull my shawl tighter around me. I could light a fire, I thought, and quickly dismissed the effort. Instead I waited.

"Miz Lucas?" I startled as I heard Quash.

I wasted no time. "Are you sure you know where Ben went? Are you sure you can catch up to him?"

Quash nodded.

"All right then." I handed him a letter with the Lucas seal. "In case you get stopped. You are on plantation business. You are to go toward Garden Hill on horseback. I'm assuming he is only traveling at night to avoid being stopped, so perhaps you will be able to catch up to him."

I stepped up to Quash and squeezed his arm. "Be safe, Quashy. You know how much we depend on you." The sudden thought of losing Quash too seemed to go off like a gong in my skull. "Please—" I swallowed.

Knowing Ben was gone and in danger because of the

callous words I'd shouted in anger was sitting on me like a millstone. Did he know how much he meant to me? Had I let him know how very much he was … valued?

That I could lose Quash too made my fingers shake.

I was sending him toward freedom with a letter clearing his passage.

He could run away.

He could choose to leave here too.

How much had I been able to do because I had Quash always by my side?

Quash's burnt bronze skin offset his piercing eyes as he waited for me to finish my thought.

"Please come back," I finally said.

Quash nodded.

Turning around, I went back to the window and heard Quash's footfall as he made his way out. "Quashy?" I called softly on impulse, an earlier conversation that had taken place in this very room suddenly carouseling around my head. A thought niggled at me, an outlandish and shocking one. But one I knew would not let me go. "Did—did he love her back? Your father, the white man? Did he return your mother's love?"

I kept my back turned as I asked. My face was a faint, pale apparition on my view of daylight breaking over the landscape outside the window. I saw Quash's reflection as he stood in the shadowy doorway behind me.

His head lowered a fraction. "Yes, Miz Lucas. Yes, he did."

Quash left the room, closing the door gently behind him.

My hands clutched the sill, my knuckles turning white. The corners of my eyes pricked and stung. And I couldn't move until long after the first light of the day washed my reflection from the window.

And with it everything became clear. I was only surprised I hadn't recognized it before now.

That Ben had left before knowing how very much he was ... loved.

It was impossible of course, and Ben perhaps had known how impossible it truly was well before I did. I thought over the painful way he had kept his distance even while I craved his friendship.

I laid my forehead upon the glass pane and prayed.

Thirty-Six

Hours became days, and nights became endless. Only a week passed, and it could have been months.

I sent Togo to town to procure much-needed necessities from the market and deliver a letter to Charles regarding the indigo affair. The account books took much of my time, and I tallied and retallied hoping to see a way we could avoid encumbering Garden Hill. We could make it. Just. But there would be no extra money for further consultants or infrastructure. And I asked myself if I'd have to set my indigo project aside.

The rain came and went, the storm subsided, only to be followed quickly by another. The palm roof peeled clear off our new schoolhouse, and Sawney and Pompey got to work immediately to repair it before I could even ask them.

Cromwell appeared at my door three days after Quash left to find Ben. "No news, I suppose?"

"No." I sighed.

"I want to thank you for sending a man after Ben."

I swallowed. "Of course. Though I did it for his safety, not as a favor to you."

"Of course. Thank you all the same." He sat, without being invited, and irritation surged through me.

"What else can I help with? Have you finished packing your belongings?"

"That's just it. I, uh, well the thing is ... well, this is rather awkward. I cannot afford passage home."

My eyebrows pulled high.

"And, well, I do not have much to return to. My brother and I—"

"So you were all bluff and bluster?" His brother was probably as tired of him as I was. A thought occurred to me. "Why would you want to add a wife to take care of?"

"Well, I thought—your mother, she—"

"You thought I came with a dowry or some such? Perhaps my father's sugar plantations in Antigua? Well, I'm afraid those are mortgaged as well. You have done a fine job making our already precarious position that much more dangerous. Well done."

He hung his head. "I'm sorry."

"Pardon me?"

"I said, 'I'm sorry.'" He gritted the words out with effort.

"Sorrys don't pay our accounts unfortunately. I can't afford to pay your way home either. You'll have to win the money at cards, I imagine. I am sending a letter to your brother updating him on your actions and asking him to remunerate us on the loss of our investment in you."

Cromwell's ruddy color leached from his face. "You wouldn't."

"I will, and have. The letter left with Togo a few days ago."

"Oh, my God ..."

"Yes, pray if you want to. Who knows what truth there is in this Christian scheme? My praying has not done much for me recently. But what beautiful joy there is in allowing Him responsibility for our misfortunes. It certainly makes one's culpability easier to bear."

He swung his head side to side as if impressed by my little speech. "You are far too intelligent for a woman."

"I'll take that as the compliment you no doubt meant. Now if you'll excuse me? I'm sure you must have packing to finish." "Where will I go?"

I smiled grimly. "For my part, I simply want you out of my sight."

I looked down, back at the books, not seeing anything except the hopelessness of my position.

Cromwell stood, and I sensed the mean streak in him coalescing into solidity as he formed his words.

"You are a pitiful excuse for a woman," he spat. "It would seem I had a lucky escape."

"Mr. Cromwell." I glanced up at him briefly. "You, sir, are a pitiful excuse for a ..." I paused. "I was going to say gentleman. But ..." I picked up my quill giving my head a dismissive shake. "You're just pitiful. Now, if you don't mind ..."

His chair screeched along the floor, and, mouth set in a line I imagined was tight with rage, Cromwell walked out.

THE PACING I DID in the next few days was enough to wear a hole in the wool rug on the study floor. I tried to keep myself busy. I began teaching Polly her French again, and then enlisted her to help me teach the Negro children their letters. Due to the off-and-on nature of the rain and our out-of-commission schoolroom roof, I'd started tutoring them in the study. Mother didn't utter a word. I'm sure she could feel the disdain for her foolishness emanating off me in waves and dared not cross my path.

Some days when the weather was nice and we learned outside, we managed to get Lil' Gulla to join us. We made letters from sticks laid in the dirt. Baby Ebba would watch and squeal as the children and I jumped from letter to letter, calling out the sound as we went or counting rocks and stones and arranging them in shapes. My smiles for others most days were forced. But the mornings with the children were the exception, the only time I could keep Ben and Quash—and of course my financial predicament—from my mind.

Sarah, having recovered from her miscarriage, had reverted to helping out in the house and with the children. No longer able to hold my gaze with the defiance she once had, she averted her eyes whenever she saw me. Perhaps her defiance had bled out of her along with her baby. Or my lack of retaliation or punishment for her deeds had broken her in a way Starrat had never managed to accomplish. She'd also taken it upon herself to collect and dry herbs and make salves to stock in the small infirmary cabin Quash had built. I did not interfere with her quiet assimilation into plantation life. She had suffered enough. We all had. Her pride could have what it could salvage.

I cursed myself for pouring so much energy into indigo at the expense of everything else. Was I any better than Cromwell? I'd gambled, and I'd lost.

Togo returned from town. As he unpacked the goods onto the kitchen table, I could see he bore no return letter from Charles Pinckney. Disappointment skewered my already fragile heart. As if he could sense my deflation, Togo looked up, his giant face troubled.

"What is it, Togo?"

He sighed and scratched his head. "Mrs. Pinckney, she sick."

Oh no. Perhaps she'd had another miscarriage. The image

of Sarah flashed before my eyes. I squeezed them closed, pushing away the memory.

"Their lady, Bettina, she tell me, Mistress very weak and tired. Bad head and she getting the fever many times."

I sighed, relieved it wasn't what I'd been thinking. Still it was worrisome. Mrs. Pinckney was so stalwart. So robust. I'd never known her to complain of so much as a sniffle or a flea bite. Not like Mama, who was always poorly and under the weather, snapping at Polly and me and blaming it on her head. If Mrs. Pinckney felt ill, she must truly be feeling bad. I was also relieved to know that there was a good reason for the lack of a letter from Mr. Pinckney about my failed indigo experiment.

"Miz Bartlett, she say she behind on her letters to England and will send you one soon."

I nodded. "Thank you, Togo."

He lowered his eyes. "Quash, he come back? Or Ben?"

My throat closed. I could barely answer. "No. Not yet."

GOING OVER ALL OUR ACCOUNT BOOKS, I plotted a way to stretch the last money from the rice out into the next year.

There were tools and upgrades we might put off buying. Luckily, the slave cabins didn't need any improvements this year since Quash had done such a good job on their upkeep. We would sell some of the benne seeds and our other produce at the market.

I penned a quick message to Mr. Deveaux asking him if he might be interested in purchasing some of our cows. Selling them to him, over anyone else, would mean we might have hopes of buying them back at some point. The islands were still paying a good price for our timber from Garden Hill so that would help. Next year we could plant more indigo to add to the plants I hoped would come back.

We would try again. We had to. As long as we were able to hold on until then. The alternative, that Father would mortgage Garden Hill, our most profitable land, or lose the properties entirely, just simply didn't bear thinking about.

I wrote again to Miss Bartlett and thought of her uncle reading my words.

Togo brought the *Charles Town Gazette* anytime he was in town, and I noted all the marriages among my so-called peers that had recently occurred. *Mr. John Drayton to Miss Charlotte Bull.* And I did feel a modicum of envy, though I'd rather die than ever admit such a thing to Mama.

Essie fussed over me, assuring me Quash would be fine and would return soon. She seemed careful not to mention Ben. "What do you know?" I asked her once when the omission seemed so glaring I felt it was lumbering around the room like a great black mass. She shook her head, but I could tell she was worried. And she kept checking that her charms beneath my bed were still there. "I won't touch them, Essie, I promise," I said, mildly amused though a little chilled.

And then several weeks later, a stranger rode into Wappoo bearing a letter addressed to *Lucas of Wappoo.*

It was Polly who came running into the house.

"There's a man on a horse," she'd yelled.

"Shush," Mama snapped. Mama was stiff-backed but frail, sitting on the end of the settee closest to the fireplace, having made it downstairs after weeks in her room. "Don't shout. It's unladylike."

Polly glanced at Mama, mumbling a vague apology, then turned to me. "'Liza," she burst. "He asked me if we own a slave named Quash."

My stomach lurched violently as though a rock dropped into it. My ears and fingers tingled and went cold.

"Come, 'Liza," Polly beseeched.

I was frozen like I'd stepped out of life for just a moment. Then the world came rushing back, and I blinked, bringing Polly into focus.

Quash.

I stood and followed her outside.

Thirty-Seven

For the crimes of running away and conspiring to organize a slave uprising, a slave named Quash of Wappoo, along with two others, had been arrested. They were to be tried in court in Charles Town.

After delivering the news and letting Indian Peter water and feed his mount, the stranger took off back down the road. I raced upstairs with Essie, hastily preparing to travel.

"Togo will have to accompany me to town. Will you let him know?" I asked Essie.

"Essie come too, chil'," she said, and I nodded gratefully. I'd have to arrive at the Pinckneys' home largely unannounced. It couldn't be helped.

"Can I come too?" Polly asked from the doorway to my room. I could see on her face that despite asking she already expected a negative answer. Sadly, I obliged.

"But it's so boring here alone with Mama. And now Essie will be gone too."

I walked over and pressed her smaller body against mine. I made a mental note to look into the cost of sending her to school if we could afford it next year. "I'm sorry, dear one. I don't know how long this trial will last or if I'll be successful in freeing Quash and Ben."

Polly gasped. Her hand covered her mouth, her eyes filling.

For me too, just saying it aloud caused a tight band of panic to seize my chest. Then an alarming thought occurred to me.

"Good Lord," I muttered. How would I even speak for Ben? I didn't own him. Cromwell did.

I didn't know if Cromwell had stayed in Charles Town or continued on elsewhere. "We must hurry, Essie."

THE VOYAGE TO TOWN by water was choppy and perilous. I had to put complete faith in the fact the boat and its hardy Negro rowers knew the journey with such familiarity. Bilious sails of nausea unfurled in my gut, gusting from side to side in tandem with the rocking vessel. I was delirious, my mouth flooding with saliva. The air was thick with dense fog, and there was no landmark to focus on as we rocked our way through the wet cloud. I emptied the contents of my stomach twice over the side of the boat into the thick gray water. Neither episode brought relief.

I DIDN'T KNOW HOW MUCH TIME WE HAD before the trial began. Waiting in the Pinckneys' front parlor for their man to announce my arrival, I worried my lips between my teeth and wrung my hands to warm them. If only there'd been a fire lit in the grate in this room. With many more rooms to use, and no visitors expected, it wasn't surprising for there to be none. I hoped I wasn't inconveniencing them too much, especially with Mrs. Pinckney being poorly.

I made a decision then. I would use money from the rice harvest when it was delivered to buy Ben from Cromwell. I'd force him to sell, if necessary. And then, I clenched my fists at the rightness of my decision, I would set him free. He would be a free man. Benoit Fortuné would be a free black man.

My heart almost floated up out of my throat.

I would help him build a reputation for indigo-making. He would do well. He would be able to buy land. I gasped aloud at my revelation. He would be freer than I would ever be.

I knew we could ill afford it right now, but I'd figure out a way to do it anyway. But first, sweet Lord above, I had to get both he and Quash out of this frightening nightmare.

The sound of the door brushing open made me turn.

Charles Pinckney's bright face instantly sobered to a frown at whatever he saw upon my expression, and he took three long strides toward me.

"Eliza, my dear. What is it?"

I opened my mouth to speak but snapped it closed again and attempted to swallow down the fear that had become a large rock inside me. Tears pricked, and before I could try again to form words, Charles had me pressed against his pipe tobacco and sandalwood-scented coarse wool waistcoat.

A deep rumble sounded against my ear as he cleared his throat and then set me away from him.

The loss of his warm, tight comfort sent a chill through me, and I shuddered. He called for the fire to be lit. "What is it?" he asked again.

"Quash and Ben have been arrested on charges of rebellion." The words tumbled out. "I must go and speak on their behalf. Ben ..." I paused and swallowed. "Ben ran away," I admitted. "And I sent Quash after him. Ben was headed south, where all runaways seem to head, so I'm sure the militia is always on the lookout. I sent Quash with a letter clearing his passage, and I don't know if he lost it, or they didn't give it credence, but a militia man showed up at Wappoo. He told us Quash and two others were under arrest for conspiracy to organize a rebellion." I took a breath. My voice had grown thin and panicky.

Charles walked to a small three-tiered oval table made from mahogany and opened a stoppered crystal decanter. He poured a deep, dark red liquid into a cup and brought it to me. "Port. It will calm you."

I took it and sipped dutifully.

"So he told you Quash was under arrest?"

"Yes."

"And you say Ben was with him?"

"He said Quash and two others." I frowned. "I don't know who the third could be."

"And I have to ask …" Charles winced. "You are sure Quash didn't take this opportunity you gave him to abscond or to join forces with other rebels?"

"No. There is no way."

Charles was silent.

"It's true," I said earnestly. "He had a chance to leave during the Stono uprising, but he didn't. Not only that, I believe he protected us somehow."

Charles' eyebrows grew close. Perhaps he didn't believe me, but it was the truth. "And Ben?" he asked.

I shook my head. The thought that Ben would join some form of rebel cause was preposterous. Although, I suppose he could be forced if they knew of his abilities. "Ben just wants to be free. He is very skilled and could potentially be quite wealthy. There is no way he would risk freedom by deflecting into some kind of skirmish." I blew out a breath.

"But I should mention ..." I dropped my eyes. "Both Quash and Ben have the ability to read and write."

"And I suppose you taught Quash?"

"And Ben," I admitted. Had I handed down a guilty verdict just by educating them? I squeezed my eyes tight.

Charles took in a long audible breath through his nose. "If the authorities know this, it's no wonder they assume the worst. We'll have a devil of a time getting them released."

"You'll help me? I came for advice. But, Charles, I—if you'll help, I—thank you," I finished, my voice wobbling.

Charles looked at me fondly. "Honestly, Eliza, there isn't much I wouldn't do for you." He smiled fleetingly, his handsome face troubled. "Now, let's not dilly dally. We'll see if we can avert a trial altogether. I'll just go and inform Mrs. Pinckney."

"Oh." I gasped, aghast at myself that I hadn't asked before now. "How is she?"

He grimaced. "Not well, I'm afraid. Though the doctor says he can find nothing wrong. But she tells me she awakens with fever at night, feeling hot when the air is chilled. She says her bones ache, though that comes and goes. And weak. She feels so very weak. It has quite confounded us all, I'm afraid."

I pursed my lips in sympathy. "I'm so sorry."

"Well." He forced a smile. "She'll be happy to have you visit with her—"

"Oh, I knew it was you!" Miss Bartlett's cheerful voice just barely preceded her through the door. "I saw Essie, and my heart gave a little jig to think you were here!"

"Dear Miss Bartlett." With effort, I pulled my mouth into a smile. "Yes, though I wish it was under better circumstances. I'm in town to rescue two men from jail."

Her eyes widened. "Oh! Do tell me all!"

THE STENCH OF UNWASHED BODIES and excrement at the jail under the courthouse wafted out to the street. I pulled a muslin to my nose and carefully stepped over the cobblestones and drains as Charles and I made our way to visit the bailiff.

A small beady-eyed gentleman, whose name I forgot two seconds after hearing it, confirmed he held a man by the name of Quash. We stood in a stone room with wooden shelving and numbered boxes along one wall.

"He mulatto?" the man asked, scratching his head and then picking a lice bug between his thumb and forefinger and flicking it toward the wall behind him.

"He is," I responded and shuddered, feeling my own skin itch in response.

"Well, sir," said Charles, "I do believe he may have been mistakenly apprehended. He and his companion, Ben, a darker skinned Negro, were traveling on plantation business up the Combahee to Mistress Lucas' other plantation, Garden Hill."

"There ain't no Negro by the name of Ben. And all due respect, Mr. Pinckney, he was in the company of some men we've been searching for for quite some time. You may have sent him on plantation business, but that is not how he was spending his time."

I opened my mouth to jump to Quash's defense. Charles quickly shot me a look, and I stopped.

"If he's lucky, and it turns out he ain't the one what been rounding these fellas all up, he may get off with a whipping. But the leader? He's gonna be hanged."

I clenched my fists, my teeth tight, trying to stifle my gasp of horror. "I'll be speaking in his defense," I managed before Charles could stop me. "He is an honorable slave."

The bailiff snorted.

I thought about what other name Ben might go by and got

nothing. "And you're sure there was no slave named Ben?"

"We ain't got none by that name," the man snapped, irritated.

Perhaps Quash hadn't caught up with Ben yet. Equal parts relief he wasn't imprisoned and dread that he was still out there somewhere washed through me. If Quash and Ben weren't together, then Ben was very likely gone. Perhaps forever. I couldn't think of that right now. I tried to keep my spinning mind blank.

"Can we see the prisoners?" Mr. Pinckney asked. "To be sure."

"Can't do that. But here's the belongings what were found with them," he said turning and hauling a wooden box from the lowest shelf and setting it on the wood counter with a thump. Inside was an assortment of flint stones, dried meat, rope, a small knife, and—I froze.

A small leather pouch sat innocuously to one side. It looked almost identical, but darker, to the one Ben wore around his neck. That was alarming in itself, but more so was the small cutting of yellow lutestring ribbon curled next to it. I slowly put my hand inside and touched it gingerly.

"That was inside the leather pouch, along with some stones and such. You recognize it?"

I swallowed. "Yes," I said, remembering the coil of yellow ribbon Papa had sent us from Antigua before the King's Birthday Ball. "I believe it belongs to me." How did Ben have a piece of my hair ribbon?

"Stole it, did he? Well, we can add that to the charges."

"No." I startled. "No, it's all right. I gave it to him."

The bailiff frowned, and I felt Charles Pinckney shift uncomfortably next to me.

"Regardless, the pouch looks like it belongs to the man you say you do not have," I said thickly. "Ben. Not Quash."

"Well, the militia said they took it from your man Quash. He was half drowned and lying on the riverbank when they came across him. Tried to get away into the river when we raided the rebel encampment, but we hauled him out quick enough."

"That makes no sense," I said, confused about him being in a rebel encampment. "What did he tell the militia?"

"Concocted some story of a boat full of rice going down in the 'Santilina' and bein' carried by the water." The man shook his head. "They'll tell you anything."

My pulse pounded in my ears, the voices of the bailiff and Charles Pinckney growing tinny as my vision narrowed. "A ... a boat went down?" *Santilina*? Our boat from Garden Hill always traveled through the St. Helena Sound. I swayed and felt Mr. Pinckney's warm hand grasp my upper arm.

If it was our boat Quash spoke of, then it would have been carrying our last rice harvest.

Thirty-Eight

"What is it, Eliza?" Mr. Pinckney urged. The crease between his eyebrows was as deep as I'd ever seen it. "What is the matter? Please. Can you tell me?"

I stared up into his concerned eyes, noted the small brown flecks within the gray blue I'd never noticed before, his smooth skin beneath the coarse afternoon stubble. The pipe smoke scent of him that calmed me even now when my heart felt like it had bled out and left a limp gelatinous skin flopping around inside me.

For a thankfully brief but inexplicable moment, I was seized with a jealous rage that men like Charles Pinckney weren't asking for my hand. Saving me from having to be in situations like this alone, fighting for my existence like one of those hungry wild dogs on the Charles Town wharf. Perhaps even Mr. Pinckney himself as a husband I could have borne. Enjoyed even. Perhaps loved. He was so very, very dear to me.

And I wasn't alone right now, was I? Charles Pinckney *was* here. Except he was already married. And men like him didn't marry scrappy, ambitious little hoydens.

I turned away, shocked at the turn of my thoughts and clutched my head. Guilt flooded me that I could even think of

Mr. Pinckney as my husband when his wife, my dear friend, lay ill at their home.

I was a fickle girl. A selfish, fickle girl.

"Do you not want to tell me?" Mr. Pinckney pressed.

"My mother was right; my father should have never left me in charge." My words came out in a whisper. "I've lost it all."

"Come," said Mr. Pinckney gently. "Let's get you home. We can come back here in the morning."

"No! I mean, no. Please. Can you please ask again if we can see Quash? I *must* ask him what happened. He mentioned a boat. The future of our plantations depends on it."

Mr. Pinckney stared at me with his warm eyes for a beat, and I wished for a clue to his thoughts. "Very well."

QUASH WAS BROUGHT INTO A SMALL STONEWALLED CELL we were waiting in, a man supporting each of his arms. He could barely stand under his own weight. His face was swollen. The whites of his eyes contained crimson pockets of blood. Like his veins had exploded into his eyeballs. His hands were behind him, presumably tied.

My breath left me in a rush.

Unconsciously, I stepped toward him, only for Charles to hold me back.

The two burly escorts dropped him in the vicinity of a bench.

"Careful!" I cried, but they walked out, stationing themselves outside the open door of the cell we'd been allowed to use to see their prisoner.

I tugged my arm free of Charles without much resistance

and came slowly toward Quash, crouching in front of his lowered head. He was filthy. I doubted he'd been escorted to the privy since he could barely walk, so the smell of him was overwhelming.

"Quashy?" I said tenderly. "I came as soon as I heard. I'm so sorry." My voice broke. "We'll get you out of here, okay? Can you tell me what happened? Did you find Ben?"

I went on when there was no response. "Please, Quash. What about the boat, they said you told them of a boat going down?"

His head moved.

"Is that yes, Quash?"

"Yes." He scratched out the word. His neck bore rope marks.

I swallowed my panic at that news, stuffing it down as best I could.

"Our boat? The boat from Garden Hill?" I managed.

He nodded.

Oh, Lord. I swayed, my crouched legs spasming. It couldn't be. *Oh my God.*

Our rice was on that boat.

Everything was on that boat.

Quash wouldn't have gotten on any other boat except ours, and only if he'd found Ben.

"So—so you found Ben?" I choked in a whisper. "And were headed back? Is he here? Is Ben here?"

Quash shook his head.

"Where is he?" My voice had taken on a high-pitched panicky breathlessness.

Quash shook his head again, his eyes closing.

"What does that mean, Quash? Did he get away? Was he captured too?"

Quash was still for a long moment. The distant clanking

sounds of the jail and the wheezing of one of the guards a few feet away made the silence in our stone cell all the more deafening.

Then Quash looked up at me with those bloody, awful eyes and shook his head. "No," he said. "Ben. He done gone. The storm. The water too strong. I tried. It took him from my hand." Quash paused, his body beginning to tremble. "His soul ... his soul done swim back to Africa."

The concerned voice of Charles Pinckney, then the bailiff, vaguely registered, though I had no idea what words were uttered.

Quash's dark, broken eyes swam before me.

My heart felt like it had melted in my chest, my body filled with a raging torrent of blood in the aftermath, drowning me from the inside. I closed my eyes and let the current pull me under.

Ben was dead?

Ben was dead.

"WELL," MISS BARTLETT WAS SAYING. "Uncle will, of course, do what he can."

I sat by the fireplace in one of their guest bedrooms, staring despondently into the dancing flames, a shawl over my knees.

"But you will have to go and speak on his behalf. It does all look rather suspicious. Being found with an acquaintance of the notorious Jemmy. He was the Stono ringleader you know? He was a slave at Fenwick Hall. That's just across Wappoo Creek from you, isn't it?"

I could almost imagine demon faces forming and melting

one after the other in the flickering flames.

"Oh, and a letter came from your mother inquiring after your well-being." Miss Bartlett didn't seem at all put off that I wasn't answering her.

Finally, I looked up at her earnest face and then around the handsomely appointed room with its perfectly needlepointed and embroidered damasks, silks, and tapestries. Essie pushed the door open with her hip, entering the room holding a tray of tea and benne wafers. The wafers, she'd informed me, were Mr. and Mrs. Pinckney's favorite teatime accoutrement, made in the traditional West African way and baked crisp.

"My aunt will be down shortly to check on you," Miss Bartlett said as she poured some warm oolong tea into delicate china cups with gold leafing on the rims.

Mrs. Pinckney was coming to check on me? I should be the one checking on her. She was the one who had been so ill recently. But *I*? I must have had a sickness of the mind, for I could not muster the energy required to move a muscle. Neither for speaking nor moving. At night, I lay in the middle of a too-large and too-soft bed and cried. Water simply flowed from my eyes in an endless torrent. When I awoke, I could barely see for my swollen lids. The salt of endless tears must have ravaged my eyeballs, such that even air stung them mercilessly. And so I kept them mostly closed.

Charles visited me twice. The second time, we were alone, and he took my hand. "Was he—" he started, then stopped himself with a frown. "Was he—" he tried again. "Did you—" He blew out a breath and released my hand.

I grabbed his hand back, knowing he needed a response. Needing his comfort. Now more than ever. But I couldn't answer him. Eventually I let him go with no answer.

Essie came to me during the night, when sleep finally claimed me only to bring dreams. Dreams not just of Ben drowning but my whole family on a primitive raft made of willow sticks lashed together. Polly, Mama, Father, George, and little Tommy even. My father's face was thunderous. Mama screeched at me.

Essie brushed my damp hair from my temples. "There, chil'," she cooed. "You jus' dreamin'."

"But it's real, Essie," I managed once in the deep dark well of night. "Ben is gone. He's gone, Essie. Forever. It's all my fault. You don't understand. I—I—"

"Shush now." She stopped my words before they could be uttered. And I'd wake in the morning and Essie would be gone.

I was alone with the wreckage of all my ambitious choices. The utter wasting of a man's life and talent. I should have bought him immediately so I could set him free. Why hadn't I? Why had I let Cromwell hang freedom over his head, putting him in that awful position? Betray me or never be free?

I tortured myself with what-ifs.

If he hadn't needed to run for the chance of freedom. If I hadn't been so ambitious. If I hadn't left for the ball. If I'd had the means to buy his freedom early on. Would he have stayed and helped me, or would he have taken his freedom and left me to figure out indigo on my own? If I'd had the chance to buy him his freedom, would I have done it? Or would my selfish need for success have made me keep control of him by any means possible, by keeping him enslaved?

I knew the answer deep in the most horrible parts of myself.

He'd contained more knowledge and skill, and more purpose, than almost any white man I'd known. And it was lost. All lost. The loss of all that incredible knowledge drifting to the bottom of the ocean was a tragedy all on its own.

He'd saved my life once. And given the chance, I hadn't saved his. I had stalled, questioned, and worried. And every moment I'd wasted had sealed his fate.

Maybe Quash was right. Perhaps Ben's soul would make it back to Africa. Maybe he'd be reunited with his grandmother once again. If Africa was his heaven, then that's where he belonged. He was finally free. How could I even think of wishing him back?

Yet each morning I wished his death was but a dream.

My selfishness knew no bounds.

How I made it to the courthouse the following week, I cannot say. The days seemed to be carried out in a fog of sorts.

I sat in front of the judges and told them about Quash's service to our family, his trustworthiness, and then I told them the frightening story of the morning of September 9, 1739, when I had been just sixteen years old.

"On plantations all around me ..." My voice trembled, echoing in the too-large room. Charles smiled encouragingly at me. "While many attended church in St. Andrew's Parish," I went on, "many of those who stayed behind that Sunday were murdered, as you know, their plantations burned to the ground." I stopped and made the sign of the cross as I relived the fear of that morning and out of respect for those whose lives were ended. "Those slaves came by boat along our narrow creek. Headed for the Stono River. I saw them with my own eyes. They made calls like the sounds of animals. Unless I had seen them I would have thought strange and unusual beasts to be about. They beat drums and carried with them a spirit of threat and malevolence."

I looked around the wood-paneled courtroom. To Quash and two black men I did not recognize who glowered at me with open hostility.

The small gathering of folk in the rows behind me were hanging on my words with rapt attention when I glanced at them. "Something turned them away," I went on. "Or should I say, someone. Only after the boat and its occupants finally moved on without even attempting to dock at our land did Quash emerge from the brush where I had not seen him, and he went to wipe away some kind of sign or warning he had posted upon the dock." I paused and heard a few quick inhales of breath behind me. "He had quite obviously made it clear that Wappoo slaves were not joining the rebellion, and that their landowners were to be left unharmed."

One of the judges, a red-cheeked man with white bushy eyebrows that matched the shoulder-length white wig he wore, glared at me over a thick, round monocle. "As dramatic a story as that is, Miss Lucas, it doesn't tell us he didn't later elect to be involved in a further uprising. Do you have anything else to add?"

"May I interject, Your Honor?" Charles spoke up. "As a character witness?"

"For Miss Lucas? That won't be necessary. I know her father, and I am quite sure she isn't lying to the courts. However, her story doesn't have much to do with today's proceedings."

"I understand. I was offering to be a character witness for the slave Quash." There was an audible intake of breath around us. Charles, undeterred, went on, "He often drives the Lucas family to town, and therefore I have had occasion to see him and converse with him in various settings. I believe him to be honorable and he was indeed carrying out an order to retrieve a runaway slave when he was apprehended."

"Was he successful?"

Something sharp and stinging filled my ears, nose, and throat. But I forced words out before Mr. Pinckney could go on. "Yes, Your Honor." I blinked rapidly. "He was successful and was returning on one of our boats from Garden Hill up on the Combahee River. We have suffered a terrible loss as the boat went down in the St. Helena Sound. And unfortunately the Negro slave who was running away ..." A hot tear escaped down my cheek, and I cursed my inability to keep myself together. "Drowned." I finished on a whisper.

Deciding to avoid further mention of Ben, I went on. "Quash almost drowned and in the process must have lost the papers I'd given him permitting his travel. It was likely an act of God that saved him by washing him to shore. And I must thank the militia men for finding him so he could be returned to us."

There was a beat of silence. "Very well, I release the slave mulatto Quash into the care of Miss Lucas of Wappoo with the understanding that any further evidence as to his guilt coming to light will mean he will need to be returned here."

I released a pent-up breath.

"Thank you," I said with force to the court. "And thank you, Mr. Pinckney," I added quietly to the stalwart and dependable man at my side.

"Actually, I think it was all you, Eliza," Charles said, his voice soft under the cover of voices that erupted around us. "How could one look at you in this courtroom, you tiny slip of a woman with those large expressive eyes and that fantastical story and not do as you ask? I think you have long underestimated your power."

He turned and strode toward the bailiff who stood with hastily drawn up papers for Quash's release.

I swung to Quash.

He nodded at me solemnly.

I nodded back.

Quash was released into our care, and Charles insisted we return to the Pinckneys' home in town so Quash could eat and rest before we headed back to Wappoo. Charles really was the most remarkable and thoughtful man.

As we trundled along the bumpy cobbled streets in our open carriage, I brought a shaking hand up to adjust my bonnet against the cold wind whistling between the buildings. The iron sky bore down heavily.

"What will you do now?" Charles asked.

The heaviness sitting deep in my gut, underneath my crushing sadness, was guilt. A massive ballast stone of it, weighing me down.

"Now," I responded, watching the myriad buildings that comprised Charles Town roll by, "I am admitting defeat. South Carolina bested me. Her fertility and her promises sucked me in, and I drowned in her marshy swamps." I warmed to my dramatic and fanciful poetry. "I've been strangled and choked by her ropes of dripping Spanish moss." I glanced at Charles whose eyes held pity. I hated that.

"I shall write to Father and let him know. He will mortgage our last property if he hasn't already. Perhaps we could forfeit on one of them, Waccamaw, and Mr. Manigault can find a ready buyer for it. I saw Laurens chatting to Manigault at the King's Birthday Ball, likely putting his ear to the ground for such a fortuitous event," I muttered. "I'll be pleased not to have to think about that ghastly Starrat anymore. Then, I imagine, we will wait for either my father or my brother George to fetch us back from here."

Mr. Pinckney and Quash both stared at me.

"What is it?" I asked, alarmed at their twin expressions of dismay.

I didn't recognize this defeated version of myself either.

Thirty-Nine

The sky, with no clouds to keep us swaddled, was cold and blue. The sun danced artlessly across the indigo water.

As we crossed the now calm Ashley River and entered the mouth of Wappoo Creek toward our land, it was as though I was a different person.

I'd left with hope in my heart, and I returned without even a heart in my chest. I was filled instead with the weight of my failures. If I slipped overboard I knew the heaviness inside me would pull me down faster than the drag of my voluminous dress.

I WROTE TO MY FATHER about the boat accident and the loss of the rice and the Negro man. I couldn't even call him Ben. My father would know when he read it. It was a matter-of-fact missive, devoid of flowery prose or excess sentiment.

Most things were now to be conducted in this manner. As though part of me had to be kept locked up tight, and any break in the seal would spring too many leaks for me to contain.

In fact, as the letter to my father dried, I picked up my

quill again and struck through the word "the" in front of Negro man, and wrote "a" Negro man.

I closeted myself away at our plantation, only keeping in touch by occasional written word, and waited for time do its healing work. Time trudged by so slowly. I was a butterfly pinned by my wings to the canvas of my mistakes.

Dear Miss Bartlett,

After a pleasant passage of about an hour we arrived safe at home, as I hope you and Mrs. Pinckney did at Belmont. But this place appeared much less agreeable than when I left it, having lost the pleasant company that then enlivened it.

I feel lost. What was once so clear has been obscured. I find myself turning more and more to faith. Perhaps this Christian scheme is but an illusion, but it is an illusion I readily subscribe to, and must cling to dearly. Perhaps if everyone believes, it will be so.

Your most humble and obedient servant,
E. Lucas

Dear Mrs. Pinckney,

To my great comfort I hear you are perfectly recovered of the indisposition you complained of when I was in town. I hope permanently.

At my return hither everything appeared gloomy and lonesome. I began to consider what alteration there was in this place that used to so agreeably soothe my pensive humor, and made me indifferent to everything the gay world could boast; but found the change not in the place but in myself …

My determination in hindsight was futile. What was a girl thinking becoming mad with such silliness? Your friendship through my folly is greatly appreciated.

—Eliza Lucas

To the Honorable Charles Pinckney, Esq.,

I think my silence requires less apology than my writing ... I have had a very great cold so that I could not hold up my head or see out of my eyes to write a line ...

Or perhaps Miss Bartlett will tell you the real cause of my affliction. I am a ship with no rudder.

You justly observe a completion of happiness is not attainable in this life, to which truth I readily subscribe ...

Mama bids me tell you she is quite ashamed of the troubles our people gave you.

Your humble servant,
Eliza Lucas

To Colonel Lucas,

I hope that you will do me justice to believe your not hearing from me for some time past was purely the effect of accident.

Your dutiful and obedient daughter,
Eliza Lucas

Forty

Sarah came to see me. She was thinner than I'd ever known her, her spirit dimmed.

I closed my volume of John Locke essays and waited wearily. I'd been attempting the fruitless exercise of keeping my mind occupied.

Sarah said nothing, her head bowed and her hands clenching and unclenching at her sides.

"What is it?" I asked, and I couldn't help remembering the last time she'd been in the study. How she'd stood in the same spot with her haughty demeanor and her unwillingness to help me. Even though she'd finally relented.

For what good it had done. I still had no idea if she had true indigo knowledge and I no longer cared.

"Speak!"

"It were my charm."

I sighed. "What are you talking about?"

"I cursed the thing you loved the most."

She looked up at me, her eyes wide, her hands still fidgeting.

Swallowing. "I don't believe in charms. I believe in God."

She shook her head. "It were me. It were my fault."

"Sarah," I said with exasperation, "it wasn't your fault

the indigo was ruined. I already know what happened. And I know exactly who was to blame. The list is long. But you are not on it."

"I no talk of the indigo. I mean Ben."

The sound of his name from her lips ringing out into the silent room was a slap across the face. My head even turned involuntarily, my breath leaving me.

"Get out," I managed after several moments.

With a soft sound she moved, her knees bending. She lowered herself to the floor.

"What are you doing? Get up."

Her head stayed bowed.

"This is ridiculous," I snapped. "Sarah, get up."

When she didn't respond, true to her stubborn nature, I slapped my book down on the desk.

What was this? Was she bowing to me? Apologizing? What? It was dramatic and uncomfortable. I stood and walked quickly to the door of the study. I needed air.

Stalking out of the study intent on going outside, I quickly changed my mind and went instead to my room, leaving Sarah in supplication upon the floor.

I startled Essie who was leaning under my bed with a stiff brush to get the dust up from the crevices.

"Lord, chil'." Her hand pressed to her chest and she rocked back on her bare, pink, and cracked heels.

"Am I to see every one of you on the floor today?" I asked, swiping at my cheek, and told her about Sarah.

Essie listened quietly but didn't dispute nor support the claim. A short while later I was relieved to find Sarah gone from the study. I looked around to see everything as it was, then walked to the gun cabinet, the door of which had come loose again. Sealing it shut, I took a deep breath and resumed reading. My head hurt.

Dear Miss Bartlett,

Have I told you I saw a comet? Perhaps the comet Sir Isaac Newton foretold should appear in 1741, and which, in his opinion, will destroy the world. How long it may be traveling down to us, he does not say.

Meditating on the shortness of life gives me no pain at present, and I hope I have not inspired you with an unpleasing gloom. There is a disgust at the separation of soul and body to human minds, but that is in great measure to be overcome by the beliefs in the Christian religion.

—Eliza Lucas

Dear Miss Bartlett,

Per your inquiry of the comet: The comet had the appearance of a very large star with a tail; to my sight, about five or six feet long. It's real magnitude then, must be prodigious. The tail was paler than the comet itself, and not unlike the Milky Way.

The brightness of the comet was too dazzling for me to give you all the information you require, but I am inclined to think by its modest appearance so early in the morning it didn't permit every idle gazer to behold its splendor; a favor it only granted to those few that take pains for it.

How was it dressed? I conclude if I could have discovered any clothing it would have been the female garb. Besides, if it is any mortal transformed to this glorious luminary, why not a woman?

The light of the comet to my unphilosophical eyes seems to be natural and all its own. How much it may really borrow from the sun, I am not astronomer enough to tell.

Your most obedient servant,
Eliza Lucas

Dear Miss Bartlett,

I assure you the sight of a comet is not the only pleasure you lose if you lie late abed in a morning; for this, like every other pernicious custom, gains upon us the more we indulge it. First, because by losing so much of our time, we lose so much of life. Secondly, because it is unhealthy. Thirdly and lastly, because we lose by far the pleasantest part of the day.

An old lady in our neighborhood is often quarreling with me for rising so early as five o'clock in the morning and is in great pain for me lest it should spoil my marriage for she says it shall make me look old before I am so.

I reason with her thus: If I should look older by this practice, I really am so; for the longer time we are awake, the longer we live. Sleep is so much the emblem of death that I think it may rather be called breathing than living.

I send herewith Mr. Pinckney's books, and shall be much obliged to him for Virgil's works. Notwithstanding, this same old gentlewoman has a great spite at my books and had like to have thrown a volume of my Plutarch's Lives into the fire the other day! She is sadly afraid, she says, I shall read myself mad.

Your most obedient servant,
Eliza Lucas

Forty-One

By the end of winter, I'd had enough of looking at the forlorn fields where the indigo had grown. I interrupted Quash midway through his reading a section of the Bible aloud to me one morning in the study.

"Quash, I need you and Togo to till up the indigo fields, pull the remaining plants, and get rid of the seeds we have. We'll plant rice."

Quash looked up as I spoke but said nothing.

"Maybe not rice." I frowned, remembering the price of rice had dropped so much of late. "Maybe cotton."

Quash left my request unanswered and returned to reading. I should have been insulted. Instead I crawled back inside my own head again, wondering where my request had even come from.

I'd been doing everything possible to avoid having to make a decision about the indigo. I didn't want to till it all up like I'd just asked Quash, but we couldn't grow it again. What would we do with it? I didn't feel confident in what I'd learned, and I scolded myself for this weakness of character that must still be a hangover from grief. There was nothing wrong with making another attempt. Yet, I was paralyzed by the very idea.

My dear Miss Bartlett,

I have found a raison d'être. I am engaged in the rudiments of law to which I am yet but a stranger. I hope it will make me useful to any of my poor neighbors. We have some in this neighborhood who have a little land and few slaves and cattle to give their children and never think of making a will until they come upon a sick bed and find it too expensive to send to town for a lawyer. If you will not laugh too immoderately at me, I'll trust you with a secret. I have made two wills already!

I know I have done no harm for I learned perfectly and know how to convey by will estates real and personal, and never forget in its proper place, him and his heirs, nor that it is to be signed by three witnesses in the presence of another.

After all what can I do if a poor creature lies a-dying and their family takes it into their head that I can serve them? I can't refuse.

A widow hereabouts with a pretty little fortune begged me to draw her a marriage settlement, but it was out of my depth and I absolutely refused it. So she got an abler hand to help her. But I couldn't get off from agreeing to be one of her trustees to her settlement.

We expect my brother George very shortly. His arrival will, I suppose, determine how long we shall continue here. I never expected to lose my heart in South Carolina. It will be heartbreak indeed to leave.

Your most obedient servant,
E. Lucas

Forty-Two

 T he indigo crop came back with all the vengeance of a hurricane roaring in from the Atlantic. It covered the fields from edge to edge, tangling and climbing over itself to fill every available space. I never knew if it came back from the seeds already nesting in the soil despite my asking Quash to clear the fields or if he'd deliberately ignored me and actually sown the seeds himself.

I did not ask and Quash remained silent on the subject.

Quash had begun rebuilding some of the dwellings with a new building substance we'd heard about named "tabby." Similar to daub, it was combined with oyster shells to give it more heft and consistency. For a brief moment I wondered if we should rebuild the main house, and then I remembered with despondency that we probably wouldn't be here much longer. Quash collected barrows of oyster shells from the shell midden on our bluff that had been there, according to Quash, since Indian days. He burned them white then bade me come and watch as he immersed the burnt shells in water and I saw them miraculously and instantaneously disintegrate into powder. He mixed the powder with sand and more oyster shells and packed it into wood casings he and Pompey had made where it dried into a hard foundation. Little by little they built the wall higher, moving the casing up a bit and pouring the new tabby onto the hardened level beneath. I was impressed with his experimentation and his skill, and so I let him continue learning. And perhaps part of me thought if he was busy elsewhere, he wouldn't pester me about the indigo plants.

For my part, I kept myself busy learning law, mastering the harpsichord my father had sent Polly and me for Christmas, and imagining anything else I could harvest that wasn't indigo.

I'd begun visiting the Woodwards again with Mama, looking forward to Tuesdays with a fervor that was almost unnatural.

Miss Bartlett never did come to visit me at Wappoo, having to return instead to London. And suddenly I became so very aware of the fact that all my letters to her had really only ever been for Mr. Pinckney, knowing he would read them. Somehow, even though we'd started out with this being the case, I had convinced myself otherwise. And now that I no longer had the veil of corresponding with Miss Bartlett to hide behind, I found myself quite unable to write with as much vigor.

When Mrs. Pinckney sent word for me to call upon her, my shame at the realization of how dependent I had become on writing to her husband kept me from responding right away.

So it was no surprise one afternoon when Charles Pinckney showed up unannounced, dancing down the lane on Chickasaw, his coattails flying behind him. Lil' Gulla was the one who came running up to the house to announce his approach, so we could all go outside and see.

"My dear, Miss Lucas." He smiled as he dismounted, and my words dried in my throat.

I was desperately happy to see him, of course, but my recent concerns for how important he'd become to me prohibited me from showing my usual joy. He and Mrs. Pinckney, and of course dear Mrs. Cleland, were some of my closest friends and soon I would have to say goodbye to them too.

"I'm sorry." He was immediately downcast when he noticed my lack of response. "I should have sent word. I was just hearing a case up near St. Andrew's church. And I have brought some letters for you from England."

So it was not my absence that brought Charles here. I swallowed a fleeting stab of egotistical disappointment and shook my head. "No, no. It's fine. I was just overcome for a moment. It is so very wonderful to see you."

"Likewise. It has been far too long since you have seen us in town. Mrs. Pinckney has been ill again." He scowled and looked out toward the creek as he spoke. "And still no explanation from the doctor."

It felt like a gentle reprimand, and it was deserved. What a careless friend I had been. I'd write to her more often. "I'm so sorry to hear it. Please tell Mrs. Pinckney she is never far from my thoughts."

"She'll appreciate that." He smiled. "And when she is feeling better, we wish to invite you on a tour of some of the upper neck plantations and the countryside. Before you"—he cleared his throat—"excuse me. Before you leave. Goose Creek, St. John's, Middletons' plantation at Crowfield. I've heard the gardens are spectacular. I thought—Mrs. Pinckney thought—you would be particularly interested in Crowfield."

"I should very much like that," I responded, genuinely cheered by the prospect of the gardens I'd heard so much about. "Thank you."

"When will you leave?"

"My father has sent George to fetch us. But with tensions at sea like they are, it may be a while before he arrives. Then we shall have to pack up the house and resettle the slaves."

"You won't leave them?"

"We may. We'll have to see what plans the new occupants have for the land. And I should hate to leave them to a harsh fate."

"May I say ... You have greatly impressed me with your eagerness to learn the law."

I smiled thinly. "It's an effective way to employ the mind from useless moping. But, I'm afraid the gentleman author is not nearly as good a teacher as you at explaining complicated issues."

We walked to the house. My mother made a rare and brief appearance downstairs and took her unread letter with her when she excused herself.

A few moments after her departure, we heard a pained sound, followed by a muffled thud. When we rushed out of the parlor we found my mother sitting in a puff of skirts at the bottom of the stairwell clutching the letter to her chest. Her face was pale.

"Are you hurt?" I asked.

She shook her head.

"What is it, Mama?" I asked after ascertaining there really was no injury. Charles and I assisted her to the settee.

"It's Tommy," she wailed. She handed me the letter.

It was from our guardian, Mrs. Bodicott.

I was not at all sure my heart would ever truly mend regardless of the passage of time. Each new tragedy chipped away at the jagged fissures so there would be no way to fit the pieces back together. This time it was my poor, dear, sweet little brother Tommy, with his temperate disposition and his eagerness to please. His illness had turned grave and we were to prepare for the worst. My breath hitched.

How arbitrary was the hand of death. Why not take the lives of evil men rather than innocent boys?

In that moment, though I'd thought I had begun to

mend, keeping myself busy and becoming passionate again about learning, this time with the intricacies of law to keep my mind occupied, all I could see was the hopelessness and fragility of life.

I swallowed my grief to attend to my mother. After I saw Mama settled upstairs and Mary Ann bringing her some chamomile tea, I returned to find Charles ready to leave.

"Must you return so soon?" I asked as I descended the staircase. My voice wobbled.

He stood in the hall below, his hat in his hands, turning it in his fingers as he regarded a lithograph I'd hung of huntsmen on horseback, hounds scrapping at their heels.

He'd startled as I spoke and now watched my descent, his eyes thoughtful, and unless I imagined it, wistful. "How have you been, Miss Lucas? I mean before this new bout of tragic news. For which, I must say, I am deeply sorry."

"Thank you. And fine." I shrugged, lightly belying my inner anguish. "I have come to terms with the fact that our leaving here is a product of my own doing—"

"Eliza."

I held up a hand and descended the last few steps. "It's true, Mr. Pinckney. There are no two ways about it."

"Charles. And no matter what you believe," he said heatedly, "I will say that I have never met a woman, or man for that matter, with as much courage, integrity, and sense of purpose. That you will even take the blame when it is so very clearly out of your control astounds me. I will always admire you. You are remarkable." He shook his head. "The things you could accomplish—"

In a fit of madness to stop his words I laid a finger lightly across his lips. Unthinking.

I snatched it back.

Charles sucked in a sharp breath.

"I'm so sorry," I gasped, horrified, and turned my back to gather my wits.

Behind me Charles was utterly still.

"You must not say such things to me," I whispered, my voice squeaking as I fought to control my emotion. I stepped away to put distance between us. "I … I depend on them too much. You make me feel as if I can accomplish anything. And yet in the light of day I can't. It …" I swiped a tear from my cheek. "It's too much."

Charles was quiet so long I began to think he had left. But when I turned around he stood in the same spot. His expression struggled between a sort of pain and devoid of any discernible emotion.

Minutes ticked by.

"The indigo," he started. "You *can*. You—"

"Stop. Please. I can't."

"Even if it meant you could stay? You won't do it?"

"It won't make a difference!"

Charles swallowed visibly, his lips mashed tight together. His eyes were dark, and his jaw clenched. "It would make a difference. It would to South Carolina … and"—his throat moved heavily as he swallowed again—"and it would to me."

We regarded each other.

Charles had ambitions. Much like I'd had once upon a time.

I wondered what he saw when he looked down upon me. I barely reached his chest in height.

I wanted to ask him what he meant but fear held me back. We were already in a strange hinterland of intimacy. "Thank you for your visit," I said instead.

Charles nodded stiffly. "Please think about our invitation. Seeing you would cheer Mrs. Pinckney immensely."

"I shall."

Forty-Three

Word came from Mr. Manigault in Charles Town that there'd been some kind of accident up on our Waccamaw plantation. Starrat was dead. A gunshot to the head as he slept.

I gasped as I read it. Not from grief but from the shocking nature of the death. His sins must have finally caught up with him.

In the note, Mr. Manigault asked me if I had anyone else in mind to appoint to the position. Surprised we even had a say in the matter given that we had defaulted on the property, I simply replied that he could appoint whomever he wished. Perhaps there were no buyers for it yet. No mention was made of an inquiry. I laid down my quill and tossed a sprinkle of sand across the ink to blot it.

A gunshot.

I stood suddenly and marched across the study to the gun cabinet, flinging the door open.

There the gun sat, idle and untouched. I closed the door again and returned to my desk. And I couldn't help but breathe easier knowing that Starrat was no longer inflicting himself upon this earth.

By the end of September, the indigo crop was waist-high.

In the early mornings, on days when I was not teaching Quash, I'd stand at the edge of the fields and dare myself to try again. Some of the indigo plants, ironically the ones closest to Ben's cabin, looked as if they would be the first to bloom. I stubbornly watched them day after day. The indigo elements trapped inside the leaves, now at their most potent, were calling to me like the most deafening siren's song. So loud, I felt I should physically cover my ears.

Whenever Quash caught me contemplating the indigo, he would stop whatever he was doing and watch me. Waiting for something.

I'd glare when I saw him, and he'd simply nod once.

Even if I could be successful with making indigo this time, my lot was cast. We were to return to Antigua. My brother George was on his way finally, not to take over the estates I'd been keeping for him and my father, but to rescue the womenfolk from my disastrous failures. So why would I even bother? It would break my heart further to finally succeed only to have to leave it all behind.

In October, I received news that Mrs. Pinckney had taken a turn for the worse. My heart ached for Charles. How distraught he must be. I made arrangements to visit Belmont as soon as possible.

Mrs. Pinckney lay before me, her head nestled on lovingly propped pillows, her skin so pale as to be almost blue. But that was not the most worrisome. All along her skin, on her hands, her arms, now her forehead and cheeks, dark dots and pools marred the pale perfection of her skin.

The doctor had said she was perhaps bleeding beneath her skin, as if she'd been stabbed by tiny swords hundreds and thousands of times, yet without the surface wounds to show for it. It was terrifying. Charles lay exhausted upon a settee next to the dying fire. I'd sent him there immediately upon my arrival to get some rest. Gaunt and haggard, his eyes were so full of heartbreak I almost couldn't stomach looking at him. It was a blow to my own heart to see him broken in such grief and helplessness to aid his wife.

Mrs. Pinckney stirred, her parched and cracked lips opening slightly.

I leaned forward. "Mrs. Pinckney?" I whispered so as not to wake her husband.

Her eyes flickered open to slits and took several moments to focus on me, and she tried to smile. "Eliza," she managed. Her voice was thready and rough.

My eyes filled in spite of myself, and I swiped at them hastily and attempted to return the smile through my worry. "Yes. It's me. I made Charles rest." I squeezed her hand gently. Even the slightest pressure Charles said would cause the bleeding to worsen.

She winced though I'd barely applied strength.

"I'm sorry."

She shook her head. "I—I'm glad you're here. I ..." Her throat made a parched snapping sound as she tried to swallow.

There was a bowl of broth on the side table. I brought a small spoon of it to her lips, hoping it would help. She took it gratefully.

"Charles said you ... your indigo came back," she managed weakly.

I nodded. "Indeed. For what it's worth. But my brother George is set to fetch us back to Antigua. We'll be leaving as soon as winter ebbs and we can find safe passage." My heart felt like stone as I recounted our plans. Mother, of course, was beside herself with joy. To see George, for one thing, but another that she'd finally be getting her wish to return to Antigua. And then she'd have her sights on England. A plan I was not averse to. I didn't have the heart to tell her that it was unlikely as tensions had risen yet further and now there was talk that the English and French would soon declare against each other.

"No. You must try."

"Try?"

"The indigo," she croaked. "You must ... try."

"Hush, do not fret on my behalf."

She closed her eyes, her brow creasing as if she attempted to muster more energy.

"I should leave you to rest."

"The letters," Mrs. Pinckney whispered.

"Pardon?" I asked, not sure I'd heard correctly.

"Can you read the letters to me?"

I frowned. "What letters?"

"Yours," she said. "The ones you wrote these last few years. I saved them."

"To you?"

She attempted to smile again. "To Miss Bartlett."

My stomach lurched, and a lump burned its way up to my throat. My letters to Miss Bartlett that had been intended for her husband? "Why?" I managed.

"Please." She sighed, her eyes closing with another grimace. "Please read them."

I looked around me. The room, done in the palest of greens, held a small writing desk in one corner. Though I could see nothing upon it. Charles twitched and shifted in his sleep. My eyes scanned the room, over the mantel, around the walls, and back to the bed.

There.

There was a stack of letters tied together with a strip of thin leather on the table on the opposite side of the bed. I rose, my belly heavy with an odd sense of guilt, and went to retrieve them. Sure enough I recognized my own hand.

Resuming my place, I untied the bundle.

Unsure what to do since Mrs. Pinckney seemed to be sleeping again, I hesitated.

"Go on," she said thinly.

I swallowed and retrieved the first one.

"My dear Miss Bartlett," I began.

At the end of each when I thought she was asleep once more, Mrs. Pinckney would bade me continue.

I read about the comet, about my business, my plans, and my schemes. I read about teaching the Negro children and two mockingbirds that had nested beside my window. I even, my nerves lodged high in my throat making reading almost impossible, read about how I'd been lacing my stays and listening to the mockingbirds and been moved to poetry, having penned a few amateur lines. How I could have written to Miss Bartlett about my state of undress, knowing Mr. Pinckney would be reading my words, caused shame to beat its way through me. My cheeks burned, my heart hurt, and a feeling not unlike seasickness hurtled around within me.

Mrs. Pinckney lay still, her face again in peaceful repose.

I stopped reading aloud, swallowing hard. But my eyes were drawn down to the pages and I kept on, this time absorbing the words silently and incredulously. I could see my grief at the loss of the first batch of indigo, and my loss of Ben, burning through beneath my words. And I saw also how I'd used the letters to work through my grief and find my way back to the living. But I hadn't stopped then. I'd begun to shamelessly flirt, and impress, and invite coquettish banter about philosophy, and people, and books, and poetry.

And law.

I'd begun learning about the one thing Charles knew best. The law.

I found myself gasping aloud in horror, my hand across my mouth.

"It's all right," Mrs. Pinckney spoke from the bed, causing me to startle. Her eyes were open, wider now, and watching me.

I shook my head. I opened my mouth, but I had no words.

"It is." She nodded. "That's why I wanted you to read them. I wanted you to understand. I knew you didn't. Your heart is so pure."

"I—I don't understand."

"I'm dying, Eliza."

I shook my head more frantically. My throat ached and tears burned. Unable to hold them back, I squeezed my eyes closed and felt them slide down my cheeks. "No. No, you're not."

"I am," she said gently. "It may be weeks. It may be days. But I know that I am. Charles refuses to accept it."

My gaze couldn't help darting in the direction of his sleeping form. He was utterly still, and I wondered if he was awake and listening.

Mrs. Pinckney let out a long sighing breath.

I reached for her hand as carefully as I could. It was cool to the touch. I laid my forehead upon it, in supplication to one of my dearest friends. In apology. In pity. In helplessness to do anything to ease her suffering.

"Forgive me," I said.

"There's nothing to forgive." Her hand fluttered in mine, holding on to me. "He won't ask you," she said. "He won't want to dishonor me. When the time comes, you'll have to ask *him*."

I lifted my head, wiping my eyes with my free hand. I was confused. "I don't understand."

"Yes. Yes, you do," she said and smiled. "Don't make him wait to find happiness again."

Forty-Four

Again I found myself at the edge of the fields.

I replayed Charles' plea over in my head. *It would matter to South Carolina.*

Charles often spoke about the tyrannical government in Georgia led by Oglethorpe. How we needed less input from the British Crown, not more. If I could prove indigo was a successful crop, who was to say other planters couldn't grow it?

Deveaux, Charles, perhaps some others.

Perhaps if my attempt could have far-reaching effects beyond just helping me, that made it less of a selfish endeavor. God knew, the failures and the sacrifices should be given a chance to mean something.

Looking at the profusion of wild indigo in front of me, I wondered if I could remember all that I'd learned. Maybe I could just try some. A small amount. Then if it didn't work again, no harm done. But if it did, it could be my gift to Charles, and to Mr. Deveaux for helping me in the beginning. It would be a gift to Togo and Sawney and Sarah and all the slaves who possessed this knowledge. And it would be a gift to this colony of South Carolina.

I would give Deveaux some indigo seed in return for his woad seeds and his advice.

My success would also be an apology for Ben's sacrifice. How he could have loved these plants, and watched them, nurtured them, and then deliberately ruined the gift they offered him went against everything I'd thought I'd known about him. But the need for the human spirit to be free could apparently outweigh anything, even the passions of one's own heart.

I took the small dirk that hung at my waist and before I could talk myself out of it, began cutting stalks. I searched for the perfect branches. The leaves were deep and resonant in their color, the tiny pink flowers just beginning to bud. I filled up a handful. Then an armful. And then I kept going.

I looked up as Quash found me. His eyes, liquid brown, were somber. "Yes?" I asked.

Quash flicked his gaze behind me, and I turned only to realize Togo was already working with me, cutting branches off the bushes. He too had one eye on me as he worked.

Nonplussed I looked back at Quash. His hand was outstretched toward me. Upon his palm lay Ben's small leather pouch.

With a quick inhale, I laid down my armful of indigo and the knife at my feet, never taking my eyes off Quash's offering. My fingers reverently traced the contours of it. This talisman had been upon Ben's person his whole life as far as I could remember. Essie had told me it was where he kept his memories, his protections, his hopes, and his dreams.

"Ben," Quash started. His voice was rough. "Ben tell me to give to you."

I swallowed. "Why did you wait?" But I knew why and didn't expect Quash to answer. I hadn't been ready to believe in Ben before. Quash saw my belief in the indigo as my willingness to believe in Ben. A breath shuddered out of me. Gingerly taking the object, I turned it over in my hand. Soft, worn supple and smooth for the most part, its opening was stiff. I closed my hand around it. "Thank you."

Quash nodded. A single nod. "It weren't Ben," he said. "Crom'all tell Ben to throw more lime in. Ben, he say no. Crom'all come back with horse whip. Still Ben say no. Crom'all he tell him, you stupid Negro, you do what I say. And he tell Ben he will never make him free if he don't do it."

My chest squeezed and my nose stung. I blinked rapidly. This was how I'd thought it happened. Them fighting, Cromwell threatening Ben's future freedom to force Ben's hand.

"But Ben, he still say no," Quash said, his tone almost incredulous.

"What?"

"Ben, he say no."

My hand covered my mouth, and I could feel my eyes growing wide in shock. The event was long past, but all this time I thought Ben had chosen his freedom over helping me.

Nausea hit. A sickness climbed up my throat.

Quash shook his head, lost in his story. "Crom'all, he grab lime sack. Ben, he fight to get it back. We all scared Ben fightin' a white massa.

"All of us, we watchin' coz we be there beatin' the indigo water. We think, Ben gon' be killed for fightin' the white massa. But Ben he bigger, he has Crom'all on da groun'. We scared for Ben if he kills white massa, so we pullin' him off. Crom'all he say, alri', alri'. So Ben done let 'im up. And, it happen so quick, Crom'all he grab sack and throws all in."

Water slid over my fingers that covered my mouth, and I realized I was crying. My other hand, squeezing Ben's leather pouch, was pressed to my breast.

We stood there, the three of us, for long minutes. The call of birds and hum of insects the only sounds close by. Far off, I could hear the jabber of other voices, and the strike of a tool upon stone. A breeze swam through the ocean of indigo around us, pulling on my skirts and wafting through the leaves. It picked up my hair, tickled my neck, and iced my wet cheeks.

Then with a hand that shook, I attached the pouch to the cord at my waist that usually hung my small knife and swiped at my cold cheeks with the back of my arms.

"We've waited far too long," I snapped at Quash and Togo. "Let's get on with it." I bent to retrieve the knife at my feet and started cutting again. "Take only the perfect branches. Leave the rest to mature and go to seed. We won't need much to prove we can do it."

THE WEATHER WAS WARM, and it took only six days for the leaves to start bleeding into the water. I took a crystal glass from the dining room, ignoring Mother's protestations and dipped it into the indigo vat every hour of every day and far into each night, capturing water and leaves and holding it up to the horizon or my lantern.

Not sure what I was looking for, except Ben's description of the leaves giving up their offering. It took my breath away the moment I saw a thin trailing smoke tendril of blue. Thinking perhaps I'd imagined it through the facets of crystal that caught all manner of colors, I hurriedly dumped the contents of the glass back into the vat and tried again. Yelling for Quash, in a most unbecoming manner, I drew the attention of everyone nearby, and shortly we were all gathered around the vat, me perched at the top of the ladder, holding a crystal glass aloft like some kind of religious ceremony.

Quash shouldered his way through, his face split into a wide grin. Within a couple of hours, Quash ordered the stoppers removed from the side of the large square vat. I watched in wonder as dark teal water cascaded out of the holes into a lower trough.

Togo, Sawney, Pompey, and Quash took first shift. Armed with paddles that looked like massive oars with holes bored through, they began a rhythmic beating through the stained water. It was back-breaking work and shortly sweat poured from their bodies and soaked their clothes.

Mary Ann stoked the large cooking fires. It would be a long few days.

Instead of all of them trading out, a new body would join and each man would shift around the vat, one of them stepping out for a long break before stepping back into the rotation. I thought they would only rotate through the men, but I swallowed thickly when I saw Sarah step up and take a spot. Tall and proud, she took up her position and within minutes had slid into the same rhythmic pattern.

The water sloshed and churned, foam forming and spinning into a flower atop the surface. The liquid grew thicker and darker so incrementally as to trick the eyes into believing it had always been so. Shadows lengthened, the sun casting us in gold. And still the beating continued.

It continued through the night. How much I'd missed by being away at the ball! I could almost feel Ben's presence here with us.

Essie brought me a shawl and dinner of hot soup.

The moon rose. As it reached its zenith, I stood, shedding the shawl, and before Pompey could join in the rotation again I put myself in his place. Grabbing the thick pole, the wood smooth under my fingers, I pushed and pulled it back and forth, rolling my wrist as I'd watched Quash do to move the paddle with the most resistance against the flow of liquid. Forcing it through the holes. Forcing it to let the night air into its depths. I gasped at the weight of the water, tired after mere moments. I gritted my teeth and continued.

Togo began a soft deep melody and soon other voices joined. Pompey stood close, and as I faltered, my arms and the muscles in my shoulders and back no longer able to keep from screaming, he reached for the pole and replaced me, never missing a beat.

As the sky began seeping silver, the liquid was deep as midnight. Quash put up a hand and the beating stopped. The liquid continued to spin and swirl. Sawney approached with a small sack. Setting it on the ground, he untied the top to reveal the sand-like contents. Lime. I recognized it as lime made from the oyster shells. Dipping a cup, he handed it to Quash.

Quash took it, and stepping up on the lip of the trough, sprinkled it across the surface.

Then he, Sawney, Togo, and Indian Peter resumed their spots and began beating the water again.

Essie, Mary Ann, and Old Betty, Quash's mother, stood next to me on either side. Even the children had gathered. It was as though they knew magic was about to occur, and no one wanted to miss it.

The first few rays of sunlight hit the top of the liquid, and I stifled a laugh of wonder. The foam was a spinning flower on the surface. It was heavy and deep, dark blue, throwing back an iridescence of purple. As they beat the liquid, it grew thicker and thicker as if the water was rejecting all of its blue, the indigo pigment being too strong of a burden to hold down. Like the water was trying to separate itself and return to what it was before it had been forced to accept its role in making indigo.

It was no use, my smiles could not be contained. The

children whooped and clapped. I leaned forward and trailed a finger through the blue scum and held it up in the morning light. It was like paint!

Joining in the laughter, I locked eyes with Quash and boldly swiped a finger of blue across each of my cheeks. His eyes widened in surprise, and then he threw back his head and laughed.

The children, seeing what I'd done, laughed delightedly and did the same, though it wasn't as visible upon their dark skin.

"The indigo lady, the indigo lady," Lil' Gulla chanted and began dancing around me. Soon all the children had joined him, and I laughed and clapped along to their song.

As the joy ebbed into contented satisfaction mixed with exhaustion, I helped Quash and Sawney skim the pigment into a waiting flat tray where it would dry before we could cut it into cakes.

Mary Ann and Sarah were already at the trough dipping pale swathes of fabric into the remaining green liquid to see if the water held any more dye.

The fabric emerged green, but before our very eyes began to deepen to blue as the liquid met the morning air.

It really was some glorious alchemy.

I turned to look at the fields still full of wild and untamed indigo plants billowing behind me in the morning breeze off Wappoo Creek and again marveled at how anyone could have conceived that this lustrous stuff would be hidden in so unhandsome a plant. And to think I had almost given up.

I glanced up at the cerulean sky and out to the morning haze upon the creek. "Thank you, Ben," I whispered, then sought Quash.

"Quash," I said, approaching him and touching a hand to his forearm. "Thank you."

He did not pull away from my touch. "Thank you, Miz Eliza," he said and nodded his head once.

All the pigment we could capture was spread onto the trays. I tried to calculate how much we had. Perhaps six pounds? I'd try to cut the cakes into one pound increments.

It was deep and dark and rich—indigo dye in its purest form. And I knew without a doubt we had succeeded. Was it as good as French indigo? There was only one way to find out.

I would send some to the trading houses in London to be tested against French indigo. All of a sudden, my easy acceptance of leaving South Carolina when George arrived was like an ax lodged in my heart.

The Negroes were singing. And it brought the sting of tears to my eyes. I breathed in their melodious voices and basked in the exultance.

Today we had all taken part in and witnessed a miracle.

We would be forever linked together in our shared experience. My joy was their joy. My success belonged to them.

Epilogue

1744

M y brother George paced in front of the open campaign desk in the study of our Wappoo home. If I squinted just right, he was like an apparition of Father. The same height and build. The same thick, lustrous hair. But his youthful skin shattered the illusion each time he turned to me.

"A tenant has been found to take over here at Wappoo," George said to me. "So we shall have no more time to dilly dally in packing up the house. We should aim to book passage by May at the very latest."

I nodded absently, agreeing with his assessment. May would be a temperate time to travel. Warm breezes and, of course, well before the threat of Atlantic hurricanes. I sat on the wing chair in Papa's study where Quash had often sat to read. George strode to sit behind the desk I'd occupied for the last five years.

How had I found myself back on this side of the desk staring at a man who looked like my father, listening to him decide the terms of our future? My future?

I would be leaving my beloved South Carolina. Oh, how it had worked its way into my heart. And I would be leaving dear friends. I counted Quash and Togo among them, though I'd say no such thing aloud. And Charles Pinckney. I would miss him most of all.

In January, as we had arrived in Charles Town to meet George, we'd received news of Mrs. Pinckney's death. Though we'd known it was imminent, it was no less of a shock. And seeing Mr. Pinckney's haunted face as we laid his wife to rest pierced my heart with even more grief.

My brother asked questions about our accounts and which ones needed to be settled before leaving, begrudgingly impressed we were not actually in too much debt. I listened and answered, even though I was thinking of how I'd sat with Mrs. Pinckney long after she'd had me read my letters aloud; long after her husband's breathing had resumed and evened out and he was no longer eavesdropping.

The sky beyond the window of our study was pewter gray and ominously still, an early spring storm was on the way. I thought of the land that was no longer Lucas land, our dwindled fortunes, our plans to return to Antigua as if our stay here in South Carolina had never happened. As if the time had never passed. As if I had never existed upon this land nor attempted accomplishing the impossible. As if I had never succeeded.

How long would we have before we'd be booking passage? I wondered if the indigo plants had dropped enough of the seed we hadn't collected, and if the fields would be prolific again this year, or if they'd freeze where they stood.

With a thick swallow I acknowledged it would no longer be my concern. There was a new owner of the land, and a new occupant for the Wappoo home had been named and would take residence as soon as we left.

A small boat heading along Wappoo Creek approached our landing and stopped. I watched Lil' Gulla race down to greet it, then return at a run. Behind him, walking slowly toward the house, a black mourning band tied around his upper arm, was Charles Pinckney. I acknowledged how my heart raced with joy at the sight of him, and I allowed myself the small indulgence.

He was handsome still, despite his stark features that had been honed by his helpless battle against his wife's illness and death. His shoulders were broad, and he walked with strength of purpose.

"But I have nothing to offer," I'd said to Mrs. Pinckney.

"You are everything he needs," she'd replied.

My brother was in midsentence.

I stood.

"Eliza?" George asked.

"We have a visitor," I said. "Do excuse me."

I hurried from the room, out the front door, and down the porch steps.

Charles Pinckney halted when he saw me. His eyes matched the winter gray of the water behind him. But while the water looked cold, his eyes were warm. Even in their sadness.

"You did not ride Chickasaw this time?" I asked by way of greeting. My nerves were suddenly jangling in my chest, making it difficult to remember how to converse in a normal manner. I longed to hold him to me and ease his pain.

His mouth quirked. "It is wonderful to see you, Eliza. I despaired of you ever coming to town, so I thought I should pay you and your family a visit."

I was shamed by his light comment. Though he meant no seriousness, it was true. I'd witnessed him bury his beloved wife, my dear friend, and then I'd hurried back to my solitude. Poor Mr. Pinckney. How alone he must feel. "We have been busy making arrangements to leave for Antigua." I winced as I spoke, then forced a smile. "There always seems to be more to do. Come up to the house, I'll ring for tea. Please tell me, how have you been?"

"Actually ..." He looked around him. "I was wondering

if we might take a short walk? I have news to impart."

I glanced toward the house as if asking permission. But truly, whose permission was I asking? My mother and I barely spoke to one another anymore. I'd sooner ask Essie. Technically, George was the one to ask permission from even though he was more than three years my junior. It was laughable. "Of course."

I stepped forward, and Mr. Pinckney surprised me by holding out his arm. I hesitated a moment before laying my hand in the crook of his elbow. It seemed small on his coat sleeve. He also looked down to where I held him. Did he too marvel at how tiny my hand seemed?

"My little visionary," he murmured.

"Excuse me?" I was unsure if I'd heard him correctly.

He shook his head, a small smile about his lips. "Let's walk," he said. "Show me your indigo. It *is* still your indigo, is it not? Not the land beneath it but the plants? Their seeds?"

I let out a breath. "Yes. I hope the seed drops before we leave." A wave of melancholy circled my throat, and I swallowed to move it away. "I should like to give some to you. Along with instructions. And perhaps you could see your way to acquiring some of my Negroes?"

Charles stopped.

"Mr. Pinckney. I, I apologize. That was forward. You have your own people. It's just that if you wanted to produce the dye, we have learned. *They* have learned. They would be invaluable. And Quash is so very talented. A carpenter even. He could be a builder—"

"Hush," Charles said, his voice soft. He laid his other ungloved hand on my own, and I started at the feel of his hot skin upon mine.

The breath left my lungs.

"I have news," he said.

"Oh." My cheeks burned in mortification. "Oh yes." How

desperate must I sound? I couldn't beg him to buy our slaves. He was so very dear to me, sometimes I forgot myself.

"I received news from London today. They have tested your indigo dye."

The world around me seemed to narrow down to the man in front of me. To his words. I spun to fully face him, snatching my hand from his arm. My fingertips pressed to my mouth.

"What—" I struggled to make sounds to form words. "What did they find?"

Charles took my hands from my mouth, clasping them in his own. "They found it to be equal, or superior, to French indigo."

"They ..." A wave of emotion flew from the depths of my chest and I half gasped, half sobbed. "Oh. Oh my." I swallowed, and tears sprung to my eyes.

Charles, now blurred in my sight, smiled and nodded.

"Oh thank the sweet Lord. It worked. It worked! Oh my word. Are you sure?"

"Yes. I'm sure. Well done. You have so much to be proud of."

With the piercing joy came a sweet and bitter agony. It hadn't been soon enough to save the Lucas family. But at least I could help Charles. "And Mr. Deveaux," I said. "I must give seeds to Deveaux also. He was so very encouraging at the start. In fact, I wouldn't have known to score or soak the seeds if it wasn't for him."

Charles nodded.

"But not to Laurens. He's on his own. Don't let him have any."

"You can do as you wish."

I smiled through my tears, then chuckled. "We did it," I managed, then joy burst forth in a full laugh. I wanted to dance around in circles.

"You are smiling and crying at the same moment," Charles said, and then he pulled me close.

I fell into his warm embrace, my cheek against the rough texture of his coat. The smell of pipe tobacco, sandalwood, and salt breeze invaded my senses. I would miss this man most of all.

A warmth started deep in my belly and burned through me to the tips of my fingers and toes. *You are everything he needs.* Mrs. Pinckney's soft voice rode on the breeze off the water.

I pulled away, my hands swiping at the remaining tears that were not soaked into his jacket. "Oh, forgive me."

"Hush, Eliza."

"Mr. Pinckney, I—"

"Please. Call me Charles. Call me Charles at least once before you go." His gray-blue eyes burned into me with a sudden intensity.

I swallowed, gathering my strength. "Charles," I said softly. I took his hands again and looked up into his face. "I know I am young. And I have nothing to offer you except some seeds. But I do not want to leave this place. And when I think of leaving, the one thing I think about most, with the most crushing sadness, is leaving you." I took a breath. "I—"

"Eliza." My name broke on his lips, his face tortured. Full of something I could not read.

I'd shocked him. Horrified him, perhaps. "I know it's too soon," I rushed on. "I loved your wife, dearly. I, I ..." My voice failed me under the weight of the emotions struggling to climb from my heart. "It's too soon, I know. Time is not on our side."

"My age," whispered Charles. "Time is not on *my* side, you mean."

He clutched my hands harder. His jaw was tight and his eyes vivid. The breeze blew a lock of his hair free. "I never thought ... I never dreamed you might feel ... I have loved two women so very deeply for so very long. I thought I was about to lose another."

The breath left my chest at his admission, leaving my heart gasping. I reached up and brushed the stray lock of his hair behind his ear.

"Could you love me, Eliza, my little visionary?"

My throat ached. "I do, Charles. I do love you." My heart flew up and out of me as I spoke the words. "Will you marry me?" I asked him. "Will you marry me and keep me here?"

He smiled, and the world seemed to brighten all around us. "I will. And we will parcel out your seeds among our friends. We will grow your indigo and whatever else you'd like to try. And we'll build a legacy together."

"As long as Quash helps us." I smiled back at Charles.

He shook his head. "You imp." His eyes danced with merriment. "Fine. I will include Quash, and anyone else you wish, in those plans."

"Everyone. Even Essie must stay with me."

"Anyone you wish." His voice was serious and tender. This man knew me better than perhaps my own family. He had seen my weaknesses, my mistakes, my ambitions, and my shortcomings. Yet, he loved me.

"And Quash ..." I took a deep breath. "One day I'd like him to be free."

Mr. Pinckney's expression never wavered in his regard. "Anything you wish."

"I think we'll do great things together, Mr. Pinckney," I whispered, overcome.

"Charles," he corrected.

"Charles," I said.

THE END

—

"Having our passions in due subjection to our reason is the greatest victory that can be acquired, and perhaps 'tis a lesson the easier learned for being early taught."

—*Eliza Lucas*, 1722–1793

—

Afterword

Eliza Lucas and Charles Pinckney married in May of 1744 in a small ceremony at St. Andrew's Parish Church. Her only dowry was her slaves and the crop of indigo still growing upon the land that was no longer owned by the Lucas family. Her family returned to Antigua without her.

Allowing the indigo to go to seed, Charles and Eliza shared the seed out amongst several planter families in the area.

Later that same year, England and France declared war against each other, and, no longer able to buy indigo from the French, the English paid a bounty per pound of indigo from the colonies. Within a few years, the French were so threatened by Carolina indigo, they made the export of indigo seed from their islands a "capital crime."

Indigo went on to become one of the largest exports out of the colonies, laying the foundation for colonial wealth that shaped United States history. The Winyah Indigo Society, formed by planters to commemorate the source of their wealth, endowed, supported, and survived the American Revolution. It also funded one of the first free schools in South Carolina. Just before the revolution, the annual export of indigo amounted to the enormous quantity of 1,107,660 pounds.

Eliza herself signed a document of manumission freeing

Quash from slavery in 1750. He continued to work for the Pinckneys, acting as paid carpenter and architect in the building of the Pinckney house on East Bay. He was well remunerated and bought property in Charles Town from Charles Pinckney as well as several hundred acres along the mouth of the Santee River, becoming a planter himself. He bought his daughters out of slavery for $200 each. He renamed himself John Williams.

John Laurens' son, Henry Laurens, went on to make his fortune in slave trading. It is estimated that eight thousand souls passed through his markets.

Eliza fell deeply in love with Charles, and after his sudden death in 1758, wrote:

> The greatest of all human evils has befallen me. I have lost the best and worthiest of men, the tenderest and most affectionate of husbands.
>
> 'Tis not in the power of my words to paint my distress.
>
> My nights have passed in tears and my days in sighs without a single exception since the fatal twelfth of July when I was deprived of what my soul held most dear upon this earth …
>
> How uncommon a loss I have met with.

Eliza and Charles' son Thomas went on to develop and sign the Pinckney Treaty that gave the United States use of the Mississippi River for trade, setting the boundary between the United States and Spanish colonies. And their other son, Charles Cotesworth Pinckney, was one of the Founding Fathers of the United States of America and represented South Carolina at the Constitutional Convention in 1787. Active in both state and national politics, Charles Cotesworth did much to shape the educational and cultural institutions within South Carolina.

Upon news of Eliza Lucas Pinckney's death in 1793, President George Washington, at his own request, served as a pallbearer at her funeral, laying her to rest in a cemetery in Philadelphia.

Two hundred years after her death, Eliza Lucas Pinckney was inducted into the South Carolina Women in Business Hall of Fame. In 2005, a new chapter of the National Society for the Daughters of the American Revolution organized in her honor, and named itself the Eliza Lucas Pinckney chapter of the NSDAR. And this year, 2017, the "Miss Eliza" 2018 Junior Doll, representing all the strong women of Colonial South Carolina, will be unveiled at the Continental Congress of the NSDAR in Washington, DC.

To this day, the South Carolina state flag is blue in honor of indigo.

As so eloquently put by her descendant, Ms. Harriott Horry Ravenel in 1896, "When will any New Woman do more for her country?"

A Note from the Author

Dear Reader,

In September 2013, I attended an indigo exhibit at the Picture This Gallery on Hilton Head Island, South Carolina. The exhibit featured many different types of artists who used or were inspired by indigo. There were dyers and textile makers, jewelry makers, painters, and a lady who was a living Eliza Lucas Pinckney, and who stayed in character all evening.

I overheard a conversation the gallery owner was having with one of Eliza's descendants who was in attendance. I caught snippets of a story that would light a fire in me. It was a story about a sixteen-year-old girl who ran her father's plantations in her father's name. "This girl," the unknown person said next to me, unaware of my eavesdropping, "made a deal with her slaves: she would teach them to read, and in return they would teach her the secrets of making indigo."

Now, I realize I am not a historian. But I do know that there once lived a remarkable girl whose name, outside of Charleston, has mostly been forgotten. And the need to tell her story became so overwhelming that I couldn't ignore it. I told myself that if I could tell her story in such a way as to capture her spirit and her fire, and introduce her back into our consciousness, then I must try.

The story that you just read was based on true events and historical documents. However, as with any fictionalized version of history there are elements that had to be created to demonstrate character or give fabricated reasons for actions where the truth behind certain deeds has been lost to time.

Most of the slaves on the Wappoo plantation you read about were real, except for Essie and Sarah. Starrat was real and was indeed a witness on a deed to mortgage their property that I found, though perhaps not as vile. I have no idea if the Mr. L whom Eliza refers to in her letter to her father is in fact a Laurens, but based on her vehement rejection of his marriage suit (her exact words "the riches of Peru and Chile had he put them together could not purchase sufficient esteem for him to make him my husband" crystallized her character and made me laugh out loud), I imagined it must have been someone memorable whose principles were at odds with Eliza's. When I learned about how young Henry Laurens went on to make his fortune in slave trading, I felt he and his father fit the bill perfectly.

Nicholas Cromwell was real and so was his sabotage of Eliza's indigo attempts. She never refers to a Negro indigo maker in her letters that are available in *The Letterbook of Eliza Lucas Pinckney*, however, there were a few things that led me to create Ben. She asks her father to send someone, and upon first read I felt it was someone she knew. In other letters to her father she appears to defend the innocence of her friendship with someone unnamed. I believe many historians have assumed it was Charles, and while their friendship and her flirtations in her later letters to Miss Bartlett (and Charles) could support that argument, her defense of this mysterious friendship was, in my opinion, far too early to be attributed to Charles.

Later, in documents by her descendants (*Eliza Pinckney* by Harriott Horry Ravenel), there is a mention that her father did indeed send a Negro man to help her, and that it was well known in the family record that he did so. But who was this man? He is never referred to again.

A boat with Lucas rice and "a" Negro man really did go down in the St. Helena Sound. One afternoon when I was in the Addlestone Library in Charleston, I found the written document in the Pinckney Papers of this entry of the boat, and to my surprise saw that the author had written "the a Negro man." From that moment on, I became convinced that there was more to the story. And so Eliza's childhood friend Benoit Fortuné was born.

Forgive me, dear reader, for any anachronistic mistakes, either accidental or willful, or for any besmirching of the character of ancestors long dead. My intent was purely to revive the memory of a remarkable young girl, who perhaps due to her youth or her gender, or being eclipsed by the accomplishments of her sons, was largely forgotten by history.

When you visit Charleston today, much of the Pinckney history is anchored in the life of Charles Cotesworth Pinckney, Eliza's son. You cannot even visit her Wappoo land anymore. It changed hands several times and is now a suburban housing development in an area known as West Ashley. Though a quick look at the road names in that area that I cross referenced with an old plat map show Indigo Pointe Drive, Eliza Court, and Betsy Road. I suppose someone knew the land's significance.

Largely, Eliza and what she accomplished has been forgotten. She married well, that's what people remember. There is no surviving portrait of her, and she has become known in some circles as Charleston's most elusive face. Far from a sweet, genteel lady in history married to a powerful man (though she may have become those things too), she was ambitious, she was headstrong, she didn't always conform to society's expectations, she made friends with whom she chose and not who was expected, and she didn't have an idle bone in her body.

The letters in this book are largely taken from Eliza's real words. In most cases, they are direct excerpts from longer letters. In very rare cases, letters are adjusted, combined, or slightly embellished. And one letter in particular, the one to her father asking for the indigo maker to be sent, was filled in almost entirely by me, the original letter being unavailable. The prayers are all her original words. I suggest anyone with further interest in Eliza pick up *The Letterbook of Eliza Lucas Pinckney*.

It was not available at the time of writing this book (2015), but since then the "living Eliza," Peggy Pickett, has compiled a robust biography of Eliza published in early 2016. I highly recommend this for those seeking to understand more about Eliza's life. It is listed in the bibliography that follows.

Eliza Lucas captured my imagination and didn't let go until I'd told her story. It may not have been 100 percent accurate, but she was heard loud and clear. Almost three hundred years later, I guess that's all she can ask for.

—Natasha Boyd

ACKNOWLEDGMENTS

During the course of my research, I met many helpful people and read many books that touched on Eliza's life or the lives of those of the time. Special thanks go to Andrea Feeser (author of *Red, White, and Black Make Blue*), Margaret "Peggy" Pickett (the living Eliza, who has recently published Eliza's biography), Donna Hardy of Sea Island Indigo (who immediately returned my call for help in understanding the dye-making process and who is reviving the long-lost art of indigo-making at her farm in Georgia—as I type this, my fingernails are still stained blue from a wonderful day learning the secrets of indigo on Ossabaw Island, one of the only places left you can find "indigenous" indigo).

And I have so many others to thank. The volunteers of the Pinckney Project (in particular Jill Templeton and Cator Sparks) and the Charleston Museum, who are raising money to restore one of Eliza's dresses and also raising awareness of Eliza herself. The Charleston Historical Society, housed in the Addlestone Library, who politely put up with my amateur questions about how to find documents. Dianne Yarbrough Coleman, whose illustrated biography of Eliza will hopefully be published soon and whom I have stalked for visual inspiration on Facebook! And all the people along the way who've answered my questions, inspired more questions, and supported my telling of this story. Especially my agent Nicole Resciniti who gave me the courage to take the leap. Thank you to the descendants of the Lucas and Pinckney clans who have looked after and donated their family documents to libraries, universities, and historical collections around the United States.

Thanks go to my family. In particular, my husband

and sons and also to my mother, for their indefatigable support.

Thank you to Karina Knowles; Alan Chaput; Dave McDonald; Judy Roth; Jennifer Wills; Rick Weiss; my editor, Madeline Hopkins; the whole team at Blackstone for believing in me and this book; and anyone else I missed whose fingerprints are on this manuscript.

Discussion Questions

1. Eliza, by all expectations, was an eligible prize. She was young (which meant she was malleable), and her family had land. Yet in her accounts and letters there is rare mention of more than an occasional interest in suitors. Apart from Mr. L, whom she soundly rejects in a letter to her father, and the obscure Mr. Murray, we don't hear much about it. Do you think she didn't find them worth mentioning since she had no intention of marrying, or was she really such a nonconforming lady that potential suitors didn't quite know what to do with her?

2. It is clear from the currency issues Charles was dealing with that colonists were already beginning to chaff under British rule even as early as the 1740s. Why do you think it took another thirty years or so for there to be a revolution?

3. There is no surviving picture or likeness or even description of Eliza that exists today. She hardly discussed her own looks. But, after reading her story and getting to know her character, do you have a sense of her in your mind? Almost as if her character is what made up her likeness? How do you picture her?

4. Do you think Ben really did die, or do you think Quash told Eliza he was dead so that Ben could be free and Eliza could grieve his loss? Why would he do that?

5. Do you think Eliza and Charles Pinckney were in love before the death of his wife? Do you consider this infidelity on the part of Charles?

6. In this story, who do you think killed Starrat and why?

7. Eliza was twenty-one and Charles Pinckney was believed to be around forty-five at the time of their marriage. Did you think about their age difference as you read the story? How do you feel about it?

8. In this story, Eliza's mother seems to be working hard toward getting Eliza married off. Do you think her mother was only doing what she thought would benefit Eliza, or was she thinking of herself?

9. It was clear that Eliza wasn't exactly a fan of the institution of slavery. Do you think she could have done more to work against the system, and do you think she could have succeeded in producing indigo with paid labor instead of using unpaid slaves?

Further Reading

Edelson, S. Max. *Plantation Enterprise in Colonial South Carolina*. Harvard University Press, 2006

Feeser, Andrea. *Red, White, and Black Make Blue*. University of Georgia Press, 2013

Goodell, William. *The American Slave Code in Theory and Practice*. New York: American & Foreign Anti-Slavery Society, 1853

Graydon, Ness S. *Eliza of Wappoo*. Columbia: The R. L. Bryan Company, 1967

McKinley, Catherine E. *Indigo: In Search of the Color that Seduced the World*. New York: Bloomsbury, 2011

Pinckney, Elise. *The Letterbook of Eliza Lucas Pinckney 1739–1762*. Edited by Marvin R. Zahniser. University of South Carolina Press, 1997

Pickett, Margaret F. *Eliza Lucas Pinckney: Colonial Plantation Manager and Mother of American Patriots 1722-1793*. Jefferson: McFarland and Company, 2016

Pickett, Margaret F. and Dwayne W. Pickett. *The European Struggle to Settle North America*. Jefferson: McFarland and Company, 2011

Ravenel, Harriott Horry. *Eliza Pinckney: Women of Colonial and Revolutionary Times*. New York: Charles Scribner's Sons, 1896

Rogers, George C. *Charleston in the Age of the Pinckneys*. University of South Carolina Press, 1980

Weir, Robert M. *Colonial South Carolina: A History*. University of South Carolina Press, 1983

Williams, Frances Leigh. *Plantation Patriot: A Biography of Eliza Lucas Pinckney*. New York: Harcourt, Brace & World, Inc., 1967